When We Were Legends

Shelbie Mae

Book Cover by Hannah Linder

Chapter images by Clay Groot

Dedication

To the One who thought I was worth saving.

Prologue

Marigold

The origins of many legends are unknown. But not the legend of me.

Perhaps I'm being presumptuous in describing myself as a legend, or perhaps I'm telling the truth of things. I'll leave that for you to decide.

My story began when I forced my eyes open.

Darkness as black as a womb surrounded me. I bolted upright at the sensation of flutters across my skin. My touch sent leaves dancing to the black ground.

I swiveled my head, trying to peer into the darkness.

A vision—no, a dream—hung at the edges of my consciousness. Two men atop a cliff. Their silhouettes facing one another before one figure fell over the side.

Not wishing to dwell on the terrifying image, I used my fingers to assess what I couldn't see.

Grit marred my face. Was it dirt or something else? Twigs tangled my hair while sweat seeped through my thin T-shirt. My bare feet poked through dried leaves.

Where was I? How did I get here?

Squinting, I braced my hands on the ground to push myself up. My vision adjusted to the faint glow of the moonlight filtering through the canopy of tree branches overhead.

The haunting cries of a Great Horned Owl echoed through the stillness of the night while a soft rustling of leaves sounded behind me.

What hidden dangers lurked in these woods? Was it a massive bear? A stealthy wolf? Or perhaps a silent mountain lion?

Despite my intense scrutiny, all that met my gaze were the dull trunks of trees.

Run, Marigold. Run.

Wait ... I knew my name!

Marigold.

And yet the path that led me here remained shrouded in mystery, a puzzle begging to be solved.

Branches reached out like skeletal fingers, scraping across my face as I clambered to my feet and sprinted. No sounds stalked me. I slowed my sprint to a steady jog, then eventually a cautious walk.

Was I moving deeper into the woods or inching closer to civilization?

My foot snagged on something uneven, causing me to stumble. Pain seared through my leg as I fell, smashing my knee upon a jagged rock. Warm blood trickled from the wound, tracing its way down my leg and bare foot.

I gritted my teeth to stifle a cry. With no choice, I forced myself upright and continued.

Minutes passed as I hobbled forward, agony pulsating through every movement. The bark of swaying trees sounded like the eerie creak of an opening door, and the rustling leaves above me whispered secrets of the darkness I had yet to uncover.

My head throbbed. I tentatively probed the tender spot, biting back a scream. This wound must be the origin of my memory loss. I needed a doctor or a first aid kit.

Without warning, the dense woods gave way to a clearing, and my wounded foot hit a flat surface. My arms windmilled to keep me upright. When I regained my footing, I took another step onto a dirt road.

A thin sliver of moonlight illuminated a thicker route stretching from left to right, and a smaller one continuing straight ahead.

A driveway.

I stumbled down its trail and found a house with a truck parked out front.

What hour was it? Should I knock?

Yes, I needed help. My head throbbed from an unknown injury, my knee burned from my fall, and my cheeks pulsed with open cuts from wayward branches.

I knocked on the door.

Tap. Tap. Tap.

No response.

I knocked harder.

Thunk. Thunk. Thunk.

Still met with silence, I fumbled along the doorframe until I found a doorbell to ring. The chime pierced through the night, prompting shuffling footsteps and an overhead light flickering to life.

"Who's there?" It was a young man's voice. *Good.* At least I didn't give an old man a heart attack.

"I need help." Squinting at the sudden brightness, I shuffled backward as the door swung open.

A man in his early thirties stood before me, purple bruises marching up the left side of his face. One of his eyes swelled shut, and his clothes appeared ruffled. His hair stuck up in all different directions.

"Who are you?" he said, holding himself upright against the doorframe with his forearm, eyes squinting.

"M-Marigold," I stammered.

"What's wrong with you?"

The sensation of dripping blood warmed my arms, legs, and face. What must he think of the bloodied woman on his doorstep? "Can you help me?" I asked. "Please?"

"Come closer. I can't see you."

Safe men didn't wear bruises like beards, did they? He appeared too inebriated to make any sudden moves. I inched forward until the porch light illuminated me once again, exposing the extent of my injuries.

He frowned at the sight of me. "Come in. There's gotta be a first aid kit around here somewhere."

The man slurred his words and his breath stank of alcohol. He was drunk and battered. But I got the impression that he wouldn't harm me.

"Are you sure?" I asked. In reality, *I* wasn't sure if I wanted to follow this man into his house. While he might not hurt me, he didn't appear to be in good enough condition to help me.

He clutched his head, blinked, and then gestured for me to enter.

If he passed out I could leave. Or use a phone. Something.

Our shoulders brushed as I wiggled past him and stepped into the house. "I don't want to get your home dirty."

He barked a laughed. "This dump? No way. Follow me."

I tiptoed behind him. Hardwood floors and carpet cooled my scratched feet like ointment as he led me to a bedroom with rumpled bedsheets. Beyond was a bathroom suite with a tub and sink. After rifling through a cabinet, he dumped two musty towels onto the countertop. Our footprints stood out on the dusty linoleum tiles.

The man swore after setting the cloth on the counter. "I gotta turn on the hot water. Give me a sec before you run a bath."

No water? Who was he, and why did his house look like it was unlived in?

I halted him with a gentle touch on his arm. "What's your name?"

Breaking away from my grasp without meeting my gaze directly, the man mumbled over his shoulder as he vanished into another room: "Levi."

Chapter One

Levi

I discovered the body on Lillian's wedding day.

The welcoming fragrance of decaying leaves, mossy rocks, and bark enveloped me as I hiked Ghost Mountain, a ridge in southern Tennessee. I was minutes from the trailhead when I deviated toward the edge of legendary Skeleton Cliff out of habit, a ritual ingrained in me since my father's tragic demise at its base three years prior.

I neared the ledge, my boots inching closer to the fabled precipice, causing a pebble to break free from the cliff and bounce out of sight. The weight of my pack shifted dangerously as I leaned forward.

Shock sent me scrambling backward until the weight of my hiking backpack pulled me onto my backside.

The vivid blue sky stared down at me as I lay there, wondering if I hallucinated the body. After all, I *had* been hiking on the mountain for a week without any human interaction. Maybe I imagined it.

Crawling to my feet, I took a hesitant step forward. Another step. Then one more.

Yes. An unmoving form with a mane of hair splayed around her head rested on the rocks below.

This side of Ghost Mountain—the side with the three-hundred-foot rock face called Skeleton Cliff—wasn't popular.

Legend claimed that bones of Civil War soldiers were found at the foot of the rock. As the story goes, the dead haunted the mountain and its hollers. Hence the mountain's name—Ghost Mountain.

I checked my watch and swore. Only four hours until the wedding, and I still needed a shower. The pungent smell of my own body odor made me cringe. My truck was parked a five-minute hike away, followed by a challenging twenty-minute drive down the winding switchbacks to the valley floor.

My gaze fell upon the tragic scene below, and another curse escaped my lips. Momma would slap my ear if she heard me. She'd raised a fine southern gentleman who knew better, but etiquette was hard to uphold when there was a dead woman three hundred feet below.

Muscles tensing, I contemplated my two impossible choices. Hike to the dead woman or rush to Lillian's wedding.

As a groomsman. Not a groom.

My number one goal in life, besides trying to erase Lillian from my heart, was trying to prove that my dad didn't commit suicide. If I hiked to the woman, I might discover a clue. Maybe their deaths were connected somehow. This might be my only chance to prove to the townsfolk that my dad, Duncan Shaw, was murdered.

Leaving her didn't seem right. Sutton was a small town, after all. I may have gone to school with her. Her death would likely stir up gossip like dust behind a tractor.

Cell service on the mountain was sporadic, which meant I couldn't call the police until I reached the valley.

A name popped into my head.

Jackson Miller.

Sheriff of Sutton.

He would be at the farm right now, preparing to wed the woman I loved. He had the power to make the arrest I'd been craving since the day my daddy died.

Yes. Reporting directly to Jackson was the right choice.

I scanned the foliage. A bunch of red cardinal flowers with velvety petals caught my attention. I pinched their stems to create a small bouquet, and then I dropped them over the edge as a sign of respect. "Rest in peace," I said.

I clutched my backpack straps tighter, leaving behind the picturesque vision of the soybean, hay, corn, and cattle farms that dotting the valley. The forest enveloped me in its cool shade as my boots crunched over roots and rocks.

Five minutes later, I gripped the handle of my truck. It creaked as I pulled it open. I hadn't locked it for two reasons: One, this was Ghost Mountain, Tennessee, where hardly a soul locked their vehicles. And two. People didn't venture to Skeleton Cliff.

But someone evidently had.

The woman and the man who pushed her must have seen my truck as they hiked to the cliff.

Dirt and leaves flung forward as I shifted into reverse and kicked the accelerator. Jerking the wheel, I avoided a tree and then threw the engine into drive before swerving onto the main road. Some might call the move reckless, but I was more familiar with this mountain than the curves of Lillian's body.

My tires slid around switchbacks like water around bends in a creek as I drove toward the farm.

Sutton sat at the base of Ghost Mountain.

I was performing my customary rolling stop at the sign in the valley when the song "Sunflower Dress" played on the radio. My tires left marks on the asphalt as I jammed my foot against the accelerator to drown out the chords I knew by heart. A burning rubber smell filled the open cab windows.

Why were the radio stations still playing this song? It should have been retired from rotation years ago. "Sunflower Dress" was my first hit in Nashville, and of course I wrote it for Lillian.

Before she left me.

Before Daddy died.

And before I gave up everything to prove that he was murdered.

I swerved a right onto Ghost Mountain Farm Road. This road wound its way through the heart of the sprawling three-hundred-and-fifty-acre farm, connecting every corner with a dusty embrace. I was born and raised on this land, and I knew every inch of it. The land was a quilt of cow pasture and growing land. Years had stitched it into my skin, a blanket of my past, present, and undoubtedly future.

This place was home. A warm compress for my cracked-open soul.

I passed the fence my daddy and I built together, and a pang resounded in my chest. His ghost lingered in most places I looked. I saw his shape in the woman who died on the rocks and his heart in the weathered white picket.

The jolt of hitting a familiar pothole sent my head lurching against the truck's ceiling, momentarily distracting me from thoughts of the body, my father, and Lillian. I'd hoped that hitting the pothole at full speed might knock the memory of them from my brain, but it didn't.

Swerving around an oncoming white GMC Sierra, I approached the cluster of four farmhouses that lined the road ahead. Most days, the farm road carried tractors and equipment. But in a few hours, it would become a parking lot for the nuptials. Lillian intended to get hitched in the old red barn, the place we'd planned to get married.

Turning onto what I dubbed Farmhouse Row—a name unofficial but deeply personal—I traced the path leading to the homes erected by my father and Samuel King when they first laid claim to this land. Each structure held echoes of their labor and love, standing as monuments to their shared vision for this farmstead.

I passed the first farmhouse that held the Ghost Mountain Farm Store. Momma and Mrs. King sold homemade jams there, along with hand-stitched quilts and everything in between.

The next farmhouse I approached belonged to Mrs. King and Lillian. Yes, my ex. She was the literal girl next door.

Momma and I lived in the third farmhouse.

And Ezra King—Lillian's big brother, my former best-friend-turned-enemy—called the fourth and final house his home.

Our relationship with the Kings—the very people we lived feet apart from—used to resemble a black-and-white sitcom. But now it mirrored a crime drama. Ghost Mountain Farm, initially established by my dad, Duncan Shaw, and Samuel King, had been the genesis of all these homes standing before me. But then everything fell apart.

As I sat in my truck parked outside our farmhouse, Momma emerged from the front door clad in a vibrant rooster-patterned apron over her dress. A string of pearls swayed on her neck as she hurried toward me.

One week ago, I hiked into the shadow of Ghost Mountain for solitude, much like Jesus did when He went camping in the wilderness. I didn't tell Momma where I was going. I had simply vanished.

The lemon-yellow hem of her dress danced at her ankles as she rushed toward my truck.

I cut the engine.

"Where's Jackson?" I asked, slamming the door.

She halted, a flour stain covering the giblet of a rooster on her apron. "Why do you need to see him?"

Taking hold of her elbows firmly, I confessed, "It happened again."

She leaned in and sniffed my breath. "You haven't been drinking." Her eyes widened in approval.

"No. I was on the mountain. I had to get away." I couldn't stand to watch Lillian put the finishing touches on her wedding.

Momma's hands, spackled with batter, brushed my cheeks gently, her expression softening with concern. "Levi . . ."

A knot formed in my throat. I couldn't talk about Lillian. Not now.

I gently guided her hands back to her sides. "When I was coming back, I hiked by the cliff. Momma, I found a dead body there. A woman. I gotta report it to Jackson. He did it again. Ezra killed someone else."

She gripped my forearm, her brows furrowing. "Don't start this, Levi Shaw. Ezra didn't kill your daddy. You know how he died."

She couldn't say the words. She didn't believe what the whole town of Sutton believed any more than I did. But it was easier to trust a computer-generated suicide note than to face the truth. "Dad was murdered."

"Levi, you didn't know your dad the way I did. Ezra didn't—"

"Where's Jackson?"

"Whoever you saw must have jumped. You know the history of the cliff."

I did. Numerous people had stepped off the edge of Skeleton Cliff and into the afterlife. But not my dad. He would never do that.

I gave up my life, my career, and my fame to discover how he had died, and this was my first lead in three years.

"Where's Jackson?" I repeated.

Momma sighed. "You promise you won't hurt him?"

As if I could. Jackson Miller was over six feet tall, a former member of the military. He'd press my face into the dirt before I could lift a hand. "I have to tell him about the girl."

She nodded at Ezra's home. "He's there."

That's all she had to say. I jogged across the yard toward Ezra's house, a charming white structure with pristine leafy-green colored shutters and a flawlessly maintained porch. Ever since his daddy went to jail and mine died, Ezra had taken over the farm as its foreman.

Voices hollered and laughed from beyond the door. I barreled inside, ran thought the living room and into the back of the house. Four men in impeccably pressed pants resembling hay, crisp white dress shirts paired with suspenders and ties in shades of evergreen, clustered around the kitchen island.

My identical outfit awaited me in my room next door. The colors and attire were all things Lillian and I had talked about when we planned our wedding. Seeing our vision displayed like this reminded me of what a foolish idea it had been to agree to be a groomsman.

It was Jackson who caught sight of me first; his close-shaven wheat-colored hair accentuated his clean-cut appearance with not a hint of stubble on his defined jawline. "Jackson, can I talk to you?"

The chatter quieted as they swiveled in my direction. I focused on the tallest man present.

He nodded once and then came to stand in front of me, saying nothing.

I avoided Ezra's piercing stare from the other end of the kitchen. "Can we talk outside? Alone?"

Jackson scrutinized me, still silent.

"I have something to report."

He straightened his tie, all business. "Of course." He followed me onto the porch, letting the screen door slap shut behind him. "What's this about?"

Jackson Miller was the tall, brooding type. At least I assumed he was brooding. He rarely spoke.

"I found a body," I blurted out. The gentle melody of a distant stringed instrument wafted through the air, mingling with the scents of cow pastures, hayfields, and vast stretches of corn and soybean fields.

His unwavering brown eyes bore into me, his brows raised curiously.

Steady. That's the thing he had that I lacked. This man was predictable, reliable, and unshaken. "Where?" he asked. Straight to the point.

"At the cliff. Just now. You have to arrest Ezra."

He sighed. "Levi, Ezra has been with us the whole time. He didn't—"

"He could have left in the night."

"Who was it?"

Jackson and I grew up in Sutton. Small towns were nice and country. Small towns were also just that—small. Everybody knew everybody, or at least someone in their family. "A woman. I didn't have time to hike to the bottom to identify her."

"I'll call the station and have them retrieve the body."

"And you'll arrest Ezra?"

Then he said the most words I'd ever heard from him: "Levi, I know your families have history, but this isn't the time to work out old grievances. Thank you for telling me about the girl. I'll make sure her death is investigated. Rest assured, we will find out what happened."

"But—"

"Do you want to ruin Lillian's wedding by arresting her brother? Besides, if there isn't any concrete evidence, then I have no right to make an arrest."

He was right. I didn't have any real proof. I could only hope the deputies would collect something that could be traced back to him.

"Levi?" Jackson's voice broke through my thoughts.

Startled by his continued presence beside me, I responded, "Yeah?"

"Go get ready."

Chapter Two

Ezra

The sweet vintage Malbec in my goblet lost its sweetness and turned as dry as a Sancerre wine at the mere sight of Levi. Standing alongside Jackson's two groomsmen, we now waited for the two men to return from their private discussion. The two men beside me sipped from glass beer bottles, but I'd never cared for the cheap stuff. Wine was richer in both flavor and price than beer, and I liked expensive things.

Unfortunately, I was broke.

After a few moments, I ambled out of my kitchen with its dark elegant dark walnut cabinets and pristine white granite countertops into the living room.

Peering through the window that overlooked the front yard, I spotted Jackson on the porch with his phone pressed against his ear. Levi was nowhere to be seen.

"I need a team at Skeleton Cliff for a body recovery."

My hand trembled, causing the wine to slosh out of my glass. A body recovery? Who had Levi found in the hills?

I was still hovering near the couch when Jackson reentered the house.

Pretending not to have overheard his phone call, I tried to act nonchalant as I asked, "Is Levi coming to the wedding?"

Jackson pocketed his phone. "Yes."

With a nod, he brushed past me and headed back into the kitchen. Too bad my almost-brother-in-law lacked personality. I relished the fact that he was a better catch than Levi Shaw. Lilly insisted he was quite interesting once you got to know him, but I hadn't met that charming side of him yet.

I wasn't the type of person to throw parties. This bachelor bash was my attempt to lure Jackson into confidence with me, brother-to-brother, but he spoke less in this situation than when issuing warnings to me for fighting in bars. In those moments, my fists flew faster than my good reason could stop them.

My temper was like a second voice inside my body, but I hadn't always been this way. I hated losing control. Ever since my father went to prison for laundering money, and I quit my job at the Bruno Vineyard Winery in the Smokey Mountains of Tennessee, something underneath my skin splintered apart, and I was left trying to keep a dark current inside of me at bay.

I threw back the last sip of wine and then returned to the kitchen. Jackson wasn't speaking to me, which was the reason for this soiree. No need to stick around.

"Please, excuse me," I said to the men. I grabbed two fresh wine glasses by their stems, along with the freshly opened bottle on the counter, and exited through the sliding glass door.

Humid Tennessee heat slapped me in the face like a wet washcloth as I stepped into the fenced-in backyard.

A garden stretched beyond the faded wooden fence. A vineyard would be more enticing, but I was stuck on this putrid farm. Ghost Mountain Farm was in danger of bankruptcy, and I was doing all I could to keep it profitable.

This piece of land in southern Tennessee held generations of memories within its soil. My father had worked hard for it, and I couldn't let him waste away in prison for nothing. I envisioned a haven awaiting his return, a sanctuary for my mother's solace, and a place where Lilly could cherish her past through rose-tinted glasses.

Someday, when I could save enough money, I'd leave the farm and buy land in the Tennessee hills where I'd build a small wedding venue next to a cultivated vineyard. Then, I could be the overseer of my world, rich in burgundy grapes and scarlet sunsets.

But until then, I must keep this farm afloat.

That task seemed to grow more challenging each week.

Pushing dark thoughts aside, I nudged the gate nestled within the pristine white picket fence with my hip as I made my way past the Shaw residence and toward my childhood home.

Giggles floated down from the upstairs window, where Lilly and her bridesmaids were immersed in wedding preparations. The orchard echoed with the cheerful chirping of birds, while tantalizing scents of roasting meat slathered in BBQ drifted on the gentle breeze.

Yes, there were pleasant things about this land. The aged tire swing that smelled of rubber, and the way mother's kitchen reminded me of sticky icing on cinnamon rolls. The fields outside transformed from a dry brown hue to lush green every summer, a seasonal spectacle that never failed to captivate me.

Mother swung open the squeaky screen door before I could knock. "Is Jackson all right? He's not getting cold feet, is he?"

"No, Mother." I kissed her cheek. "He's acting like his normal, unshakable self."

She rose on her tiptoes to tame an errant strand of brown hair that had escaped my hairline. "You look so handsome."

Mother appeared pristine in her creamy pink mother-of-the-bride dress. "You're looking beautiful yourself. Can I see Lilly?"

She shook her finger at me. "Not with that red wine. You'll ruin her dress."

"Please?" I gave her my most arresting smile.

With a shake of her head, she relented. My smile had worked from as young as I could remember. Mother stood at the bottom of the stairs and hollered, "Lillian, Ezra's here. Can he come up?"

I refrained from mentioning that I could have screamed up the staircase myself, but this was Mother's house. She'd always done the yelling for us. Hearing her reminded me of years past.

Moments later, a line of girls filed down the stairs. "She says you can come up," the girl with wine-colored lips, and a perfectly symmetrical face said. I couldn't remember her name. She was one of Lilly's friends from nursing school. Maybe she'd married a famous country artist? Lilly's life was almost grocery-store-magazine worthy too. Until Levi messed it up.

Typical Levi.

"Don't you dare let Lillian have that wine," Mother said.

"I won't let her ruin her dress, Mother." I gave her another peck on the cheek before I ascended the creaky stairs, a nuance that had been a part of the house since I was a teenager. I never made it far when trying to sneak out. A smile lifted on my lips at the memory.

Lilly met me at the landing, resplendent in a white gown and a flower crown.

"Wow," I said. "You look . . . magnificent."

"And you look debonair. Is that a vintage Malbec?"

"Should I have brought something else?"

"Mother won't let me drink a drop of anything but water, and you know how much I love wine. Bring it inside. Quick, before she takes it away."

She pulled me into the room that once sported a weathered blue marker sign declaring "No Boys Allowed," an attempt to bar me, Levi, and his brother Colton. Lilly was the princess of the farm. The only girl born of the King and Shaw families.

Her room hardly resembled the teenage girl oasis it used to be. The pink floral bedspread had been replaced by a pristine white duvet embellished with delicate ruffles. A potted fern on the dresser replaced her old stereo. The walls were adorned with framed paintings capturing poignant moments of human connection: a mother embracing her toddler, a grandfather tenderly holding his wife's hand, and two lovers locked in a graceful twirl.

The most noticeable change was the absence of scattered clothes on the floor. "Has Jackson turned you into a neat freak?"

"Not completely, but he has forced me to become better organized. It's not bad, I suppose, but I'm used to knowing where everything thing is, even when it's a mess."

I gave the room a nod of approval. My home was immaculate. As was Momma's. Being tidy was a personality trait Lilly hadn't inherited. Thankfully Jackson had encouraged Lilly to adopt some of his military-style cleanliness. "I like it this way."

"Of course you do. The only thing you leave lying around are wine glasses."

She knew me too well. "And cork openers," I said cheekily.

"Naturally." She grinned. Looking around the room, she sighed. "I'll miss this place."

I carefully poured two glasses of wine, giving her time to mourn her past as she embraced her future.

She leaned forward to take a delicate sip from hers. "I can't risk getting a drop on this dress."

19

She looked like the Ghost Mountain Farm princess she was. Flowers graced her hair, and her makeup enhanced her natural features instead of hiding them. "Nor would I desire you to."

Her eyed rolled back into her head as she closed her eyes. "Mmm, this is great. I'll only have a little. I want to be sober for my wedding."

"No worries, little sister. I didn't come to intoxicate you."

She peered at me over the rim of her glass, her wide mascara-coated eyes blinking curiously. "Why are you here? Are Jackson's friends too dull?"

"They're all right. I came to tell you that Levi's arrived."

She set down her glass and said, "He made it?"

"Why do you sound excited? He broke your heart. I don't understand why you invited him to the wedding, let alone asked him to stand. It's weird."

"Levi and I are friends."

Lillian's lingering feelings for Levi were clear. I suspected Jackson knew as well, but she'd left Levi in spectacular fashion. She was marrying Jackson. It was clear which man she cared for more, even if she still held old feelings for Levi.

"He wants to be more than your friend. Trust me." Good thing Levi didn't know she still cared.

"It won't matter after today."

I considered telling her about the body Levi discovered, but I decided to spare her undue curiosity or stress. Jackson could share it with her later if he chose.

"I could kick him in the balls for disappearing and missing the rehearsal dinner. Where was he?"

Levi had been carousing in the hills, nursing his misery and probably drowning in drink. I shrugged as I again considered telling her about the body. But I couldn't give her that kind of shock before her wedding. "I'm not sure. But that's not the only reason I came."

She sank onto the bed as though it were made of cotton clouds.

I leaned against the dresser. How could I voice this next part without sounding like a weak fool? "I wanted you to know that I'm honored you're allowing me to walk you up the aisle."

Her hands disappeared in the folds of fabric.

"It shouldn't be me," I choked out. Our father hung like a mist over our lives, present but untouchable. He should be the one escorting Lilly.

Her gaze met mine. "I know," she said, her voice cracking. She tilted her face upward. "Stop making me cry. I'll ruin my makeup."

"I'm sorry. I just wanted you to know he's proud of you, even if he can't be here."

She used a tissue to dab at the moisture under her lids. "He called me today."

I tried not to sound shocked. "He did?"

"Yes. He told me to enjoy every second with every person." She grinned. "He also requested that I tell you not to get into any brawls. He wishes you'd call him more."

I didn't call because my father asked too many questions about the farm. Questions I could never answer without lying to him. My father knew me too well. He knew when I was deceitful.

"Promise?" she said, taking a sip of wine.

I frowned. Did I miss something? "Promise what?"

"Not to lose your temper."

I circled my wrist as I took a bow. "As you wish, Milady." But we both knew it wasn't that simple. When you shook a bottle of soda, it exploded. Pressure sucks the space from an object. The same happens to my blood when the right pressure is applied. "I'll avoid Levi."

"I wish you two could be friends again."

Irritation rippled through me. "Why? He means nothing to us."

"He'll always mean something to me."

Her confession turned up the pressure under my skin. "He shouldn't."

"You can't erase history, Ez. It follows us everywhere. I accepted what happened between us, and I'm much happier now."

I finished my glass of wine, unwilling to venture into talking about the past. "See you on the field?"

She let my abrupt end to the conversation stand. "I can't wait." Her smile returned.

I leaned in to kiss her cheek before leaving. "I love you, Lilly, and I'll do whatever it takes to care for you and Mother while Father is away. I just wish I didn't have to. It's not fair."

"I love you too, Ez. I've got Jackson now. You can let me go, okay? One less lady to take care of."

I stood. "I'll never stop looking out for you."

"Nor will I for you."

I walked to the door. "I'll tell your entourage to reassemble."

She laughed, rising to finish her wine. "Take the Malbec, or one of them is bound to spill it on me."

The girls traipsed up the stairs as I descended. Mother was nowhere to be found. She must have escaped to her bedroom to continue getting ready.

Retracing my steps toward my home, a fluttering paper by the shed caught my attention. My backyard, enclosed by weathered white picket fencing like the neighboring farmhouses, housed a shed in the far corner for my gardening tools.

I stooped to retrieve the paper and scanned it. Then I crumpled it.

In the center of the yard stood a fire pit I'd created myself. The area encircling the pit shimmered with polished whites stone, while white pebbles snugly filled the gaps between the slabs. Though I rarely made a fire, flames had licked the black sky last night.

This paper should have been destroyed with the rest. Nobody could know the truth it held.

There weren't any other papers in sight.

Good.

I brought it back to the fire pit and peeked inside. All ash.

I threw the crumpled bank statement inside and then found a lighter in the shed.

Orange flames devoured the evidence with a satisfying crackle. Smoke burned my nose as I collapsed into one of the Adirondack chairs around the pit.

The farm felt like a noose cutting into my windpipe. Although my father admitted to the money laundering that sent him to prison, I had a feeling he was covering for someone. Duncan Shaw.

Levi and I hated each other because I believed his father was responsible for my father going to prison, and he was convinced that I killed his father in retaliation. Neither of us could prove the other wrong.

Last year, when the crops were bad, I wondered if my father did launder the money. The farm was one harvest away from ruin.

But no. He couldn't have.

If I didn't act, then the land my father had worked so hard for would no longer belong to us.

Family history—vanished in an instant. Along with a place to live and my dream of being a vineyard owner.

Back when I left my favorable job at the Bruno Vineyard winery, life had felt bleak, but now it felt like a death sentence.

Was I willing to place my entire future on land that had the potential of becoming lost? I didn't want to, but I must. It was my duty to provide in my father's absence. Besides, I needed the money to carve out my place in the world.

Levi's figure flickered in the kitchen window of the Shaw house. How dare he live as though there was no responsibility? How dare he break Lilly's heart and smugly accuse me of murder? Especially when I was the one providing a home for both him and his mother.

Indignation simmered, but I promised Lilly that I wouldn't brawl on her wedding. I'd promised.

Levi disappeared from view.

The wind rustled the leaves from branches above my head as I worked to calm the rage underneath my skin.

I couldn't, but I also couldn't let Lilly down.

Abandoning my seat, I marched toward the shed, drew back my arm, and forcefully slammed my fingers into the sturdy wood.

The aspect about my episodes of outburst that remained a mystery to most was the agony that drove them. It wasn't about inflicting harm on others (though Levi sometimes deserved it); it was about releasing the unbearable discomfort festering inside me. One strike didn't suffice.

The skin on my knuckles split upon impact with the wood once more.

Pain seeped from my body, offering slight relief, but not enough.

A third strike tore more flesh from the bone.

Then, just as I struck the wood for the fourth time, fingers clawed into my arm. A throb pounded through my temples as my chest heaved.

Mother's touch on my bleeding hand was gentle yet firm. "Stop," she commanded, her voice cutting through my anger.

I clenched my jaw, fury still coursing through me like a relentless fire.

The shards of betrayal threatened to tear me apart. If broken hearts could be weapons, then I would forge them to seek vengeance against Levi and his kin for all they had stolen from us.

Another shard broke off my heart as I looked into Mother's sad eyes.

My father crushed her heart first. And I might break it again. I'd do anything to keep the land that she and Lilly loved so much, even if it meant getting myself into a heap of trouble.

I didn't have money, but I was determined to make some.

No matter what it might cost me.

Chapter Three

Levi

The groomsmen and I stood on either side of a magnolia tree while white petals drifted down upon us on the light breeze like flittering fairy wings. Flower petals dusted the ground while Father Hosea and Jackson Miller positioned themselves front and center.

The gathering crowd, bedecked in pastel dresses and ties, rose from their wooden folding chairs as the music changed. My heart might dry up in my chest if Lillian went through with marrying Jackson. I couldn't imagine life without the possibility of being with her again.

How could I possibly be watching this? I'd been a fool to accept her invitation to stand at the wedding.

The crowd faced the rear, waiting for her to appear. I stared at my feet, watching as an ant scurried across my decorative boot.

I couldn't bear to witness Lillian walk up the aisle, her gaze on Jackson alone. If brides had jitters on their wedding day, then ex-finances had internal seizures. How could she ask me to stand here? Technically, it was Jackson who had asked. We were friends—I guess—but I got the impression that she was behind it.

Curiosity lifted my attention off my boots. I peered at Jackson first. He looked the way that I imagined I did—terrified yet hopeful. Perhaps Lillian would see my face in the lineup and choose to walk toward me instead.

A man could hope.

Unintentionally, I followed Jackson's gaze to where she'd soon appear.

My breath caught as I first glimpsed the crown of her head emerging, followed by the rest of her form gradually materializing. She cradled a bouquet of sunflowers, ferns, and Queen Anne's lace in the crook of her arm.

Emotion clogged my throat as her eyes passed over me and landed on Jackson.

Her dress appeared to be an extension of nature itself; the fabric resembled petals unfurling from the earth rather than mere human craftsmanship. Lace covered her shoulders, while white satin sheathed her body. Her hair, the color of rich mountain soil, was elegantly pinned up with wildflowers woven through the strands, creating an illusion of a natural crown gracing her head.

I wanted to brush my hands from her neck to her hips, to her head, and then kiss her until she breathed my name into my mouth.

But she wouldn't meet my gaze. I might as well be invisible to her.

Her lips resembled the soft pinkish red hue of a ripened peach at dusk, while her eyes shimmered like emerald pine needles. A sun-kissed, golden glow caressed her skin, giving her an ethereal radiance. Her bare nails and lightly blushed face showcased her natural beauty, akin to a creature of the hills. A woman birthed straight from God's creation.

And I was the snake who had deceived her. I whispered lies into her ear. Told her I'd take her with me. Said I'd call her every night. Tried to convince her that my music would never come between us.

I didn't intend to lie, but that didn't change the fact that I had left her behind, forgot to call after late-night shows, and allowed the music create a rift in our relationship. I didn't believe that high school sweethearts—especially those born from Tennessee small towns—could break up.

I was wrong.

She and Ezra stopped at the front of the aisle as Jackson approached. He shook Ezra's hand and then took Lillian's. I clenched my fists to smother my emotions, fighting both love for Lillian and hatred for Ezra.

For the next twenty minutes, I focused on remembering every detail of the body I'd seen at the bottom of Skeleton Cliff. Lillian and Jackson tied their lives together in front of the town of Sutton and God Almighty while I contemplated the unnamed woman.

Most people avoided the precipice. Too many ghosts roamed around Skeleton Cliff. While it made sense that the woman might have committed suicide, I couldn't shake the idea that her death was related to Dad's.

Besides the legend of soldiers, the cliff was once a hub for rock climbers. That is, until tragedy struck, claiming the lives of two seasoned mountaineers. With no reason for the calamities, folks whispered about ghosts.

A decade ago, a high school girl ended her life there. Seven years ago, a man used the cliff as a gateway into the afterlife. Soon after, my dad died in (presumably) the same way. When a third accident nearly took a climber's life, local authorities hung signs, and thrill-seekers left Skeleton Cliff in search of less haunted adventures.

The sound of applause and whistles jerked me back to the present. Lillian and Jackson were locked in an embrace, their bodies intertwined as they shared a passionate kiss. I believed in the sanctity of marriage. Lillian was Jackson's wife now, and I could do nothing about it.

I was simply too late.

A banjo solo reverberated through the barn, its notes intertwining with the twinkling lights casting a warm glow. The potluck organized by Lillian was top-notch. There were five variations of mac 'n cheese, alongside vibrant kale salads dotted with cranberries and almonds, golden cornbread, crispy sweet potato fries, and an array of farm meat samples grilled or smothered in barbecue sauce.

I sat at the wedding table and downed unattended glasses of champagne to quench the thirst that seemed to parch my throat.

The music transitioned to a slow acoustic guitar number, and the crowd watched as Lillian and Jackson shared their first dance on the hay-strewn floor. I drained another champagne—the matron of honors' glass, maybe? Most of the wedding party circled the dance floor.

I tore my stare from Lillian and found Ezra standing by the open barn doors, sipping from a brown bottle. I shook my head, noticing red stains on his knuckles.

It was clear that he was drawn to conflict like stray cats attracted to a bowl of food, much like how I found solace in two fingers of whiskey when faced with my own demons.

My mouth watered at the thought of whiskey. This champagne wasn't giving me the buzz I craved.

Fresh air washed over me as I strod out the rear doors, escaping the din of clanging silverware. I sidled up to the artisan-crafted bar that was strung with twinkle lights and ordered a whisky sour.

Lush green grass swished underneath my cowboy boots as I meandered toward a game of horseshoes, a frosty drink leaving damp trails on my fingers.

The sun setting over the mountains set the undersides of leafy trees in a golden glow.

I pressed the cool glass against my forehead as a form at the bar caught my attention.

Ezra.

I downed the rest of my drink in two gulps and veered in his direction. "Did you kill her?" I blurted out, my hand instinctively reaching for his arm. The glass slipped from my grasp, clinking as it hit the ground.

He jerked out of my grip. "You're drunk."

I was far from drunk. "I found her, you know," I said. "The girl you left on the mountain." If I were lucky, he'd incriminate himself.

He closed his eyes and sucked in a deep breath. "Levi, let's be civil. This is Lilly's wedding."

He never reined in his emotions. What was he hiding? "I know you did it. I'll prove it. You killed my daddy, and now you killed her."

His arm stiffened as he lifted a fresh glass of wine to his lips. "I don't know what you're talking about."

"Don't play dumb. I know you—"

In one languid motion, he slammed the wineglass onto the bar and wrapped his arm around my neck, covering my face. "Shut up. You're pathetic," he spat in my face. "You're using your father's death as an excuse to drink yourself off the earth. Please drink away. But don't drag me and my family into this when your father is the one who sent mine to prison. Blood is thicker than water, old friend."

A slideshow of memories played through my head when he said, "Friend."

I recalled the days we spent digging holes and then using the dirt to construct bike ramps, building the treehouse with our dads, and playing hide-and-seek in the cornfields. But amidst these warm recollections, a stark image intruded—my father lying lifeless in a casket. And then a figure lurking in the shadows at the back of the church. The only person with enough hatred to kill.

The man I grew up with who used to be my brother. The man holding me in a headlock.

The fleeting vision flashed away within a second, jarring me back to reality. I sucked in a deep breath, recognizing the strain in his voice, the telltale signs of mounting anger, and I silently welcomed it. My heart ached with sorrow, seeking an outlet for my anguish. And here stood Ezra, unwittingly becoming that conduit.

Our bitter exchange gathered onlookers. Two men in dress shirts. One with his hand clamped over the other's mouth.

I reached up and twisted my fingers into Ezra's slicked-back brown hair, tugging until he released his grip on my face.

When his fingers loosened, I stumbled away. "I won't let you get away with killing her," I said.

His face flushed crimson, chest rising and falling rapidly. With a sudden jerk back, his fist collided with my cheek. Pain exploded through my face as I tumbled onto the grass, blood trickling from my nose.

Fury coursing through me as I wobbled to my feet. Perhaps a whiskey sour before a fight was a bad idea. Too late now. The taste of pennies filled my mouth as warm liquid dripped over my top lip.

I swung at Ezra. He blocked it, using my momentum to hurl me away from the onlookers.

The smell of soil filled my bleeding nose as I flopped onto my back, landing on the damp soil. Grumbling, I slammed my fists into the earth. Ezra stood with his hands at his sides, watching me as I sprang up as fast as my buzzed head would allow. I faked a left swing first, and then I cut him across the jaw with my right knuckles.

As he staggered back, blood trailing from his nose to his lips, he spat contemptuously aside. Doubling over, I charged at him, ramming my shoulder into his middle. We crashed down together in a tangle of limbs and fists.

A high-pitched squeal pierced the air, halting our struggle momentarily. "Stop."

The familiar voice brought us both to a standstill. Ezra pushed me away and rose to his knees while I rolled onto my back, gazing up at the darkening sky.

"I can't believe you two," Lillian scolded. "Y'all couldn't go one day without pitching a fit? Get inside, Ezra. You promised."

Feet shuffled, mummers whispered, and boots thudded on the dirt. Her head entered my vision like a rising sun, radiating authority.

"Get up," she said.

I did.

"It's my wedding day, Levi. Why would you provoke him?"

"How do you know I—"

"Because I know you. *Both* of you. You can clean yourself up now and act like a gentleman, or you can go home. Your choice."

I couldn't look her in the eyes. "Yes, Ma'am," I said. At that moment, she reminded me more of my momma than the girl I used to share my dreams with.

"What are you fixing to do? Shape up or get out?"

"I'll leave."

She sighed. "Levi, I love you. I do. But you need to stop being selfish. I understand that you're unhappy and wish we were still together, but you chose this. You forgot all about me. Your broken heart is no reason to beat on Ezra."

Did she say she loved me? The ring Jackson that slipped onto her finger a few hours ago spoke a different story. "He punched me first. And I never forgot you."

"I don't care who got physical first. I'm finishing it."

"Yes, Ma'am." I rose and brushed off my pants, then I took a different path around the barn instead of through it.

As I turned to leave, she called out after me hesitantly, "And Levi . . ."

I paused mid-step with my back turned toward her. "Yeah?"

"Don't call me 'Ma'am.'"

"Sure thing." I caught a glimpse of regret in her eyes as I turned to look at her. A thin film of tears misted my own.

She was right. I still wished we could be together. But she was wrong about Ezra. Her love blinded her. Did she not see the blood on his knuckles when he walked her up the aisle?

Father Hosea waved at me and hurried over. "Son?" He'd shed his priestly robes for a black suit. His customary steel-toed cowboy boots poked out from the bottom of his pressed pants.

"Hello, Father Hosea."

He pointed at his nose. "You've got blood."

I wiped it with my shirt sleeve.

"Dear boy, what happened? Never mind. I heard you found a body at the cliff today?"

News in this town traveled faster than email. "Yes."

"Was it Shelly Hooper?"

My mind churned like a tractor engine. Shelly was about six years older than me. She worked at the hair salon in town and still lived with her momma. "Shelly Hooper? It could have been. She was too far down to identify."

He shook his head. "Her momma hasn't heard from her in a few days. I worry . . . let's not talk of such things. That cliff is a wretched place." He shuddered. "We'll all know when the police release the identity. I hate performing funerals." He smiled and pointed to the barn. "But weddings are grand." He clapped my back. "Levi, just remember that hatred is bad for both the body and the soul."

And then he walked away, leaving room for Momma to swoop in.

She grabbed my arm. "What happened?"

So much for making a clean escape. "I shouldn't have come."

She studied my expression intently, probably searching for any hint of my thoughts. "I'd hoped that today might be different," she said. "When you disappeared for a week, I expected you to return home too drunk to stand at the

32

wedding. But then, when you got out of your truck and walked in a straight line, I thought you'd done some healing."

"My time away only reminded me of how much I love Lillian. Then, when I found the body, I knew Ezra . . . "

Her fingers tightened on my arm. "Don't talk about him that way. He's like a brother to you."

"He hates me."

"You've given him ample reason to, always accusing him of murder."

"But has he ever denied it?" I shook my head. "Not once."

"Ezra would never—"

"Did you see his knuckles tonight? They were bloody."

"Probably yours."

I shook out of her grasp. "There was blood on his hands before he hit me."

She released a heavy sigh. "Levi, you can't keep doing this. Courtney and I are weary of you dragging the King and Shaw name through the mud. Folks are tired of it too."

"But if I can prove that this girl . . . "

"She must have fallen. Maybe she left a note. I'm sure the police will sort it all out."

No one believed me. The town revered Ezra King as the savior of Ghost Mountain Farm. They didn't dare consider that his temper might be deadly. I was certain he harbored lethal intentions toward me.

A sudden memory—probably prompted by alcohol—flooded back to mind: Dad's cabin. I hadn't thought of the place in months. If I was serious about discovering who had killed him, I would have gone to that secluded place years ago.

Ghost Mountain held much of what its eerie name implied. Ghosts. But Dad's cabin carried a distinct shadow . . . the shadow of *him*. If I went to the place that he loved, then maybe I would discover the truth. Either that or sink into memories.

"I'll stay at the cabin tonight," I said.

Momma's clutched the folds of her dress. "But nobody has been there since he passed."

"I know."

"So why now?"

As I glanced back at the barn illuminated by twinkling lights, a glimpse of Lillian's white dress fluttered through the open doors. "Because I have nothing more to lose."

———

Ezra

On my second glass of wine, a napkin plugged into my nose to stanch the blood, I caught sight of a familiar face amidst the twinkling lights.

Squinting, I took another sip and watched him. He relaxed against the rear barn doors, a glass of brown liquid in his hand as he smirked at the festivities.

I would have ignored him except for the niggling knowing that he hadn't been invited.

Jake Tanner was my friend. Not Lillian's. And he had spent the last five years in prison. I'd heard a rumor that he had returned to town. This encounter marked my first glimpse of him since his rumored comeback.

As I drew closer, he acknowledged me with a subtle nod but made no effort to change his relaxed posture. His jeans were starched and clean, sticking out like a fox in a henhouse compared to the pressed dress pants that the other men wore. Clinging to his lean torso was a faded purple Polo shirt that seemed well past its prime.

"Hello Jake," I said, stopping next to him.

The banjo twanged a solo. "Ezra," he said, keeping his gaze on the drunken dancers.

"I don't believe you were on the guest list."

"Nice to see you too." Raising his glass to his mouth, he shot back the rest of his drink. "You're correct. I wasn't invited, but most brides and grooms don't detect a gent abusing their free bar when they've had a few too many themselves." He winked at me.

Jackson Miller didn't touch alcohol, and Lilly was far from drunk, but they were too preoccupied with each other to notice the presence of my old friend.

"I gather you crash weddings often," I responded. "Give or take a few years."

He grinned. "Correct. It used to be a pastime of mine before my sentence, and it continues to be one after. In fact, this is my second wedding crash since freedom found me." He ran his fingers through his slicked-back brown hair, and his clean-shaven jaw accentuated his mischievous smile.

"So what are you doing these days?"

"Coming here wasn't all play. I had hoped to see you."

I tilted my head in intrigue. "Oh?"

"My probation officer would be thrilled if you offered me honest employment."

I folded my arms against my chest and asked, "How would he feel about your trespassing on private property and stealing booze?"

He shot me a look. "I can't tell if you're serious or not."

"I'm not. Partake," I said, giving him a playful slap on the back. "Consider it my apology for not being able to take you on." I could hardly pay the few farm hands we had, let alone hire another.

"That's too bad." Stepping outside, he craned his neck to gaze at the weathered barn, then he shifted his attention to the darkening field.

I'd seen that look on his face before. Right before Jake had suggested that we graffiti the side of the high school building. I didn't give in, but he did. And then he paid for it with a one-week suspension.

"What are you thinking?" I inquired as he retreated further from the barn.

Following him, I settled beside him on a bale of hay. The dry grass poking through my slacks emitted an earthy aroma of straw that tickled my nose.

"Nothing you'd be interested in."

Jake had been arrested for weapon and drug trafficking, and I suspected he now pondered new ways to make a buck. He might be the perfect person to help me acquire money off the books. I'd already exhausted all the legal avenues.

"Perhaps I am," I said.

He studied me. "You're a hard one to read, King."

"Are you still working, or did prison reform you?"

"Oh, I'm reformed all right. I won't be a drug or gun mule for nobody. But . . ."

"But what?" I prodded.

His grin, which was exposed from the light streaming through the barn, was playful. "You're messing with me, King. You've always been cool, but a little too out of my league. You know what I'm sayin'? I ain't falling for your tricks, man. No way. I ain't going back behind bars."

"Jake," I said, keeping my voice low and serious. "Allow me to be candid with you. Your particular skill set could be of great use to me right now."

"I'm great at landscaping. You need a landscaper? Nobody'll hire me. That's why I came out here."

"I'm interested in your landscaping business if it makes me money too. Do you understand?"

He grasped a handful of hay from the bale and shoved a piece into his mouth, causing me to nearly gag. "Are we talking about landscaping or," he lowered his voice, "*landscaping*."

"Whichever one puts money in my pockets."

"Bro, you want to go into business with me?"

Would I regret this later? Without a choice, I let the words fall from my lips. "I do."

His forehead met mine as he leaned closer and whispered, "You better not be messin' with me. If you want to do the big one, I think this place would be perfect."

I looked around at the barn. "Here?"

"Yeah. It's secluded."

I still wasn't sure what kind of business we were referring to. But if it made me a profit—and if we didn't get caught—then I was willing to try.

Still, I needed clarification. "Are we talking about landscaping a green plant?"

"I don't know, bro. What are *you* talking about?"

Lilly's high-pitched scream of joy startled me. She twirled inside the barn in her wedding gown while Jackson watched with a grin. Momma stood beside Mrs. Shaw, sharing whispered conversations and radiant smiles. The barn was otherworldly tonight, glowing with lights, revelry, and enchantment. The magical atmosphere put me at ease.

I had to keep this.

Not a soul lingered behind the barn now. I seized the opportunity and said, "Shoot straight with me. You want to use my barn as an indoor pot farm?"

Jake squinted, still trying to gauge my intentions. "You said it. Not me."

"If I'm the one taking the risk on my property, I'll split it eighty-twenty."

"And I'm bringing the brains. Sixty-forty."

"I'll put your name on the farm payroll to appease your parole officer. Seventy-thirty," I proposed.

Jake leaned in, a sly grin playing on his lips. "I know a guy who can do the trafficking."

"Deal."

He nodded. "Deal."

As I finished the last sip of my wine, preparing to leave, Jake gently guided me back into my seat and asked, "What's got you willing to associate with someone like me?"

I withdrew from his touch. "Sheer and utter desperation."

Chapter Four

Levi

T he beam of my headlights blurred the brown trunks of trees and the
gravel edges of the road as I drove toward the cabin, swerving to keep my
truck from scraping the guardrail.

If the police pulled me over—which was unlikely because of their preoccu-
pation with the body—then I'd explain that I hadn't been drinking and driving.
That was true.

I hadn't taken a sip since I closed my truck door.

Scratch that.

A drop hadn't passed my lips since I packed the flask into the guitar case with my Martin D-28.

George Jones' song "He Stopped Loving Her Today" that played through the stereo distracted me as I wove around sharp turns. I'd found this George Jones album tucked into the driver's door pocket—one of Daddy's old CDs. Growing up, we listened to everything from Elvis to Johnny Cash to even Maroon 5. On Sundays, he'd play music from Aretha Franklin, Whitney Houston, or Fred Hammond.

Apart from passing a solitary car, the road stretched empty before me until a row of mailboxes signaled the upcoming turnoff. Maneuvering onto the winding dirt path, I counted each driveway methodically:

One. Two. Three.

Then it was time to make the turn.

Each property along this secluded route was shrouded by thick woods and at least half a mile separated them from one another. The drive trailed the inside of the mountain, while the homes faced the valley. Dad's cabin materialized as I neared. The twin beams of my headlights pierced through a few dusty windows, brightening the solid red door.

This log cabin, a sturdy structure aged over seventy years, stood as a testament to time. From the front, it looked like an average log cabin, but its backside was unique. Whenever dusk descended over the far-off mountains, a cascade of light would splash across the valley in such vibrant colors, showcasing God's beautiful handiwork.

Stepping out of the truck, I was greeted by the rustling of leaves and the resonant hoot of a Great-Horned Owl. The wind carried whispers through the trees as gravel grated beneath my boots. Trying to clear my spinning head with a shake, I gazed at the cabin which momentarily swayed before steadying itself.

I used the flashlight from my phone to maneuver the dark driveway, then I unlocked the front door. The metal hinges squeaked with disuse as I pushed it open.

A dusty, moldy scent overwhelmed me as I hooked right and walked down a hallway. Three doorways framed the walls.

To my right lay Colton and my bedroom, while Dad's master bedroom occupied the left side. At the end of the hall loomed an entrance leading downstairs. Carpeted stairs muffled beneath my boots as I walked through the third door and into the basement.

Using the flashlight, I maneuvered around stacks of boxes and toward the breaker panel. Dust particles tickled my nose relentlessly until a sudden sneeze erupted from me, sending sharp pain reverberating through my head.

After flipping the main breaker to the On position, I tested a light. The fixture hummed to life, casting a soft glow over Dad's old storage area, filled with boxes containing his collection of books, VHS and cassette tapes, records, CDs, and who knew what else.

Turning off the light, I stumbled back upstairs, ignoring the kitchen and living room as I turned straight into the master bedroom. If there was any evidence to support that my dad had been murdered, then I would find it here. Besides, I needed sleep.

I snapped the light on and cringed.

A thick layer of dust coated everything. The place smelled like stale air and disuse. Squinting through the dimness, I observed the items beneath the dust: an outdated comforter on the bed, neatly arranged shoes in the closet, nightstands overflowing with novels by Clive Cussler, Stephen King, James Patterson, and Nicholas Sparks.

This made me smile.

The music that my dad had listened to, the books he once read, and the movies he'd watched encompassed a broad range of tastes.

Moving toward his desk positioned in front of windows framing a view of the valley below—a serene writing spot—I surveyed the cluttered workspace. Journals, sheets of paper, and books made the area look like something from the home of a hoarder rather than a bestselling author and music legend's desk.

I lifted a stack of papers and blew off the dust, sending a puff into the air. The text appeared part of his original manuscript that had later become a bestseller. The paper had yellowed and the ink faded, but I still enjoyed holding something he had once created. Dusting off a journal, I flipped it over to see Dad's messy script.

When I held his words, I felt like he was near enough to clap me on the back and say, "How's your next song coming along, Son?" I wished he were that close. And I wished I was still writing songs or that Lillian hadn't left me.

Those dreams were nothing but smoke.

I snapped the journal shut then stumbled back to the truck to collect my belongings. The cabin enveloped me in an overwhelming presence, heavy with memories of my father. It was like tying a cow to my ankle and jumping into the sea. The pressure was crushing.

Placing my guitar case gently on the bed, I unlatched it and searched for my flask. Nestled snugly against the velvet lining and next to the weathered instrument lay the gleaming metal container. With just one sip, it was already drained. The craving for more was insatiable.

Leaving the bedroom, I ventured into the living room. A hearth covered one wall while an ancient box TV, still attached to a VHS player, occupied one corner. Several couches encircled the space, creating a cozy yet worn-out atmosphere. An archway seamlessly connected the kitchen to this communal area.

After a quick search, I found a dusty and unopened bottle of George Dickel Rye Whiskey in Dad's liquor cabinet. I didn't bother pouring it into the flask. Instead, I took it with me as I ambled into the living room and sank onto the sofa in front of the TV. Dust billowed from the cushions, making me cough.

Lost in swirling thoughts under the influence of alcohol, I contemplated my next steps.

A VHS deck nestled under the TV, surrounded by a collection of weathered tapes neatly arranged on the shelf. Setting the bottle of whiskey on the coffee table, I crawled across the ground, popped a plastic video into the slot, and pressed a button on the remote the size of a grown man's shoe.

The screen flickered to life, casting a grainy image. In the scene, a girl ran through a house with her boyfriend chasing her. When he caught her, he pushed her against a wall and screamed at her. She cowered as he pounded his fist into the drywall beside her head. With a sense of unease settling over me, I shut off the movie just as they were about to lock lips.

My brain swam in an alcohol-induced haze as I staggered toward the sliding glass doors that led to the deck with the bottle of George Dickle clutched in my palm. The night had draped Tennessee in darkness like a heavy cloak when I stepped onto the wraparound porch. Inhaling deeply, I welcomed the warm breeze that erased the stench of the stuffy house. The sky stretched for miles, and the moon shone like a muted bulb overhead.

Nostalgia enveloped me as I sank into an aged wicker chair, its twisted wood screeching in protest.

Three or four times a year, Dad would bring Colton and me to the cabin so that Momma could have a weekend in solitude. We'd spend hours hiking these hills, foraging, and building huge fires in the yard beyond the porch. We cooked venison steaks and shot squirrels.

Then, when we arrived home, Momma had a fresh pie awaiting us on the table, her face glowing clear and young again. She'd smile at Daddy and kiss him long and deep, thanking him. Colton and I didn't know we'd caused our momma her gray hairs. Thinking back on the way we'd run around with hatchets, and the bones we broke, it was no wonder she needed time to let Dad take over.

What Momma didn't realize was that those weekends nourished us kids too. I think they helped Dad as well. He did "manly" things with us. These were the weekends when we learned how to shoot guns and dress deer.

My mind swirled as I gulped a long pull from the bottle, trying not to wallow in these memories.

Thoughts of Daddy stirred memories of his passing, which in turn led me to think of Ezra, and then Lillian, her absence a painful realization. I would never hold her hand or kiss her lips again.

Tears burned my eyes. After taking another long swig, I ambled back into the bedroom and fell onto the desk chair. Dust billowed around me before dissipating.

Emotions surged within, begging for release through my pen and onto a blank sheet of paper in the form of song lyrics. I found a blank journal and began to pour out my soul:

I remember holding her hand
She used to look at me like I was her world
She wore that wedding dress like a Tennessee mountain queen
But it wasn't me who made her twirl
Never again will she be my girl

I scratched the pencil over the words. *Lame. So lame.* Turning to the next blank page, I wrote.

The Mountain Girl

My pen hovered above the page, its tip poised to inscribe the next words. Titles didn't come to me in the same effortless manner that song lyrics did. Why did I write *The Mountain Girl*? I preferred the mountains, but Lillian cherished the valley. She was made for fields of wildflowers and sunflowers, not the rivers and hills.

I kept writing, and as my pen continued its journey across the paper, I met a girl unlike Lillian.

From a cold night she awoke
Breathless and searching
She was born in mountain cloak
With river eyes
And marigold hair
She wore the scent of pine
Of her love the mountain bespoke
It set her upon her way
She fell upon the doorstep
Of a gentleman astray

-

He loved her like the one he lost
But he didn't know how much her love would cost
He kept her hidden away
Loved her gently
But she didn't stay
She left him like he left his last love
The wild mountain took her away

-

He loved her from afar
Not crossing the threshold of her heart
Until she was ready to let him in

He gave his everything to be hers
He cast his heart upon the rock
She took it as a sign
The mountain brought her to him
And they loved together for all time

The words read more like a ballad than a catchy country song. I dropped the pencil and finished the bottle of whiskey.

Standing made me sway.

Placing my guitar gently on the floor, I felt the weight of my duffel bag as I set it down beside it. With a forceful thud, I pounded my fist into the bed, displacing the dust.

Darkness overtook me before my ear grazed the worn pillow.

I thudded my empty shot glass on the bar counter to get the barkeep's attention. Each smack of the glass sent a sharp pain through my skull. I smacked again and again until the noise startled me awake.

With eyes barely open, I slowly sat up in bed, greeted by a sliver of moonlight seeping through unfamiliar curtains. I blinked away the haze. The sheets tangled around my waist smelled old. It wasn't until my gaze landed on Dad's journals and books scattered across the desk that recognition dawned on me; this was his study where I had been reading before drifting off. I had dreamt that I was at a bar.

A persistent knocking roused me further from my haze, and I groaned. Who would be knocking at—I checked my phone. 2:47 in the morning?

New aches and pains greeted me as I forced my body out of bed. Alongside of the throbbing head, every movement sent reminders of Ezra's violent outburst:

pain radiated from my cheek, jaw, and eye socket where his blow had landed. Even my fist felt stiff and sore in the spot where I'd punched him back.

Good. That meant he was hurting, too.

The leftover sound of a shot glass pounding wood echoed through my skull with each step. My eyes refused to peel open. I flipped on the outside light before unlocking the door. "Who's there?" I groaned with lidded eyes.

"I need help." A girl's voice. Urgency rang through her plead.

The squeaky hinges made me wince as I opened the door.

She stood on my stoop wearing a T-shirt wet with dew and blood. Her bare, scratched feet and blood-streaked legs spoke of a harrowing journey. She held her arms across her chest, shoulders hunched and eyes wild with fear. She took a few steps back at the sight of me.

I rubbed my eyes. Maybe I was still dreaming. "Who are you?"

"M-Marigold," she stammered from the shadows.

This couldn't actually be happening. "What's wrong with you?"

"Can you help me? Please?"

"Come closer. I can't see you."

A young woman in her mid-twenties stepped into the light. The longer I observed her, the more certain I became that this was not a dream. The cuts marring her face, arms, and legs were all too real. The blood was real. Her fear was real.

The headache drumming between my ears made her form pulsate before me. "Come in. There's gotta be a first aid kit around here somewhere."

"Are you sure?" She considered me, gaze lingering across the bruises stretching from my temple to my jawline, and the disheveled state of my clothes.

The porch light glared down on us like a stadium spotlight on my whiskey-fogged eyes. I held a hand to my forehead to steady myself before leading the woman inside.

She pushed past me and stopped on the dusty threshold. "I don't want to get your home dirty."

That was funny. "This dump? No way. Follow me."

I led her to the bathroom attached to Dad's bedroom. After finding towels in the cabinet, I remembered the hot water and swore.

There was no point in starting the tub without hot water.

She stood shivering by the sink.

Placing two towels gently on the edge of the tub, I maintained a cautious space between us. "I gotta turn on the hot water. Give me a sec before you run a bath." I turned to leave the room.

She placed a delicate hand on my arm and asked, "What's your name?"

"Levi," I said before walking away.

———

Marigold

Dust as thick as carpet covered the entire bathroom floor. Was Levi a squatter? Did I stumble from one dangerous situation and into another?

Leaning against the counter, I squeezed my eyes shut as a memory surfaced. An image of a man with dark hair and bright brown eyes fluttered to the screen of my mind. No, they weren't bright; they were fiery, blazing with an intensity that bordered on fury. His brows furrowed together as his spit a torrent of anger.

The recollection made me shudder.

I recalled fleeing from him, only to be cornered in the living room. That's where he caught me and pressed me against the wall, his voice a thunderous roar that sprayed spittle on my face as he unleashed his anger. Trembling, I instinctively shielded myself as he struck the wall beside my head, sending drywall cascading into my hair.

I snapped my eyes open to banish the image from my mind.

First, I had dreamed of men fighting on the edge of a cliff; now, a vivid memory of a man abusing me surfaced. What sort of girl had such violent and tainted dreams?

Did that man leave me in the forest for dead?

The events of the past hour lingered like an ominous shadow. Dried leaves rustling underfoot. Elusive animals darting out of sight. Branches clawing at me relentlessly.

Fear that suffocated me.

Struggling to recall anything else beyond this nightmare, I strained to conjure images of driving through familiar streets or glimpses of home. Yet, nothing emerged from the depths of my memory.

I tried to remember something else—such as driving to the woods. A name besides my own. Even images of my home and where that was located. And yet nothing surfaced.

The sound of footsteps distracted me as Levi returned to the bathroom. He was average built with the lean, muscled arms and the legs of an athlete. His thick hair, a blend of blond and brown hues, was cropped close on the sides with a wave on top. Purple and yellow bruises splotched across his cheekbone, nose, and eye, giving him an air of mystery that contradicted his age—somewhere between late twenties and early thirties, if I had to guess. Not much older than me.

Grimacing from pain, he reached up to touch his ear before meeting my gaze with a squint that gradually sharpened into focus. His piercing blue gaze traveled up and down my body. "Are you okay?"

I used my forearm to wipe a thick layer of filth off the mirror and examined my reflection.

Twigs and leaves were entangled in my thick wavy red hair. Superficial cuts covered my face, neck, and arms, which were otherwise dotted in freckles. Dirt and blood clung to my green T-shirt.

Shifting my attention away from the mirror, I inspected the bottom half of my body underneath the bathroom light. The lacerations on my legs burned. My knee was warm and sticky with drying blood where it had collided with a rock, while my feet stung with open cuts.

I wrapped my arms around my tummy to keep from panicking and said, "I-I don't remember."

"It's okay. Take a deep breath." He inhaled a lungful of air and then exhaled slowly, gesturing me to do the same. After a few breaths, he said, "How did you get here?"

The pain surged back. "Where is *here*?"

"Ghost Mountain."

Did he say Ghost Mountain? Did I wake up in a fairy tale? No, that would be crazy. "Where?" There were mountains in lots of states. Was I in Colorado? California? Or somewhere else altogether?

He closed his eyes and pinched the bridge of his nose, and then winced. He must have forgotten about the bruises. "What happened to you?"

I wiped a trail of blood off my arm. "I could ask you the same question."

He sighed. "You're in Tennessee. The closest city is Chattanooga."

Straightening my posture, a flicker of recognition sparked within me. "I think I'm from Chattanooga."

"You *think*?"

Struggling to free a tangled twig from my hair, I admitted, "I'm not sure."

"Looks like you got a pretty good gash on your head. That injury might be why you can't remember."

My fingers hovered over the injury.

"Is there someone you can call?"

"I don't remember anyone." It wasn't a total lie. The man who had yelled at me was hardly someone I could turn to for help. Besides, his name and any contact numbers eluded me.

"You should clean those cuts and go to bed. Maybe things will be more clear after you sleep." He turned on the faucet in the clawfoot tub. The water gushed brown before turning opaque.

I wrinkled my nose. "Does it always look like that?"

"This cabin was my dad's. I haven't been here in years." He scrubbed away the grime with his bare hand and then plugged the drain. "I'll sleep in the spare room. You can have the queen bed."

The neglected state of the bathroom made sense now with his revelation about its disuse. But questions lingered in my mind: Why hadn't his dad been here? When was the last time the sheets were washed? Could I trust this man not to hurt me?

My head throbbed. I didn't have the energy to find another shelter.

As Levi headed for the door, I called out, "Do you have soap?"

"Huh?"

"Soap." I gestured toward the water spilling into the tub, its steam enveloping the room in warmth. "For the bath."

He stumbled to the closet, muttering as he pushed odds and ends around. Finally, he produced a bottle of Mountain Fresh shampoo and set it on the counter, leaving a faint ring in the layer of dust. "This is the best I can find. That is, unless you wish to smell like a man."

The desire for cleanliness outweighed any concern for scent. "I don't care what I smell like."

He shrugged. "Pick whatever you want."

The sharp whiff of alcohol invaded my senses as I sidestepped him, trying not to recoil. Of all the doors I could have knocked on, I chose the house of a drunken man.

As he turned to leave, my bloodied heels grazed against the denim fabric of my shorts as I knelt before the bathroom cabinet. "Levi, wait."

"Yeah?"

I hated asking. "Do you happen to have any extra clothes?"

Inspecting my torn T-shirt, the too-short shorts, and the blood and dirt that marred them, he furrowed his brow. "Just a sec." With hands pressed against his temples as if to contain his throbbing headache, he disappeared briefly.

Moments later, he returned and handed me a pair of gym shorts and an oversized T-shirt. "Sorry, this is all I've got."

"It'll work. Thank you."

"I'll see you in the morning," he said wearily, clearly eager to sleep off his hangover. I nodded in response.

As he reached the doorframe, he halted and said, "I forgot to ask. What's your name?"

He had asked, but his drunken haze must have erased the memory. "Marigold."

"Marigold," he mumbled, squeezing his eyes shut. "I'm sorry. I need to lie down." He closed the door behind him.

Listening intently until his footsteps faded away, I cautiously tested the door-knob to ensure he hadn't locked me in. It creaked as I twisted it open. Grimacing at the noise, I gently closed it again, hoping he hadn't heard.

I sighed with relief, thankful for the silence that followed.

The pain of my cuts faded, giving way to a deeper ache that gripped my bones. I felt like I'd hauled a body up a hill on my shoulders. What if I had? What if I'd killed the man from my haunting memory? Could the blood staining my skin be from more than just my own wounds?

No. I was just tired. Bone tired.

I turned off the faucet and eased the clothes off my battered limbs. My knee stung as I settled into the water and then leaned my head against the back of the tub, careful to avoid the tender spot.

It took mere seconds for blood and mud to blur the outlines of my legs beneath the filth. I washed the cuts and my hair as best I could. Then I allowed myself to relax.

When the water cooled, I pulled out the plug, hauling myself out of the bathtub while muddy water circled into the drain. My small pile of clothes looked pathetic on the floor; my underwear too dirty to wear again. I had no choice but to go commando for now—at least until I could figure out what I was doing at . . . what did Levi call it? Ghost Mountain?

I slipped into his shorts and T-shirt, opting to skip the discomfort of putting on my sweaty bra. I left everything as tidy as possible before opening the door to the bedroom.

The space felt abandoned, the air stagnant like it hadn't boasted an open window and welcomed a fresh breeze in years. Dust blanketed much of the stationery items. Rectangle shapes cut through the grim on the desk, indicating the books and journals resting atop it had been recently moved. I was too tired to inspect the room further.

I peeked out the door, but there was no sight or sound of Levi.

With no other choice but to trust him, I climbed into the bed that stank of musty old sheets. Determined to ignore the unpleasant smell, I burrowed into the fabric and rested my head on the lumpy pillow, waiting for sleep to whisk me out of this nightmare. For now, at least.

Chapter Five

Levi

Muted sunlight filtered through the windows, warming the backs of my closed eyelids. Groaning, I rolled over and pulled the quilt over my head, but the thin patches of blanket did nothing to block the sun's rays. Giving up on seeking refuge in darkness, I sat upright and rubbed my face.

Confusion clouded my thoughts as I glanced around. Why was I sleeping on a twin bed, and where was my phone? I fumbled in the creases of the quilt until I found the device.

It was nine fifty-five in the morning on Sunday. The day after Lillian married Jackson.

She had said "I do," and I retreated to the cabin like a dog licking his wounds.

I fell back against the old mattress, intent on languishing through the afternoon.

Wait.

My body rocketed up, the image of a red-headed woman flashing through the haze in my mind.

I had to sleep on the twin bed because this mysterious woman woke me in the middle of the night. Was she still here?

I threw off the covers and plodded toward the bedroom wearing only my pants. I'd been too tired to remove them last night. Buckles and buttons didn't mesh well with my fingers when I was drunk. I must have pulled my T-shirt off because my chest was naked, but I had it on when I answered the door during the night. Right? Did I even go to the door, or was this woman merely a dream?

Approaching the bed where strands of hair the color of autumn maple leaves peeked out from under the blankets, my doubts dissipated.

She was no dream.

What was her name? A flower?

Marigold.

That was it. Marigold.

Yes, it fit her. Her hair was the color of marigolds.

Why did marigolds remind me of something? What was I forgetting? Something more important than a woman? Not likely.

I sat in the desk chair, its worn leather cooling my back. The legs squeaked, but the woman remained undisturbed in her slumber. A brown journal sat open on the desk. Was it one of my dad's?

No, that didn't seem right. My brain begged me to remember. But what had I forgotten?

Curious, I leaned closer to decipher the words inscribed on the page.

From a cold night she awoke
Breathless and searching
She was born in mountain cloak
With river eyes
And marigold hair
She wore the scent of pine
Of her love the mountain bespoke
It set her upon her way
She fell upon the doorstep
Of a gentleman astray

The handwriting was mine, but the journal must have been Dad's.

A hazy recollection emerged from a night fueled by whisky; an attempt to compose a song about Lillian had transformed into this poetic creation.

My intention was to come to the cabin to uncover proof that Dad didn't die by his hand, yet instead, I found myself immersed in a tale spun under the influence of alcohol. A ballad about a woman. Then I passed out, woke up when Marigold arrived on my doorstep, helped her, and then passed out again.

"Morning," the woman's voice said from behind me.

I swiveled in the chair to face her. She sat on the bed, my rumpled T-shirt hanging loose over her shoulders. Did I give that to her?

Yes, I did. In the bathroom.

Fragments of the night began piecing together like scenes from a blurry film reel.

"Morning," I echoed, pretending she hadn't startled me. "How are you feeling?"

She eased a freckled hand to her head and winced. The soft morning light filtering through the window exposed all of the freckles and cuts on her skin. "My head hurts." She relaxed against the pillow. "My whole body hurts."

Was she wearing a bra? I forced myself to focus on the journal instead of her chest. I didn't ogle women, even when I was sloppy drunk. Momma taught me better.

She had amnesia, right?

"Do you remember anything?" I asked.

"My name."

I narrowed my gaze at her. "Only your first name?"

"No, the whole thing. I'm Marigold Anne Rivers."

Her blue-green eyes struck me at the same time as her surname. I turned to the journal.

With river eyes
And marigold hair

What the . . . ? I snapped the book shut and pinched the bridge of my nose. I must be going mad. "Are you hungry?"

She nodded, grimaced, and placed a gentle hand at the base of her skull.

The gesture reminded me of the bruises on my own face. With any luck, Ezra looked similar. "We'll go to my momma's house. She's a great cook, and she might have something for you to wear."

The woman covered her chest.

"Sorry, I didn't mean it like that," I stuttered. "I meant she'll have more . . ." Why was I struggling to talk? "Feminine things."

She uncrossed her hands. "Oh. All right, then." She stepped out of bed, stretched, and rubbed her eyes. As she passed by, I caught a whiff of pine emanating from her tousled hair.

She wore the scent of pine

A question nagged me, but I ignored it. I was hungover and nothing more.

———

As I parked in front of the farmhouse, Marigold didn't move. The morning sun highlighted the cuts on her face, arms, and legs.

I glanced at my momma's house, trying to see it through her eyes, noticing the weathered shutters and porch in need of a fresh coat of paint. The neglected roof was littered with leaves that should have been cleared months ago.

"Did your mom plant those?" Marigold asked, fixated on the focal point of the front yard.

Momma's garden.

Red and pink geraniums spilled out of flower pots that lined the wrap-around porch. Beds of marigolds, sunflowers, and Gerber daisies hugged the house.

"Yes."

She hopped out and slammed the truck door. "I like her already."

The spicy aroma of bacon greeted us as I pushed open the creaky screen door. Marigold stepped cautiously inside, her eyes darting around as she absorbed every detail.

I brought her here for clothes, yes, but also to ask Momma about her. Momma knew most folks who lived within a fifty-mile radius, and Marigold couldn't have simply appeared out of nowhere. She must have family somewhere nearby.

"Right on time," Momma called from the kitchen. "It appalled me when you didn't show up for church, Levi Shaw, but I figured you'd crawl back down the mountain for a good breakfast."

Marigold stopped in front of Momma's hutch adorned with an array of vibrant rooster plates, delicate rooster teacups, whimsical rooster salt and pepper shakers, and various other glass bird trinkets.

"Levi, where are you?" Momma appeared in the dining room through the swinging kitchen door wearing the familiar rooster-themed apron layered over her church dress. Her eyes widened as they fell upon a stranger, a woman engulfed in my oversized clothes without a bra, her gaze fixated on the collection.

"Momma, this is Marigold Rivers." I introduced her.

Marigold turned toward Momma, tucking strands of her unruly red hair behind her ears before offering a tentative smile.

"Rivers? I don't know any Rivers. Where are you from?"

I swallowed. This couldn't be right. She had to know Marigold's kin.

Momma watched me collapse onto the couch. "You're more hungover than I suspected," she said. She turned back to Marigold, waiting for an answer.

"I, um . . ." She twirled a strand of her hair. "I don't know where I'm from."

Momma squinted. "Are you on drugs?"

I stood. "No, Momma. She's hurt and might have amnesia. She knocked on the door after midnight and had a giant gash on her head."

Momma stared at the ceiling and crossed herself as if she were in church. "The Lord works in mysterious ways. I thought you were crazy when you said you were going to the cabin, but you were following the Lord's direction." She smiled at Marigold. "I hope he treated you properly."

She nodded. "He let me sleep in the master bedroom, although it's a little out of sorts."

Momma laughed. "My Duncan always loved that place. God rest his soul. Nobody's been there since he passed."

Marigold cast me a look. Her eyelashes framed large oval eyes. Even in the darkened interior I could make out the blue-green color.

"Come into the kitchen," Momma said.

Marigold pointed at the glass doors of the hutch. "I like your collection."

Momma's face brightened at the compliment. She was the only person I knew who cared a lick about roosters. Most people, including me, found them to be annoying. But not Momma. "You do?"

"She's kidding," I said. She had to be.

"No," Marigold insisted. "I admire roosters. They speak up when no one asked them to."

Momma shot me a pointed I-told-you-so look.

Marigold perched on a stool at the kitchen island as Momma flipped sizzling bacon and fluffy pancakes. I concocted my signature hangover remedy, a steaming mug filled with half coffee, half milk, crowned with a dollop of whipped cream and a sprinkle of cocoa powder.

"Want one?" I asked Marigold, raising my mug.

"What's in it?"

Her freckled nose wrinkled in distaste as I told her. "No thanks."

"What do you like to drink?

She thought for a moment. "Pink lemonade mixed with sweat tea and crushed mint leaves."

"That sounds heavenly," Momma chimed in. "Levi, will you pour her a cup of orange juice?" She beat the skillet of eggs on the stovetop coils.

I sipped my hangover brew before grabbing the orange juice pitcher. "That stove coil is on the fritz. Momma won't let me hire someone to fix it."

Momma held the skillet aloft until the coil turned orange. "It's not broken, just testy."

Marigold rounded the island, popped the dial off, inspected it along with the misbehaving coil, and said, "If you have a toolbox, I think I can fix it once it's cooled."

"You fix stoves?" I said, incredulous.

She shrugged and returned to her chair. "I enjoy fixing things."

I set the juice down on the counter in front of her. "You don't know where you came from, but you know you like roosters and fancy lemonade, and you know how to fix busted appliances?"

"I wish I could remember more. I sense who I am, but I can't see the entire picture. It's like looking through your periphery."

59

"You poor dear," Momma said, expertly flipping a bubbling pancake.

"Are you sure you don't know a family with the surname Rivers?"

Momma slapped a pancake onto a plate. "I've never heard that name around here. I've also never seen a man or a woman with your shade of hair. I expect it's genetic." She returned her attention to Marigold. "You can't remember anything else, dear?"

She squirmed. "No."

"I'm sorry. I don't mean to pry. You probably need sleep," Momma said. "You can stay with me if you'd like."

"Or me," I offered.

Momma's eyes widened. "I'm not sure that's proper."

"We're not dating, Momma. I think I could help her remember."

"You do?"

Good question. But I masked my doubts as I said, "Maybe."

"When will you have time to nurse her back to health when you're working? That is, if you still have a job after running away."

I grimaced. I didn't tell my boss or the school district that I was leaving. Not my smartest move.

"I only work in the afternoons." I turned to Marigold and said, "I'm the high school football coach." Something inside urged me to keep her close. She was unlike any woman I'd ever met, and I wasn't sure why.

Momma spun toward Marigold. "We're talking about you as if you have no say. What do you think? Where would you like to stay?"

She bit her bottom lip. "I don't want to inconvenience anyone."

"You wouldn't bother either of us, dear," Momma said. "But I can say without remorse that I'm the better cook."

"I-I think I'll stay at the cabin for now," she said. "If that's okay."

Momma pointed her spatula at me. "You take good care of her. Hear?"

"I will. Promise." I snapped my fingers. "Speaking of which. Do you have any clothes she could borrow?"

"Lillian left a bag of hand-me-downs at Courtney's house. She and Marigold appear similar in size. I'll fetch them after breakfast."

Momma piled the plates with food, then we migrated to the dining room. After we were settled and said grace, Momma pointed her fork at me in an unladylike manner. "I need to talk to you, Levi."

I braced myself, anticipating a lecture on how to treat a woman, how to cook, or how to clean. But instead, she said, "Father Hosea asked if the body at the bottom of the cliff could have been Shelly Hooper."

Marigold's fork halted halfway to her mouth.

Momma noticed. "I'm sorry, dear. This isn't a pleasant table talk."

My mind hummed like a tractor engine. I already had this conversation. "He asked me last night, but Ezra would have no reason to kill Shelly."

"You get that fool-brained idea out of your head," Momma said.

The hangover drink wasn't strong enough. Did Momma have whiskey in the house? No. She dumped it down the drain when I started coming home drunk. My mind was a mess. I needed to get sober or get drunk.

Marigold forked a bite of eggs into her mouth. She needed me sober.

"So, you don't know if it was Shelly?"

I shook my head. "No. I told Father Hosea that the girl was too far down to see."

Satisfied with my answer, Momma turned to Marigold. "Do you remember hitting your head, dear?"

Marigold cut her pancake. "No. I woke up in the forest and stumbled into the cabin."

"You don't remember how you got to the mountain?" Momma asked.

She stared at her hands. "It felt like I was waking up from a dream."

Another line of my poem surfaced in my mind:

She was born in mountain cloak

No. No. No.

I couldn't let my thoughts wander. The implication had no foothold in reality. Marigold could not be the girl I wrote about. It was impossible.

Momma's gaze flickered between Marigold and me, her lips drawn into a tight line. Then, as if reaching a decision, her expression transformed into a radiant smile, and she gave an enthusiastic clap. "After we get you those clothes, I will send you home with groceries. You should rest, dear. I'm sure Levi can convert the boy's bedroom into a nice place for you."

Marigold seemed to force a smile as she said, "I'll take my plate to the sink and then look at the stove, if that's all right."

Marigold wore a pair of Lillian's Daisy Dukes and a scoop-necked white T-shirt, her forehead rested against the truck's window as she dozed. She might be wearing Lillian's clothes, but there was an undeniable air of difference about her.

As I navigated our way up the winding mountain road, I couldn't help but worry. The question that had been lingering at the back of my mind all day finally broke through my thoughts.

What if Marigold was the girl in my ballad? What if, somehow, my words had come to life?

Levi left me alone in the bedroom to rest—but every time my eyes dared to shut, the haunting image of two figures standing on a cliff edge invaded my mind. A surge of terror raced through my veins as I recognized the falling man.

Levi.

Sheets stiff with disuse pooled around my waist as I sprang up, panting. My head pulsed, begging for sleep, but I couldn't bear the thought of dreaming about death.

Two sharp knocks reverberated through the room, causing a spike of pain to shoot through my aching head.

"What?" I said.

Levi's voice sounded muffled from behind the door. "Can I come in?"

"I guess."

The sound of squeaky door hinges sent a knife of agony through my brain as he entered.

My body dipped toward him as he sat on the edge of the bed. "Can't sleep?"

I returned my ear to the pillow and curled on a side, closing my eyes. "My head hurts."

The bed sprang back as he went into the bathroom. "Want some Tylenol?"

Although I trusted Levi—especially after observing his interaction with his sweet momma—I was still wary of his bruises. After seeing the red Tylenol mark stamped into the pills, I took both of them with the offered water and then lay back down.

He set the glass on the nightstand. "I'll let you rest."

———

A sense of déjà vu pressed against my consciousness as my eyelids fluttered open.

Where am I?

Confusion clouded my thoughts—but then the events following my awakening flooded back when I saw Levi sitting in the chair at the desk.

The muscles in his biceps twitched as he slammed a book closed, a guilty look on his face. "How are you feeling?"

I moved without the usual ache, prompting me to rub my eyes. "Better."

"Care for some fresh air outside? I can fetch you something to drink."

Specks of dust danced in the sunbeams, casting an amber hue over the room's walls. My stomach rumbled, confirming that I'd slept late into the afternoon. "Sure."

"You'll love the view." Levi tried to lead me out of the bedroom, but I paused at the sight of a tattered guitar case. "Is this yours?"

"Yes." He returned and set it on the bed. The hinges creaked and snapped as he unclasped them. A beautiful instrument gleamed from the velvet. I pressed my palm against the strings and felt something warm that wasn't tangible, like love, radiate through them.

Touching the dented body, I said, "You're either really good or really bad at playing this."

He gave a deep chuckle. "Some folks think I'm talented, while others say that I have a thing or two to learn."

"Will you play for me?"

Closing the case with a click, he replied, "Later. Come outside first."

I followed him down the hallway, noticing the sun-kissed hue of his arms, hinting at hours spent beneath open skies. He led me through an outdated living room and then onto a deck overlooking the valley. The view showcased farmland and a stream wandering between rolling hills, patches of fields on each side. The town of Sutton looked like a cluster of boxes at the foot of the mountain.

The deck sprawled widely against the second-story facade, supported by long lumber poles that anchored into the dirt below on a level patch of overgrown yard. Faded wicker furniture furnished the deck, once pristine white but now weathered and peeling from exposure. Overhead, a canvas canopy fluttered in the breeze, secured by sturdy poles.

Settling onto a wicker bench, I stretched my legs from beneath the shade of the canopy until my toes basked in the warm sunshine.

"My momma has been texting me nonstop, reminding me to keep you rested, hydrated, and fed."

Clouds drifted across the sky like puffy balloons, while birds twittered in the trees. "I'll be fine if I sit here for a spell."

"Be right back." Moments later, he returned holding a mason jar. "Try this."

Ice clinked the glass as I tilted it to my lips. The flavors of sugary pink lemonade, tangy sweet tea, and fresh crushed mint danced on my taste buds like an unexpected yet delightful kiss.

"You remembered my favorite drink?"

Levi's grin could have outshone the sun itself. "It was unique. I've never heard of mixin' those together."

Wood creaked as he sat beside me. Now that my mind was clear, curiosity bubbled up within me. "What happened to your dad?" That was a bold place to start.

He chipped crackling paint off the bench using his fingernail. "It's a long tale."

"I've got time."

He sighed. "I'm not sure it'll make much sense."

I took a sip from the jar. "Why don't you try?"

His leg bounced in a frantic cadence as he regarded me. "Do you recall the row of farmhouses where my momma lives?"

I nodded. "I can't remember anything from before last night, but my short-term memory is fine."

"That's fair." He flicked a chip of paint to the deck. "My daddy and his best friend, Samuel King, built those homes. My daddy married my momma, and Samuel wed a nice lady named Courtney. They started Ghost Mountain Farms together." His story came to a sudden halt, but I could tell there was more he wanted to unveil.

"That's simple enough," I said. "Keep going."

"Samuel took care of the farm finances, while my daddy pursued other passions. Things like writing novels and making music." He looked over the valley. "Four years ago, Samuel was sent to prison for laundering money through the farm. A year later, they found my daddy at the bottom of a cliff. I think someone pushed him, but most folks believe he stepped off the ledge."

My heart quickened. The remnants of the drink left my mouth dry, and the glass made a clinking sound in the jar as I struggled to control the trembling in my hand.

Levi took the glass from me and set it on the wooden floorboards below. "Are you okay?"

"Your . . . your dad was pushed off a cliff?" The nightmare replayed vividly through my mind.

"I can't prove it yet, but yes. I expect so." He narrowed his gaze at me and asked again, "Are you all right?"

"No . . . yes. I mean, I don't know. It's just . . . " I covered my mouth with quivering fingers. The sheer terror of such a fate was overwhelming, and it sent a wave of panic coursing through me.

Levi's hands rested gently on my shoulders, a reassuring weight that grounded me in the moment. His touch spoke of safety without words. "Listen," he said, eyes widening. "You're safe here."

My fingers nervously found their way to my throat, a physical manifestation of the unease that had settled within me. "I haven't been entirely honest with you. There is something that I do remember."

"Tell me." His voice was a soft murmur, coaxing me to share.

I took a deep breath and then recounted the harrowing memory of the men on the cliff. As I spoke, Levi's touch on my shoulder offered silent support, his fingers applying just enough pressure to convey understanding without overwhelming me. I finished with, "The man who was being pushed was you."

Levi's grip on my shoulder loosened as he processed my revelation. "Me? You must have dreamt about my daddy."

Fear clawed its way back into my chest at his words. "How could I dream something from *your* life?"

He hesitated before speaking again. "Is this all you remember?"

"There is one more thing. But I'm too ashamed to share it."

"Why?"

"Because it makes me sound weak."

"I doubt that."

I told him about the man whose eyes blazed with anger and fists clenched in fury. "The thought of living with someone like that, loving them . . . it's unimaginable to me."

Levi taped the edge of the armrest of the bench like a distracted drummer. "Did he have dark hair?"

"He did." I leaned away to look him in the eyes. "How do you know?"

He shrugged. "Lucky guess."

That certainly was not a guess. "Do you know something about me?" Maybe I wasn't truly without hope. Maybe Levi could fill in some of the missing pieces for me.

He shook his head. "I've never met you until last night."

Disappointment weighed down on me like a heavy blanket. "But how . . . "

"It was just a guess. Okay? It's nothing."

"Do you think that man is responsible for my head injury?"

Levi pinched his lips together, then said, "Possibly."

My mind felt as disorganized as a drawer with haphazardly tossed clothes; memories jumbled and incomplete.

Overwhelmed by emotion, I covered my face so he wouldn't see my misty eyes. Levi enveloped me in his arms reassuringly, his muscles strong as he cradled me. "Shh. You're safe. You haven't lost all of your memories."

His words failed to stop my racing mind. My reality was too daunting to ignore. I had amnesia, and I was currently living off of the kindness of a stranger. I couldn't remember my family, my past, or my life in general.

Was it the altitude that caused my breaths to shorten or just sheer panic constricting my chest?

Levi's grip on my shoulders tightened as he drew back. The faintest trace of stubble prickled his jawline, and those dark bruises were hard to ignore. "Slow down, Marigold. Take a deep breath." He drew me closer until our gazes met at eye level. Purple and green rimmed his left eye. "Breathe with me." He demonstrated by sucking in a slow and deliberate lungful of air, then he let it out.

Initially gasping for air as if submerged underwater, tears pricked my eyes as panic overtook my body.

Gradually, Levi's composed demeanor and measured breathing seeped into my frantic state. Though fear still raced through my bloodstream, I could finally draw in a full breath again.

Cupping my cheek tenderly, he asked, "Better?"

"Only slightly."

Maintaining his gentle hold on my face and locking eyes with mine, he asked, "What's your favorite flower?"

I paused a moment as I considered this. "The crocus."

"Why's that?"

"Because they're eager to bloom even when frost might destroy them." Newfound peace now eased my heartbeat.

The pad of his thumb rubbed circles against my cheek. "And your second favorite flower?"

"Marigolds. Because of my name." My pulse slowed further.

"And your third?"

"Daisies. Because they're playful." My heart resumed its normal rhythm.

Levi wiped a tear from my cheek with his calloused thumb. "You see? Not everything is lost. Deep down, you still know who you are."

I brushed aside his hand, uncomfortable with the warmth it offered. He was still a mystery to me. And it was best not to get close to a stranger. Yet, I couldn't deny the comfort it had given me, how I wished to lean into him and the safety his closeness evoked.

Leaning away, I asked, "How did you know about my love for flowers?"

He smiled. "Because you admired Momma's."

Shifting on the creaky bench, I asked another important question. "Who hurt you?" I asked, gesturing toward the bruises darkening his cheek and temple, marring his otherwise handsome features. I knew if I touched the colors on his face, he would wince.

"Now it's my turn to confess." His smile faded. "I left out parts from my story."

This is why his closeness scared me. I didn't know him. "Why?"

"Because it's a lot of information."

I leaned forward to retrieve my drink from the deck where Levi had gently placed it earlier. Curling my legs beneath me, I settled against the arm of the bench, waiting with my brows raised.

He eased his arms back across the seat. "I'm the oldest of two boys. My brother Colton lives in Nashville and works as a sound engineer for a record company." He held up two fingers. "Samuel and his wife Courtney had two kids too. Same age as Colton and me. They named the first Ezra. He runs Ghost Mountain Farm. We used to be like brothers." He folded down his middle finger. "Their second child is a girl named Lillian." It seemed as though his decision to not elaborate on her was deliberate.

A flicker of recognition crossed my mind from our earlier conversation at breakfast. "You think Ezra is the one who pushed your dad off the cliff? That's what you said to your mom, right? You also assume he's responsible for the death of the woman you discovered yesterday?"

"Very good. Yes. I suspect Ezra murdered my dad. I think he was upset enough about Samuel going to prison and having to move back to the farm that he harmed my dad in retaliation."

"But your mom doesn't think so."

"No. The police found a printed note with my dad's name. But the thing is, he loved to write longhand. The note couldn't have been written by him. My Momma is heartbroken and wants to move on. Believing my old man died that way is easier."

"What does that have to do with your face?"

He avoided my gaze. "Ezra and I had a discussion at Lillian's wedding last night."

Lillian. Ezra's sister. "A discussion that involved your fists?"

"Something like that."

"And I'm wearing Lillian's clothes?"

He swallowed as he took in the sight of my outfit. "Yes."

The woman in me recognized his hurt. I realized what he wasn't telling me about Lillian. "You loved her."

He averted his gaze.

"Did she love you?"

He still wouldn't look at me. "Once upon a time."

"You still love her," I said.

"I didn't say . . . "

"You didn't have to."

He stood. "Are you hungry? I am. I'll start dinner." He shut himself inside the cabin.

A gentle breeze stirred the leafy canopy above, causing it to sway. It arched higher than it should. After a quick perusal, I noticed a single loose knot securing the canvas to the eye hook. I may know very little about myself, but I did know that I liked things to be in order. If they weren't, I fixed them until they were.

The information Levi shared lingered in my thoughts like a delicate petal caught in the breeze as I shifted the bench beneath the flapping canopy.

His dad died under suspicious circumstances. He didn't trust his former friend, Ezra. He was still in love with Ezra's sister, Lillian.

I ran through the names in my mind: Samuel and Courtney were the parents of Ezra and Lillian. Meanwhile, Levi's mom and dad had two sons—Levi and Colton.

By the time I'd untangled Levi's confessions, the canopy was tightened.

Levi slid open the door. "Mac n' cheese is ready on the stove. It came out of a box. Momma wasn't kidding when she said she was the better cook."

Sitting down beside me, he turned his gaze upwards before meeting my eyes. "Did you change something?"

I gestured toward the spot I had tightened while he was away.

His brows rose in surprise. I simply shrugged.

Exhaling heavily, Levi attempted to find a comfortable position on the bench, but it only squeaked in protest with every move he made. Eventually giving up, he sat as stiff as a plank of wood. Nestling beside him on the bench, but not too close to touch, I took a sip of my drink and asked, "Are you okay?"

"Yeah, why?"

"You seem restless."

It was his turn to shrug now.

"Why don't you play your guitar?" I said. "I'll decide if you're any good."

He clapped his hands on his thighs. "Yes. Perfect."

Moments later, he cradled the instrument by its neck, settling into position with a dramatic flair. He forced a fast melody into the dusk around us, his fingers moving with confidence and familiarity along the frets.

My mouth dropped open in awe. This man wasn't just good at playing the guitar; he was great. The worn dents on the guitar's frame bore witness to consistent practice and dedication.

As Levi finished the song, his eyes drifted shut before he launched into a comfortable refrain. Brief pauses between notes left me hanging on each sound, making me wonder if there was more beneath the surface.

I tapped him on the shoulder. His fingers stopped as he rested his arm along the guitar and asked, "What do you think?"

"Where are the lyrics?"

He leaned the instrument against the deck. "I don't sing."

That didn't seem right. As certain as I knew the order of my favorite flowers, I was sure Levi Shaw had a voice for singing.

"Yes, you do," I said.

"No, I don't."

"You do," I insisted.

A shadow crossed his features. "Not anymore."

Before I could press further, he abruptly changed the subject. "I'll get dinner."

With a sense of agitation hanging over him like a cloud, Levi left the guitar resting against the cabin and then disappeared inside.

Approximately three minutes later, he returned and pressed a bowl of cheesy noodles into my hands. The sun dipped toward the horizon, casting a warm glow of orange, pink, and red that mingled with the encroaching darkness.

With my fork poised between my fingers, I mustered the courage to ask the question again. "Why don't you sing?"

He kept his attention plastered on the sunset. "I just don't."

Frowning, I looked back at my food. He had opened up about his father's passing and his family troubles, so why was he so reluctant to share his voice?

As the fiery orb disappeared behind the edge of the earth, Levi and I cleared the dishes together. Levi then busied himself changing the sheets while I bathed. Upon returning, I found him engrossed in the same leather book I'd seen him reading this morning.

"What are you reading?"

He snapped it closed as he glanced up. "Nothing." He looked over my T-shirt and night shorts. "I'll leave you to sleep. Tomorrow, we can arrange for you to move into the other bedroom. Or you can have this one."

"I'll sleep in the other room. This feels like a man's room." My cheeks flushed as I continued hesitantly, "Would . . . would you mind sitting with me until I fall asleep? And have been asleep for a while? I don't . . ."

"You don't want to have the same nightmare," he finished for me.

I exhaled, relieved that he understood. "Yes."

He gave a brief nod. "I'll sit here until you fall asleep. If you need me in the night, I'll be just down the hall."

"Thank you."

"You don't have to thank me," he said, and then he turned off the light.

Chapter Six

Marigold

A bump shook away the flog of sleep as I blinked my eyes open. I found myself nestled in a queen-sized bed beneath brown sheets and a plain gray comforter. My surroundings came into focus, revealing the dust-covered room as memories flashed back to mind like a disjoined film reel:

Waking in the woods. The two men on the cliff. An abusive lover.

Yesterday.

Levi, Beth, the rustic cabin, the guitar, shared dinner on the wooden deck overlooking nature's canvas, and the tranquil descent of the sun.

The last recollection was Levi's comforting grip on my hand in the dark bedroom as I slipped into a deep sleep. A dreamless one at that.

Another sudden thud followed by a scuff prompted me to rise from bed. What was Levi doing?

Hugging my arms across my chest, I shuffled toward the noise. Levi stood disassembling a twin-sized bed frame in the adjacent bedroom.

He stopped, a screwdriver clutched between his teeth. He spit it into his hand, then said, "Did I wake you?"

I swept aside a heap of thick, wavy hair from my face. "What are you doing?" A second twin bed occupied the corner, its bare mattress propped against it.

"I'm moving one bed into the basement so we can convert this into your new space."

The room was veiled in a thicker coat of dust compared to the master bedroom, triggering an unexpected sneeze.

He grimaced. "Don't worry. I'll clean before I go to work."

Where did he say he worked again? "At the school?"

He nodded. "I'm the football coach, so I don't have to leave until two-thirty."

Yawning, I stretched my arms skyward. Upon lowering them, I caught Levi fixated on . . . what exactly? My legs? The T-shirt I wore? It was hard to discern, but his face bore a strained expression.

Did the shirt look wrinkled? Was my hair a mess? I dropped my hands and covered myself self-consciously. "Let me change first, then I can help you."

When I returned to the bedroom, Levi was gone. Clanging noises and murmurs from the kitchen steered me in that direction. The counters, sink, and cabinets begged for a thorough scrub.

Levi stood hunched over a metal bowl, a whisk in his hand. "Pancakes for breakfast. Do you want bacon too? Momma sent us home with plenty of food. She knows what I can and can't cook. It's hard to mess up a recipe that requires only water, eggs, and pancake mix."

I smiled, a sharp pain shooting through the cut on my cheek. Wincing, I touched the spot.

"How are you feeling today?"

I feel like a helpless girl with no past. I didn't want to remind him I was another mouth to feed. I'd show Levi that I was useful and valuable, not merely broken and questioning.

"My entire body aches, but I'm much better than yesterday. What can I do?"

He gestured toward the table. "You can wipe that down, then take a seat."

I sprayed and polished the wooden table, along with the surrounding four chairs. Then I filled two glasses with orange juice and placed them next to two woven straw mats.

Once done, Levi presented me with a stack of pancakes and a plate of bacon. My stomach grumbled at the smell of butter and maple syrup.

He said grace, then we heaped our plates with pancakes, thick slices of melty butter, and gooey homemade syrup from a mason jar.

The morning sunlight streamed through the windows on each side of the front door, warming the inside of the cabin. Through the back sliding glass doors, the picturesque valley unfolded before us, adding to the sense of comfort and security enveloping us.

"Can I ask you something?" I ventured as Levi paused mid-bite, his bacon strip balanced between his fingers.

"Sure." He set the bacon back on his plate.

"Why have you stayed away from this cabin for so long?"

He swallowed, his Adam's apple bobbing. "This place holds painful and poignant memories and each one stings with the absence of my dad. This was his castle on a hill. His oasis. I couldn't bear the thought of coming here, not seeing him, and being greeted by the ghosts of memories."

I dared to ask a bolder question. "Why did you come when you did then? I mean . . . " I set my fork down. "Are there homes nearby? I keep wondering what I would've done if you hadn't been here."

"I'm sure any of the neighbors would have helped you." He then turned his attention to his plate as though that was the end of the conversation.

"But why did you come?" I couldn't figure out how he had arrived on the very same evening I did.

Metal clinked against ceramic as he set his silverware on his plate. "Because I needed to get off my butt. Lillian got married, and I had no choice but to move on. I'm also certain that if Dad was depressed enough to walk off that cliff, there would be evidence here. So I've been trying to keep an eye out for potential clues."

"But you think Ezra is to blame, right?"

He shrugged. "Yes. Maybe I'll find something that points in his direction."

I needed to put the pieces together. "So, you just fell asleep and woke up to me knocking on the front door?"

"Pounding is more like it," he said with a grin.

"And you . . . you don't know where I came from? You don't recognize me at all? Not even my name?"

He seemed to intentionally avert his gaze. "I never met you before Sunday morning," he admitted, a hint of mystery lingering in his tone.

Curious, I probed further, prompting, "But?"

"It's just . . . " Levi sighed. Then, finally meeting my gaze, his eyes held a glint of recognition as he confessed, "You remind me of a girl I read about."

———

After breakfast, we returned to the bedroom where we finished disassembling the bedframe. With synchronized efforts, we maneuvered the bulky pieces down into the basement labyrinth of stacked boxes, then set to work cleaning. We dusted, vacuumed, and polished every surface until a zesty lemon scent enveloped the second bedroom.

"We could fit more furniture in here," Levi said. "I saw a bigger bookshelf and a desk downstairs."

"You think?"

Sweat beaded my forehead by the time we hauled everything upstairs.

The desk was small and simple, but the etched legs gave it character. A dark wood chair with a plush green velvet seat made for a perfect accompaniment. We set a quaint lamp with a tasseled shade on top of the desk, then Levi arranged unused journals and an assortment of pens and pencils nearby.

"I love it," I said.

"Since you made me carry this bookcase upstairs, I'm guessing you're a fan of reading?"

"I believe so."

"What's your favorite book?"

"The whole Little House on the Prairie Series."

We knelt together beside the small shelf, transferring books to the larger one. The collection was evidently shared with his brother. *Hatchet*, *Eragon*, *The Chronicles of Narnia*, and The Lord of the Rings Trilogy were all well used.

"Which was your favorite?" I asked.

He found a worn copy of *Tom Sawyer*. "My brother Colton has always enjoyed fantasy and dragons, but I like that a normal boy could unearth treasures in his normal town. And maybe get into some mischief along the way."

"Has anyone found treasure here?"

He laughed, the sound rich and deep. "No. Only legends of ghosts here."

"Ghosts? I thought the name of the mountain was metaphorical."

"All stories start somewhere." He winked at me then checked his watch. "I've got to go."

"When will you be home?"

"Hopefully by six or seven. Will you be okay here alone? I could drop you off at Momma's house."

A hand-stitched quilt adorned the twin bed nestled in the corner—a creation from Levi's mother years ago. The bookshelf held half its capacity with boxes of books awaiting exploration in the basement. After less than forty-eight hours, this cozy cabin was already starting to feel like home. "I'd like to stay."

"I'll see you in a few hours," Levi said. He stepped forward and raised his arms as if preparing for a hug—but then he awkwardly angled for the door instead.

I wandered down the hall, watching as he climbed into his truck. The bruises on his face were deepening by the hour, yet an undeniable sense of security enveloped me in his presence.

My head throbbed, reminding me of the gash near the back. I should rest. Perhaps pick some flowers for my room after I awoke.

As I settled on the twin bed, I prayed I would awaken with a head full of memories.

———

Levi

I reread the email from my old buddy Drew before climbing out of my Chevy.

Levi,

Please come to my office before practice.

From,
Drew Brown
Sutton High School Principal

I hadn't found myself in the principal's office since my teenage years. No doubt the email had something—or everything—to do with my disappearing act last week.

The scorching touch of the sun-warmed metal seared my hand as I pushed open the glass door of Sutton High at three o'clock, striding inside as if my paycheck wasn't at stake.

The hallways whispered with an eerily silence as I made my way to the office. Dented lockers and faded carpet brought back memories of kissing Lillian between classes, laughing with Ezra, and doing just enough schoolwork to stay on the football team.

A woman with curly silver hair looked up as I entered. It was Bett Woodward, or Mrs. Woodard, the same woman who wrote my tardy slips in high school. A few more wrinkles lined her face, but she still wore her trademark leopard print glasses held in place with a beaded strap around her neck.

She slid them down her nose to look at me. "Why, if it isn't Levi Shaw? Drew said you'd be stopping by today." She cupped a hand beside her mouth, leaning in as she said, "The superintendent and board asked him to speak with you. But you didn't hear that from me."

I pinched my lips together and playfully mimed locking my lips shut. With a smile, I whispered, "How much trouble do you reckon I'm in?"

She waved away my concern. "I wouldn't be too worried. You're a good coach, and everyone seems to love you. It's not like there is a line of men applying for your job. Besides, you played college ball."

In this town, my limited two-year college football career followed by a life-altering ACL injury didn't seem to matter to anyone. They saw me as a success story.

Mrs. Woodward, I mean, Bett, as she insisted I caller now that I was on the school faculty, adjusted her glasses on her nose. Drew will be out soon. What have you been up to?"

The poor woman must be tired of talking to moody teenagers.

Instead of jabbering about myself, I told her about my momma. Bett soaked up the information about herb gardens and peach trees like it was sweat tea made by God himself.

When there was a lull in the conversation, she said, "You're the one who found Shelly Hooper, aren't you?"

Gossip multiplied quicker than wild barn cats in Sutton. Had the police released an official identity?

Bett must have known more than I did. "Yes, I found a body. It was Shelly?"

The rhinestone beads adorning Bett's glasses' strap sparkled in the fluorescent light as she scanned the area, ensuring our conversation remained private. "Yes," she whispered. "Word 'round town says it was Shelly Hooper. Poor girl. I remember her attending this school. She was always going home sick."

She tapped a finger against her temple. "Not your usual flu, mind you. No, she had what them doctors today call . . . " She searched for the word. "Bipolar or something? It's just terrible how she died. Seeing as only three years ago, Duncan . . . " Realization seemed to dawn on her as she recognized her audience and she fell silent mid-sentence.

Drew's door opened, saving us the embarrassment of continued conversation.

One of my football players walked out. Tall, lean, and muscled. Trevor Goodman. He brushed past me without making eye contact and let the main office door slam behind him.

Drew emerged wearing pressed slacks and a white shirt with a colorful tie. Observing him like this tempted me to laugh, but I swallowed it back.

"Thank you for coming, Levi. Please come in."

With a somber expression, I obeyed his command. This was certainly not a time for jokes.

"Let's cut to the chase," Drew said as he shut the door behind him. I wasn't as familiar with *this* Drew—the one with the slicked-back hair and thin lips.

"The board is fuming. That stunt you pulled last week was irresponsible." He settled behind his desk and continued. "And then word got out that you were in a brawl on Saturday evening at Lillian's wedding. Really, Levi? What if some of your guys saw you throwing punches?" He gestured at my face. "You can't hide those bruises. It's clear as water what went down. Some of the board members are asking for your resignation."

I sat uneasily in the chair opposite Drew, shame pressing down on my shoulders. This was the chair reserved for delinquents. Seven days ago, losing my job wouldn't have mattered. But now, with Marigold, I had a reason to earn a living. I had to take care of her.

Earlier that morning, as we cleaned together, I found myself watching her and wondering about her history. Why did she resemble the girl I wrote about?

"Levi?"

I jerked my head toward Drew, embarrassed that thoughts of Marigold had distracted me from this important conversation.

"I'm sorry, Drew. You can tell the board that my decision was rash and emotional. I won't let it happen again."

He perused me from a reclined position. "I get it. All right? We grew up together. We used to play football and cause all kinds of mischief. I can't imagine how it must feel to lose someone like Lillian. But Levi—we aren't boys anymore. We work with juveniles. We have a standard to live up to and must remain excellent role models, an example worth following."

He was poking at my fight with Ezra. Did he want to cast stones? Fine. None of us were free from sin. "Weren't you the one who lit a tapestry on fire at church while trying to light a candle?" I asked.

A smirk tipped his mouth as he pointed a pen at me. "We were children back then."

I extended both hands. "As surely as you asked for forgiveness, I am now asking for mercy. A second chance."

Drew tapped the pen against his desk, clearly deep in thought. Finally, he said, "A written apology should suffice. Have it in my inbox before lunch tomorrow. I'll grease some wheels and make sure everyone knows you're contrite."

Tension melted from my shoulders as I released a breath. "Thank you, Drew. You won't regret this."

"I hope not." He gave me one more stern glare before breaking into a smile. "Now that the serious business is done, get on the field and get those boys ready for their first game."

"Sure thing." I stood. "Why was Trevor here?"

He dropped his pen on a legal pad and crossed his arms behind his head. "He and William got into a fight today. Something about a girl. I told him he'll have to tighten it up if he wants to keep playing. These guys look up to you, Levi. There are consequences for poor decisions. I don't want to be the bad guy if you lose yourself again. You'll have to tell these boys something about your injuries. I recommend you use it as a teachable moment."

Trevor and William drew eerie parallels between Ezra and me. Boys who were friends one second then enemies the next.

A thought nagged at me: *You and Trevor were in this office for the same reason. A fight. But the difference now is that you should know better.*

Should I?

Trevor and William were fighting over a girl. Ezra and I were fighting over the life of my dad. There was a big difference.

But you don't have any proof.

I pointed at the clock. "I should get going. The boys will be in the locker room shortly."

Drew rounded the desk to shake my hand. "Keep your head down, Levi. Stay out of trouble. Everyone is watching."

I left with a nod. Bett waved as I breezed out the door, the rhinestones from her glasses strap blinding me.

My nagging thought was right. I didn't have any proof that Ezra killed my dad. And if nothing changed, I never would.

Chapter Seven

Levi

F ive days ticked by, each one weighted down by the sudden appearance of Marigold and her possible connection to the woman I wrote about in *The Mountain Girl*. Her resemblance to that woman was uncanny.

Was I going insane?

I knew of one man who could help dispel or confirm my fears.

Old Man Donner.

However, with the scrutinizing eyes of the school board tracking my every move and Marigold healing from her injuries, it wasn't until the Saturday following her sudden appearance that I found time to visit the reclusive hermit.

"Are you sure you don't mind if I leave for an hour?" I asked Marigold as she arranged a cluster of flowers on her dresser. The room was overrun with plants in various stages of decay, occupying nearly every available surface. If she stayed here long-term, she might just deplete the land surrounding the cabin of its floral splendor.

"I'll be fine," she said. "I'm feeling better."

The gash on her head had completely healed, and the cuts on her skin were now wispy red lines ringed with new white skin.

"Do you need anything before I leave?"

"No thanks." She walked past me and stepped into the hallway. "I'm going to play in the shed."

"Marigold, you don't have to fix every mower, weed eater, and bike chain in sight."

She'd spent the entire week sitting in the sunshine, tinkering with Dad's outdated equipment and toys. Soon, the entire shed would have workable hardware. Not a bad option, but she should be getting some rest instead.

Marigold slipped her feet into her shoes. Well, technically they were Lillian's old shoes. "I'm enjoying myself," she said with a cheerful tone. "I can't just sit around and read another book. I want to be useful."

She walked out the front door, waving back at me over her shoulder. "See you soon."

I couldn't suppress a grin. Aside from Lillian, Marigold was the most attractive woman I'd ever encountered. Watching her work elbow-deep on a lawn mower with grease streaking her arms was almost too much for me to handle. She stirred a warmth within me that I had only felt with Lillian.

The hot summer air blew through my open window. The song "Yours" by Russel Dickerson played on the radio as I turned onto Old Man Donner's driveway.

Old Man Donner—or *Donner* as my dad called him—was one of the few men I remembered Daddy strumming guitars with. He hadn't crossed my mind in years. Not until Marigold appeared.

Donner, being one of the oldest people in Sutton, knew mountain lore better than anyone around here. I was confident that he could tell me why the words I wrote resembled a real-life girl.

Maybe he would even know a thing or two about the mystery surrounding my dad.

Marigold was a coincidence I simply couldn't ignore. Her dream about two men on a cliff could be straight from my subconscious. Not to mention, her memory of the abusive boyfriend was a scene from the film I'd watched the night of her arrival.

Was it my fault she couldn't remember who she was or where she came from? Did I *write* Marigold into existence?

I shook my head, a sardonic laugh crawling up my throat. Impossible.

Parking behind Donner's rusted red Dodge, I let my hands fall to my thighs. The idea that I was about to ask a recluse if I could have written someone into existence was absurd.

Releasing a weary sigh, I swung open the door of my truck. Stepping out onto the cracked pavement, I made my way across the uneven sidewalk toward the weather-beaten house.

The front steps creaked as I approached the solid wooden door. An odd sight halted me—a vintage soda machine bearing a faded blue and red Pepsi logo sat nestled against the edge of the wrap-around porch.

Steeling myself, I advanced toward the door, contemplating whether to turn back. Instead, I rapped my knuckles against the wood.

Footsteps shuffled toward me from the other side. "Who's there?"

"Levi."

There was a clunk. Was that the pump on a shotgun?

"Levi who? I don't know a Levi."

I angled my body away from the door, imagining a gun pointed at me through the wood. "Levi Shaw. My dad was Duncan Shaw."

There was a momentary pause.

The lock clicked and the door swung open. Donner stood wearing blue jeans, a button-down shirt, and a sleek black vest. He might be a hermit, but he was known for getting gussied up for any day ending in the letter *y*. A shotgun hung from his dark arm, and a cigar hung between his thin lips.

He plucked the cigar out and exhaled a breath of smoke. "Levi Shaw," he said. "Why, you look as fine as rain in August."

"It's good to see you," I said.

He had warm brown skin and a puff of curly gray hair upon his head. "What in Sam Hill brings you here? I don't reckon I've seen you since you were no taller than my waist." He leaned his shotgun against the door frame.

"It's been a while." I ran my fingers through my hair. "Do you mind if we talk?"

He brought the cigar to his mouth while he regarded me. "Duncan Shaw's boy, eh? Yeah, I reckon I got time for Duncan Shaw's boy. I wouldna recognized you if you didn't mention you were his boy. How old are you now?"

"Thirty."

"That so? Well, son, why don't we have a seat on the porch, and you can tell me what's on your mind? Nobody comes to visit me unless they're sellin' somethin' or got somethin' on their mind. I reckon you're the latter."

"You are correct, sir."

As he moved silently behind me, I noticed his bare feet padding along the wooden planks. Despite being dressed nice enough for a formal occasion like church or a wedding, he had opted out of wearing shoes. His yellowed toenails seemed almost fused to his knobby and twisted feet.

"You want something to drink?" He angled into a weathered chair that bore the marks of homemade craftsmanship. Gesturing toward the soda machine, he pointed out the quarters nearby and said, "There're quarters there. Help yourself."

"Sure." My hiking boots clunked across the porch as I approached the towering machine emitting a soft hum and gentle glow.

Beside it sat a worn card table displaying an old cast-iron skillet overflowing with quarters. "What would you like?"

His chuckle reverberated around the wood beams. "Son, even you don't know what you want. The machin'll tell you."

I understood what he meant as I tried to decipher the unmarked buttons. Why were there no labels? I stuck in four quarters, relishing the sound they made as they struck the bottom of the tray, and pressed a button. A metal can came loose and fell with an echoing crack. I pulled out a Pepsi.

When I refilled the quarter slot and hit the button again, a can of beer dropped into the dispenser. I handed the Pepsi to Donner, my mouth watering for the alcohol.

"I pressed the same button twice," I said.

He snapped the tab on his drink and clinked the metal against mine. "That's the beauty of fillin' the thing yourself. You can put whatever you feel like in whatever slot. I never know what I'm gettin'. Your daddy helped me install that marvel. I haven't seen many folks since his passing 'cept when I go to town, but nobody talks to me much."

Taking a seat beside him, I admired the tranquil view around us. Our trucks were parked in the shade of the trees hugging his circular driveway. A plain wooden barn stood next to an unpaved path leading into the woods. Unlike some rural homes in the vicinity cluttered with trash and debris, this land was pristine.

Donner drew from his cigar before taking a gulp from his soda. "What brings you here, son?" His voice sounded tired.

Placing my beer on the porch, I leaned forward with my elbows on my knees. "I have an unusual question."

He closed his eyes as he inhaled the tobacco. "Why, me?"

"Because you and my daddy were close, and they say you know more about this mountain than anybody else around here."

He slowly opened his eyes. "So it's about the mountain then. Git on with it. I ain't gonna live forever."

I played with the tab on my beer. "Something strange happened a few days ago. I might be crazy. But . . . "

"Spit it out, son."

I recounted the details of the wedding, the secluded cabin, the haunting ballad about the mysterious girl, how I suddenly passed out and then found Marigold. "When I woke the next morning, she seemed familiar even though I'd never met her. She resembles the girl I wrote about. I wonder if she's . . . am I crazy?"

Donner gazed past the driveway, but I suspected he peered at something far away in his mind, a memory only he could see. Then he sighed and said, "Son, are you asking me if you wrote this Marigold to life?"

"I know it sounds nuts—"

"Yes," he interrupted. "It's possible."

"What?"

"It's possible," he repeated.

I both feared and expected this answer. "But how?"

His chair creaked as he leaned back. "It happens."

"How?" I persisted, like a record with a scratch.

He took a deliberate drag from his cigar. "Because I've done it myself."

The chirping of birds in the nearby trees mingled with the hum of the soda machine behind us, creating an eerie silence following his confession.

When I recovered my voice, I asked, "You've written someone? Who?" Maybe I wasn't bananas—or maybe we both were.

"That's the problem, son. Once you write them onto the mountain, you can't change what you've done. You gotta live with that for the rest of your life."

He spoke like the existence of Marigold could be a bad thing. "What do you mean? Who did you write?"

He answered my question with a question of his own: "Do you know why mommas and daddies worry about their kids from the moment they hear their first heartbeat until the moment that mommy or daddy passes from this life?"

"No, sir."

He slapped his soda can on the arm of his chair with a clank. "Cause you can't stop fretting about something you're responsible for. It's worse when the thing you made turns out to be bad."

I waited for him to continue.

"I once sat in this house and wrote about the kinda son I wanted. Wasn't married. Just over the age of forty. Saw my odds of meeting the right woman fadin' by the day. I didn't mean to do nothin' reckless. So I wrote about a twelve-year-old boy I could teach to shoot and fish."

He chuckled and shook his head. "Next thing I know, there's a little white boy on this very porch. He's got no idea where he came from or how he got here. I took him in and fed him. The more time I spent with him, the more I began to recognize him. Not from town, but from what I wrote. I did everything I could to find his mommy and daddy, but they didn't exist."

Dots swam before my vision. Was it the beer or Donner's words? My chest tightened. I pressed my head between my knees, trying to suck in a lungful of air.

It couldn't be true. What Donner said was impossible. Crazy.

I forced out one word: "Who?"

"Who what?" he said.

"Who did you—"

"You know Jake Tanner?"

I lifted my head and looked back at him. "Yeah. But he's my age."

Donner nodded. "Yep. The boy I wrote about that day was his daddy. Fredrick Tanner. Everyone in town knows Fred as my boy. Jake is my grandson

91

by association. When Fred showed up, I told people he was my nephew. That made sense because he was white, so there was no way he could be my own flesh and blood. My half-sister was mulatto. After a year, nobody batted an eye when he started calling me Daddy. I said my sister down in Florida died, and no one checked my story."

"I was a poor father," he continued. "Gave Freddie too much rope. He did what he wanted. Got into drugs and junk. Then he had a son. Jake ain't no different. The apple didn't fall far from the tree.

"All the drug runnin' and weapons in Sutton," he said. "Those are my fault. Fred's in charge of all that. Jake just got out of prison a few weeks ago, and I fear it won't be long before he's right alongside his daddy sullying up this mountain."

Fredrick Tanner was Donner's son? That made him Donner Tanner. I'd never known him as anything but Old Man Donner—or simply *Donner*.

"Have you tried talking to him?" I asked.

He laughed. Then tears trickled down his cheeks, and he slapped his knee. "Oh, son. You got lots to learn. 'Course I talked to him. I've talked to both those boys, but they ain't gonna listen. They in it for the money. No, son, I wasn't firm with Freddie from the git-go. I messed him up, and now he does his own thing. It's too late. You say you wrote a girl?"

I nodded. "Her name's Marigold. And she's more woman than girl."

Donner sat back in his chair. "Pretty name. Where is she now?"

"At the cabin."

He shook his head. "The first year is the hardest."

"She won't remember anything from before?"

"Son, there *is* no before. Don't you get it? You wrote this girl." He pointed his cigar at me. "I shoulda done what you done. If I wrote a girl and had a baby with her—with her permission, of course—instead of writing a kid from the git-go, then maybe I wouldn't be in the mess I'm in today."

The weight of this responsibility felt like a tractor on my chest. "But she knows her entire name, as well as her likes and dislikes. She just doesn't have any long-term memories."

"And she won't either. Her life started the night you wrote her. Sure, she might be normal for her age. She'll know most of the things you do, I reckon. Freddie knew everything a twelve-year-old boy should. He even knew some movies and books of the time. But nothing 'bout his history."

"What—what do I do with her?"

He spat a wad of brown liquid off the porch before answering. "Whatdya mean? She's a girl, ain't she? You treat her the way your momma taught you to treat a girl. And on top of that, you protect her. You're all she's got in this world. You darn well better keep an eye on her."

"But she doesn't belong to me. She's a human."

He jabbed a finger at my chest. "And don't you forget it."

This revelation was too much. I stood and paced the porch, trying to process. "How do I explain her to people?"

Donner took another drag of his cigar. "Son, that's entirely up to you. I'm not gonna tell you how to run your affairs. All I gots to recommend is that you don't run 'em like I did mine. You take care of that girl."

How could I have so easily accepted the outlandishness of Donner's explanation? Could he be speaking the truth, or was I fated to be the next crazy old man out on the mountain?

Maybe Marigold's memories would return. Maybe Donner was wrong.

Yet, a deep intuition in my heart told me he wasn't mistaken. The unsettling truth loomed over me, causing my throat to constrict.

I swallowed. "I could use another beer right now."

Marigold

I'm not much of a better cook than Levi, I thought as I inspected the pasta. The spaghetti sauce came out of a can, and my attempt at homemade rolls had turned into dense, brown spheres due to.overcooking. Thankfully, the kitchen carried a comforting aroma of garlic and herbs that enveloped the room. My only consolation.

Levi walked through the door and kicked off his boots. "Smells good in here."

"The rolls are like rocks, but the insides might be salvageable."

He reached toward the cabinet and pulled out a glass bottle of amber liquid. As he brushed passed me, I caught a faint scent of alcohol on his breath. With the bottle in hand, Levi headed to the table that I'd spruced up with flowers.

Had he gone to a bar? He hadn't stank of alcohol since the night we met.

"Are you hungry?" I wanted to ask him if he was okay, but his avoidance of my gaze and swigs from the bottle deterred me.

"Sure."

I plated the food and set them on the table. Levi took a bite without saying grace—unusual behavior for him.

Breaking my roll in two, I discovered its softer interior. "Where have you been?"

"Driving," he said.

"To see a friend?"

He shrugged. "I don't have many friends."

I'd gathered this. His brother Colton was the only guy he had spoken of. I tried a different approach. "Did you visit your momma?"

He took another swig from the bottle. A big one. "No." Then he finally met my gaze, and his eyes focused. "Are you . . . " He stopped and cleared his throat. "Are you happy here?"

Confused, I focused on slathering butter on my roll. "I'm comfortable."

I would be happy if I could regain my memories, but that wasn't happening. Not yet, anyway. But I still had hope that they would return. Or maybe my family would come looking for me.

"What do you remember?"

This topic was at the forefront of my mind almost every minute of every day. "I remember waking in the woods, watching you fall off the cliff, and an abusive boyfriend."

"No, I mean—what do you remember? You said your favorite book was *Little House on the Prairie*. You had three favorite flowers and a favorite drink. What else do you remember?"

"Oh." I'd been so focused on my long-term memory: Who were my parents? My siblings? Where did I live or go to high school? Yet he wanted to know about me, not my past.

I thought for a minute. What *did* I remember?

"I like salted caramel candy, and—"

"Did you go to college?"

What was wrong with him tonight? The alcohol had turned his behavior sour. "I think so, but I can't recall where or what for."

"How many states are there?"

"Why are you asking me this?"

"Do you know?"

"Of course, everyone does. Fifty."

"But you can't remember anything from the night before we met?"

Pushing my plate aside, I stood. "We talked about this earlier. No, I cannot."

He trailed from the kitchen to the deck, where a gentle and warm breeze carried wisps of my hair off my neck. If dandelion dust could truly be wished upon, I would wish for my lost memories to return. It would be my first wish from a genie, and my only wish upon a star. Why did he have to remind me that the one thing I wanted most—the return of my memories—was out of reach?

Levi must have sensed my change of demeanor because he said, "I'm sorry."

I didn't bother turning to face him.

"I didn't mean to push you."

The sun dipped toward the horizon, a daily delight I'd never tire of. I could watch the sunset from this cabin every day.

"Why are you drinking?" I asked.

"It's Saturday. I needed a break."

"I think there's more to it than that."

"Do you want to finish dinner?"

Dinner was a failure. "I'd rather listen to you play the guitar." Every time I heard him play, something came to life in my head and my heart. It was like the music was a part of me.

"Okay."

I couldn't ignore the way he placed the bottle of whisky next to his chair upon returning with his guitar.

Though he didn't sing aloud, I sensed there were words swirling in his mind, waiting to be unraveled. Someday, I would find them.

In between songs, Levi indulged in sips from the bottle. Soon, his once-clear eyes grew bloodshot and hazy. Dusk crept closer, and I no longer felt like crying. We should finish dinner before Levi lost his drink all over the deck.

My stomach rumbled. "Let's eat."

The food had cooled during our musical interlude, but our hunger overrode any desire to reheat it. We finished and stepped outside to admire the sun's grand finale.

Levi held his guitar by the neck and said, "I'm sorry."

"You already apologized."

"I know, but—do you like me?"

I tore my gaze from the sunset. "You're drunk."

"I want to know."

"You're acting strange."

He took another gulp of whiskey before I snatched the bottle away. "I wasn't done," he protested, slurring over his words.

"I think you are."

"Do you like me?"

"I don't know what you're asking, and I won't try to reason with a drunk man. Come on." I clasped his hand, guiding him back into the house. I dropped his hand as soon as he stared at our intertwined fingers, as though this connection held significance. His behavior confused me, as did his reluctance to tell me where he'd been.

He fell onto the couch and reached for the remote.

"You should go to bed," I said, pouring the rest of the brown liquid down the drain.

"Not tired. Wanna watch a movie with me?"

With a wistful glance at the vibrant horizon through the window, I threw the bottle into the trash and then settled beside him, curling my legs to my chest.

Halfway through the movie, he stood. "Be right back," he said, then disappeared down the hallway.

When he didn't return, I went searching.

I found him passed out in bed. The cabin gleamed spotless after my extensive cleaning efforts throughout the past week. I'd even lit candles throughout every room in an attempt to eliminate the musty odors. This particular room smelled like notes of walnut and vanilla.

"Goodnight," I whispered, flicking off the light.

"Wait." His voice was a whisper.

"What?" I whispered back.

"I want to know if you like me."

I knew he was beyond inebriated and probably wouldn't remember this conversation tomorrow. But still, what did he mean? Did I like him as a man? A housekeeper? Football coach? I had yet to have the opportunity to truly know him.

Instead of asking him to elaborate, I chose honesty. "You're my only friend."

His fingers found my face in the darkness and he cupped my cheek, then fell back onto the bed, sleep claiming him with gentle breaths.

Chapter Eight

Marigold

"**M**arigold, are you almost ready?" Levi rapped on my door, his voice muffled through the wood.

I stood in front of my closet with no idea what to wear to a football game. After almost two full weeks, my memory remained a blank canvas.

After fixing every machine in the shed, I'd moped around the house. The anticipation of the game offered a welcome distraction, yet I found myself at a loss when it came to choosing an outfit.

Checking the closet one more time, I slid on a white dress with sunflowers embroidered along the skirt and bodice. The raised flower stitches rippled beneath my fingers as I pressed them over the length of the fabric.

"I'm ready," I said, swinging the door open.

Levi lounged against the arm of the couch in the living room, wearing a casual pair of khaki shorts and a navy blue polo emblazoned with Sutton High Football on its front pocket. He sucked in a breath at the sight of me.

I threw my arms up in uncertainty. "You hate it, don't you? I don't know what to wear."

His gaze lingered over the dress, moved to my face, then roved back down to the dress.

"Levi." I waved my hand to get his attention.

He finally regained his composure.

"Is this appropriate for a football game?"

"Is that from Lillian's wardrobe?"

"Yes. Should I change?"

"She threw it away. . ." he mused, his gaze distant as though he weren't talking to me but through me.

This dress clearly meant something to him. And to Lillian. Perhaps he'd purchased it for her. "I'll change, but I need to know what to wear. It's blazing hot out there, and I want to be comfortable."

He shook his head and gestured to my room. "May I?"

"Yes. Please. I don't think I've ever been to a football game before."

He picked out a pair of jean shorts and a navy blue T-shirt that matched his polo. "Football games are informal." He checked his watch. "And we should hurry."

I wanted to ask him about the significance of this dress, curious to know why he looked at me like I was a ghost. But we didn't have time. Maybe I'd have a chance to ask later.

Later. In the future. Such an elusive concept. A notion I had clung to for almost two weeks now; waiting for mornings that would bring back memories or moments that would trigger forgotten recollections.

But *later* never arrived.

I felt like a blank book with scribbled notes near the middle. I wanted to read the beginning. But it was as though it was unwritten.

Forcing a smile, I walked to the entry where we kept our shoes on a mat by the door.

"You okay?" Levi asked.

I didn't fool Levi. The swiftness with which we learned to read each other was astonishing. In less than two weeks we'd become close friends.

"I'm fine."

"You sure?"

"Yes. Let's go."

He held the door open for me.

Good. I'd managed to fool him.

Ezra

I threw a handful of popcorn in my mouth, crunching on the salty and buttery goodness as I walked to the bleachers to find a seat.

In a town like Sutton, attending a few high school football games each season was the equivalence to attending church on Christmas and Easter. I'd prefer to be on a date at a French restaurant with red wine and delicacies, but I wasn't a heathen.

Not wanting to draw attention to myself, I walked to the end of the home section and ascended the bleachers to the very top.

"Hey, man."

I stopped and turned to find Jake rocking the bleachers as he made his way toward me.

Just this afternoon, we'd outfitted the old barn with grow tents, lights, and a huge padlock with chains on the door. Folks considered my family well-to-do and my association with Jake might waggle tongues. Not the attention I wanted while staring a pot farm.

If the weed was as lucrative as Jake said, I'd consider growing another haul and putting the money aside to buy a vineyard. Then I'd stop farming for good. My father could take over once they released him from prison.

"You got an extra ten?" Jake asked.

"Are you seriously asking me for money?" I had precious little.

"Just a ten. I need more Skittles. They don't have these in prison." He held up an empty bag.

Thankfully, no one seemed to have overheard his comment. "Hush, man."

"Everybody knows who I am and where I've been."

He was right. But still.

To keep him happy and quiet, I gave him a five.

"Thanks, man." He slapped me on the back and ambled toward the concessions.

Among the crowd, a flash of red hair stood out to me. Perched atop the bleachers, just below the announcer's box, sat a young woman. She had long crimson hair that almost reached her waist—a sight hardly seen in Sutton.

She must have sensed my stare because she turned in my direction.

Her fiery hair, creek curves, peach-colored lips, and luminous eyes gave her the appearance of a forest dryad. A dangerous yet irresistible beauty.

Would it be polite to ignore her now that we'd made eye contact? I had no desire in talking to anyone this evening. My mind was too full of worries and hopes, both regarding the farm.

The least I could do was say hello.

She averted her gaze as I moved closer. Did she want to be left alone?

When I reached the top of the bleachers, I sat a few seats away and waved.

She didn't reciprocate. Instead, she set her elbows on her knees and stared at the field with a forlorn expression, her red mane framing her face.

She was not from around here. Nobody in Sutton had hair that color. Had she taken a seat in the home section when she meant to sit with the away team?

And why did she appear so lonely?

Sighing, I walked parallel to the top bleacher seat to settle beside her. Perhaps I was entranced by her mysterious aura, or perhaps it was the ingrained chivalry instilled by my mother. She taught me to open doors for women, listen when they talked, and treat them with respect. My upbringing drove me closer when all I wanted was to retreat to solitude.

She startled slightly as I sat beside her and I offered her my popcorn. "I don't think we've met."

She ignored my offer. "Do you know everyone?"

I pulled the popcorn back. "Everyone in Sutton, yes. But not you."

She narrowed her gaze at me. "I'm Marigold."

"That's a pretty name. Are you here cheering for Sutton?" A child three seats over dropped his popcorn. It cascaded through the slats in the bleachers, causing him to erupt in wails.

"Yes. Sutton." She watched the mother console her son.

"I hoped so."

"You hoped so?" She turned back to face me, the sunset highlighting every freckle on her face.

"Yes, because I shouldn't fraternize with the opposing team." I pointed to the opposite side of the bleachers where parents and kids here to support the away team were bedecked in red and white.

A gorgeous smile carved her cheeks as her gaze followed the direction of my pointed finger.

"Do you have a younger brother playing in tonight's game?"

She swung back toward me. "No. I'm new in town."

"I gathered as much."

"That's right. You know everyone." She brushed the hair from her shoulder. "I'm friends with the coach."

Irritation made my fingers twitch.

Wait a second . . . was she wearing Lilly's clothes? Mother said Levi found a woman on the mountain with amnesia and she'd given Lilly's donated things to her. This had to be her.

Amidst the uproar of the announcer's thundering voice, any attempt at conversation was futile. The crowd stood and cheered as the teams ran onto the field. They introduced the coaches and starters to more applause.

Marigold and I didn't stand, and because we were in the very top row, nobody seemed to notice.

When the kicker served the ball to the opposing team and the scoreboard started ticking down the minutes, she turned to me and asked, "What's your name?"

Levi must have told her horrible things about me. If I told her my name, she might find a new seat. I would have welcomed that just mere minutes ago—but she intrigued me. Why was she sad? Did she truly not have any memories? Could I make her smile?

I answered her question with a question of my own: "How do you like Sutton so far?"

She brushed over my redirection. "It's small but cute. I like the mountain."

Ghost Mountain was an island mountain, separated from her sisters, the Smoky's. The Smoky's were preferable, in my opinion. There were more wineries there.

"What do you like about the mountain?"

She lifted her elbows from her knees as she straightened her posture. Had our conversation distracted her enough to forget why she was feeling downcast? I hoped so.

"The mysteriousness of it. Who wouldn't be fascinated with a place called Ghost Mountain? Do you know any legends?"

"Ah, so you like stories."

"Yes. I love to read, but I get fidgety. Like I should be doing something more productive with my time." She tucked a heap of hair behind her ear. "I guess you didn't ask about that."

"I enjoy learning about you. And, yes, I know a few stories, but not many. I've never been particularly fascinated with the lore. When you grow up in the shadow of it, it becomes commonplace."

The bleachers reverberated with the thunderous stomping, rhythmic clapping, and exuberant cheers of the fans as Sutton High clinched a touchdown. Marigold smiled and whooped along with them.

When the crowd settled, I said, "I'm glad to see you're looking happier now."

Her lips quirked into an embarrassed smile. "Was I that obvious?"

"You appeared melancholy. May I ask why?" Why was I asking her personal questions? I shouldn't be attracted to a woman who had ties to Levi.

She tapped her head. "I . . . um . . . " She rubbed her hands over her thighs. "I don't remember much of my past. I'd prefer not to talk about it."

Not wanting to scare her away, I acquiesced. "That's fine." I looked around, trying to think of a non-intimidating change of subject. "What's your favorite candy?"

And with one simple question, we had fuel for an entire football game's worth of conversation. We chatted about our favorite types of candy, the town of Sutton, and the mesmerizing sight of the sun setting over the rolling hills. Amidst the cheers of parents and the rhythmic beats from the band's halftime performance, we shared stories and laughter.

As the game progressed into the fourth quarter, she said, "I need to run to the snack stand."

The snack stand? How quaint.

I escorted her through the dark to the concessions counter where she ordered four hot dogs.

"You should have mentioned you were hungry," I said. "I would have bought food for you." Correction. I would have tried with the last three dollars in my wallet.

"These aren't all for me. Two are for Levi."

The buzzer reverberated through the night. The game was over. The crowd erupted into a frenzy of victory for the home team.

Marigold and I held back as the crowd surged toward the exit. I couldn't allow Levi to see me with her. I didn't want to deceive her, but what else could I do?

We ambled behind a set of grandparents toward the parking lot where she walked straight to Levi's truck —the same truck he used to drive Lilly home with in high school. She opened the unlocked door and placed the hot dogs on the front seat.

I had to slip away unnoticed before Levi caught sight of us together.

"It was nice to meet you, Marigold," I said in a rush.

"Likewise. Thank you for sitting with me."

Over her shoulder, I noticed as Levi spotted her in the crowded parking lot.

"See you later," I said, then turned and hastened away.

Levi

Ezra was talking to Marigold.

I pushed past my boys and navigated through the crowd toward my truck.

An over-packed minivan smashed its horn and slammed on brakes as I walked in front of it. I gestured apologetically and hurried to the side of the road.

Catching sight of me approaching, Ezra pivoted. Not up for a fight today, I see?

I had no intention of hitting him. Not on school property with the team watching. I couldn't afford another reprimand from the board.

Marigold faced his cowardly form as I reached her. Harsh beams of headlights pierced the night from various angles, making me squint.

"What did he say to you?"

She spun around to face me. "Who?"

I gestured toward the direction Ezra had disappeared.

"Him?" she said. "We talked during the game."

Had he known who she was? The way he hurried away suggested he did.

"He didn't tell you his name?"

"I guess not. Why? Who is he?"

"That's Ezra."

She whipped her head around to look at him. "The man you think—"

"Yes."

"He didn't say."

"Because he knew I wouldn't approve."

She leaned against the grill of the truck. "He didn't seem malicious."

"Everyone in town thinks he's innocent. Except me."

"Everyone?" Her voice held surprise.

I needed to return inside to congratulate the boys. "Are you okay waiting in the truck for a few minutes? I need to grab my duffle bag." I handed her the keys.

"Sure."

A niggling feeling accompanied me into the locker room where I high-fived and praised the boys for their victory. Despite the elation of our first win of the season, an unsettling emotion lingered, casting a shadow over my joy and exhilaration. However, I couldn't identify its source.

After I ushered the last boy out and locked the doors, I found Marigold sitting in the cab of my pickup truck waiting for me.

"Congratulations," she said when I climbed in beside her.

Her praise stirred warmth within my chest. The last woman to encourage me, besides my momma, was Lillian. She had congratulated me after every football game and gig. I didn't realize how much I'd missed it.

As I remained silent, unable to muster a simple "thank you," Marigold lapsed into contemplation. I still couldn't identify the emotion I felt after seeing Ezra.

Returning to the cabin, Marigold's demeanor turned somber. I owed her an explanation for my reaction to Lillian's sunflower dress, the one I wrote a song about that still received airplay on the radio.

How could Lillian dump it into a bag of donation items? Did she think of me so little?

No. She'd simply moved on.

Before Marigold could shut herself in her room, I said, "Do you want to share a drink with me on the porch?"

She slipped off her shoes and tossed her socks aside. "What drink?"

"Pink lemonade and sweet tea?"

A grin tugged at her lips. "Only if you add mint."

After preparing the drinks, I flicked off the kitchen light and cautiously made my way to the deck. I found her on the bench, waiting for me, her legs tucked beneath her, the moon's faint glow highlighting her pale face.

"Here you are," I said, offering the mason jar to her.

She said nothing as I settled beside her, our thighs brushing slightly. Over time, I'd grown more comfortable with her nearness. We could be side by side on the couch or the bench without recoiling.

"Are you okay?" I ventured.

Ice clinked her in her glass, and I glimpsed the moon's reflection on its rim as she tilted it to her lips. She sighed. "I can't remember who I am."

If Donner's theory held true, her memories would remain elusive, though it was the one thing she desired the most. How could I uplift her spirits?

"I wanted to apologize for the way I acted earlier."

This got her attention. She tilted her head in my direction, listening intently.

"That dress you tried on before the game. Lillian used to wear it. Seeing you wear it brought back memories."

She took a sip of her drink. "I suspected it was special."

We lapsed into silence. I'd rather not tell her about the song. Or how I lost Lillian and my dad in less than two weeks. How I felt like a failure for squandering my career in search of my father's murderer.

Three years had passed since then, yet the truth remained elusive. Perhaps delving into Dad's journals would provide some answers. I'd been too distracted by Marigold's appearance and my desire to keep my job to read them.

"How long ago did you and Lillian break up?"

Taking in a breath, I leaned my head back. The indigo sky resembled a canvas that God had punctured with a fork, pinpricks of stars dotting its expanse.

"She broke up with me three years ago, but I'd rather not talk about it."

"It's still painful?"

Yes, I wanted to shout. Yes, it hurt to see the woman I thought I'd marry fall in love with a man she deemed better than me.

"What can I do to uplift you?" I asked, trying to change the subject, desperate to help her find happiness in her situation. The situation I brought her into.

"Help me remember," she said.

She wanted the one thing I couldn't give her.

Darkness enveloped us, refreshing air sweeping off the trees. Not cold, but cooler than the scorching days in the valley.

My hand found Marigold's fingers in the darkness, and taking a risk, I clasped mine through hers. She didn't resist. When our skin touched, I realized the emotion I'd been unable to name.

Jealousy.

The realization stunned me because two weeks ago I deemed it impossible to love anyone except Lillian.

I didn't love Marigold, but seeing her talk to Ezra sparked something I thought I'd never feel again.

I needed to learn more about her, about writing, about the magic of the mountain.

There was only one person I knew to ask.

Chapter Nine

Levi

M id-morning the day after the football game, I parked my Chevy behind Donner's red Dodge. Marigold's slender waist peeked between the hem of her shirt and her jean shorts as she twisted to release her seatbelt, tempting me to—at the very least—hold her hand. Swallowing back my impulses, I hopped out and hefted my guitar case from the bed.

Marigold fell into step beside me. "Who did you say lives here?"

"An old friend." I suspected Donner would be thrilled to meet her. The girl I wrote into existence.

As we ascended the porch steps, I tried to ignore the growing awareness of attraction that lingered within me. Ever since acknowledging my jealousy the previous night, my perception of her had shifted. Her smile, her unwavering trust in me, even the curve of her jaw now held a different significance. She was no longer just a stranger; she was someone who stirred an undeniable attraction within me. I fought against it for two crucial reasons.

One. She didn't know I'd created her.

And two. Dating your roommate was never a good idea.

To prevent myself from dwelling on that thought any further, I knocked on Donner's door.

"Who's there?"

Marigold whirled toward me. "He isn't expecting us?"

I raised my voice. "Levi and a friend."

The door swung open to reveal Donner dressed in his Sunday best attire. A turquoise turtle pendant encased in silver gleamed from the twisted leather stands of his bolo. He leaned a shotgun against the inner wall before centering his attention on Marigold.

"Why, don't you look purdier than a picture?"

She extended her hand gracefully. "I'm Marigold."

He shook it. "Your name is as purdy as you are." Then he turned to me. "To what do I owe the pleasure?"

I lifted my guitar, remembering those evenings bathed in hues of the sunset when my dad and Donner strummed their strings on the porch, while Colton and I took aim with BB guns at squirrels. "Do you remember how to play?" I asked Donner. "Or have you become as rusty as your truck?"

He grinned, revealing yellow tobacco stained teeth. "That ole truck ain't worked for a few months, but I still know a thing'er two about strings."

Marigold perked up. "Your truck is broken?"

The girl couldn't help but fix broken things. With her attention diverted, I could speak to Donner alone.

"Sure is. I don't care enough to get'r fixed. Not with all this delivery stuff nowadays."

"Do you have tools?"

He scratched his head. "Sure. But why—"

"I'll fix it," she declared before he could finish his sentence.

Donner leaned toward me and whispered, "She serious?"

"As serious as a car accident."

He gestured toward the back of the house. "Sugar, you can try to fix that dump. Tools are in the shed out back." With that, he tossed her the truck key and she disappeared around the corner of the house.

Donner watched her go with an amused glint in his eyes. "I reckon it's more likely to snow in July than for that purdy girl o' yours to fix my heap. You best fetch us some sodas while I grab my banjo. My oh my, are you a sight for sore eyes. Thanks for not forgetting this ol' man."

Quarters clinked into the soda machine, drowning out the morning birdsong as Marigold rummaged through a toolbox. The truck groaned in protest as she turned the key to test it.

A can of Sprite tumbled into the dispenser tray, followed by a beer and then a Coke. I took a sip of the cold Coke before popping open the beer with a hiss.

Donner emerged from the house, sporting a towering ten-gallon hat and cradling a shiny vintage banjo. "You know how to play one o' these?" He plopped into the chair beside mine and accepted the beer I offered.

I cracked open a Sprite. "Marigold, you thirsty?"

She was engrossed in tinkering beneath the hood with her sleeves rolled up. She didn't hear me as she worked elbow-deep in the engine.

I set the soda on a third chair. "Yeah, I can play the banjo."

"Your dad was wonderful."

"I can only remember him playing guitar."

"Oh, he definitely had skills beyond that."

Marigold dragged a bright orange bucket from the bed of Donner's truck and placed it between the headlights. With focused determination, she leaned underneath the hood, then hopped down and shimmied beneath the grill with a wrench.

"That girl is somthin' else," Donner remarked.

My guitar nestled comfortably against my thigh, its smooth curves familiar under my fingertips. I played a scale. "I like her," I admitted.

"Nobody can blame ya for that, son."

I should seize this opportunity to ask my questions while she was preoccupied.

"How does writing actually work?"

He scoffed. "You're tellin' me you've lived here your whole life and you still don't know?"

I set the guitar aside. "Should I?"

He threw his hands up in exasperation. "Kids these days don' know nothin'. They have no respect for the land. The legends. I suspect it's for the best, though. But you . . . "

"Are you talking about how Ghost Mountain was named after the Civil War soldiers?"

"Blimey," Donner said. "Do you think that's how the mountain got its name? I thought only city folk believed that bologna, not a boy born in the shadow of the mountain. No, this mountain got the name Ghost Mountain long before the Civil War set men's hearts against one another."

What was he talking about? "But the stories—"

"Are true enough. Yes. But they're only part of the picture."

"How do you know?"

The lines on Donner's weathered face seemed to deepen. "I'm old, Levi."

Could he be older than I'd originally guessed? Anything was possible after what I'd already experienced. "Are you saying you've been here all these years writing?"

Donner spewed his mouthful of beer across the porch. "Is that what you think I am? Some kind of immortal being?" His body shook as he coughed, his hacking giving way to belly-splitting laughter. Amusement rattled his chest right before he sucked in a lungful of air and started the entire process again.

Of course, Donner wasn't immortal. There was no such thing. Yet his words wove a mystical ambiance around the mountain as if the ancient trees whispered of times past, eras they had witnessed but would never reveal to me.

Deflated, I slumped back in my chair, waiting for him to finish laughing at me.

When he'd composed himself, his eyes were wet with tears. "Son, you keep me young. My sides haven't ached like that in years."

Afraid to open my mouth and risk embarrassing myself further, I sat silent.

Finally, Donner caught his breath and grew more serious. "Now listen here, Levi Shaw," he said. "I'm a man. Same as you. I've just lived a few more decades, but I'm surprised your daddy didn't tell you these things."

I leaned forward. "What?"

"You wrote about Marigold in Duncan's journal?"

"Yes."

"Did you ever see him write?"

"Sure. He was always tinkering with a fresh story idea."

Donner sighed and relaxed against the chair. "So he told you nothin' about writing?"

A clank and a grunt sounded from beneath the truck.

"You okay?" I hollered out toward Marigold.

"I'm fine," came a muffled yell in response.

I turned back to Donner. "My dad read books to us like they were as essential as food. He loved words. He scribbled in notebooks and typed on a keyboard, but he didn't ever share what he wrote. I don't think he ever finished another novel. He couldn't keep his passion for one story lit for too long."

"That sounds like Duncan. He lived with his head in the clouds. I just can't believe . . . "

I waited for him to complete the sentence.

"I can't believe he didn't tell you that he was a writer too."

Everyone knew Dad was a writer. He'd even written a bestseller. But Donner wasn't talking about that. He was implying ...

"My dad wrote someone? Like—like how I wrote Marigold?"

Donner slapped the arm of his chair. "Whydya think we were such good friends? He came to me, same as you, asking questions and seeking guidance."

"Who did he write? Is my momma . . . " I couldn't bear to voice that thought.

"No, no, keep your britches on, now. Elizabeth is a local girl. I knew her daddy."

"Then who?"

He shrugged and sipped his beer. "Dunno. He never told me. We talked 'bout it an awful lot, but he never enlightened me."

How could Dad keep a secret like this? Who had he written into existence? Maybe his best friend, Samuel King?

Donner followed my train of thought. "I've always wondered if it was Samuel too. I can't be so sure, but there's a good chance. Are you sure you knew nothin' about writers before you came here askin' me questions?"

"No."

"Hmm." he hummed. "That's surprising. I woulda thought Duncan would have at least told you the legends. The history of the mountain."

I braced my elbows on my knees and eased my head into my hands. Dad may have written Samuel King. How could this be?

Donner continued, "Legend says there are a few writers every generation. There ain't no rhyme or reason as to who they are. It seems to run in families. Heck, we might not be the only ones alive with the ability. It's called Ghost Mountain because ghosts live here. Not real ghosts, mind you. But people born from ink and pen. Your Marigold is a ghost because accordin' to the rest of the world, she don't exist."

He scratched the scruff on his neck. "I suppose it makes sense the stories faded to legend. It wouldn't do for all folk to know others had powers. But still, you're Duncan's boy. You oughta know."

My mind still tried to wrap my thoughts around Dad and Samuel King. "So, how does this work? If my dad wrote Samuel here, then how did he become a legal citizen? How did you get papers for your son, Fred?"

He waved off my question. "Ah, that's not a big deal. We got papers for Fred easy enough. I'm sure even your daddy coulda helped Samuel get forged papers. I don't reckon he ever applied for a passport. The legal system had little reason to look into him."

"But wouldn't they have discovered his papers were false when he went to prison?"

Donner considered this. "Good point, boy. I dunno. I don't have any proof that it was Samuel he wrote. It coulda been anyone."

"I wish he were still here." The words rushed out like a fresh wave of grief instead of a simple statement.

Donner's hand settled on my back. "I know, son. I know."

I'd never asked him about my daddy's death, but suddenly, knowing his opinion was important. "Do you think my daddy killed himself?"

Donner withdrew his hand and sat back. "I dunno, son. I dunno."

"But if you were to guess. Do you think he would've stepped off that cliff?"

Donner pursed his lips then shook his head. "No. I don't believe he was that type of man."

"But he was creative, passionate, and emotional." For the first time, I tried to convince myself to believe what so many others did.

My mouth spouted off the excuses and explanations I'd been told. "Maybe he struggled with depression. Or anxiety. Maybe his passions overflowed into emotions he couldn't handle."

"He was passionate about life," Donner said. "His creative outlets spilled into everything he did, but I don't think they poisoned him."

He fitted the banjo into the crook of his arm and played the strings. A lifting melody cascaded over the porch like an evening breeze.

Bubbles burned the back of my throat as I gulped back the soda.

Marigold was still underneath the truck.

"Should I tell her how she came to be?"

Donner sighed, deep and heavy. "Son, that's a tricky one. Do what ya think is best."

My foot tapped in irritation. "That doesn't help when a flesh and blood person is searching for her lost memories that don't exist. How am I supposed to break the news to her?"

Sadness filled his eyes. "I don't have the answers. This life ain't easy."

"Did you tell Fred?"

He ran his calloused fingers over the strands of his bolo, a thoughtful expression on his face. "I tried once, but Fred was grown by the time I got around to it. Grown people don't believe in the impossible like a kid. Maybe if I told him sooner." He shrugged. "So, to answer your question—no, Levi Shaw. I won't tell you what to do. All I'm gonna advise is that you treat her good."

"What does that mean? She's not a little boy who needs a father. Should I date her? Marry her? Bring her to the nearest town and let her find her way? How do I keep her safe?"

"Levi." Donner's voice was gentle. "This is your story. I can't write it for you."

He must have sensed my unease because he played a merry tune on the banjo. "You listen here, boy. I don't want nothin' to do with messin' up your life. You do what you feel is right, and I'll pray it turns out well."

We both watched as Marigold dug her heels into the dirt, tinkering underneath the truck. She wiggled out, climbed into the seat, then cranked the key. The engine roared to life with a determined rumble.

Donner sputtered on his beer while Marigold waved us over. I held back a laugh.

Donner and I left our instruments to inspect her handiwork. She backed away as Donner approached.

"Dang, girl," he said in awe. "You is somethin' else, aint ya?"

She wore a proud smile and offered him the key.

He raised both hands defensively. "Naw. You fixed it, you keep it."

Her smile faltered. "What?"

"You heard me. I don't need this heap. I got another in the barn." He gestured toward the closed wooden structure.

"You mean it?"

"Sure. As long as you can drive a manual."

A grin tugged at her lips. "I think I can."

"You *think*?" Donner said.

"I'm seventy percent sure I can drive a stick shift."

Donner's laugh was more like a howl. "Girl, you gotta do better than think. You gotta know, or else you'll burn the engine before you leave the driveway." He pointed at the grassy path leading into the woods. "Why don't you two take a drive?"

She cleared the bucket and toolbox away from the grill and jumped into the front seat.

Donner slapped my back as I passed. "You make sure she's safe, hear?" He winked at me.

The truck hummed as I closed the door. Dirt smudged Marigold's shirt, and a twig dangled from her hair. With one foot on each pedal and hand poised on the gearshift, she was ready to take off.

"Before you start—"

She shifted into first gear, eased off the clutch, and accelerated. The truck jerked and then evened as she worked the clutch.

I hurried to attach my seatbelt, only to realize she hadn't bothered to fasten hers. She was a whirlwind of impulsiveness and beauty.

Sliding across the bench seat, I attempt to secure her seatbelt as well.

"What are you doing?" she questioned, just as a pothole jotted us upwards, making me hit my head on the roof.

"Ouch!" I exclaimed with a laugh. "Please slow down before we end up in a ditch somewhere. Let me help you with your seatbelt."

"We're not even on the road."

"That's true," I agreed. "But you might hit a tree if you keep this speed."

"I will not." She didn't even tap the brake.

She ignored my advice and continued at her reckless pace. As I leaned over to fasten her seatbelt, another pothole threw me off balance, causing my hand to accidentally land on her thigh before I quickly withdrew it. She cast me a stern, disapproving stare.

"Sorry," I said. "This would be a lot easier if you weren't driving like a maniac."

She smirked, focusing on navigating the rough terrain ahead.

Finally managing to secure her seatbelt and then mine amidst the truck's swaying motion, I advised, "You should slow down for the potholes. There's more than one way to damage a truck."

The ride eased a bit. "How am I doing?"

I gripped the handle. "You can work a manual, but I think 'drive' is a generous term."

She reached out and slapped my arm playfully. "Are you saying I'm a bad driver?"

"You said it, not me."

Her laugh filled the cab. "This is fun."

"I'm glad someone is enjoying it." I pressed my palms against the truck's ceiling to balance myself as she careened through yet another divot in the earth. The road veered up a hill. She shifted like a pro. "Turn up here," I said, pointing at a clearing. My body lurched forward as she braked. "Easy, girl. Don't hesitate. Just do what you know to do."

She shot me an exasperated look before smoothly shifting gears, braking again for a sharp turn, and then seamlessly adjusting once more. Was it wrong of me to hope she stalled out and left us stranded in the woods together? Maybe she'd let me hold her hand as we strolled back to Donner's place. I braced myself for the return trip.

When we reached the house, I made a show of throwing myself out of the truck and pretending to kiss the ground.

"How'd she do?" Donner called.

"I'm lucky to be alive," I said.

Marigold pocketed the keys. "He's nothing but a big baby. I did great."

Standing up, I shrugged nonchalantly. "We're in one piece. That's the best I can say."

She shoved me playfully then strode toward Donner.

Sitting down on the porch steps, Marigold hesitated, holding out the keys to Donner. "You aren't seriously giving me your truck," she insisted.

He cradled his banjo with a twinkle in his eye. "How 'bout this? You can keep the truck, but in return, you swing by once a week to do my grocery shopping. I'll pay ya. My legs ain't what they used to be for all that drivin' every week."

"Really?" Marigold's eyes widened in disbelief.

"Sure," he drawled.

She leaped from her seat and enveloped the old man in a tight hug. "Thank you! This means the world to me. I've been searching for something meaningful to do, and—"

"Hush, girl," Donner spluttered. "Don't go gettin' all sentimental on me now. The truck is a dump anyway. She never woulda felt the road underneath her tires again if you ain't fixed her. And I'm too old to be drivin'. You're doing me a favor."

We lingered on Donner's porch as the sun dipped lower in the sky, passing the time with games of soda machine roulette and twanging strings, while being regaled by his tales of yesteryears.

It seemed like an ordinary day that could happen anytime, one that could easily blend into any other—but it was anything but ordinary. Because in that moment, a subtle shift occurred within me.

It felt as though a piece of my heart that held onto Lillian was finally loosening its grip, creating space for Marigold to settle in its place.

Chapter Ten

Marigold

The sun warmed my shoulders as I inspected the back of Donner's Dodge. The stubborn gate refused to fold down. With a determined push, I pressed my weight into it and heard a crack before it dropped further than expected, startling me.

Great. A broken part.

I could feel my neck gradually tanning under the relentless afternoon sun as I tried to jerry-rig the misaligned parts into position. Nothing worked.

The sudden sound of tires popping on gravel drew my attention to the driveway. Levi wasn't due home from work for several more hours.

A silver Ford Bronco parked behind Donner's truck. Ezra King stepped out.

Yesterday, Levi and I visited the quaint Catholic church with its towering steeple and enchanting stained-glass windows. Ezra had also been present.

He lied to me that night of the football game. Betrayal and acceptance warred within me as I tried to reconcile the lie with the kind man I'd spoken to for hours.

The sunlight reflected in his sunglasses as he meandered to where I sat in the bed of Donner's truck.

"Hello," he said, removing his sunglasses and hooking them to the collar of his shirt.

"What are you doing here?"

He shoved his hands into his pockets. "I wished to speak to you."

Wished to speak to me? Who talked like that? Placing my foot on the rear of the Dodge, I vaulted over the gate of the truck and sat on the rail with my feet in the bed. "You could have spoken to me at church yesterday."

"True, but Levi was there, and I didn't want to cause a scene."

I recalled the purplish bruises on Levi's face, though they had now softened into faint shadows tracing his cheekbone. The man in front of me was responsible for those marks.

I couldn't reconcile the murderous man Levi spoke of with the congenial companion I'd conversed with at the football game. Should I be afraid of Ezra or accept him as a friend?

"Why do you hate Levi?" Neither man seemed to be the type to throw punches at a wedding, yet they both had.

"Do you mind if I sit?" he withdrew his hands from his pockets and gestured toward the opposite side of the truck from where I sat.

I pointed to the rail across from me, unwilling to forgive his betrayal so easily.

He launched over the broken tailgate and faced me. "It's cooler up here than in the valley."

Still irked that he'd omitted his identity, I snapped. "Are you here to talk about the weather?"

A slow, sad smile played on his lips. "No. I came to apologize. I realized who you were shortly after we met. I didn't want you to think ill of me, so I omitted my name."

"And now you feel guilty?"

"Not really, no. I'm glad we had the opportunity to get to know one another. I came here because . . . " He paused, bracing himself against the rail. "I care about what you think of me, and I worry that you've only heard dreadful things from Levi."

Interesting. Levi believed Ezra had murdered his father—but the mysterious man I met at the football game, and the man who sat before me now, did not exude any hint of malevolence.

Killers didn't apologize. Or so I suspected.

If he wasn't a murderer, he still raised suspicion. "I can't trust you."

"Because of what Levi told you?"

"No. Because you lied."

"Which is why I am here asking for forgiveness."

Huffing, I spun my legs over the side of the truck and then hopped, landing in the dirt.

"What were you doing when I parked?" he asked.

"Trying to fix this," I said, slapping the metal. "But I need a new part."

"How about a used yet intact part?"

"You have a spare part for a 1996 Dodge Ram sitting in your shed?"

Rocks crunched beneath his weight as he spun off the truck bed onto the driveway. "No, but the farm has a truck graveyard. I'm not promising you'll be able to find what you seek, but it's a free place to start."

Still reluctant to continue our conversation about forgiveness, I asked, "You busy right now?"

He grinned. "Follow me."

———

Ezra

The rusted old truck trailed behind my Bronco as we descended the mountain. Considering it was a manual transmission, Marigold did an excellent job easing around the steep twists and turns.

She parked in the lot outside the last farmhouse—my house—and stepped out. Her wavy red hair dropped halfway down her back as she shoved her keys into her back pocket.

"Where is this truck graveyard?" she asked, a smudge of grease marring her jaw.

"Near one of the back pastures. C'mon. We'll take a golf cart."

"You have a golf cart?"

"This farm is over three hundred acres. Or we could take my truck if you'd prefer."

She shook her head. "The golf cart sounds like fun."

"Have you been to the farm before?"

"Yes, twice. The day after I . . . met Levi. And then yesterday, after church."

I wanted to press for more details, curious to know what she was leaving out of her story. But I decided against it. For now, at least. "Have you had a tour?"

"Not yet."

Taking a chance, I extended my arm toward her. "Will you allow me to be your guide?"

She hesitated, then intertwined her arm with mine. "As long as we end up at the truck graveyard."

"Of course, Milady." I gestured toward the farmhouse before us. "As you can see, this is my house. You've been to Beth's. Next up is my mother's. Then the farm store."

She plucked flowers from the community co-op garden, caressed ripe peaches in the orchard, giggled at the cows grazing in the pastures, and marveled at the furrowed rows of soybean, hay, and corn fields.

To my astonishment, Marigold had a way of dispelling all of my worries. As we strolled and talked, her arm lightly brushing against mine, a sense of contentment washed over me. It was almost . . . joyful.

"Is the golf cart in there?" she asked, pointing toward the old barn.

My worries swept over me once more. Inside were four grow tents concealing marijuana plants flourishing under artificial light. Only Jake and I were privy to this secret operation hidden behind the padlocked doors.

What would she think if she found out?

I came to the cabin this morning to ask for forgiveness, but I also intended to inquire about her thoughts of me. After I rushed away at the football game, and then as I watched her in church yesterday, I realized how much her perception mattered to me.

Had Levi painted me as a monster?

Why did I care?

I wasn't sure. But I did know that I enjoyed her company, and I didn't want her to view me as a criminal—even if I was one.

"No, the golf cart is this way." I steered her toward a newer metal barn located a quarter mile away, housing an array of farm equipment.

Entering through a side door of the monstrous metal structure, we were greeted by dim lights casting shadows on tractors, combine harvesters, and broken irrigation pipes. The faint aroma of cow manure and hay mingled in the air, yet Marigold didn't flinch at the smell the way most girls would.

"Over here," I said, gesturing toward the little green golf cart positioned to the right of a wide barn door. With a push and a metallic creak, I widened the door enough for the cart to pass through smoothly.

Marigold slid into the passenger seat beside me. I cranked the key in the ignition, and we swerved out the door.

"This is a unique farm," I noted as we drove. "Because of its size and the diversity of dairy cows and harvesting crops, it's the biggest and most well-known in the area."

Watching the fields blur past us, she said, "That could also be because of its name."

I smiled. "Yes. Ghost Mountain Farm sticks with you, huh? Tell me about your truck."

Perspiration moistened my hairline as she told me about Old Man Donner and the part-time job opportunity with him. Her eyes sparkled at the prospect of earning a few dollars, igniting a strong desire in me to offer her a position at the farm.

I was drowning in debt. Jake was on the payroll for legitimacy. I had no margin to hire her.

Marigold's presence evoked memories of a girl I'd encountered in Italy.

I knew I wasn't made for farm life. So after graduation, I left Sutton to backpack the world. But I only made it to Europe. Italy captivated me with its vineyards, Roman structures, Florence art, and picturesque waterways in Venice. The allure was heightened by the company of Alessia, a captivating Italian woman I'd met in Amalfi. She made me feel like my true self. We boated around Sicily and wandered through vineyards, sampling various types of wine and cheeses.

And then she dumped me for a wealthier American tourist.

I left Italy soon after, yet my passion for grapes and wine lingered.

These memories wouldn't leave me as I roved the farm in a golf cart with Marigold. Both girls—Alessia and Marigold—saw me beyond my responsibilities, allowing me to embrace a sense of boundless freedom.

To my family, I was a brother and a son. To Levi, I was a villain. Yet with Marigold, I found solace in being myself.

The truck graveyard came into view.

"It's just up here," I said, surprised to know that a younger version of me—that carefree spirit—still lived deep within my psyche. Perhaps this mystery girl might carve the dark edges off my soul and reveal the boy I was before my life crumbled.

Veering right, we jolted over a grassy path of fallow field toward a cluster of abandoned and rusting machinery—a red and green tractor. They loomed large beside three cars stripped of their wheels. Scattered around were eight pickup trucks in various stages of decay, adding splashes of color to the desolate scene.

Marigold hopped out the second we stopped and asked, "Do you have a toolbox?"

I pulled one from the back of the golf cart. "Right here."

Finding the tools she needed, she went to an old Dodge and started tinkering with the tailgate.

I casually leaned against the side of a blue Ford F-150 and asked, "Where did you learn to fix trucks?"

She shrugged, her hands still working on the tailgate. "I dunno. It's not just trucks. I can fix almost anything."

I raised an eyebrow, intrigued. "Is that so?"

She ignored my question and asked, "Can I take a piece off this one?"

I crossed my arms. "That's why these trucks are here. Harvest what you need." Trying to keep the conversation light, I said, "I don't mean to pry, but . . . why can't you remember where you learned to fix things?"

She huffed. "I don't want to talk about this."

"Why?"

With a swift motion, she extracted the piece from the truck and held it up. "Because it's none of your business."

"I didn't mean to pry."

She spun around, the truck piece in her palm. "But you did."

"I apologize."

"You're doing a lot of that today."

I nodded. "True."

She stalked to the golf cart, pocketed the piece, and loaded the tools into the back. "Can we go?"

"Yes," I said. I wanted to ask more without offending her. "You don't recall your family or birthplace?"

We hit a bump in the road, causing the cart to jolt. I focused on her solid jaw as she clenched tightly, grinding her teeth.

"No," she gritted out. "But it sounds like rumors about me are already spreading."

I averted my eyes back to the road ahead. "Have you asked the Sheriff to run your name through the database? He might be able to locate your family. He's my new brother-in-law."

Her voice lifted with hope. "You think he'd help?"

"Yes. He's an excellent lawman." Hopefully not good enough to discover my new operation, though.

"When can I talk to him?"

Perhaps we could spend more time together. "Would you like to go now?"

"Truly?"

I nodded. "We can take my truck."

She squirmed in excitement as though unable to contain her joy. I drove the golf cart to my house and parked in the front lawn underneath the leafy shade of the giant tree.

Marigold hesitated before entering my Bronco.

A pang of anger pricked at me. "Marigold?"

She looked at me.

"I can only guess what Levi has told you about me. Let me assure you. I would never hurt you."

Her eyes studied me a few seconds longer. Then, without a word, she unlatched the door and hopped inside.

Marigold and I lingered by the reception desk inside the Sheriff's office. His secretary, Joy, tapped her pink dagger-like nails on the phone. "Do you have an appointment?" she said with a bored expression on her perfectly contoured face.

"No."

It was hard to miss the heavy black eyeliner that curved at the corners of her eyes. "Sorry, he's too busy."

"Ezra!" Jackson's name echoed through the entryway. "I have a minute."

I couldn't tell if he was granting me access because of my familial relation or because my presence intrigued him. I'd never come to the sheriff's office willingly before.

Exchanging a knowing glance with Marigold, we stepped inside the spacious office.

"Ezra." He gave a gruff shake of my hand. "What brings you here today?" Intrigue it was.

Papers cluttered the top of his desk. A sure sign he was busy. Usually, Jackson's space was immaculate.

"This is Marigold." I gestured to her as she shook his hand. "She was wondering—"

"Can you help me find my family?" she finished for me.

Jackson motioned for us to sit in the chairs opposite his desk. Without saying a word, he corralled the papers into a neat pile.

Marigold looked at me expectantly. I subtly motioned under the desk for patience—signaling that he would address her question eventually. Jackson was a man of few words.

He stared at us for forty seconds. Yes, I counted.

"I heard about your case around town," he finally said to her. "Tell me your version of how the events unfolded."

"I have no memory of anything in my life before Saturday, July twenty-seventh," Marigold offered.

"But you know your name?"

"Yes." She twisted in her seat.

"Then you remember something. What else have you got?"

She intertwined her fingers in her lap, clearly nervous. "Maybe an abusive boyfriend."

"What do you mean, *maybe*?" Jackson's tone was firm, demanding answers. This, along with his military background, is what won him the Sheriff's office. Folks felt safe with his no-nonsense attitude and precision-like questioning that got him results.

I gave her hand a gentle squeeze, but she didn't seem to notice.

"I have a vague memory of a guy who hit me. It's hazy."

"Do you remember his name?"

"No."

Her cold fingers trembled beneath my touch.

With a deep sigh, Jackson pressed on. "Do you recall your last name?"

"Yes. I'm Marigold Anne Rivers."

He stood and turned to a wooden filing cabinet behind his desk. Fingering through slots, he found the one he was looking for and extracted a slip of paper. "Can you complete this form?"

She tugged free of my grip, still seemingly unaware that I'd held her hand. "I can fill out my name and address," she said, reviewing the paper. "I'm living with Levi Shaw."

Jackson gave me a pointed look as if to say, *what kind of game are you playing?*

"No social security number?" He asked, turning back to face her.

"No."

"Birth date?"

"No, but I'm twenty-six."

"Do you have a phone number at least?"

"Yes," I said.

She frowned at me, clearly confused.

"I'll give you my old phone," I said.

"I was referring to a phone number we could trace back to an identity," Jackson clarified.

She shook her head.

"Fill out your name and address," Jackson said. "I'll see what I can do." After she filled out the few items, he said, "Come back in two weeks."

"Two weeks?" she said, her voice raising an octave.

"Yes. I'm sorry. There are pressing matters I need to attend to."

As I glanced over the papers, words like *drug*, *trafficking*, and *Sutton* caught my attention.

Did he know?

I had to play it safe. I held out my hand. "Thank you for your time, Jackson. We'll be back in two weeks."

Marigold's sagging shoulders reminded me of a wilted flower as we returned to my truck.

"Hey," I reassured her. "Don't lose hope. He might find something."

She tried to smile. "Hopefully."

"Let's get you back to the farm and I'll give you that phone."

Her spirits lifted like a flower blooming under sunlight as she asked eagerly, "Truly?"

"Yes. I have an old one I was about to toss. You may have it."

"Are you lying to me to make me feel better?"

I held out my hand for a shake. "No. Promise."

When she shook, I felt the warmth of her fingers thaw a section of my soul. Jackson's warning look pierced my memory. She lived with Levi.

What exactly was I getting myself into?

Marigold

An unread message blinked on my phone's screen when I arrived home. I tapped it open while exiting the truck.

> **Ezra:** Let me know if you need more truck parts. See you in two weeks.

A sudden tap on the window made me drop the phone with a yelp.

Levi raised his hands apologetically. "Didn't mean to scare you." His muffled voice was barely audible through the closed door.

Granules of dirt stuck to my fingers as I fumbled along the floorboards to retrieve the phone. Finally finding it, I grasped its metal frame just as Levi pulled open the door.

"Were you at Donner's?" he said, then he noticed what I held. "Where did that come from?"

Shifting out of the truck, I landed on the driveway. Ezra was right. The temperature was cooler on the mountain than in the valley.

Producing the Dodge part from my pocket, I said, "I was at the truck grave-yard savaging for parts. Now I can fix the tailgate."

"Who told you about the truck graveyard?"

"Ezra," I said. "And he's the one who gave the phone to me."

I'd contemplated how to present these offerings to Levi and concluded that being straightforward was the best approach. I couldn't stop them from loathing each other, but I also couldn't be swayed to hate either of them because of their word against the other.

From my perspective, Levi was a good guy. And so was Ezra.

Levi's grin disappeared as he said, "Why were you with Ezra? Marigold, he's dangerous."

I released the tailgate and began working with the tools I'd left in the back.

"He's trying to steal you from me."

I paused. Yes, this thought had occurred to me—but when we were in the golf cart, Ezra looked at me like he was surprised to like me. I didn't know exactly who Ezra was or what he was capable of, but I knew he wished me no harm. He'd seen my hesitation before getting into his truck, and he'd spoken to me with care.

No, Ezra King was not a threat, but I wouldn't pretend to know his intentions for Levi. Thus, I didn't plan to get stuck between them.

This didn't excuse his mishandling of information at the football game.

I'd keep an eye on him. "He was a gentleman," I said.

Levi's shadow loomed as he approached the area where I worked. "He acts that way with everyone. He's playing you. You can't see him again."

Standing up straight, I addressed Levi calmly but firmly. "Levi," I began, choosing my words carefully. "You helped me when I was hurt. You've given me a place to stay. But you cannot tell me who I may and may not speak with."

His hand lightly gripped my wrist. "I only want to protect you."

I moved away from his touch. "And I appreciate that. But can you trust me?"

"I know Ezra better than you."

"Levi, when you answered the door that night when you were drunk and bruised, I could have fled. But I trusted my intuition and stayed. Allow me that same trust with Ezra now, too, okay? I needed this part, and he helped me get it. He gave me the phone and I'm grateful. Aren't you?"

I didn't share about my trip to the police station. I wanted one thing, one hope, that was mine to dream about at night.

"Ezra is the one who gave me the bruises."

Levi wasn't going to drop this. Turning my back on him, I worked the broken piece off the truck. "Can I fix this?"

"Marigold, if something happened to you I—"

"Would understand that I'm an adult capable of making my own decisions and even making my own mistakes?" My back remained turned.

"I would never forgive myself," he said, and then he walked away.

Chapter Eleven

Levi

I leaned against the wooden headboard, guitar across my legs as I looked toward the ceiling. Then, setting the instrument aside, I tiptoed down the hallway and listened outside Marigold's door.

Nothing.

Our argument still made me wince. She didn't understand. The weight of her past, present, and future haunted me. If I had given her life, shouldn't I keep her safe?

On the other hand, she was right. I couldn't chain her to a radiator and expect her to be happy. She had to experience life, make mistakes, find friends, and choose a path.

I went back to my dad's room and sunk into his desk chair.

Since learning about this miraculous gift of writing, my goal at the cabin had changed. No longer solely focused on unraveling the mystery of my father's final days through his written words, now my quest was to unearth the journal that held the power to breathe life into its characters. Who did he write into existence? And who was my dad really?

To discover my dad's colossal secrets, I knew that delving into each journal scattered around this bedroom would be my first step forward.

I flipped through the pages of a composition notebook resting on his desk. I might as well start here.

Two hours later, I determined the journals in this room contained snippets of books, scenes, and diary-like entries, but there was nothing from the year he'd passed, nor any characters that could have walked off the page.

"Who did you write, Dad? Did you tell them what you did?"

I considered confessing the truth about Marigold's origins, but I worried she'd think I was crazy. After all, if she told me that she'd created me with ink and pen, I'd write her off as being "not all there."

Writing someone into existence was the stuff of fairytales.

If Marigold and I were characters in a book . . .

An idea took root.

Was Marigold's appearance a fluke? Or could I do it again?

With shaking fingers, I found the journal where I'd written *The Mountain Girl* and set the pen to paper.

Faithful as a friend true
He appeared on the mountain running through

With golden fur and a long snout
He stole his master's thawing heart
Four paws and floppy ears
The dog was happy for all his years

I placed the pen beside the journal.

Now what?

Did Marigold come into existence the moment I wrote her—or was it sometime later? She could have stumbled through the woods for an hour before finding the cabin.

Less than a minute passed before I heard a bark.

My chair smashed against the bed frame as I rocketed up and raced out the front door. Blackness enveloped me as I careened to the driveway, rocks poking my bare feet.

A form rushed toward me and landed its paws against my stomach with a fearful whimper. I caught its furry head against my chest and tried not to vomit.

It worked. How was this possible? Fur wiggled between my fingers. The dog pushed off and ran toward the light that streamed through the open door.

"Wait!" I yelled. But the animal bolted inside faster than I could catch it.

Chasing after, I finally found the dog in the kitchen. It had parked itself by the refrigerator.

Observing him up close, the creature hardly resembled a typical canine. It was the ugliest mutt I'd ever seen. He was on the small side of medium with long droopy ears, a pudgy body, and a short yellow coat. He looked like a golden retriever who lost a fight with a beagle.

Maybe the trick to writing was simple. Don't force it. When I had penned Marigold effortlessly, she had emerged as a vision of beauty and femininity.

Not so with this mutt.

The dog set his paws on my chest as I knelt to stroke his fur. I checked underneath to confirm that he was, in fact, a male.

"What's your name?" I scratched behind his ears and almost gagged. He smelled like he hadn't bathed in months.

He licked my cheek as I assessed him, holding my breath. He appeared to be young, but not a puppy. His chubby frame wobbled with eagerness, every movement exuding a contagious energy. The last time I owned a dog was back in high school when Tuck, our adventurous black lab, used to race after passing cars down the farm driveway.

"How ya doin', buddy?"

In response, he licked my bicep.

"You hungry?"

His tail picked up speed, staring at me adoringly as I stood. I swore under my breath. The evidence that I could write physical bodies into existence chilled my fevered brow.

The dog barked.

"Shh. Just a minute. I'll find you something to eat."

Bark. Bark. Bark.

"Hush, boy. I'm moving."

Marigold's door swung open. "What's going on?" She stepped into the light, clothed in cotton shorts and a tank top that left little to the imagination—especially since she wasn't wearing a bra.

The dog sat beside me and inspected her. "I found him," I said.

Her lips twisted as she studied him. "He's rather unfortunate looking, isn't he? Where did you find this . . . dog?"

"In the woods."

Her expression strained. "The same way you found me?"

I couldn't tell her the truth. Not yet. "Kind of."

She knelt in front of the animal and plugged her nose. "He reeks. And he doesn't even have a collar. Think someone's looking for him?"

"Nope. He's ours now."

"How do you know?"

"I just do. Trust me. He needs us."

She kept her thumb and forefinger pinched over her nose as she extended her other hand toward the creature. "What's his name?"

The dog had a mischievous glint in his eye. I recalled the books *Tom Sawyer* and *The Adventures of Huckleberry Finn*. Grinning, I said, "Finn, sit."

He sat.

"I guess his name is Finn," I said.

"Can we give him a bath?"

"Yes. I don't want him jumping on the couch smelling like this. I'll get a rope and some soap if you can keep him in the kitchen.

He tried to follow me.

"Wait," Marigold said. She opened a cupboard and grabbed a bag of potato chips. "Want a treat, Finn?"

He abandoned me to wag his whole body in her direction.

Ten minutes later, we stepped outside and into the grass illuminated by the porch light. Marigold held the rope while I tried to lather Finn's ever-moving body. "Can you hold him while I rinse?"

"Scrub him more."

"Fine."

Finn broke free from her grasp and shook, spraying soap, water, and dirt across her upper body.

She met my gaze with wide eyes, lips twitching. Neither of us could hold back our laughter.

Finn must have wanted to join in the fun, because he jumped against my stomach, pushing me off balance. I collapsed on my backside in the dirt.

Marigold rolled onto the grass and laughed harder.

Smirking, I corralled Finn and sprayed him with the hose.

Marigold's laughs rang through the woods. I couldn't remember a time when Lillian and I had laughed like this. I didn't know it was even possible to fall in love with another woman. Because that's what was happening. Although we bickered and I couldn't force her to see life through my lens, I was definitely falling in love with her. She was by my side at one in the morning, helping me wash the ugliest dog in the world.

Finn slipped, and the hose jerked in my grasp, dousing Marigold as she sat cross-legged on the grass with the rope in her hands.

She shrieked. "Levi Shaw!"

"Sorry."

The fabric of her tank top turned nearly transparent as she erupted into laughter.

By two o'clock we were back inside, changed into fresh clothes, and curled on the couch with our newest cabin vagabond. None of us wished to be separated.

And with Marigold's feet snugly tucked under my legs and a contented dog nestled between us, a sense of completeness washed over me.

There was no doubt in my mind now. It was possible for a once-broken heart to feel whole again.

Marigold

Warm drool dribbled onto my arm, leaving a damp trail from Finn's grinning jowls. He was sandwiched between Levi and me in the truck as we made our way to town.

"Gross. You have got to stop doing that," I said with a grimace.

Finn wasn't like other dogs. He had one or two loose screws, and his unconventional looks set him apart from the canine crowd. Granted, I wouldn't love a cute dog drooling on me either.

Levi pointed to the glove box. "There should be some napkins in there."

After finding the stack of industrial brown napkins, I used one of them to wipe away the drool. By the time I stuffed it into the door cupholder, Levi was pulling into the parking lot of the local tractor supply store.

"Are dogs allowed in here?" I asked.

"With a leash, but we don't have one. I'll just carry him."

A sharp pain shot up my back as I hopped out of the truck. I straightened to keep the sore muscle from protesting. Sleeping on the couch was not the wisest idea.

Last night, my irritation with Levi faded when I caught sight of Finn wagging his body in the kitchen. Even though he's not exactly attractive, he became an immediate part of our cabin life.

Today we awoke and realized that feeding him dry cereal wasn't sustainable. He deserved proper dog food. And so, we indulged in a hearty breakfast of pancakes, including a portion for Finn, before heading to town.

Levi hoisted Finn out the truck, and I couldn't help but chuckle at the dog's signature goofy smile, his tongue wagging. I ambled a few feet behind, watching with an amused grin.

I would miss this once I reunited with my family. In two weeks, Jackson would fill in the gaps in my memory.

Perhaps I had a boyfriend. Brothers and sisters. Maybe even a dog.

The automatic doors slid open as we approached. We must look like a family of three traipsing into the store with groggy eyes from staying up half the night.

I would definitely make an effort to visit Levi after I found my old life. He had become my strongest memory.

This was a good moment, and I wanted to remember it.

Levi led us to the dog section. He tore a collar off its cardboard casing for Finn.

"I'll hold that," I said as he picked a matching blue leash.

With Finn tethered, we ambled through the dog aisles and shopped like first-time parents. We bought the necessities, like a bed, food, and bowls—but we also left with five different flavors of treats, a bowtie, three different-sized balls, brushes, shampoos, and a few other items we thought might be fun.

I held Finn on the leash as Levi made two trips to the truck to load our purchases.

"C'mon, Finn, let's go home and fill up your doggie pool," Levi said as we jumped into the truck.

His small back expanded and contracted as he breathed, tongue lolling as we left the store. I rolled down my window and let my arm rest in the breeze, fully content in this life I'd stumbled into.

―――――

Ezra

A pang of envy buzzed through me as I saw Levi and Marigold drive past. Her window was down, hair flowing in the wind. *He* was in the driver's seat. If only that could be me.

Wait a second. What was I thinking?

I hardly even knew her.

But I wanted to know her better. Levi's hostility hadn't poisoned her. Surprising.

"Next."

I looked away from the windows and strolled over to the bank teller's station. Placing the water-damaged check onto the counter, I said, "I would like to cash this, please. The app won't read it."

"Of course, Ezra," the woman said, taking the check.

A mere two minutes later, I found myself back in the driver's seat of my Bronco, headed to the farm, thoughts consumed by Marigold.

Few things held my attention in this town. I knew all of the people and streets. Life was as simple and boring as the seasons. There were woods and fields and the mountain, but not a burgundy grape in sight.

Marigold was different in all the right ways. She attracted me like a vineyard, yet my chaotic schedule and restless spirit left me unable to fully engage with her. She belonged with Levi. I could not pull her into my sphere.

I was a dormant firework. One spark might destroy everything I'd hoped for.

To keep my dreams within reach, I had to remain invisible, a shadow in the background.

As I pulled up to my house, a figure on the porch captured my attention.

Jake stood from his perch and ambled over to me in the yard.

"What are you doing here?" I asked. "You can't sit on my porch like a lazy oaf. You're on the payroll."

He shrugged like he didn't care, but there was an air of electricity shooting from his twitchy fingers.

"I had to talk to ya."

Fear darkened my vision. Had we been discovered? "What happened?"

"It's my daddy," Jake said.

Fred Tanner? The local dope dealer and troublemaker? "What's wrong with Fred?"

"Remember when I told you I knew a guy who could traffic the pot 'cause I don't do that no more?"

He had to be joking. Fred Tanner was his guy? I might as well have turned myself into Jackson. "I hope you're kidding."

"Naw," Jake said. "He's got his hand in operations from Nashville to Atlanta. He's sorta like a contractor. He finds folks who do the growin' and then he distributes. That way, those growin' don't worry 'bout who they're sellin' to. You follow?"

I understood what he said, and I hated myself for not asking who Jake's trafficker was before we set up the barn. This was madness.

Taking a deep breath, I said, "There are a bunch of farmers between Nashville and Atlanta growing pot. But are you saying they don't get caught because they're not circulating it?"

Jake's eyes lit like he'd done something right. "That's the beauty of it, see? The growers don't leave their homes. My daddy does all the drivin' and movin' of the product. No one's the wiser."

"Who does he sell to?"

"Don't know. Don't want to."

At least Jake had some sense. "What if you're arrested again?"

"You ever hear of my daddy goin' to jail?"

Although he didn't mean to imply that my father did indeed go to jail, the question stung regardless. "No," I admitted.

"That's why I'm doin' it. I was in the wrong place at the wrong time with them guns, but if I keep myself outta trouble for the next twelve months, I can slip right back into my daddy's business and nobody'll blink."

I wanted to lecture Jake on how he could do better. He could go to college or get a real job. But as the financier of this operation, who was I to talk? It wasn't too late to pull out. Fred's involvement made things sticky. I didn't want a single thing to do with the man.

Momma stepped outside and hollered, "You coming to supper, Ezra? You can bring Jake."

Jake's eyes grew as wide as tractor tires.

"I'm making a fresh peach pie," Momma said, as if that was the push I needed.

Even from the distance, I could see the flour on the pink tulip-patterned apron she'd sewn herself. She missed Lilly and wanted some company for dinner. I wouldn't deny her that.

"Sure, Momma. We'll be there."

Jake waved in her direction.

"Dinner's at six," she said, then she patted her apron and disappeared inside.

I couldn't burn the pot and erase the evidence. If I didn't do this, Momma would lose the farm. Lilly was living with Jackson. Daddy was in prison. If she didn't have her home, she'd only have me, the son who had failed her, and I would not lose her livelihood.

The pot must stay.

Jake gripped my arm as I tried to move past him toward my house. "I didn't tell ya the bad part," he said in a whisper.

My muscles tensed at the unwanted physical contact, and I jerked away. "What's that?"

"My daddy wants to see the barn. Next week. Says he won't traffic nothing until he knows how much we got."

Fred must not come here. It would only raise suspicion. "Is it normal for him to be involved?"

Jake shrugged. "I dunno. I been gone awhile."

"Tell him no."

He shuffled as I tried to move past.

"I told him that," Jake said, "but he said he'll come anyway."

This was pure stupidity. "Does he want us to get arrested?"

"He says it's just the one time. I told him next Wednesday 'cause that's a quiet day here. He'll arrive at three."

Jake shrunk back from my stare. Sounds like I didn't have a choice. I'd make sure Fred knew he wasn't welcome. "Make sure you drive your truck. I don't want any unfamiliar vehicles on my property. Understand?"

"Yes."

"One more thing," I said. "Put on something nice for dinner with my Momma."

He nodded. "Yes, sir. Wouldn't dream of nothin' else. Can't believe she'd allow a guy like me at her table."

"She's good and decent like that. Just don't be late."

Once I was alone on my porch, I sank into a cushioned chair and surveyed the land I was risking my freedom to protect.

Only the faint scent of manure accompanied me.

Chapter Twelve

Marigold

Six days after Donner gave me the truck, I drove to his house at lunchtime, a plastic bag filled with peanut butter and jelly sandwiches resting on the passenger seat. The canopy of trees provided a welcome shade in the driveway as I parked. Stepping out, a stifling breeze greeted me. Sweat beaded above my lip and on my brow within seconds. This southern humidity was like living in a sauna.

Squirrels and chipmunks scurried along branches above my head as I walked toward the porch.

"Who's there?" Donner called out after I knocked.

"Marigold."

"Who?"

"Marigold. I'm here to buy your groceries."

The bolt slid back and the door creaked open, revealing Donner. He stood barefoot but dressed oddly formal, as though preparing for a wedding. In his hand, he held a rifle, but then he noticed my ogling and tucked the gun inside the doorframe. "I wasn't sure ya'd come."

I wouldn't tell him this was the only event on my calendar. "I keep my word," I said, holding out the bag of sandwiches. "And I brought lunch."

A yellowed grin spread across his face, coaxing a smile from me as well.

"Well, ain't you somethin' sweet. Let me fetch us some drinks and we'll sit on the porch a spell."

Sweat dripped down my temple. "Wouldn't it be cooler inside?"

"You kiddin'? I don't have no AC. The breeze on the porch'll be nice."

No AC in the sizzling South? I used the end of my tank top to dab at my glistening face. Donner ambled over to the Pepsi machine and returned with two drinks. He set an orange soda on the wide arm of my chair while I handed him a sandwich.

"This tastes like the jam I used to can," he said.

I couldn't imagine grizzled Donner canning anything. "Really? It's from Beth Shaw, Levi's mother."

He nodded. "She and Duncan are—*were*—good people. May Duncan rest in peace."

"Beth will be at the football game tonight. Are you coming?"

"Me? Naw. I don't bother with sports."

We settled into comfortable conversation. Donner asked me questions about living at the cabin, and I listened to his stories.

When we were done eating and drinking our sodas, he gave me a list and two hundred dollars. "Whatever you don't spend is for you to keep."

I read the list. "But this won't cost two hundred dollars."

"I know. Now go on now. I'll be waitin'."

An hour later, while I was loading the truck with Donner's things with a giant wad of cash bulging from my pocket, I spotted a thrift store a few doors down. Locking the truck, I went inside.

The fiasco with Lillian's dress still troubled me. I didn't like that the things I wore reminded Levi of her. I wanted clothes of my own—clothes that reflected my own style.

The prices were generous. I filled two bags with items before checking out the shoe section. After peeking inside a box set on top of the rack, I hugged it to my chest. These would make a perfect gift for Beth Shaw.

I was hoping to sit with Ezra at the football game again, but he'd admitted via text that he wouldn't be attending tonight's game. Levi said that Beth had asked about me and suggested I sit with her. That was fine by me. She'd been nothing but kind the few times I'd met her.

After purchasing the items, I packed my bags into the truck and drove back to Donner's. He was relaxing on the porch like it wasn't a hundred degrees outside with thick humidity.

"Did you find everything?"

"Yes." I reached into my pocket. "Are you sure you don't want—"

"Naw, you keep it."

There were still over fifty dollars left. Enough to help Levi buy groceries.

Donner stiffened as I embraced him. "Shuck's, girlie, you'll make me blush. Git on now or you'll be late for that football game."

It was only three-thirty in the afternoon, but I didn't argue. I helped him unload the groceries, and then I left to wash and fold my new clothes.

The high school football stadium hummed with the buzz of a carnival, complete with the scent of popcorn and sweat. Since it was my second time attending a game, I knew where the Sutton High fans sat, where the snack stand was located, and the spot where Levi would be coaching.

Although the teams had yet to arrive on the field, his presence sent a thrill of anticipation through me. Our friendship was growing over shared pancake breakfasts and quiet sunset-gazing on the porch. I adored the thought of seeing him, spending time with him, and the idea of cheering for him at one of his hometown games.

The clatter of footsteps on metal bleachers snapped my attention to the present. The marching band was warming up in the farthest section, their lively tunes reverberating through the stands.

Scanning the crowd, I spotted Beth amidst the sea of faces. She saw me approach and stood. "Marigold, I'm delighted to see you. How has Levi been treating you? Are you well fed?"

"Your cooking is far superior, but we're managing."

"Bless him," she said, and then she perked up. "I have something for you."

The rough edges of the shoe box pressed into my arm as I clutched it close. I tucked a strand of hair behind my ear and motioned for her to sit. "I have a gift for you, too."

The bleachers clanked as she perched on the edge of the metal. "You do?"

"Yes." I offered the box to her. "I found them at the thrift store, so they're not new, but they don't look used."

She lifted the lid and froze, a moment of anticipation hanging in the air.

I held my breath. Did she hate them? After seeing her glass collection, I thought for sure she'd enjoy these.

"Dear, they're beautiful."

"Really?"

She pulled out a turquoise rain boot adorned with rooster print. "Yes. Perfect. But, Dear, you shouldn't have. We're the ones who should be taking care of you."

I shrugged. "It was nothing."

Beth snapped the cardboard lid back onto the box and then rummaged in her purse. "I thought you might enjoy wearing this," she said, placing a piece of cloth into my hand.

Unfolding it, I found a green and gold jersey bearing the number forty-eight and the name *Shaw* embroidered on the back. "Was this Levi's?"

"Yes. It's his high school jersey. I think he'd like you to wear it."

"You do?" This was personal. I wasn't sure if Levi would appreciate me stepping into his private life. Yet we'd shared our most painful secrets. His losses and my memory. What could be more personal than that? But still . . .

"He'll light up like the sun when he sees you wearing it."

Not wanting to disappoint Beth, I shrugged the jersey over my T-shirt and spun in a circle. "What do you think?"

She clapped. "You look like the coach's girlfriend."

I stopped spinning.

Beth's hand slipped over her lips. "I'm sorry, dear. I didn't mean to imply."

"It's okay," I said. Did people assume Levi and I were dating? It might appear that way to the casual observer. Had he mentioned something to his mom?

Beth pointed at the field and said, "Here comes the team."

I searched for Levi as the fans applauded. He strolled onto the field, a ball cap hugging his ears and a clipboard tucked beneath his arm. He talked to another coach and then turned to the boys. His team.

As the announcer presented the starting lineup, the melody of "The Star-Spangled Banner" filled the air, accompanied by a teenage girl's powerful rendition that seemed to silence the world. Chills crept over my arms when she held the notes to the word *free*. The stadium went quiet before bursting into raucous applause.

This was small-town American football in all its glory. The community ties, the family, the patriotism, and the young men competing felt like a long-lost memory. A part of my past I wanted to capture like a lightning bug and keep in a jar.

An hour and a half later, the buzzer sounded, and the bleachers erupted in fanfare.

The team won.

I watched Levi from across the field, his demeanor composed yet radiating unmistakable excitement, even from yards away. The boys galloped toward him with triumphant fist pumps and beaming smiles. He reined them in and then lined them up for the handshakes.

"Are you going out there?" Beth cradled the box under her arm as she motioned toward the revelry on the other side of the fence.

"Am I allowed?"

As I spoke, someone pushed the gates open, and friends and family streamed onto the field.

She shooed me forward. "Go see how the coach likes his jersey."

I wasn't certain Levi would react the way Beth hoped. "Thanks for letting me sit with you."

"Don't be a stranger." She held up the box. "And thank you for the gift. I will cherish these."

She disappeared as the crowd dragged me beneath the stadium lights like a fish carried downstream. The track felt squishy under my sandals, teasing my toes as they touched the grass.

Sweaty players beamed. Parents congratulated their boys. High school sweethearts clung to each other, their eyes filled with adoration and their limbs awkwardly entwined.

The throng was so thick that I couldn't find him. Swirling, I scanned the people, searching through faces, heights, and clothing colors until a surge of teenagers parted near the exit, revealing him. His Sutton High T-shirt hugged his torso. A day's worth of stubble scuffed his jaw, and his lips widened as he shook a parent's hand.

I maneuvered around the teenagers and waved, trying to get his attention. He froze when he saw me. Uncertain, I stopped. Beth must be wrong. He hated seeing me in his jersey. With my luck, Lillian wore this scrap of cloth too.

He closed the distance between us, his hand hovering over my shoulder. "Where did you—" He stopped. "Momma."

Fingering the fringe, I said, "I hope you're not upset that she gave it to me."

He rested a hand on my back, tracing the lines of his number, causing goosebumps to skitter across my body. His touch was gentle. Loving.

"Upset? No. I think you should keep it. Wear it to every game. It looks better on you than it ever did on me."

The airy cloth suddenly felt like a weighty promise. Of what? I wasn't sure.

"Coach! Coach! Coach!" A chant rose around us. I stepped back, and Levi ducked his head. If he'd kept his gaze upward, he would have seen the teenager running toward him with a green water bottle. Instead, he was surprised when the clear liquid splashed over him, causing everyone in sight to cheer.

He swiped off his hat, searching for the boy. Laughing, he lurched and snatched the bottle away.

"Trevor, we won one game, not the championship."

Trevor laughed and then disappeared into the crowd.

Levi shook his head like a dog after a bath. "Teenagers," he muttered, but he said it with a grin. Some of his boys loped toward the locker room. "I should go. Meet you at home?"

The moment begged for a hug or a peck on the cheek, something to mark the goodbye. Instead, Levi gave me a short wave and then ran toward the school.

Confused, I fished my keys from my pocket and meandered to Donner's truck, taking in the sights and sounds as I went.

The mountain seemed quiet until I noticed all the little details. Relaxing on the deck that overlooked the valley, I heard the slap of leaves against bark, the skittering of animal feet, and the hoot of an owl. The night played a song all its own, and I loved it.

The darkness wasn't threatening anymore. I wasn't afraid that a bear or a wolf might chase me.

An engine neared, grew closer, and stopped on the front side of the cabin. The door opened and closed before the twinkle lights above sparked on. I blinked against the sudden brightness.

We found the bulbs in the basement the day after discovering Finn. Levi strung them around the canopy for extra nighttime ambiance.

He slid the sliding glass door open and asked, "Why are you sitting in the dark?"

"I'm enjoying the night."

The wicker furniture groaned as he sat beside me. His arm rested over my shoulders. Comfortable.

He ran his fingers over the jersey but stopped when his gaze landed on the item resting against the bench. My arm wrapped around its neck. "You brought my guitar outside?"

"I want to hear you play."

Sensing a shift in our relationship, I was reminded of the missing lyrics and how I wanted to help him find his voice.

He untangled himself from me and accepted the instrument.

Closing my eyes, I settled against the cushion and breathed in the sound of his melody. Life was meant to be lived with a soundtrack. I wished this was mine. What did his voice sound like? Why wouldn't he sing for me?

My thoughts were stuck in a loop.

Waking. No memories. Levi. Ezra.

The most haunting memory replayed in my mind.

Levi falling backward off a cliff. My heart pounding, realizing I couldn't save him.

Why did I have this terror living inside my head?

Ever since the night I met Levi, I'd felt an invisible magnetic pull toward him, almost like we were connected in some way. I assumed it was because he was the first person I spoke to after my head injury. But what if there was more to it?

"Do you know something about me?" I asked.

The chords faltered before falling back into place. "I don't understand what you're asking."

Why did he hesitate? "I can't get the image of you dying out of my head. It feels like we're connected. Do you feel it, too, or am I crazy?"

His fingers stopped moving. "I'm sure that wasn't me. It was my dad."

"But why would I have a memory of your father in my brain?"

"Coincidence. It was big news a few years ago."

"But I'm not from around here. How would I have heard about it?"

He picked at the guitar strings. "Am I not enough?"

The question stunned me. "What do you mean?"

He set the guitar aside and faced me fully, taking my hands in his. "If your memories haven't returned yet, maybe they won't. Can I—or, can we . . . " he gestured to Finn sleeping on a pillow in the glow of the strung lights. "Can we be enough for you? Can we be the start of a new life you build with new memories?"

I tugged my hands away from his. "It's not that simple. I need to know who I am and where I'm from." Jackson had to have the answers because Levi could be right. The hard truth was, I may never get my memories back.

The thought made me restless. I stood and walked to the railing, knees shaking.

Levi followed and then leaned his elbows against the weathered wood.

"I need to remember," I whispered.

Silence stretched between us as lights twinkled in the valley below.

"Would you like to play?"

My face scrunched in confusion. "Play what?"

"The guitar." He led me back to the bench. "I'll teach you."

"What?"

"Let's think about the hard stuff another night, okay? The boys just won, and you look beautiful in my jersey. Let's enjoy the evening. I'll teach you to play the guitar."

Thankful to have relief from my overworked mind, I accepted Levi's invitation. We sat side by side as he hefted the instrument into my lap. His chest warmed my back as he stretched his arm behind me, showing me how to hold the guitar.

Thump. Thump. Thump.

Was that my heart or his?

My skin felt like it was melting where he touched me.

"Now you try," he said, but he didn't move away. His breath warmed my shoulder as I went through the motions with my hands.

"Good. Now play around with it."

Levi's weight shifted as a gap of distance opened between us. He guided my left hand with his and used his other to trace the numbers on my back.

An hour later, I was no closer to being a guitarist, but I also wasn't thinking about the pain of my memory loss anymore. Instead, all I could think about was Levi, his closeness, and how this moment was the perfect ending to the night.

Chapter Thirteen

Marigold

Beads of sweat gathered on my forehead, trickling down as a shiver ran through me despite the warmth. I couldn't stop rubbing my thighs beneath the hem of my cutoff shorts.

Up and down. More heat. More anxiety. *Up and down.*

It had been two weeks since I'd asked Jackson to scan my name through his database. And this was the day that I'd learn the results.

Around noon, Ezra gripped the steering wheel as he drove us to the police station. Noticing my nervous fidgets, he said, "You okay?"

"What if . . ."

There were too many *what-ifs*. What if my family believed I was dead? What if I never remembered the people who loved me? What if I had an abusive boyfriend who thought he'd killed me and dumped my body in the woods?

"Do you want me to change the music? What do you find calming?"

I hadn't noticed the hum from the speakers. What kind of music did I find calming?

"I like country music when I'm happy," I said. "Acoustic covers with zero vocals when I read."

"Find a playlist you like." He handed his phone to me, and I scrolled until I found a mix of piano and guitar covers.

Minutes later, I returned to my fidgeting gestures.

"Check in the glove box for some gum," he said. "We're almost there."

"I don't want to have a wad of gum in my mouth when I talk to Jackson."

"There's some candy in there too."

In need of something to occupy my restless hands, I opened the glove box and found a package of red licorice nestled among two packs of gum. Beneath them lay a jumble of owner manuals, maps, and napkins.

The red licorice straw flipped around as I held it between my thumb and forefinger. I caught it in my mouth and bit. The sweet essence of strawberries flooded my taste buds, distracting me as Ezra parked outside the police station.

He kept his hand on the wheel. "Don't fret. I'll stay with you if you'd like."

I was strong enough to hear what Jackson had to say by myself. But I didn't want to. "Please come."

A small grin tipped a side of Ezra's lips. "Of course." He held the door for me. The same perky blonde who wore bold makeup and an overly wide smile greeted us. "Do you have an appointment?"

"Yes."

Before she could respond, Jackson called out from his office. "Come in."

He stood as we entered, extending his hand for the customary shake before motioning for us to take a seat on matching wooden chairs.

As the cool wood met the backs of my thighs, a sense of restlessness tingled beneath my skin, urging me to flee. No. I would not escape from this. I had to know.

An overwhelming silence filled the office.

"You told us to come in two weeks," I finally said.

Jackson studied me. "I know."

Ezra and I shared a look when Jackson said nothing further.

"What did you find?" Ezra inquired when the silence became unbearable.

Jackson continued staring at me. "That's the thing," he said, setting his hands on the table. Then he stood and declared, "I didn't find anything."

My insides quivered. When I lifted my hand from my leg, it trembled uncontrollably. "What do you mean?"

He extracted a sheet of paper from a filing cabinet and set it on the desk before us. "There are several women with the legal name *Marigold Rivers*, but none of them are in your age demographic. Without a social security number, there's not much else I can do. I recommend seeing a doctor in Chattanooga who specializes in brain trauma."

I swallowed around a lump in my throat. Sure, I'd considered talking to a doctor. I'd also researched brain injuries. But the thing was, there wasn't a pill or a therapy that could invite the return of my memories. Seeing a doctor when I didn't have an identity or health insurance sounded expensive and unhelpful. Maybe if my memory didn't return by . . .

No. I had to grasp onto hope. I had to believe that I'd remember who I was and where I came from.

But deep inside, I knew this:

If my memories were going to return, they would have already made an appearance by now.

Nothing inside my brain was clearing or growing sharper.

The only hope I had was the soothing balm of new memories—such as Levi burning eggs for breakfast and setting off the fire alarm. Or surprising Donner with a bottle of fancy rum I found on special at the grocery store. And Finn learning to roll over on command. Sharing conversations over sweet tea with Beth on a lazy afternoon.

A light touch on my arm jolted me back to the present.

Jackson returned the file to the cabinet, and Ezra stood beside me.

"Are you ready to go?" he asked me, his hand still cradling my arm.

I let him lead me away from the station and back to the Bronco as I struggled to accept the truth that I didn't technically exist.

I would never remember.

Hot tears slid down my cheeks. I wiped them away, trying to calm myself, unwilling to let Ezra see me this way.

To his credit, he didn't mention it. He drove us back to the farm with a piano ballad playing on the stereo. Fields passed us on either side as the AC dried the tears on my cheeks, leaving behind salty streaks.

When we arrived, Ezra got out of the truck and came around to my side, opened the door, and helped me out.

I couldn't hold back my cries. The embarrassment of sobbing in front of Ezra didn't register as much as I knew it would've if I wasn't filled with despair.

He looked at the sobbing mess in front of him and pointed behind the house. "Can I show you something?"

Now? I shrugged. I could stay here or go home and cry. The thought was enticing. At home, only Finn would witness my emotional volcano complete with lava tears. I was already here. I might as well.

He led me around the house. The garden was resplendent with red and green lettuces, spicy herbs, peppers, cucumbers, and tomatoes. Ezra guided us around the raised beds and into the orchards beyond.

A few taller trees danced along the outskirts of the peach and pear trees, towering against the cobalt-blue sky.

We side-stepped fallen peaches rotting in the grass, their pits splayed open. The orchard smelled like warming fruit, sweet and enchanting as if a fairy might flit from a tree at any moment, pixie dust in her wake. Bees hummed in the branches above.

Ezra stopped at a ladder set into a maple tree, and I craned my neck upward. Twenty feet into the air above us was a sturdy treehouse.

"Levi and I built this with our fathers when we were young," he said.

"Will the ladder fall apart?"

He wiggled one of the planks of wood that was nailed into the tree, but it didn't budge.

"No. It's still sturdy."

Uncertain, I said, "You first."

Without hesitation, he climbed the wooden planks and disappeared through a hole in the treehouse's floor. Then reappeared seconds later, his face peeking out from the opening, motioning me to follow.

———

Ezra

Peering above the floorboards, Marigold's eyes widened as she scanned the space. The treehouse was modest—a simple platform with a weathered wooden railing. But it was once my castle.

A pulley system still hung from a branch off the side. Levi and I once used that to haul rotting peaches, buckets of toy cars, board games, and even buckets of dirt up to our fort. Because we were the oldest of our siblings, we had imposed a strict ban on our younger sister and brother from entering until our parents intervened.

Marigold found a spot by the trunk and leaned against the gnarled wood, eyes puffy and red.

How was I supposed to help her? Sometimes I came up here to think. It was a safe place. A quiet haven that could allow Marigold to experience and express her emotions freely.

"Are you okay, Mari?"

Her red-rimmed eyes met my gaze, but she remained silent. "Mari?" she asked.

I shrugged, a little embarrassed. The name had just slipped out. "It's a nickname," I said. "Do you mind?"

She used the hem of her T-shirt to dab at the moisture under her eyes. "No. I kind of like it."

The pale white skin of her stomach distracted me. She looked soft and warm. I forced myself to look back at her face.

A woman like Marigold could never develop feelings for someone like me. Not with her ties to Levi. We could be friends and friends alone, no matter how much I wondered . . .

I moved to the railing, as far away from her as possible. Standing at the railing, I felt the soft peach fuzz brushing against my bicep as I leaned back against the wooden structure where the peach tree's branches met the treehouse.

"Would you like a snack?" I picked a succulent-looking piece and handed it to her.

She rolled it between her palms but didn't take a bite.

"You can stay here as long as you want," I offered. "And . . . and I'm willing to listen if you need to talk."

Her trembling lip hinted at unshed tears.

"And I don't mind if you cry," I said. "I have a little sister, so I'm used to the affair."

Her expression wavered from a small smile to sorrowful agony. Curling into herself, she wrapped her arms around her knees, the peach resting delicately in her hand.

If she were Lilly, I would have embraced her without hesitation, urging her to confide in me. But this was Marigold. I couldn't treat her the same way I treated my sister.

I remembered her hesitation to climb into my Bronco. The way she paused, probably wondering if I would kill her based on Levi's opinion. Now we were in a tree together, and I could only guess she wanted me to keep me at a distance.

"Do you want to talk about it?" I tried.

She lifted her head, noticed the peach still in her hand, and took a tentative bite. "This tastes like candy."

Not what I was thinking we'd talk about, but at least it was progress. "The trick is to pick them when they're delicately soft."

She nodded, taking another bite. "I just . . ."

I waited for her to finish.

She wiped the juice off her chin. "I don't know what to do."

"What do you mean?"

Peach juice dripped down her wrist. "If Jackson couldn't find a record of my past, then I fear I'll never know. It's been a month."

Had it been a month already? "Go on," I said.

She shrugged. "I don't know what to do. Stay here? Try to find my family? Wait to see if my memory returns?"

I adjusted my back against the wooden plank. "What do you wish to do?"

"To remember my old life."

"Yes. But if you couldn't, what would you do?"

"I'm not ready to give up that dream."

"Okay. What's your next step?"

She took another bite of peach. "As much as I hate to admit it, I think I should wait. I could search the Internet for any mention of a missing redhead. I could gather newspapers following the week I arrived and search for reports of a missing person.

Marigold was a beautiful twenty-six-year-old. If she had gone missing, there would've been colossal media coverage.

"That sounds like a good place to start," I said. "I hope you don't find living in podunk Sutton too insufferable."

She threw the peach pit into the orchard below. "I enjoy it."

"That makes one of us."

"You don't like it here?"

"No, ma'am. I'd rather live on a vineyard with a stone chalet and walkways, arches, and fountains. Cool air and liquid sunrises. I was working at a winery before my father went to prison. Someone had to take over, so I came home."

Her eyes were less puffy now. "You didn't have to."

"Didn't I? You've been here for a month now. Family is everything in a small town. Out here, you do things for family or you're heartless." I paused a moment and decided to change the subject. "What would you like to do now, Mari?" The nickname had a delightful ring to it.

"Eat salted caramel ice cream."

"Ah, yes. The post-cry ice cream. Lilly enjoys that too. C'mon, I'll take you to a spot in town."

We spent the next hour eating ice cream and talking about trivial things. At five thirty she said, "I should go. Levi will be home soon. I don't want him asking questions about where I've been."

I hugged her. "Drive safe, Mari. Until next time." And then I watched her drive toward my enemy.

Chapter Fourteen

Marigold

A thick fog hovered over my mind as I drove home from Donner's after completing his weekly grocery run.

The cloud had been with me since yesterday when Jackson told me I was unidentifiable. I knew it was akin to depression, or that it might be depression itself, but I didn't want to peek above the fog to see what was above. That would require hope, and I was running low on that.

When the mountain leveled out for a stretch, my mind drifted to the radio. "This recently requested three-year-old hit is called "Sunflower Dress" by Levi Shaw . . . "

I slammed on the brakes and parked on the shoulder of the road. My heart raced as my hand shook. I stared at the radio dial in bewilderment.

Levi was a musician? Was this why he wouldn't sing for me? He was keeping secrets. We both were. I still hadn't told him about how I'd met with Jackson.

I'd simply assumed that he'd lived in Sutton his whole life, but I must've been wrong. So very, very wrong.

The realization made my shoulders slump. Who was I to Levi? A friend he felt obligated to help, but nothing more? Not a good enough friend to share his past with obviously.

The song started, intertwining guitar strings with another instrument layered beneath.

My eyes brimmed with tears as Levi's voice permeated the confines of the truck. It sounded like evergreen boughs in the wind, the distant rumble of thunder, and the patter of rain on a window.

Then the words hit me.

He was singing about Lillian. A crown of baby's breath in her hair, her skin tanned the color of wheat, and a sunflower dress.

I swallowed a lump in my throat and covered my face with quivering hands.

The dress I'd tried on before the football game. The one that caused Levi to almost crumple at the sight of me. It used to belong to Lillian. He loved it—he loved *her*—enough to use his voice.

When he saw me, it reminded him of the girl he lost, the song, their love. And at the same time, he realized she'd thrown it away.

What happened between Levi and Lillian? I was both curious and afraid to know.

The song ended and I turned off the radio.

Why had he kept this piece of himself hidden from me?

I forced my hands to still as I took the steering wheel and shifter, checked my rearview mirror, and carried on.

Levi wasn't home yet, but football practice would be over soon. Finn pranced around my feet as I started dinner, waiting for Levi to return. I replayed the lyrics over and over in my head, trying to determine why he'd ceased to sing.

It's because of me, I reasoned as I browned ground beef on the stove.

No. It must be Lillian, I mused as I boiled noodles—my go-to dinner. I'd gotten much better since the first spaghetti fiasco. *She broke more than just his heart. She broke his voice.*

Why am I fretting? We haven't known each other long enough to share about past lovers, I rationalized as I cut lettuce. A cherry tomato rolled off the counter. I slammed my heel on it, the juice sliding between my toes.

I was deceiving myself. We'd known each other long enough. He should have told me.

Finn scurried toward the bedrooms at my stomp.

Levi had the freedom to choose what he told me, but I had nothing to offer him. No memories. He knew all of me. Every broken and missing part.

Perhaps that was why he kept his life a secret. I was empty and he was full.

The front door opened as I mixed red pasta sauce with the meat.

A moment later, strong arms wrapped around my waist and hugged me from behind. "That smells wonderful."

My heart melted at his touch, beckoning me to sink into his arms. How had I forgotten that Levi greeted me like this?

I hadn't, of course. But it was easier to dwell on the negative—such as the secrets and the pain of him not sharing. I'd rather do that than remember how he'd been showing me spurts of affection since the night he first taught me how to hold a guitar.

That evening would have been the perfect time for him to tell me that he used to be a country artist. Right? Or was I reading into things too much?

He untangled himself from me. "Did you see Donner today?"

Finn bounded into the kitchen and jumped on Levi, his rear end wagging.

"Yes," I replied.

Finn and Levi scuffled around the kitchen. Levi hadn't picked up on my morose mood. "There's a tomato on the floor."

"Oops." I feigned ignorance, masking the fact that I had crushed it in a fit of hurt and anger.

He wiped the juice as I plated dinner.

The sun burned its orange gaze on the mountainside as the three of us retreated to the porch. Finn curled on a pillow as Levi and I sat with plates of pasta and salad. "I heard a song on the radio today," I said, scraping my fork through the pasta.

Levi tensed.

"It was called "Sunflower Dress."

He set his plate down.

I shoved pasta in my mouth, tasted the garlic and tomatoes, and waited.

"Marigold." His voice trailed off.

"When were you going to tell me? Wait, don't answer that. I'd rather know *why* you didn't tell me. I've shared everything with you. The fact that you were famous enough to be on the radio seems like something you should have mentioned. What else are you keeping from me?"

He ran his hands through his hair and then rested his elbows on his knees. "I didn't tell you because it was nice to have one person *not* know what a loser I was."

I almost dropped my fork. "What?"

He shook his head with an air of disgust in himself. "Sunflower Dress" was my first big song in Nashville. There were other singles, but none as popular as that one. I was on a cusp of going big, headlining my own shows when my dad died and I . . . " he trailed off.

I set my plate next to his on the little wicker table.

He shrugged. "I moved back home to prove that my dad hadn't died the way everyone thought. I threw it all away for nothing. It's been three years and I still haven't proven anything. Most people look at me with pity, and I don't blame them. I pity me too."

If I was feeling like my normal, happy self, I might have tried to see the bright side. But instead, I said, "What happened between you and Lillian?"

He stood and walked inside.

Too offended to move, I sat with my mouth open. Did he just walk away from me?

He reappeared and set a beer on the seat between us, resting his guitar on his thigh.

One side of his mouth tipped up at my puzzled expression. "I didn't mean to be rude. But if I'm going to talk about Lillian, I need to keep my hands busy. This guitar is more than an instrument. It's my crutch, my comfort, and—" He paused, seeming to search for the word. "My barrier."

I leaned against the old wood bench and crossed my arms.

Strumming the guitar absentmindedly, he relayed the tale he should have told me weeks ago. "As you know, Lillian and I grew up together. I didn't think of her as anything more than Ezra's annoying little sister until high school. She looked different when she came up freshman year. Plus, I saw her kissing another boy underneath the bleachers and realized I hated him for it. I felt like I had dry wheat in my mouth when I asked her to the homecoming dance, and I almost fainted when she agreed. We did everything together, from playing hide-and-seek in cornfields to taking holy communion in church. Loving her made sense."

The cords turned into a melody I now recognized as "Sunflower Dress." Levi continued. "We celebrated our acceptance into the same college with pilfered bottles of beer in the old treehouse behind my house."

I didn't mention that I knew the exact spot he spoke of. I imagined Lillian's back snuggled against his chest beneath the light of the moon as they discussed their futures, laughing and dreaming together.

"I went to college with a full scholarship to play ball. She came to every game and met me after every practice. Then I tore my ACL and lost my football scholarship."

He stopped strumming, popped the cap off the beer, and took a long drink. "I moved to Nashville, waited tables at dive bars, and played on stages. Scribbled some songs. Ironically, my first track was called "Treehouse", named after the place where Lillian and I had spent so much time together. The night I proposed to her on stage, a big star named Ryker Tucker saw me perform and contacted me."

I blinked, surprised. I didn't remember who my parents were or if I had siblings or if my boyfriend abused me, but for some reason, I recognized that name. "He's very successful."

Levi tipped his beer in my direction, offering a sip, but I declined. He took a swing. "He mentored me. I toured as his opener.

"After "Sunflower Dress" went viral, we did a single together. Both successes combined had my phone blowing up with calls from agents and record labels. I was so busy singing about Lillian that I neglected to actually spend time with her, invite her to Nashville, and include her in my success. She broke up with me on the day of my dad's funeral. One week before our scheduled wedding. She couldn't handle my neglect any longer."

Soft music wafted over us as he placed the beer on the deck and strummed again.

"I moved back home. Three years later, Lillian is married and I'm in a musty old cabin looking for ghosts." He hesitated, glanced at me, then looked away.

One question begged to be answered. "Do you still love her?"

Levi's fingers stopped as he focused on the dipping sun. "I don't think you ever stop caring for your first love. I wonder what could have been. Parts of me will always love her. But the more time that passes, the easier it gets." His eyes shimmered.

I stood and ambled toward the railing, unsure how to process his confession.

The faint sound of his guitar being gently placed down resonated, followed by the echo of his steps as he approached me.

"You should have told me," I said. The valley below shimmered in a golden hue, casting elongated shadows from the scattered trees and houses onto the fields.

"Really? So when was I supposed to tell you that I let my last girlfriend down in tabloid-accusing fashion?"

I tightened my grip on the railing. "Your breakup was covered in magazines?"

"A few. Not front page, but that didn't matter."

No, I supposed it wouldn't. "Is that everything?"

"What do you mean?"

"Do you have any more secrets, Levi?"

He paused. "One or two. But don't you think I'm allowed to keep those?"

Ezra flitted through my mind. Yes, he was allowed to have secrets, but only because I had one of my own. "If you promise to share them when the time is right." I planned to do the same.

He rested his elbows on the railing, shoulder brushing against mine. "Yes, when the time is right, I'll tell you my secrets."

The birds twittered in the woods as we continued watching the sun.

"Marigold?"

"Hm?"

"Will you forgive me?"

My grip on the wood eased. As much as his omission hurt, I was a fixer, and I would not allow our relationship to remain broken. "I suppose."

My body angled toward Levi's at the same time that he faced me. The Tennessee sun infused the deck with warmth.

He inched closer. I closed my eyes as he enfolded me in his arms. My cheek rested against his chest and again, I felt the *thump, thump, thump* of his heart. I breathed out a sigh. This felt like home.

Home?

Could I let go of my desire to learn who I was and allow Levi to be my home?

Before I could consider that any further, he bent down, gently nuzzled his nose against the curve of my neck, and inhaled deeply. When the stubble of his jaw tickled my skin, I clung tighter, my fingers digging into the soft skin around his elbows.

His palms cradled my hips before enveloping the small of my back, drawing our bodies together akin to intertwining flower roots tangled in soil.

For a second, the fog hovering around me lifted, my brain cleared, and I exhaled. I belonged here. With Levi. Right now. We hadn't planned this moment, but I hoped it would linger.

I set my hand on his chest and inhaled his scent; sunshine and evergreen trees, like he spent his day on either the mountain or the football field. I wished I could press the fragrance into my pillow and fall asleep basked in the aroma.

His lips grazed my neck, igniting a trail of warmth through my core. Levi Shaw was kissing me. I didn't move. I stopped breathing. His lips curved against my neck as he said, "Marigold."

"Uh-huh?" I whispered.

"Breathe."

I sucked in air. The sun didn't warm me. Levi did. All the places he touched were liquid fire.

Pulling away, his kind and questioning eyes brushed over my face and then landed on my mouth. The rise and fall of my chest felt obnoxious as we stood there, tangled together with the last rays of sun searching for cracks of earth to brighten.

Dusk fell as his breathing mingled with mine. Neither of us closed our eyes as Levi leaned in and pressed a tentative kiss on my lips. He pulled away and held my gaze, seeking a reaction.

In response, I closed my eyes, waited for him to close the space between us.

It felt like an hour passed before his lips met mine. He kissed me with curious adoration. Craving his warmth, his care, and his song, I leaned in, eager to learn more about Levi Shaw through the feel of his skin against mine.

Before I could become breathless, he pulled away. I hated the cold that rushed between us. When I opened my eyes, I found him with raised brows and a slightly open mouth.

"What's wrong?" I asked, sensing a sudden change.

He untwined his arms from my body and set me aside, then he leaned against the wood railing, head in his hands. He let out a soft groan.

Then, Levi's back stiffened as he looked back to me. "I'm sorry," he said. "I shouldn't have done that." He raked his hands through his hair. "We can't do this. I'm sorry."

I turned away to steady myself on the railing. "Because you still love Lillian," I said. *Note to self: never kiss a guy after talking to him about his ex. It's not as romantic as it sounds.*

He stood beside me but left what felt like a field between us. "No. It's not that."

Since kissing him had never been my intention, I answered diplomatically, "Okay." But the memory of his gentle lips seared through me like a burn that does most of its damage after the heat is gone. I didn't realize how attracted I was to him until this moment.

Maybe attraction wasn't the right word. Being with Levi was safe and easy. The bruises had faded, and all I saw now was my best friend.

"I'm sorry," he said again.

Was that a tremor in his hand? "Will you play?" I gestured to the guitar. We needed a distraction.

He left me at the railing and fitted it against his body to wash us in the cleansing embrace of a melody.

Soon, dusk evaporated into darkness.

But Levi didn't sing.

Levi

The moment I pulled away from Marigold, I regretted it. Her hand rested lightly on my chest, her lips still warm from our kiss, beckoning me closer. But I couldn't allow myself to continue when I was lying to her.

As my fingers absently strummed over the guitar strings, I longed for them to be intertwined with hers, cradling her gently against me.

Yes, this guitar was my wall. Because if I wasn't holding it, I would be holding her instead.

Oh, how I wanted to.

But I couldn't.

Why did she ask if I had more secrets? I hated myself for keeping what I knew from her. Fear stopped me. I was afraid she'd reject me. Reject the truth.

My biggest secret, the one that was growing into a lie by omission with each passing day, was that I knew where she came from. I knew she would never regain her memories. Withholding this truth from her made me feel like I liar.

But if I told her, she might not believe me. Worse—she might consider me crazy.

Some nights, with Marigold asleep and Finn nestled at the foot of my bed, I sometimes dared to open the journal that breathed life into their existence.

I'd think myself insane if I didn't have the proof inside my bedroom. If I didn't know the words by heart.

He loved her like the one he lost
But he didn't know how much her love would cost . . .

How could I ask her to believe something as lofty as this?

She was a ghost of Ghost Mountain. And I, Levi Shaw, had created her with ink and pen.

I couldn't allow her to love me under false pretenses, but I couldn't tell her the truth either.

She sat a few feet away with a dazed expression, like she, too, was thinking about the kiss, wondering why it had to end.

"I'm going to bed," she said as she stood.

"Marigold."

She stopped with one foot over the threshold.

I wanted to tell her that I was falling in love with her, that maybe I already had, but instead, I said, "Goodnight."

Sighing, she left me in the darkness.

A few minutes later, I stopped playing the guitar.

As I went to my bedroom, I noticed that her door was closed. Finn's nails clicked on the hardwood behind me.

For hours I lay awake, contemplating my two options. I could tell her the truth, or I could keep it from her. As I gave into the heaviness of my eyelids, I realized both options would hurt her. I wasn't saving her pain by keeping my knowledge—and yet I still couldn't bring myself to do it.

Chapter Fifteen

Ezra

My clothes clung to me, sticky with humidity, as I walked to the weathered red barn concealing illegal drugs. Jake and his goon father would arrive any minute.

The key scraped against the new lock as I turned it.

Click.

I pulled the chains from the doors and opened them wide.

Two minutes later, my heat-heavy gaze focused on a beat-up Tacoma as it rumbled to a stop in front of the barn. Fred and Jake climbed out, their feet scuffing the dirt as they walked toward me.

I forgot how unkempt Fred was until he moved closer. He strolled into the barn-turned-pot-farm like he'd purchased the weed himself. If I didn't know better, I'd think he was a homeless man with his shaggy hair and rumpled clothes. How did this guy run a criminal business? He didn't look like he could rub two pennies together. And how was he supposed to help me escape debt?

The sooner this meeting ended, the sooner I could forget that Fred was a part of this. My pulse increased as he snapped his fingers in front of my face.

"Yes?" I said through gritted teeth. This greasy man had better state his business and get out, or else I might escort him out myself. With force.

"I asked you a question, boy."

Blood thumped through my veins, throbbing in my ears, keeping time with the displeasure in my pulse. Uncontrollable rage surged as Fred squinted at me, looking at me like I was a grade school yuppie.

He wasn't supposed to be here. I should be working in a vineyard in the Smoky Mountain, not stuck on this doomed farm.

I slapped his fist away. "Get out of my face," I said, my voice low and threatening.

Fred grinned with tobacco-stained teeth. "Don't get your panties in a bunch. I asked you to show me what you got goin' on here."

I enjoyed looking down into his eyes from my two-inch high superiority. "Jake will show you around." I wasn't about to give Fred a tour like he was some high baller and I was his hick dope farmer.

Jake tried to direct Fred's attention to the plants. Fred ignored him and grabbed my arm. "You show me," he said, an evil tilt to his lips. He was trying to goad me.

I remained still. "You better get your hand off me."

Fred didn't move.

Jake froze. The sun shining through the open doors cast his shadow across the hay-strewn floor. He sensed the tension thicker than barn dust between Fred and me.

I twisted my arm until I clenched Fred's wrist, and then I jerked until his hand was behind his back. The old man was surprisingly fast. He wrenched away, slammed the side of his fist against my temple, and kicked me in the knee.

I stumbled but didn't fall. My chest heaved.

Without thinking, I reacted on impulse.

Fred shuffled back as I caught my balance. He was a few feet from me when I lowered my shoulder and ran.

My legs locked and my boots slid across the floor when I heard a gun cock. With waning momentum, I stopped a foot from the barrel of the pistol that Fred aimed at my chest.

Jake stood in the barn's doorway. The shape of his shadow changed as his arms rose in a reflexive surrender. "Fred," he said, neglecting to call the man with wild eyes his dad. "You know I can't be around them things. I'll get sent back to prison."

Fred spat chew to the side. Dark tobacco dribbled from the corner of his mouth. "Shut up, Jake. This ain't about you."

Only my lips moved. "You didn't have to bring a gun."

Fred twitched his wrist, making the gun slide back and forth. One second he pointed it at my left shoulder, and the next at my right. "Didn't I?"

I didn't answer.

Fred shook his head like he was speaking to a petulant child. "You're like your old man."

The words rattled me to my core. I was nothing like my father. Samuel King was a good man. I still held fast to the belief that he was innocent. I, consequently, was an abhorrent person. I hated the farm he had sweat and saved for, and I was, indeed, a criminal.

"You know why your old man's rotting in prison?" Fred asked. "Not 'cause he's a crook. No, I knew your daddy, and I know a lot of sinful men, but your daddy ain't one of 'em. Your daddy wanted more money than he needed, and he didn't stop when he should have. He couldn't control himself. Looks like you can't either."

Everything he spewed out of his mouth was wrong. "Put the gun down, Fred."

"Yeah, toss that thing outta here. You ain't bringing it back in my truck. I will not—"

"Shut up, son," Fred said. "Or I swear I'll shoot you and force you to shut you up."

No protests came from Jake. We all knew Fred wasn't bluffing. He'd shoot his own son if it made him a buck.

"You wanna see the plants, Fred? Look around."

He spat again. "This trip was never about the plants, little King."

My muscles twitched. If he aimed the gun at anything but my chest, I'd wrench it from his grasp. "Then get out."

Fred stepped closer. Maybe now was my chance. But I wasn't sure I could snatch the gun before he shot me. His twitchy index finger hugged the trigger too tightly.

"I'm not leavin'," he said. "Not until I do what I came here to do."

He wanted me to ask him why he was here, but I wouldn't.

"Good boy," he said. "Do what you're told."

I recognized his taunt for what it was. "Speak or get out." My words were tight and throaty.

Fred considered me. "I'm here because my guy in Atlanta wanted to make sure you understand the rules. You promised him a product and he expects his money. Understand?"

"I didn't sign a contract. I don't have—"

Before I could finish, Fred lunged at me. I angled back, trying to stay clear of the gun, but the weapon gave him a backbone. He sprung for me, smashing the butt of the pistol against my head, and then he stood watching as I wavered. I caught myself on a beam of wood as my vision blackened and then returned in hazy focus. Wet, hot liquid streamed from my temple. I squinted up at Fred, the coward.

He backpedaled when, bracing myself on the wood, I forced my knees to lock and stand. Fred was just out of reach again, the gun still pointed at me. Pretending to be the guy in charge, he said, "How much did you spend starting this operation?" He gestured around him.

I ground my teeth, hating that he had me under his control with that stupid gun. He'd shoot me if he felt threatened. I couldn't reach him, and my head was throbbing.

Fred assessed the area. "This'll be a decent batch of dope, and I doubt you got the means to move it without me. Where does that leave you?" He tipped the gun from my chest to the spot between my eyes. The barrel was an unblinking black hole. "It leaves you with no profit for your investment," he continued. "You wanna make a few dollars? You need me, and you need the nice men in Atlanta. They may have invested nothing, but they're still invested. You got it?"

If I fronted the money, then I had the most to lose. Not Fred or his mysterious men.

"I see what you're thinking," he said. "Let me put it this way. Now that we know about what you got here, we expect your cooperation. Otherwise, we'll take the dope when it's done. If you wanted to do this on your own, you shoulda kept it a secret. Think of us as managers. Either you give us our cut or we take it. Understand?"

If Jake wasn't my only help, I'd fire him for putting me in this situation. Now we had thugs in Atlanta involved? On the same property where my mother lived. If anything happened to her . . .

My temple felt warm where Fred hit me. "Leave."

"I gotta be sure you understand."

I looked Fred in the eyes. "It doesn't look like I have many choices."

He lowered the gun. "Then I guess you understand."

"Get out."

Jake stepped toward me. I held up my hand. I didn't wish to hear him apologize. He knew his old man was dirty, but he must have underestimated his criminal involvement. He wouldn't be waving guns around and making threats for an organization that he wasn't entangled in.

After they left, I slid to the barn floor with my skull throbbing and red dots dancing in my vision.

Anger swelled through me.

I sat on my knees, turned, and pounded my fist into the beam of wood I'd been leaning against. My knuckles were bruised, but the pain didn't appease my fury.

I punched the wood again.

And again.

And again.

Streams of blood trickled into the webs of my fingers, then down my wrist. The color reminded me of wine. A spiderweb of blood radiated from my knuckles. Pink and red flesh covered the bones.

What had I backed myself into?

Marigold

Donner's truck was a Godsend, but it was also older than a dinosaur. Nineteen-ninety-six wasn't too old, but with all the parts needing replacement, it seemed ancient.

After Levi left for football practice, I climbed inside the cab and coasted down the mountain. I planned to visit the truck graveyard to scavenge for parts that might help me fix the window, not the AC, because fixing the window was cheaper than replacing the AC unit.

Not wishing to make the trek to the truck graveyard by myself—and unsure if it would be considered trespassing—I planned to start at Ezra's house. We hadn't seen each other since the day we spoke to Jackson, but I doubted he'd mind an impromptu visit.

A cow lowed as I ascended the porch steps and knocked on his door.

One minute passed. Then two.

I knocked again.

I heard the sound of footsteps, and then, "Mari?" The barrier between us muffled his voice.

"Sorry I didn't text or call. Can we take a trip to the truck graveyard?"

"I must apologize," he said, still keeping the door closed. "I came down with something." A cough followed his words—one that definitely sounded forced and fake.

How stupid did he think I was? "What's going on?"

Ignoring my question, he said, "I'm fine. Just have a little sniffle. I wouldn't want you to catch it."

I peeked through the frosted glass set high in the door. Nothing but the ceiling was visible. I crossed to the closest window and squinted inside. I could only see his leg from the thigh down, which was clothed in a pair of gym shorts. It looked like he sat in front of the door, blocking it.

"I can see you," I said, tapping my knuckles against the glass.

"Please, Marigold. I can't see you right now."

"Why?" I watched him scramble to his feet, still mostly out of sight.

"I told you. I'm not well."

Something wasn't adding up. "You sound fine."

"I know, but I'm ill." He fake-coughed again.

Ezra's charade was about as convincing as the nursery rhyme claiming a cow could jump over the moon. "I'm not stupid, Ezra King. I know you're not sick. Open this door."

What had caused me to be so bold? Ezra and I were mere acquaintances, but the fix-it part of me knew something was wrong, and I wanted to help him.

Taking a gamble, I marched forward and twisted the door handle.

Locked.

What if? I returned to the window and tugged upward. The pane slid until it hit the top of the runner. "You should invest in screens," I said, climbing inside.

He angled his body away. "No, Marigold."

"I'm not leaving until you tell me what's going on."

He held his palm up and kept his face to the side, watching me from the corner of his eyes. "I'll tell you later. Please go."

I pushed his hand aside and scurried to stand in front of him. The sight of him made me fall back into the wall. He caught my forearm to straighten me.

A red gash rimmed in green and yellow marred the left side of his face from above his eyebrow to below his cheekbone. Blood trickled from the center, down his cheek, and onto his white T-shirt. When he tried to shield himself from my perusal, I saw his hand. Raw flesh and oozing blood made the knuckles look almost unrecognizable.

"What happened to you?"

He dropped his arm and pretenses with a sigh. "You might as well come inside now that you've seen me."

I followed him to the living room where bandages, gauze, ointments, and a bowl of murky water lined the coffee table.

I sank onto the couch beside him as he pulled a washcloth from the bowl and wiped the line of blood off his cheek.

When he didn't say a word, I pressed him. "Tell me how this happened."

He sighed but said nothing.

"Please," I said.

He gave his head a little shake and then chuckled. "It was nothing. One of my workers arrived drunk this morning. I told him to go home." He dipped the washcloth in the water and then wrung it out.

"Let me," I said, taking the cloth.

He continued as I cleaned his brow, his temple, and his cheekbone. "I told the guy to go home. Driving to work under the influence could get him in trouble with his probation officer."

When he didn't continue, I asked, "So, what happened?"

He shrugged. "He was drunk and angry and threw a few punches."

I tapped his wrist. "And you hit him back?"

"I tend to hit first and think later."

Levi's face was a bruised and molted mess the night I'd met him. It was Ezra's fists that had done the damage then, too. I'd chosen to forget this darker part of my new friend, but this story couldn't be true. Fists didn't make indentations like the one on his face. Knuckles couldn't become raw from hitting flesh.

My hand halted its ministrations as I considered his narrative. "Tell me what really happened," I said.

Ezra leaned back into the cushions and groaned. "Mari, why do you have to be so infuriatingly, insightful, and devastatingly honest?"

I held my breath when he called me *Mari*. Why did I like that so much? Of course, he was flattering me to keep me from learning the truth. "I'm not an idiot."

"No, my dear, you are not."

"Will you continue ignoring my question?"

He leaned forward and set his elbows on his knees. "I acquired these battle scars by doing what's best for my family and this farm. I won't tell you anything else. Can you trust me?"

The answer was simple. "No." If Levi hid his past as a musician from me, then I could only guess what secrets his enemy was hiding.

Surprised, he sat up and lifted his brows. "Your honesty hurts."

"Trust is important, and you're lying."

He straightened. "Don't attribute judgment before you know all the details. I understand I'm withholding certain aspects of my life from you, but there is a reason. If you can't trust me, then I request you honor my privacy."

I reared back. He had a right to his privacy. But this . . . these wounds were serious. Could I drop the matter without some form of explanation?

"I'm not judging you. But I don't know you well enough to blindly trust either."

His face hardened. "Is your hesitancy because of what Levi told you about me?"

Levi told me that Ezra was dangerous. Clearly he was right. But I couldn't accept that Ezra was a murderer. "No. Levi has nothing to do with this."

"I find that hard to believe."

A drop of blood seeped from his temple and slid down his face. I caught it with the cloth. "Let me bandage this."

He found a piece of gauze and tore a long strip of tape. "Do you have these items on hand all the time?" I secured the gauze to his face.

"I live on a farm. It's smart to have first aid supplies handy."

I felt the calluses on his hands as I used the cloth to clean his knuckles. He was avoiding the question. "Ezra, I'm not accusing you of anything, but I'd like to know that you're safe. Fists didn't cause these injuries."

His shoulders eased as he sunk into the cushions. "Does that mean you care for me, Mari?"

"Of course I care." The realization surprised us both.

His gaze met mine, his strong jaw covered in rugged stubble. The side that wasn't bruised was handsome, his dark brown, almost black hair a mess from the path of his fingers.

He twisted his hand until he held my wrist. Water and blood from the cloth dripped onto the leather couch as we stared at each other.

Drip. Drip. Drip.

I ached to wipe the moisture away, but he still held me.

"How much?" he asked.

Our thighs grazed. His fingers warmed my wrist. The atmosphere in the room shifted.

I pulled my hand away, sensing his attraction.

A few days ago, Levi and I had kissed. I thought it was perfect, sweet, and loving, but then he broke away and pushed me out. I would not grow close to another man, especially when someone from my past could find me and whisk me home.

"I care for you as a friend," I said, not wanting to complicate our relationship.

I could tell that he sensed my discomfort as he leaned back. "I'm sorry, Mari. I'm not myself."

I looked around the space at the sleek flatscreen TV, the hardwood coffee table, and the black leather couch we sat on. Ezra and Levi couldn't be more different.

"How are you?" he asked. "The last time I saw you was—"

"The day I lost control of my emotions. I remember. That's not why I'm here. I came for a truck part."

He squeezed his eyes closed and grimaced. "I can bring you in a few moments."

Realizing how much pain he was in, I backtracked. "We'll try another day."

He reached for a bottle of pain medicine on the table. After swallowing the pills, he relaxed again. "Does Levi know about the police station?"

I hugged a decorative pillow to my stomach. Frustration over my lost memory, Levi's confusing kiss, and the truck that wouldn't stay fixed overwhelmed me. Why couldn't one thing go right? "No."

His voice sounded gentle. The awkward tension in the room had vanished. "Why?"

"Because there's nothing to tell. I'm a nobody. And besides, I can't let Levi know that I was with you. If I lost his friendship, I'd have nowhere to live."

"Mari," he said. "I don't mean to sound impulsive or crass, but you're always welcome here. In my home."

I didn't respond.

"And as far as you being a nobody, that's not true. You are very much a *somebody*, and I hope to get to know you better. As friends, of course," he added.

My eyes misted, but I didn't cry. Or maybe I did because in the next second, his bloodied hand wiped a tear from my cheek, and at that moment, his violence became tenderness. He was a combination of passion and pain, anger and beauty.

Ezra set his hand back in his lap and watched me.

He didn't understand the buzz in my head that roved my consciousness for a memory, a speck of who I was. He couldn't know how my chest sometimes felt empty, devoid of the fullness I should have for people and places. Yet, in that moment, he had eased the hurt.

I looked at his oozing knuckles. Regardless of what he hid from me, Ezra was a good man.

I could learn his secrets later.

Chapter Sixteen

Levi

Marigold sat beside me in the cab of my Chevy wearing cut-off shorts and a sporty green tank top with a racer-back.

We'd been flirting with the fallout of our kiss for almost a week. I never should have kissed her.

But I wished to do it again.

I couldn't. Not without telling her the truth. The distance between us was uncomfortable, but we could heal and move on.

Our eyes met for the briefest of seconds before I looked back toward the windshield. Her hair was pulled into a pony at the base of her neck. It was the first time I'd seen her with her hair up, and it was just as lovely as when it sprang wild around her face.

"Where are we going?" she asked.

"I told you it's a surprise."

We bumped onto an almost-forgotten road with cracked pavement. Green shoots sprang from the crumbling concrete. Animal trails veered into the woods. I steered the truck off the disintegrating road and parked on the shoulder.

She tucked an uncooperative strand of hair behind her ear and met me at the tailgate as I slung a backpack out of the bed. "This way." Twigs snapped and leaves whooshed as I foraged into the woods. "There's no trail. Stay close."

Hiking on Ghost Mountain was similar to hiking in the Great Smoky Mountains. A mist obscured the woods in an ethereal haze. Rich brown tree trunks rose from the ground with gnarled bark that stretched upward to reveal dark green leaves, lush with robust veins and dewdrops. Boulders and slabs of rock protruded from the earth along the landscape to create an enchanted forest feel.

Moisture stuck to my legs, arms, and cheeks as I tugged the backpack straps tighter and moved into the untamed woods.

A cold breeze swirled around me. In the past, I'd imagine a ghost greeting me as I walked its territory. But I knew better now. Ghosts were real. They were flesh and blood. One walked behind me. Still, the cool, otherworldly fog felt like a premonition. A warning or an invitation.

The tranquility of the woods invited my mind to wander.

I remembered the day Lillian's dad was arrested. I remembered the night she broke up with me in an alley filled with shattered glass. Glass she'd thrown against the walls. I remembered my dad in the casket. And then I remembered Shelly Hooper's broken body on the cliff.

The wintry wind rolled around me again and I looked over my shoulder. "Do you feel that?"

She stopped. "Feel what?"

"A cold breeze."

She stilled. "No."

A sense of urgency filled my chest as the swirling chill turned my head.

Above us, etched into the bark of a towering oak tree, were initials inter-twined within a heart. Marigold's eyes met mine, drawn to the intricate carving. The heart, positioned just above my eye level, bore the letters *DES & Courtney* in a declaration of love that had weathered the years.

She stood beside me, both of our gazes upward. "What was your dad's middle name?"

I inhaled. "Edmond."

"Duncan Edmond Shaw and Courtney? Isn't your mom's name Elizabeth?"

My hands clenched my backpack straps tighter. "Yes."

"Do you know any Courtneys?"

"One."

"Who?"

The straps dug into my shoulders. "Courtney King."

"Ezra's mom?"

"Yep." I eased my grip. "It must be somebody else's initials. My mom and dad were high school sweethearts. Their love was so deep that my mom will never marry again."

Who else in Sutton had the initials *DES*?

They couldn't have belonged to my dad. The notion was impossible. His name and Courtney King's didn't belong together.

Marigold's footsteps trailed away from the tree where I still stood. "What were you saying about a chilly breeze? Now I have goosebumps. I overheard someone say there are ghosts on this mountain. Do you believe in ghosts?"

Did I believe in ghosts? Yes. In the most literal sense possible.

I met her gaze. "Yes."

She appeared shocked by my response. "Because it's called Ghost Moun-tain?"

I nodded, forcing my feet to move. "There are legends about the mountain and how it got its name. Stories too. My favorite is about a mountain man and his love affair with a ghost. My dad told the story to me."

Her muscled legs trailed behind me. "Tell me."

I relayed the tale as I led her away from the tree and toward our destination. "A mountain man once fell in love with the ghost of a woman who died at Skeleton Cliff. He saw her form at the bottom as she searched for a way up. There was no path. The precipice was too steep," I said. "But don't let the legend fool you. It's not hard to hike down. For the sake of the story, we'll assume there's no way."

"Okay." Her voice held interest.

"The man came to the cliff every night to meet the woman he loved."

"How did they fall in love if she was a ghost?"

We passed a massive mound of rock that disappeared into the mist above. "I dunno. Doesn't matter."

If Marigold was a ghost, then I could guess how the man fell in love with his ghost. Falling in love happened fast. Maybe that's why they called it *falling*.

"Okay, I'll stop interrupting."

"Thank you," I said with a grin in my voice. "The deeper they fell in love, the more ways they tried to bridge the gap between them. He tried ropes. She tried climbing the mountain and the trees.

"They couldn't find a solution. Finally, the mountain man said, 'I'll jump to you. Maybe I'll join you as a ghost.' But the ghost refused. She said she'd rather live with him alive than risk his death and no chance of them being together. But he believed that if he jumped, he would be reunited with her in spirit form."

"Did it work?"

I held a branch back so it wouldn't slap her in the face. "No. He died."

She flicked my bicep. "That's a terrible story. Is that the end?"

"Yep, that's the end."

"Why is that story your favorite?"

The sound of the creek trickled through the woods. We were almost there. "Because he found a girl he was willing to die for."

"Would you have died for Lillian?"

I paused. "I think so."

"But you're not sure?"

"Listen," I said. "Hear that?" I was grateful for the distraction, unwilling to talk more about Lillian.

She stood still. "Water?"

"Follow me. Few people know about this."

She held my shoulder, using me as a shield through the last of the branches.

A river flowed swiftly past us. Clear crystal water diverted around river stones and sheets of rock.

Marigold wound around me to approach the waterfall. Icy mountain water crashed thirty feet into a small basin. Droplets landed on her eyelashes as she neared. The scent of mossy rocks and raw, unfiltered river bathed us in mountain glory.

Her eyes glittered. "Why don't people know about this? I could sit here all day."

I led her to a large, flat rock that jutted into the creek. We sat on a dry section as the river whooshed by. "It's not on any maps, and it's a long hike if you don't know where you're going." I leaned back on my elbows beneath the canopy of leaves shading the rock. "I found it on one of my solitary hikes, and I've never told or shown anyone. It's my secret. Now, I guess it's our secret."

She reclined beside me as the mist dissolved and the sun poked through the dark green leaves above us. "It's beautiful. I—"

I pressed my index finger to her lips. "Shh, you hear that?" I removed my finger.

She quieted and focused on listening to the rushing water, the rustling leaves, birds calling, and the sound of squirrels skittering along branches.

"I only hear the woods," she whispered.

"Exactly," I said. "Isn't it one of the most beautiful things?"

She relaxed on her back and stared at the swaying trees, listening, feeling the breeze. Because she was so enraptured by the oasis, she didn't notice me looking at her, admiring her beauty. The smattering of freckles across her nose were no larger than the point of a pencil. Yes, I'd seen them before, but not in this light.

Sitting up, she dragged her sweaty socks off and set them with her shoes. "You ever been swimming in this creek?"

"No. The water is freezing."

"It's over eighty degrees out here. I'm sure it'll be nice."

I sat up. "No way. I'll watch."

She gave me a mocking grin and said, "Baby."

"You gonna swim in your clothes? Those won't be fun to hike back in." I unzipped the backpack. "While you act crazy, I'm gonna eat lunch. We have fresh gourmet PB and Js."

She snatched the backpack from me. "No, you're coming with me. We'll eat afterwards." She peeled her tank top off and then unbuttoned her pants.

"What are you doing?"

She shimmied out of her shorts and then stood on the rock, pretty much naked other than her red sports bra and white underwear.

"Stop staring," she said. "Don't worry. I'm not taking these off."

The curve of her hips and the perfect circle of her navel captured my attention. When my gaze traveled upward, I found a riot of freckles dancing along her chest.

She grinned. "Coming?" There was something in that grin. She wasn't trying to seduce me; she was simply comfortable in her skin.

When she turned, I spied more freckles across her back. I wanted to lay beside her and play connect the dots all day long.

Suddenly, cooling in the creek seemed like the perfect idea. "Fine." I took off my shirt and stripped to my boxers.

She perched on the edge of the rock, feet in the water and teeth set in a bracing grin. "It's not too cold," she forced out.

I stepped in until the water reached my knees. Slippery river rocks made it hard to stand, so I maneuvered to a waterlogged branch and then held my hand out toward Marigold.

She stood, her body dappled in leaf shadows, and then she stretched toward me. Step by step, she wobbled forward. When her foot slipped on a rock, I lunged to catch her by the waist and pulled her to me. We paused at the center of the creek, and I kept my arm around her. If my grip traveled any lower, I'd touch her curves. I kept my hand in a gentlemanly position until I realized she could stand just fine on her own, and then I released her.

Her teeth chattered. "Not—" she gasped—"cold . . . at all."

"Hilarious," I said in a deadpan voice. I turned and climbed onto the thick branch behind us. The water didn't rise above my knees.

"Help me up."

I tucked my arm around her and hauled her beside me. Her hip touched mine.

"You about done with this madness?" I asked.

She glowed. "I feel refreshed. How about you?"

"Refreshed is one word for it." I pointed down the length of the tree branch I still held. "We can climb on this branch and walk back to the riverside." I pointed to my backpack resting on the rock.

"You first," she said.

I maneuvered around her and hauled myself onto the tree. With careful hand placement, I crouched and then crept along the slippery waterlogged bark until a mighty shake sent me toppling into the river. A shake that could only have been caused by one person. Marigold!

The sudden immersion of cold stole the breath from my lungs. I surfaced with a gasp. Marigold stood waist-deep in the creek holding the branch, tears streaming down her cheeks and laughter pulsing her stomach.

"You won't get away with that." I grinned.

I powered through the water and lifted her over my shoulder. A half-scream, half-laugh rushed out of her before I tossed her into the water.

Seconds later, she surfaced with mouth agape, arms wrapping around her shoulders. "That's colder than Antarctica."

The smile on my face hurt. When was the last time I had smiled this widely? "You done swimming now?"

She nodded with chattering teeth and held out an arm. I hauled her toward me, and then we plodded through the rushing water back to our rock. She lay in the sun. Her bra and underwear were soaked and see-through, but she didn't cover herself.

Her sense of self-worth and acceptance attracted me more than her body. How had my brain and my words created a girl like this? I'd never met a woman with no physical insecurities.

She reached her arms toward the sun. "Warm me."

"If you stay there, you'll warm up so quickly you'll want to jump back in."

"You said you brought sandwiches?"

Unlike Marigold, I preferred to cover what the water had uncovered. I sat on the rock and set the backpack in front of me like a shield. "Yep. PB and J and a few peaches."

"Sounds perfect. Will you bring them here? You can dry off too."

Proximity to her could be dangerous. The chemistry between us was as tangible as the water rushing past us. I wanted to draw her close and kiss her, tell her I didn't mean it when I pulled away from her lips all those days ago—but I couldn't give in to these impulses. I still couldn't tell her the truth.

"It's September now," I said as I moved just close enough to toss her a sandwich.

"I know." She caught the bag and folded the edges down to take a bite.

"Every September the town hosts a Labor Day event. Would you like to go with me?"

She talked around the bite of PB and J. "Are you kidding? I've got nothing else to do. Will Ezra be there?" A worried expression flitted across her face before she masked it.

"Why would that matter?"

She shrugged. "He helped me find the part for the truck, and I need to find another."

"I can take you to the farm."

"I know, but—never mind."

My body buzzed with alarm. I was missing something important, and I had no idea what it was.

"Do you—" I stared. "Would you still like to go to the Labor Day events?"

"Yes. On Monday?"

I nodded.

On the surface, the day was a success. We'd gotten out of the confines of the cabin. We'd reconnected as friends, but in the cracks of my chest, I worried that we'd opened a new chasm.

She saw Donner once a week, but did she see Ezra too? The idea was preposterous. Why would they have any reason to converse or spend time together?

But if they hadn't, why would Marigold ask about him?

I couldn't force her to see things from my perspective. I couldn't convince her that Ezra's heart was poisoned with hate.

Is this what Lillian felt when I went on tour with Ryker Tucker?

Left out? On the sidelines? Worried?

I should come clean. Tell her everything and see if she'd accept me.

No. I couldn't lose her.

She stretched out on the rock a few feet away, her eyes closed and a blissful smile on her face.

A pang shot through my chest. Had our bond deepened too much? I feared that, now, telling her the truth might feel like the ultimate act of betrayal.

Chapter Seventeen

Marigold

The sky stretched above us, a vivid summer blue that seemed to go on forever. Levi stopped the truck in a field filled with haphazardly parked vehicles.

Stepping out into the scorching heat, I felt the warm air envelop my bare shoulders. Levi had insisted I wear my bathing suit today and bring an extra pair of clothes. Why? I didn't know. The closest body of water was the Tennessee River.

An enormous cheer rose from a commotion beyond my sight. "What's going on?"

Levi hefted a small cooler from the back of the truck. He reached out his hand like he was going to take mine, but then pointed instead. "Welcome to the annual Labor Day games. This land has been abandoned for a century. Nobody owns this field."

I gestured to the paved road to our right.

Levi waved off my observation. "True, there is a road, but besides that and a single fire hydrant, there's nothing out here. A developer slated this land for homes, but when the town put up a riot and demanded Sutton stay nice and small, they gave up and left."

The sound of spraying water surrounded us as we strolled further.

Levi grinned. "What you hear is the single fire hydrant manned by the good firefighters of Sutton. You see, the games originated from a need for the poor people of Sutton to cool down. Not poor as in money, but poor as in *it's-too-dang-hot-outside*. Sutton folk need a reason to roll in the mud, and the Labor Day games give them that."

"Mud?"

"Yes, mud. Now, let me explain how this works."

I regretted wearing my cute mint green one-piece. Mud and mint green did not mix.

"They broke the Labor Day games into three facets," Levi continued. "Number one is the men." He pointed.

We emerged from the parking lot.

Men congregated around grills that appeared like mushrooms sprouting from the ground. The section of the field closest to the parking area looked like one giant and disorganized tailgate party. A tantalizing aroma wafted through the air, enough to tempt even the most fastidious of appetites.

Levi pointed in the opposite direction. "The second facet is the women."

Beth Shaw waved as we approached. She occupied the only dry patch on the field, surrounded by an assortment of tables adorned with vibrant beach umbrellas and miniature tents, all laden with every kind of picnic food imaginable.

"And third," Levi said, "Is everyone else."

The rest of the town of Sutton—anyone under the age of fifty—was covered in varying degrees of mud. The fire chief, along with a few men from the department, doused the field and overgrown weeds in water using the singular red hydrant.

Beth met us wearing a red and white sundress and a wide-brimmed hat. "You made it just in time. The football game is about to start. Some of your boys were looking for you," she said to Levi.

I stood beside her, hoping I wouldn't be invited to play football in a slippery mud pit.

Levi tugged his shirt over his head and handed it to Beth. "Gotta show them how it's done then," he said, winking at me. He kicked off his shoes and walked into the squishy mud.

The sight of his bare skin was still unsettling. At the cabin, he was careful not to blur the lines between friend and roommate. So, he never walked around in his underwear, and neither did I. And I'd never seen him without a shirt on.

Until the waterfall.

He wasn't so handsome that a girl had no choice but to look. Rather, I felt drawn to him because we kept these parts of ourselves hidden.

"So," I said, turning to Beth. "What do the girls do?"

Before she could respond, a group of girls with varying heights and skin tones made their way toward a volleyball net.

"You don't have to play if you don't want to," Beth said.

I surveyed the area. Every girl my age was on the field.

It seemed like I didn't have a choice.

I tugged my tank top over my head and placed it in Beth's outstretched hand.

"I'll be cheering for you," she said.

"Hey, Marigold. You made it."

The voice made me halt. Standing behind Beth was Courtney King from church, followed by Ezra. *Shirtless* Ezra.

I focused on his face, not wanting him to think I was interested in his athletic build. The side of his head displayed a patchwork of bruises that seemed to have evolved into an array of colors since I last saw them a week ago—as though he were collecting a rainbow on his cheek, forehead, and jawline.

"Yes," I said.

"I like your bathing suit."

I crossed my arms over my chest, more self-conscious than I'd ever been. Stripping down to my bra and panties in the woods with Levi had been nothing because we were alone. But being in a tight-fitting suit in the middle of this crowd felt . . . *unnerving*.

"See you out there," he said, brushing past me.

"Dear," Beth said. "You truly don't have to go."

I toed off my shoes and set them underneath the umbrella that she and Courtney shared. "No, I need to do this."

I took one step forward and felt the mud slide between my toes. A strand of long grass tangled around my ankle with the next step.

I took a deep breath and gathered courage. It's not that I hated mud, it's that I was still the "new girl" in Sutton. I was an outcast. An enigma with my red hair. The other girls might ask questions I couldn't answer. Questions about my past.

I can do this.

Ezra

I kept searching for Mari, and then I finally found her. Amidst the crowd, she stood in a simple suit paired with cut-off jean shorts, a wide smile and a streak of mud on her face.

Unlike me, who stole glances in her direction, Mari was fully engrossed in the volleyball game, exchanging words with the girls around her and occasionally casting a glance at Levi before refocusing on the net.

I shouldn't have cared that I wasn't the one she was searching for. But for some reason, I did.

Had I lied to her about my injury? Yes. But to be fair, I'd lied to everyone.

Could I be arrested by my brother-in-law for growing weed on the farm? Sure.

Was I the kind of guy that she deserved? No way.

But I cared about what she thought. I'd wanted to impress her from the moment we met. I'd visited the Roman Colosseum, boated in Rimini on the Adriatic Sea, seen Michelangelo's David, and tasted wine so sweet it became a part of my bloodstream. I wished for her to see the real me. The Ezra who yearned not for a life on a farm, but dreamed of nurturing his own path, exploring distant lands, and cherishing a woman—perhaps even her.

The thought was ludicrous. As much as I wanted to live in the luxury of my past, the reality was staggering. I had nothing to offer her.

I'd gone from Italy to Sutton. Grapes to cow manure. Boat rentals to golf carts.

If only she knew the real me—

A body slammed into me, knocking the breath from my lungs and sending me sideways into the mud. A whistle blew, signaling the game's ending. The man who'd clobbered me offered a hand and helped me up. "Sorry, man. I was going long for a pass. Didn't see you there."

My bare chest was sweaty, streaked with mud and blue chalk. "Who won?"

He pointed at his red chest. "Reds."

Levi's team. Of course.

The groups broke up and headed toward the shade to get water.

Seeing Levi and Marigold congregate with Mother and Mrs. Shaw, I veered toward Lilly who sat on the folded-down bed of Jackson's F-150. She stood and gave me a muddy hug. "How have you been, Ez?"

She handed a plastic bottle of lemonade to me, and we both sat overlooking the crowd. "Married life appears to be treating you well."

"All five weeks of it," she said with a laugh.

"Still. You look happy."

"And you look perplexed."

"Do I?"

She tipped her plastic bottle toward the field. "Does it have to do with her?"

"Who?"

She pointed to the tent where Mother and Mrs. Shaw talked with Levi and Mari. "Marigold. I met her at church. Nice girl. I'm glad Levi has someone." There was a note of longing in her voice I chose to ignore.

"She's okay," I said, drinking the too-sugary lemonade. My lips puckered.

"I know you better than that," she said.

"We're just friends." And that was true.

She dropped the topic. "I talked to Daddy yesterday. He misses hearing from you."

I took another pull from the bottle.

"He says that if you don't call him soon, he's going to call you."

Talking to my father was complicated. He knew the state of the farm finances. He might ask questions I didn't want to lie about.

Before I could answer, someone yelled, "Let's eat!"

"Not yet," yelled the half-drunk owner of the animal feed store. "Sledding first!"

Cheers rose from the men.

Father Hosea stepped forward wearing a pair of khaki shorts, a white polo, and a ball cap that said Sutton High. "That's my cue," he said as he raised both hands like Moses parting the Red Sea. "They have chosen me to coordinate and simultaneously pray over the sledding games this year."

The people laughed.

Father Hosea's voice carried across the field. Startled from his grilling duties, he still clutched meat tongs in one hand, using them as if conducting an orchestra rather than addressing a group of muddy townsfolk. "This year will be a bit different. The game coordinators have decided to choose the teams."

The field went dead silent.

"We'll also decide who gets to use which truck."

The men broke into arguments. "No way is anyone other than me drivin' my truck," someone yelled. "We been practicin' this for months," another called.

Father Hosea pointed his tongs at the voice. "Exactly. You've been practicing. For the record, I was against this. It's too dangerous for my liking, but that's why I'll be praying." He smiled.

"We won't make you pass over the keys to your rides, but instead of traditional two-man teams, this year there will be two winners. One driver and one sledder."

Sledding had been a part of the Sutton Labor Day Games since the invention of the truck. Vintage black and white photographs, proudly displayed in historical hangouts like The Haunt, showcased the daring spirit of 1955 Fords participating in these thrilling games.

The sledding games were conducted when the tailgate was removed and attached to the bed with long chains. The sledder would sit on the tailgate and hold on for dear life while the driver navigated an obstacle course. The atmosphere crackled with danger and excitement, often culminating in inevitable mishaps like broken bones occurring almost every year.

In years past, the driver and sledder practiced before the race to get a feel for what the other could handle. Guys who knew each other well worked best together. It was also acceptable to pimp out their tailgates to make special holds or grips. Splitting up the teams assured that there would be less predictability.

"The driving winner is the man who gets through the course the fastest," he continued. "And the sledding winner is the man who stays on the longest. But—" he held his tongs in the air for emphasis— "if the first truck to cross the finish line also still has his sledder, there is a one-hundred-dollar prize for both men. If you win only the driving or the sledding prize, you will receive only a free round of drinks at The Haunt, and one of Mrs. Goodman's peach pies."

The new rules were genius. The outcome would depend on the drivers. If they sped through the race then they might win. But if they worked through the race with their partner, they had a better chance at securing a hundred dollars. Predicting how a man would react to your speed and driving was hard. That's why men practiced. The new rules made the game total guesswork.

"This sounds interesting," Lilly said. "Are you participating?"

I took the last gulp of lemonade. "Wasn't planning on it."

Father Hosea took a folded piece of paper from his pocket and started to announce the teams. Just when I thought he was done he threw out one more sentence.

"Ezra King as a driver and Levi Shaw as the sledder using Levi's truck."

Father Hosea paused to look between Levi and me. The whole town did. He must've been attempting to bring us together. It wouldn't work.

Levi looked at me, a question in his eyes.

Would we ride?

Everyone stared.

I nodded once, and he nodded back. For public appearances, we would.

Years ago, Levi would have been my first choice. But now, I wouldn't trust him to put gas in my truck. I smirked. I was the one driving. I could toss his body off the sled any time I wanted. But the prize sounded too good. *One hundred dollars.*

If I wanted the money then I had to be smart.

Father Hosea retreated to his grill as the men found each other and ambled to the trucks.

Soon, only Levi and I hadn't moved.

I crushed the plastic bottle in my fist, handed it to Lilly, and then walked barefoot across the field to stand in front of him.

Levi spoke before I could. "Look, we don't have to do this. I don't wanna partner with you any more than you wanna partner with me. But—"

"One hundred dollars sounds good," I finished. "And they don't know the huge mistake they just made."

Marigold, Mother, and Mrs. Shaw all gaped at me.

"We could drive circles around them," I said. "Some things never change. You in?"

Levi grinned. "I'm in. For the money, of course."

"Naturally." I scratched dried dirt from my cheek and let the flakes fall to the ground. "Let's go."

———

Levi's truck was a chaotic mess, with empty soda cans and crumpled granola bar wrappers scattered everywhere. I kicked aside a sports drink bottle and slid into the driver's seat.

Ahead of us, a dozen trucks revved at a spray-painted starting line. Another dozen idled behind, waiting for the second race. Levi crouched on the tailgate, his fingers clutching the edge. Mud oozed over the edges of the metal, seeping toward his dirt-splattered calves.

Although we held a momentary truce, I considered pressing the gas pedal hard enough to throw him from the tailgate. If I did, I might be lucky enough to leave his body in the wake of another speeding truck.

No. For this race, Levi and I were partners, not enemies. If the town wanted a show, we'd give them one.

He shot me a thumbs up and I faced forward, waiting for the shotgun start.

Father Hosea stood at the starting line and waved his arms. His mouth moved, but I couldn't hear a word he said over the rumble of the trucks.

Finally, he aimed a black pistol in the air and fired a blank toward the sky.

I pressed the accelerator. My desire to force Levi's grip off the tailgate fled.

One hundred dollars.

Levi and I had won this race many times. I tapped into our shared history as we surged forward.

Levi knew how I drove. I knew how strong he was.

Or how strong he used to be. I hoped his drinking hadn't made him weak.

My truck pulled ahead of the others, spitting mud in an arc behind us, bathing Levi. He held on surprisingly well with a thick line of dirt dripping down his face.

I pressed the accelerator a little harder.

Orange five-gallon buckets served as obstacles. I veered toward the first one. Once we were out of the mud the truck moved faster, no longer dragging the sled like a spoon through molasses. I rode the brake around the first bucket and then sped toward the second.

The flash of a blue Tacoma nearing my left caught my eye. The driver wanted to cut me off at the next bucket. I checked Levi then pressed my foot to the floor. Levi ducked his head to keep the spray of dirt and small rocks from assaulting his face.

I screamed, hoping my voice would carry through the interior of the Chevy. "Hold on."

I didn't wait for him to respond. I took the next bucket without the brakes and imagined Levi white-knuckling the tailgate.

I took the corner tight. The blue Tacoma tried to follow and hit the bucket.

One more bucket and we'd be on our way to the finish line. I checked the rearview mirror. The remaining trucks were too far behind or had already lost their sledders. The ones without sledders were the most dangerous because they didn't have any reason to restrain themselves.

If I could keep my clip then we'd win.

The same blue Tacoma rode my bumper around the next bucket, his sledder still holding on, but he was more careful this time. I took the turn with the same gusto I'd taken the last two. After clearing the turn with bluey still behind, I punched the gas, and we lurched toward the finish line.

I checked the rearview mirror. Levi was still attached, teeth gritted.

Come on. Come on. Come on.

The blue Tacoma gained.

I floored the accelerator.

The finish line was feet away.

We crossed first with the Tacoma less than five feet behind.

Levi rolled off the tailgate as I drove parallel to the parking lot and stopped. The scent of burnt rubber greeted me as I stumbled out of the truck. For a moment, we were brothers. We forgot why we'd hated each other. We forgot our fathers.

Levi punched his hands in the air, fists toward the heavens. I did the same. We hollered at the sky in victory. Before I could think about what I was doing, I threw my arms around him and slapped his back. He returned the gesture, adrenaline pulsing through me.

When we pulled away, he said, "We still got it."

"I can't believe you didn't lose it around those corners."

"I figured you'd coast them."

Four years after we imploded, we still knew each other.

He pointed at my face, noticing the bruise. "What happened?"

My defenses rose. "Just a row with a friend."

"Is that what it takes to be your friend? A black eye?"

"Only if you're an idiot." I tried to smile, but I could feel my pulse rising.

Mother, Mrs. Shaw, and Marigold ran toward us. The light in our mother's eyes dimmed as they realized that winning the race hadn't mended the chasm between us. Mother hugged me, careful not to attract a layer of dirt. Mrs. Shaw hugged Levi. Marigold stood to the side.

"What did you think?" I asked as Mother pulled away. I was desperate to get away from Levi and his paltry accusations. I assumed he'd seen the bruise before the race. I must have been angled the right way to avoid his scrutiny.

Marigold's eyes darted between us.

"I'm just glad you're both okay," Mrs. Shaw said. "Why they keep this fool-hardy race in the games is beyond me. Last year, a boy had to be airlifted to a hospital. But does that stop these crazies from doing the exact same thing again this year? No, it does not. This should be banned." She looked at my mother. "I say this every year, but I mean it this time. We need to start a petition to stop this madness."

"It's just a little fun," I said.

Levi's jaw twitched as he inspected my face.

I patted him on the bicep. "Thanks for the hundred dollars."

He nodded and then led Marigold away.

Marigold

The landscape of the field changed as the sky melted against the horizon in every shade of rose.

The barbecue potluck was over, the fire chief had stopped up the hydrant, and the games were over. As night approached, people convened around four giant bonfires in the dry area of the field. Food trucks had replaced the tents, and more than a few people held guitars.

As Levi and I walked from the parking lot to the field, both of us dressed in new clothes with our faces mostly clean of dirt, I inhaled the aroma of fire smoke, popcorn, and hot dogs. We passed families roasting marshmallows, couples tangled together, and groups gathered around stringed instruments.

"This part of the day is low-key," Levi said, holding the handle of his guitar.

He laid a blanket beside a campfire occupied by one couple. The lovers ignored us in favor of making out as he unclasped his guitar case and pulled out the sleek wooden instrument. They turned when he played.

The guy did a double take. "Are you Levi Shaw?"

Levi avoided eye contact and nodded once.

He sat up and snapped his fingers. "You did a song with Ryker Tucker, right?"

His girlfriend sat up. "I love that song. Will you play it for us?"

He ignored the question. "Where are you folks from? I reckon you're new or passing through."

"Is it that obvious?" the girl said with a blush. "We're from Bowling Green, Kentucky. We wanted to get out of town for the long weekend and Ghost Mountain sounded intriguing. It didn't amount to much though. I didn't run into a single ghost, not even a fake one. Shouldn't there be some sort of haunted attraction?"

Levi chuckled. "Most folks want to keep Sutton as tourist-free as possible."

Her shoulders slumped. "That's what we gathered. The only juicy information we found was about a place called Skeleton Cliff where several people have offed themselves. Is it haunted?"

Levi stiffened. I sucked in a breath and caught a whiff of sugary caramel corn. Popcorn would be a perfect distraction. "Why don't you play for a spell, and I'll get us a snack?" I asked, touching his arm.

The girl sensed her question hadn't landed well, and she snapped her mouth shut. Levi ignored her and focused on his guitar. I left him to strum for the awe-struck—and now uncomfortable—couple as I ambled around people and fires toward the popcorn wagon.

I carried a bag in each hand when a voice stopped me. "Marigold?"

I couldn't place the tone until I turned and saw her auburn hair.

Lillian.

We met at church but had never spoken.

She sat on a blanket beside Jackson. "That popcorn looks delish. Do you mind getting me some, Jack? And Marigold, why don't you sit?" Her tone was neither welcoming nor hostile.

Jackson left.

"What's going on between you and my brother?" she asked.

A few kernels tumbled out of my bag as I faltered. "We're friends." I'd noticed the way he looked at me today. The same way he looked at me last week as I cleaned the cut on his face.

She rolled her eyes. "C'mon. I'm his sister. I can tell he has feelings for you. What I can't figure out, though, is you. Whose side are you on? You're living with Levi but getting close to my brother. Do you expect to bring them together?"

I recognized the fear in her voice. She cared for them. Why did she care for Levi?

Dusk settled as I crouched beside her, interested in learning more. "I'm friends with both of them. Only friends."

"Which one are you in love with?"

I set the bags of popcorn in my lap. "Neither."

She faced me. "I love them both. I don't know you, and I'm not sure why you came to Sutton. I hope you don't plan on breaking either of their hearts."

My retort was fast and spicy. "Whose fault is it that Levi's heart is broken?"

She turned away. "I did what I had to."

"Lil, I've got the popcorn," Jackson said as he approached. His words were like a warning, a tentative step toward quarreling wolves to make sure they didn't attack him.

We weren't fighting. We were trying not to lose our hearts. She'd thrown her sunflower dress away, yes, but she hadn't thrown away Levi.

His words repeated in my mind. *"I don't think you ever stop caring for your first love."*

We stared at each other, our eyes communicating things we didn't say.

Me: *I'm trying not to get hurt too.*

Her: *Be careful.*

Me: *I will.*

"Thanks, Jack," she said aloud. "We're finished here."

Mind reeling, I gathered my popcorn and headed toward Levi.

"Hey, Mari."

I knew who had spoken before I saw him. Only one person called me Mari. As I turned, a teenager rushed past, jarring the bags of popcorn from my hands and spilling them across Ezra King. He sat on a blanket before a crackling fire. If we were closer, flames would have vaporized the popcorn.

"Sorry," I said, kneeling to brush kernels off his shoulder.

"Not your fault. I'll buy you another."

"Don't worry about it." Heat radiated off the fire, warming one side of my face.

Did he just sigh with relief?

"I wanted to apologize," he said.

That got my attention.

He pointed at the molted colors on his face. "I'm sorry for the way I acted when you came over last week."

I picked apart a piece of popcorn and threw it into the grass. "Are you sorry for trying to turn me away or for lying about your injuries?"

He rubbed his healing knuckles. "Both," he said. "But I'm still not ready to talk about what happened. I meant what I said when we spoke about your living situation. You are always welcome with me. In a separate bedroom, of course. And I hope we can still be friends."

Levi would come searching for me if I didn't return soon. "Yes, we're friends. I still need a truck part from the graveyard."

"Ah, yes, I had forgotten. Stop by anytime this week."

I stood and brushed my shorts off, feeling the dirt caked beneath my tank top. Looking up, I caught sight of Levi standing in the light of a bonfire, watching us.

———————

Levi

Ezra grinned at Marigold. The girl I was trying to protect. His eyes crinkled and his teeth showed in that genuine good-ol-boy way the town trusted.

I wasn't fooled.

Marigold beamed back at him, oblivious to the way he could turn violent within a millisecond. He hadn't always been that way. The change had happened after Samuel went to jail and he became convinced that Dad was the one who turned him in.

The truth was, not even I knew who turned in Samuel King. When I'd asked Dad, he said he didn't know. Then, a year later, he was dead.

After that, Ezra changed. I guess I did too.

She was talking to him like they were best friends. If she was chummy with Ezra, I'd already failed her.

Today, as Ezra drove across the finish line, I'd wondered if we might mend the brokenness between us. Then I saw his face. I'd seen it before the race, of course, but I was too busy deciding if I would be his partner to focus on the massive bruise.

For a second, we were the old Levi and Ezra. Brothers of Ghost Mountain Farm. The moment passed within an instant—in the time it took for me to remember who we'd become.

If things were different, we might have been friends. But hatred and distrust were hard things to scrub from the mind.

Marigold saw me staring and wound around couples on blankets to get to me. "Sorry. A teenager spilled my popcorn."

"So, you got cozy with Ezra?" I hated the snide in my voice, but I couldn't tamper it.

A huge log popped in the nearest fire and then collapsed, sending ash into the air around us. An ember landed on her shoulder, and I smudged it out with my forefinger, smearing gray across her white skin.

"I was scheduling a time to find the truck part," she said.

I wanted to argue with her. Insist that she allow me to bring her. But I didn't want to trap her. "When are you going?" I asked in a tone I hoped sounded supportive.

She shrugged. "Maybe tomorrow."

I had to tell her about the night she arrived. If she knew, I'd hug her in the middle of these people so Ezra would know we belonged together.

But I couldn't claim her affection until I told her everything.

I tried to calm the tremor in my hand as I pointed at the food trucks. "Should we get more popcorn?"

She nodded. "I'm starving."

I nudged her shoulder with mine. "You almost always are."

"Not true," she said. "But I do love to eat."

We both laughed.

I couldn't tell her in this crowd. I'd have to wait until we got home.

Tomorrow.

I'd tell her tomorrow.

What would she think of me once she found out the truth?

Chapter Eighteen

Levi

B almy September sunshine streamed through the sliding glass doors, casting a warm glow over the kitchen table where Marigold and I were seated, indulging in freshly made pancakes.

I'd hardly slept, yet for some reason, I was wide awake. Hours had passed as I contemplated how to tell Marigold all I'd learned since the day I found her. Should I be serious? Nonchalant? Apologetic?

She drizzled syrup over her pancakes and took a bite, butter oozing into the thick brown liquid and pooling on her plate.

Two untouched pancakes sat before me. Nervous energy kept my foot bouncing beneath the table.

I stood, pushing my chair back. If I was going to do this then I needed to do it now. "Would you like to sit outside with me for a spell? There's something we should talk about."

"And leave the pancakes?"

"We'll warm them in the oven later. Please?"

Pouting, she set her fork and knife on the plate, then accompanied me to the porch.

Finn had been camped beneath the kitchen table and wasn't thrilled that we were leaving without at least dropping a morsel for him. He looked at the table laden with food and then followed us outside, his tail limp.

In the daylight, the white lights Marigold called "twinkle lights" glittered as sunlight shot rays through their glass caps.

We sat beneath the canvas canopy and faced each other.

"I need to tell you the truth," I said. What a terrible start. It sounded like I'd been lying to her.

"What?" she said.

Doubts assailed me. I straightened the lights on the closest railing and considered backtracking. What if telling her didn't shorten the distance between us? What if it made it worse?

This was a bad idea. Perhaps my confession had less to do with being honest and more to do with my desire to share my feelings. I wanted to tell her everything because honesty multiplied trust. If we trusted each other then maybe we could become more than just friends.

Was telling her a form of manipulation? I didn't want that. But what else could I do?

She moved to the far end of the bench, pulled her feet onto the wood and crossed them, facing me.

It was hard to keep my thoughts straight with her staring at me like that.

"You're making me nervous," she said.

"Don't be." She deserved the truth. I was hurting both of us by keeping it from her.

Donner may have known a thing or two about writing, but he'd never once experienced the pressure of hiding a secret like this from a grown woman. A woman I may have loved if I permitted myself. "It's about the night you lost your memory."

The wind blew through the leaves and pine branches, shifting her hair around her shoulders and face. She hugged her knees. "You've been keeping something from me?"

"No. Sort of." I fiddled with the lights once more and dug my fingers into Finn's fur for a long pet. "I swear I'm not crazy." What was I doing with my hands? This was going terribly.

"Okay," she said.

"I'm sorry I haven't told you sooner. Keeping it from you any longer seems dishonest."

"Levi," she said firmly, her blue-green eyes boring into me. "Tell me."

"Right, I'm rambling. Sorry." With shaking breath, I told her about the night of Lillian's wedding, the journal, passing out, and then finding her. "I kept this from you because I understand how it sounds."

She bit her bottom lip.

I waited for her to respond. Finn squirmed.

"I'm not sure what to say."

That wasn't a negative response. "Say what you're thinking."

Her lips pursed. Then, finally, she spoke. "Let's backtrack. Are you suggesting that you . . . *made* me? That you're responsible for my existence and the fact that I don't have any memories?"

When she put it like that . . .

Finn whined as I clutched him too tightly. "I thought it was crazy, too, I assure you. But Donner told me—"

218

"You're getting your information from *Donner*? The guy who just last week told me he names the squirrels in his backyard before shooting them for dinner?"

"You're right to be skeptical. I understand this sounds bananas. But—" I gestured to Finn. "I wrote him too."

She stared at Finn. "Why would you make something so ugly? No offense, Finn."

Finn wagged his tail and opened his mouth for a signature-smile pant. It was as if he were saying, *No offense taken.*

Turning back to me, she said, "Levi, I don't understand why you're saying these things. I knew you were still struggling with your dad's death, but . . . "

If I could script this conversation, Marigold would cycle through emotions like the wind circulated from the mountain to the valley—initially hurt, then forgiving. She'd be angry and then get over it. She'd accept my account without reservation. Then, in my wildest imaginations, she would fall in love with me.

How could I help her believe me? "I didn't make this up. Donner said it's happened before. You're not the first person to be written onto the mountain."

"Levi, please. Do you hear how crazy you sound?"

I'd been wondering if I was crazy for weeks. "Yes, I know. That's why I haven't shared this with you until now. It sounds insane. *I* sound insane. That's why I waited. But every word I've said is the truth."

She was quiet for a moment. Finally, she said, "I don't believe you."

Her words hit me like a head on collision with a truck, knocking the wind out of me. This rejection stung deeply; a fear turned reality that I detested facing head-on. "That's fair," I said. "But what other explanation could there be for you to have not have any memories?"

My brain fastened on an image, and I snapped my fingers. "I can prove it. Do you recall the morning after you arrived? When you told me about your boyfriend, and I somehow knew his hair color?"

Her confidence faltered. This had bugged her too. "Yeah."

"The exact scene you described was in a movie I'd watched the night before. You remembered something from my subconscious."

"That could have been a lucky guess." Worry lines crinkled her forehead.

"I realize it sounds nuts, but it's real. Donner explained that the mountain is named Ghost Mountain because of the ghosts born here."

She swallowed and turned her face away. "Please, Levi, don't do this. If I made you want to push me away—"

"You didn't do anything."

She unfolded her legs and stood. "Then why would you attack the thing that means the most to me? You *know* I want my memories back. You know how much I desire to know myself."

I matched her stance. "That's why we're having this conversation. I couldn't go another day without telling you."

Tears welled in her eyes. "Please, Levi," she begged. "Tell me the truth. I know you know something about me, but this can't be it."

Finn positioned himself between us as I tried to step in her direction. I halted, lifted a hand to touch her, then let it fall to my side. "It's the truth," I whispered.

"I can't accept that," she said.

"I'm not lying."

She stepped backward. "Why—" she paused, turning toward the valley. "Why did you stop kissing me?"

Finn moved just enough for me to stand beside her. Taking a chance, I touched my knuckles against her hand. She pulled away.

"Because I needed to tell you about the journal first."

She shook her head. "No. You still love Lillian." Lines of hurt marred her face.

I had to help her understand. "Part of me will always love Lillian. But I don't think about her anymore. Not since you."

"Levi." Her voice was hoarse. "Why did you . . . " Then her fist clenched, and she whirled on me. "Why did you have to lie? We were happy. I was enjoying breakfast. I think you're afraid to love someone again, so you're pushing me away on purpose. It's fine. I'll go." She walked off the porch.

"Go?" I ran after her. "Go *where*?"

Instead of answering, she marched into her room and started to shove clothes into bags.

Desperation ran through me. "Please," I said. "I don't love Lillian like that. I promise. I was starting to fall for you. That's why I told you. Not to push you away. I didn't want there to be any barriers between us." My heart pounded as my words came fast through quick breaths.

She scoffed. "I can't tell if you believe this or if you're simply trying to manipulate me."

No. No. No. This was supposed to be the total *opposite* of manipulation. How had this backfired? "I would never try to manipulate you."

Tears welled in her eyes.

This couldn't be happening. If I could reach back in time, I'd snatch the secret back, even if it broke us. At least that tearing would have been slow. This was too much, too fast.

I watched helplessly as she packed and then threw the bags into the back of her red truck.

Without a hug or even a slight smile, she left.

My heart dropped into my stomach. I'd lost Marigold.

Marigold

I didn't let the tears fall until I was rolling to a stop in the valley. They flooded my eyes, their warmth searing my cheeks.

Levi thought he could find a solution for my memory loss? He thought he could be my savior by pretending to be the man who created me?

What a joke.

The problem was this: I cared for Levi.

Tears still leaked from my eyes when I parked in front of Ezra's house.

Wait. Ezra's house?

I'd been driving on autopilot, but now that I was there, it made sense. Beth had offered to let me stay the morning after Levi and I had met. But I couldn't ask her. That would be too . . . weird.

Ezra was my only option.

Before knocking on his door, I sat for a few minutes, debating if I'd made the wrong choice in leaving Levi. I could still go back.

No. I couldn't.

The tale he spun about writing me in a book and then magically finding me on his doorstep couldn't be real. I would not fall for the lore of the mountain. Stories were just that. Stories. People didn't invent people with words. I would not be tricked into believing that I didn't have a past.

No, I didn't have any memories dating before the night I woke in the woods—but that didn't mean my existence was proof of magic.

It simply meant I had amnesia. Long-term amnesia. I still went to bed most nights hoping I'd wake with my memory in the morning. It hadn't happened yet, but it would. Someday.

At least, I hoped.

Ezra's frame darkened the screen. He pushed the door open, stepped outside, and waved.

I waved back.

With a sigh, I turned off the engine.

His voice carried across the lawn as he said, "I wasn't expecting you today."

I debated if I should trade pleasantries or get right to the point. Who was I kidding? I didn't have the guts to ask if I could live with him here on the lawn. Pleasantries it was.

"Is now a good time to find that truck part?" Maybe the opportunity to ask him about the living situation would arrive on our trip to the truck graveyard.

"It's a little early yet. I've just put on a pot of coffee. Why don't you come in for a spell?"

That might work too.

Once we stepped onto the porch, I followed him into his sleek kitchen, adorned with stainless steel appliances and a massive fridge boasting double doors. After retrieving two coffee cups from the cupboard brimming with an assortment of mugs, he poured the rich, fragrant brew from a weathered coffee pot.

As he began to pour, I halted him with a raised hand. "That's enough."

"I'm sorry. I should have asked if you liked coffee first. We've never seen each other this early. Please excuse me. Mari, do you like coffee? If so, how do you like it?"

"I prefer less coffee and more cream and sugar."

He poured in the cream and let me stir in the sugar. Then we moved to the living room couch, our feet propped on the low table, mugs in hand.

"It's a beautiful morning," he said. "I was just—"

"I need to talk."

"Okay," he said, giving me ample space to gather my thoughts. His languid posture and presence calmed me.

Telling Ezra about Levi's stories made me squirm. I didn't believe them, but they still felt private, raw, and vulnerable. Something nagged at me, and I couldn't put my finger on what it was.

I could pretend this was a social visit before driving to the mountain to seek Levi's forgiveness. Nope, that wasn't an option either.

I had two choices:

Go back to the man who lied—or I could ask Ezra for a place to stay. He was keeping secrets, but he hadn't been untruthful to me.

So far, at least.

"Levi and I had a disagreement."

He cocked an eyebrow. "So you came here to gather yourself and visit the truck graveyard?"

"Sort of. I left after the argument."

He paused. "What do you mean *you left*? You're saying it like it means more than the fact that you drove to my house, which is obvious."

This was the tricky part. The coffee mug burned my cupped hands. I'd already gotten this far.

"No. I packed my bags."

He set his mug aside without taking a drink. "I deeply desire to know what that argument was about. But for the sake of your privacy, I won't ask." He stared at me pointedly as if to say, *See? I don't need to know your secrets. We can be friends without sharing everything.*

I wasn't so sure. Not when the thing he kept from me involved a bash on his head and raw knuckles. The bruise looked the same as it did yesterday. An array of colors atop healing skin. This wasn't the time to argue.

"Thank you," I said. "I appreciate that."

He waited.

"I, um, I hoped your offer still stands."

He blinked, retrieved his mug, and took a sip. "Yes. It does."

"I'm talking about when you offered to let me stay here."

He gave a small nod. "I'm aware that's what we're speaking about, yes."

"And you're still okay with it?"

"Certainly."

I had to be sure. "Just like that?"

"No strings attached."

"I didn't want to assume."

"Mari. Stop. You are welcome here. I have a guest room."

This was easier than I expected. "Thank you."

A knock at the door startled me, causing coffee to spill over my mug and onto my shorts. I spun to see Beth and Courtney with their noses pressed against the screen as they peered into the living room.

Ezra chuckled. "Come in, Mother. Mrs. Shaw."

The door flung open. "Marigold, how are you today?" Beth's gaze darted between the two of us. She was obviously trying to discern the nature of our relationship. How could I live with Levi but be here, with Ezra? She was in for a surprise.

"Good morning," I stammered.

Ezra warmly embraced Courtney as she balanced a glass pan covered in foil. "Mari, have you met my mother?"

"Briefly. At church."

She shifted the pan to her other arm and reached out her hand toward me. "I'm Courtney King. It's a pleasure to meet you again."

Her name reminded me of the day Levi and I hiked to the waterfall and found the initials *DES & Courtney* carved into the tree. Could this be the Courtney who etched her name into the wood with a penknife dozens of years ago?

"I–I'm glad we met again." Why was I stuttering?

"Marigold is staying with Levi," Beth said. "She has amnesia."

"I remember."

I felt like a rare bird at the zoo under her scrutiny.

Ezra cleared his throat. "She's not living with Levi anymore."

Beth's brows came together to form the shape of the letter *V*. "Is Levi okay?"

"Yes," I jumped in. "He's fine."

The woman who welcomed me into her home, sat beside me at football games, gave me Levi's jersey, and greeted me with the warmest hugs now looked like I'd broken her heart. "Oh," she uttered as the spunk drained from her face.

When I left Levi, I hadn't considered how it would affect his sweet mother.

Courtney broke the awkward silence. "I brought the cinnamon rolls I promised."

Ezra accepted the offered pan. "They smell delicious."

I couldn't think straight as Beth pasted a smile over her forlorn expression. "Well, it's delightful to see you, Marigold," she said. "I should go."

Courtney didn't turn with her friend. Instead, she kept her stare on me like she was sizing me up as a suitable match for her son.

"Mother?"

She blinked.

"Thanks again for the cinnamon rolls," Ezra said.

She forced her gaze away. "Of course. They're your favorite."

"Mother and Mrs. Shaw are always baking," he said with a jovial grin, maybe trying to break the strange tension emanating from both older women. "I'm lucky to live next door."

Courtney smiled. "We'll get out of your way. Tillie Brown's husband passed two days ago, and we plan to deliver a pan of brownies and a chicken casserole."

"See what I mean?" Ezra said. "Always in the kitchen. And thinking of those in need."

Beth glanced back, then the screen door shut behind them.

The sound of crinkling aluminum distracted me as Ezra pulled back the foil on the glass pan. A whiff of cinnamon made my mouth water.

"These will pair perfectly with breakfast."

I pushed aside Beth's disappointment and Courtney's strange fascination with me to focus on Ezra's solid body beside mine and the aroma of the food. "Breakfast? I only saw coffee." I remembered the forgotten pancakes on the kitchen table at the cabin.

"Exactly," Ezra said.

I walked into the kitchen and watched as he placed two rolls on a plate, covered them with a paper towel, and then set them in the microwave. He leaned his backside against the counter as the machine whirred.

"I'm sorry for my mother's behavior," he said. "She's not normally so . . . *intense*."

I crossed my arms. "I'm afraid I've disappointed Beth."

"This is a strange situation," he said. "You living with Levi first and now me? But I think they'll warm to the idea. My mother has been protective ever since my dad went away."

Courtney's stare didn't resemble that of a concerned mother. She looked like she knew something about me. Like she knew me.

The microwave dinged.

Ezra set two forks beside the plate of warm, gooey rolls.

I wasn't hungry.

"Are you okay?" he asked in a gentle voice.

"Just distracted."

He set the sweet aside. "Would you like to get your mind off things?"

More than anything. I nodded.

"Your things are in the truck?"

I nodded again, too overwhelmed to risk saying too much and voicing my fears and sadness.

"I'll grab your bags, and then we'll go drive somewhere," he said.

Instead of arguing, I let him go.

Echoes of my argument with Levi resurfaced.

"Every word I've told you is the truth."

If what he said was true, then the eerie hours spent wandering through the dense forest aligned with a strange logic. The absence of any form of identification, the void of social media presence, and the lack of a name for authorities to trace suddenly found an explanation in his narrative. It explained why my memories weren't returning.

But Levi's story couldn't be true.

It couldn't.

Doubt clawed at my mind as I sank forward, hands meeting my temples in an attempt to quell the throbbing ache that pierced through my skull.

But what if it was?

Chapter Nineteen

Ezra

In a month, the Great Smoky Mountain landscape would transform into a fiery canvas reminiscent of the deep crimson hues swirling in my glass of Pinot Noir. The leaves would turn from green to orange.

It was surreal to have Marigold by my side, her belongings now resting inside the welcoming embrace of my home. To take her mind off things, I drove her to one of my favorite places. The Bruno Vineyard Winery.

As we sat overlooking the vineyard, I couldn't resist seeking her opinion. "How do you like the wine?" I asked.

We were two and a half hours from Sutton on the eastern side of Chattanooga.

She lifted the glass to her lips and took a sip. "It's sweet. You used to work here?"

"Yes. I was the manager until four years ago. I miss walking among the grapes and tasting their vintage flavors. Someday I wish to run a winery of my own in these mountains."

There it was. My hopes and dreams summarized in three sentences.

She set her elbows on the table. "You'd move away from the farm?"

"I'd leave that dusty, manure-stinking place in a heartbeat if it was in good hands and my momma was cared for. This . . . " I gestured toward the vineyard stretching below us against the backdrop of the Smokey Mountain. "Suits me more than a farm."

She took a sip and squinted at me. "I can see that." Her eyes were still puffy.

"How are you feeling?"

She shrugged. "It's pretty out here."

Not the profound answer I was looking for, but I understood the desire to change topics. "It is. I love the mist."

"It's like that on Ghost Mountain sometimes too."

"I know, but I prefer the Smokies."

"Even though you were raised in Sutton?"

"Yes, Ma'am."

"Why?"

I grinned. This was my opportunity.

I told her about Italy—minus the romantic parts—and how I'd fallen in love with wine. Sutton felt too small after that. I'd consider living in Napa Valley if it wasn't so far away and too hard to break into the wine business. I wanted something I could start from scratch.

The Smokey Mountains emerged as an ideal alternative—close enough to home for comfort, yet distant enough for solitude and escape from prying eyes. "What are Rome and Florence like? Did you see famous art?"

I signaled the wine attendant. "Can we please try the Rosé and get an appetizer plate?" When she left, I turned back to Marigold and said, "Yes. I saw it all."

She took a long drink of Pinot Noir. "Tell me everything."

While I told her of the sun-kissed vineyards nestled in Sicily, the server set the plate of appetizers on the table alongside two glasses filled with Rosé. My stories painted vivid pictures of encounters with the spirited locals, daring escapades into the unknown, and the uncertainty of my nightly accommodations—whether it be a cozy hostel or an open field.

Her cheeks were flushed by the time she finished the Rosé, her once swollen eyes now bright and lively.

"Where is your dream travel location?" I asked when my tales were over and we'd moved to a second Pinot Noir. She liked it better than the Rosé.

She admired the evergreens surrounding us, the dip and peak of the rolling mountains. "Home," she said. When I gave her a quizzical look, she added, "Where I come from. I want to go home." Her eyes glassed over.

I must cheer her. Speaking more of this would bring tears to her eyes. "Would you like to go for a walk? Take a drive to Chattanooga for dinner? Head back to my place?" I made sure not to refer to it as "home."

"Dinner in Chattanooga sounds nice."

I offered her my arm and stood, feeling the wine go to my head. I knew I could drive but I also knew an extra thirty minutes would clear my head. "We'll walk first. There's an abandoned cabin on this property not many people know about. It's interesting because it looks like someone just left. Nobody around here knows the history of the place."

She clutched my arm, more unsteady than I was. "Lead the way."

Levi

At ten o'clock on the day Marigold left me, I smashed my fist into the pillow and sat up, perching myself on the edge of the mattress. Telling her sooner wouldn't have changed anything. She would've had the same reaction a month ago as she did today. She would've left me.

Moonlight filtered into the dark bedroom, casting a sliver of light across the bed's end and Finn's wagging tail resting atop the blankets. I had no proof that Ezra killed my dad, and now I didn't have Marigold. I was worse off than the night I wrote her song.

Warm light flooded the room as I switched on the lamp and stood. The novels on the nightstand caught my attention. Maybe reading would help me fall asleep—or forget. Yes, forgetting was paramount to sleep.

I picked up a book and started to read, but I struggled to focus. The memory of Marigold's truck disappearing from view kept replaying in my mind. I slammed the novel shut and stood, in desperate need to leave the place that was haunted by her memory.

Finn watched from his curled-up position as I tugged on my jeans and then slipped into a T-shirt. He stayed put as I walked to the front door, not bothering to wear shoes. Grabbing my keys, I left the cabin.

The familiar feel of the steering wheel and the sound of country music settled my frustration as I drove. I had no destination in mind as I let the tune soothe me. The curves of the mountain and the twin beams of the headlights piercing the darkness calmed me with their familiarity.

Before I knew it, I was on the road that led to the school. I shouldn't have been astonished since it was the place I drove most often. Headlights by the football field surprised me. Who parked here this late?

The lights came from a Jeep Cherokee. Two figures sat on its hood. They raised their arms to block the light as I angled my truck in their direction. I recognized them.

Trevor and William.

My headlights illuminated empty brown bottles balanced around them. Smoke emanated from between Trevor's fingers. Was it a joint of a cigarette? At their age, did it matter?

I parked ten feet away with my lights blinding them. The boys slid off the hood to stand in front of the grill.

Thankful for the distraction from Marigold, I kept the truck running as I confronted them.

"What do you two think you're doing?" I asked. They squinted as I strode closer. "You could be kicked off the team for this."

They shared a glance as they recognized my voice. Trevor threw the cigarette—smelling like tobacco, not weed—on the asphalt and ground it out with his shoe. "We didn't mean nothin'. It's the first time. Swear."

My shadow stretched over half of Trevor's face and half of William's. They turned their faces away from my headlights and looked down at the empty beer cans littered around the Jeep.

The scent of alcohol taunted me. Why hadn't I taken a drink when sleep evaded me? Whiskey could numb my mind faster than a novel. My drinking habits had dwindled since Marigold arrived.

Bringing my thoughts back to the boys, I counted the bottles.

Eight beers on their first night of drinking? Not likely. Why did they get wasted on school grounds? Sutton was riddled with secluded spots—dead-end streets, hidden corners against the mountain, and desolate parking lots behind abandoned buildings—where they could have indulged without fear of consequences. Why choose here? It felt as absurd as a toddler denying raiding the cookie jar while sporting chocolate-stained cheeks. Nonsensical and unbelievable.

"First time, huh?" I remarked dryly. "How'd you plan on getting home? Were you planning on driving? 'Cause last I checked, that was illegal for adults who drank, let alone kids. You know Sheriff Jackson Miller is hard on drunk drivers."

"We were gonna call his brother." Trevor nudged William.

William paused for a moment, then a spark of realization lit up his eyes. "Yeah, my broder was gonna pick us up," he slurred.

I crossed my arms. "That doesn't change the fact that you'll both be removed from the football team." I couldn't let go of their indiscretion. Not only were they drinking. They were doing so on *school property*. Their teammates would be devastated to lose them.

My gut churned at my hypocrisy. Who was I to judge when I'd committed the same sins? But this was different. I was their role model. If I let this go and something happened in the future—a car accident or another alcohol-related mishap—then I'd be the one to blame.

Indecision twisted my reasoning. This was about more than just football. If I reported what I found, Drew would have to suspend them. Small-town gossip would ruin their reputations.

I'd once made stupid mistakes as a high schooler too. If I'd been caught, I wouldn't have played college ball, and maybe I wouldn't have become a musician either.

"C'mon, Coach Shaw," William pleaded. "We promise we didn't mean no harm. We won't do it again."

Trevor pointed at my feet. "Coach, where are your shoes at?"

I ignored his question. Encountering delinquent teenagers hadn't been on my agenda when I left the cabin without pulling on footwear. I'd just wanted to get out. "Why are you drinking together?"

Trevor stared at the broken cigarette at his feet. Upon further inspection, I saw an old condom beneath their truck. Evidently, this parking lot was used for all kinds of after-school "activities."

"Jess didn't want either of us."

I tried not to laugh. The girl they both pinned after had rejected them. I considered Marigold. I'd prefer she spurned both me and Ezra instead of being with him.

Maybe this was the first time the boys had gotten drunk. They were commiserating over heartbreak. I could relate.

"Drinking won't fix what you're feeling."

If I said one more hypocritical thing, God might smite me. I was ill-equipped to deal with these things. Chastising wasted teenagers in parking lots was not my area of expertise. I'd rather join them than berate them.

The question remained:

Would I report them?

They had great prospects. William was an excellent student, while Trevor was a gifted ballplayer. Should a typical teenage mistake—one that hadn't harmed anyone—dictate their futures?

I didn't want to be their judge. I should have simply stayed in bed.

"You swear you've never done this before tonight?"

They nodded.

"And it'll never happen again if I drive you home right now?"

Trevor affirmed, "No, sir," in unison with William's "No, Coach."

Gesturing behind me, I instructed, "Pick up those bottles and dump them in my truck."

They scurried away to gather the bottles.

Trevor sat in the passenger seat with William squished between us.

My toes curled around the gritty gas pedal as I pulled away from the Jeep. It would have taken me five second to slip shoes on. Apparently misery made us all do stupid things. We were quiet as we drove to William's house. Despite my coaching instincts nudging me to lecture them, words eluded me. Finally, I mustered, "If I ever hear of this happening again, I'll have no choice but to turn you in, understand? Jesus gave second chances, but He also taught us about consequences. Being the grandson of a preacher, you should get that, Trevor." I felt good about bringing Jesus into the conversation. It seemed more grown-up that way.

Trevor didn't respond, but William said, "Yes, Coach. Thank you, Coach," and then he hopped out. His voice came out slurred and shaky.

Good. He was remorseful for what he'd done. It could have ruined his future.

We passed the entrance to Ghost Mountain Farm on the way to Trevor's house. He didn't thank me for bringing him home. Actually, he didn't say a single word. Perhaps he'd heard the rumors and recognized what a hypocrite I was. He got out of the truck and shut the door with a nod in my direction.

I didn't wait for him to sneak inside. Whether he made it in without waking his parents wasn't my concern. As I shifted into drive and peeled away from a curb—a little louder than necessary—he spun around. If I wasn't mistaken, he flipped me the middle finger as I sped off.

I wasn't their babysitter. I was their coach. Turning up the radio, I headed back.

My pulse was too high to return home and try to sleep. I needed to do something, but what?

Donner.

Not a single car passed as I steered toward his house. At first, I assumed he was asleep, but then I noticed a flicker of light on the porch. The hot tip of a cigar on an inhale, and then a dim glow. A gun cocked before I opened my door all the way.

"Easy, Donner. It's Levi."

"What'r, you doin' out at a time like this? I coulda shot ya."

Leaves crunched beneath my bare feet as I stepped toward him. "How often do you get visitors this late, and who do you expect them to be?"

"Exactly why I could'a shot ya. Ain't no good news after a respectable nine o'clock."

The butt of the gun thunked to the wooden planks as I sat beside him and wrinkled my nose. What was that odor? He took another inhale, and I realized he was smoking a joint, not a cigar.

"Wannna drag?" Donner asked with the joint pinched between his out-stretched fingers.

"What are you doing with this?" I asked as I accepted the marijuana.

"Helps me sleep. Don't worry. I'm not a pothead. I get this from an herb doctor, not my drug-runnin' son Fred."

Weed wasn't legal medicinally or recreationally, but I was a farm boy from a small town in the south. I knew my way around a joint. I hadn't gotten high since I was a teenager, preferring alcohol as my vice of choice when I came of age. Taking a hit was as familiar to me as riding a bike.

"What brings you here this time of night?"

I passed the rolled weed back to Donner and exhaled. "I told Marigold the truth."

"I'm assuming it didn't go well if you came t' me."

"She left me for Ezra."

Donner took a drag and leaned back.

My fingers started fidgeting on the arm of the chair. "I don't know what to do. Should I try to explain myself?"

The night burned brighter in the joint's glow. "Sounds t' me like you wanna force that girl to see yer point of view."

"She thinks I'm crazy."

"So you wanna bash her head in with your stories?"

I held out my hand for the joint, and Donner obliged. "They aren't stories. I want her to have the truth." I exhaled the smoke.

"She went to Ezra," I repeated.

"So? What's that to you?"

I gave the joint back. "I'm better for her."

"Who are you to decide somethin' like that?"

I slammed my hands into the arms of the chair and shot to my feet. "I'm the one who made her."

The darkness magnified Donner's exhale. "Sit down, Son." He tried to pass me the joint but I declined.

"Listen, I'm not goin' to pretend to understand what yer goin' through, but you listen good. Hear? You are not to try and get that girl to love you. Real love don't do things like that. Real love lets the thing it loves most walk away because real love don't force itself on nobody."

The high hit my bloodstream. "I don't want to force her to love me. I just want her to see—"

"You want her t' see things the way you see 'em. You wanna tell her she's wrong and yer right." Donner interrupted.

"But I *am* right."

"Don't matter now."

"Then what am I supposed to do?"

"Nothin'. Don't speak to that girl unless it's to let her go. That's the best way to love her."

"But—"

He gave me a pointed look. "Do you love her?"

"Yes, but—"

"What do you love about her? You hardly know the girl."

I forced my eyes closed. The weed was loosening my tongue more than I liked. Donner had a right to speak his mind, considering I came to him in the thin hours of the night.

Focusing on his question, I said, "I love how free she is. I love how she not only desires to make things right, but she actually does. She's only ever been truthful to me. She loves and cares for my momma, and she sees the good in all people. I know because she stuck with me as long as she did."

"Those'r mighty fine reasons to love a girl."

My back relaxed against the chair as the weed settled in my lungs. "So, I just let her go?"

Donner dropped the smoked joint on the porch and smothered it with his bare and calloused foot. "That's right, Son. You do nothin'."

My limbs felt both heavy and light. Donner stood. "Come with me. I think it's time we went to bed."

Defeat and sadness wrapped me in a blanket as I collapsed on his couch and succumbed to exhaustion.

Marigold

The guest bedroom—as well as the rest of Ezra's house—was modern and orderly. A sharp contrast to the rustic charm of the mountain cabin.

My mind felt hazy, not just from the glass of wine we savored in the kitchen but also due to the two additional glasses at the winery and the one Ezra insisted we have with dinner before lugging my bags upstairs.

He dropped one of the garbage bags by the closet door. "You can use the dresser." He pointed to one with a large oval mirror on top. "And there are hangers in the closet." He opened the door to show me. "The mattress is nice, and the bathroom is just down the hall. I hope you don't mind if we share it."

The room was so . . . impersonal. From the dark wood dresser to the queen-sized bed with a plain gray comforter and white pillowcases. Not a single hint of personal touch adorned the space; no cups filled with wildflowers, no books strewn about, no Mason jars redolent with mint and lemonade-infused sweet tea.

Seeming to read my mind, he opened the top drawer of the dresser and pulled out a candle. "Maybe this will make it more homey."

I checked the scent while he headed to the bathroom for matches. *Lavender.* Well, that was something.

When it was lit and casting flickers across the room, he stood just outside the doorway. "Do you need anything else?"

I moved to stand in front of him, an invisible wall between us. He was on the outside of the room and I was on the inside.

"Thank you," I said. "For today. It was nice of you to show me around. And—" I touched the doorframe—"thank you for letting me stay."

"I meant it when I said you were welcome here."

He wanted me to say something. Maybe confess what had torn me away from Levi.

The wine helped me temporarily forget my morning. Levi's insistence that I was forged from words on paper and that I would never regain my memories.

It would be nice if that were true—but it would also be terrifying. Nice because it would explain so much. And terrifying because it'd mean that I was only one month old.

I blinked to erase the stupid thoughts. Levi's "truth" was absurd.

When I focused on Ezra again, he was staring at me. Had he stepped closer?

"Mari, I . . . " he paused, then said, "I'm glad you're here."

My legs felt wobbly. I leaned against the doorframe to stay upright.

"Are you okay?"

"I'm just tired," I said, closing my eyes.

He reached out and grasped my arm with a strong touch.

I opened my tired eyes to find his concerned look. Forcing strength back into my legs, I brushed off his grip and smiled. "It's nothing. I'll go to bed."

He was still staring. Had he moved even closer, or were my eyes too tired to focus properly?

"Mari, may I . . . " He sighed and then shook his dark hair. "Never mind." Spinning on his heel, he turned to go.

I was curious. "Wait."

He pivoted.

"What were you going to ask?"

His bare feet glided soundlessly as he retraced his steps, drawing closer with each stride. He was closer than he'd been before. His jeans grazed the exposed skin of my thigh. He leaned casually against the doorframe above me, and I waited for him to say the words he'd retracted.

In a hushed tone, he confessed, "I told myself I wasn't good enough for you. I still believe that. But . . . " His fingers brushed a strand of hair behind my ear. We were so close that I could smell the wine on his breath. "Mari, may I—and I might regret this in the morning—but . . . may I kiss you?"

I could refuse. I *should* refuse.

But with his face so close to mine, and the wine buzzing through me, I didn't want to. I wouldn't pretend I loved him. Yet there was something about the way he wanted me, cared for me, and called me *Mari* that made me move my lips closer.

Levi had pushed me away. Ezra wouldn't.

With a gentle grip on my ribcage and a soft exhale, his lips paused just shy of mine. The sweet scent of wine on his breath mingled with the soothing scent of the nearby lavender candle.

And then our lips met. Surrendering to the tender pressure of his kiss, I shut my eyes, savoring the gentle dance of our lips connecting and the reassuring touch of his hand against my diaphragm.

As our kiss deepened and he tentatively parted his lips against mine, seeking more intimacy, I reciprocated willingly.

Could he sense the expansion of my lungs with each breath drawn in sync with him?

When he leaned back, his breath mingled with mine as he murmured, "Mari."

My lips were still parted when he kissed the corner of my mouth. He released his hold of the doorframe and my middle. Touching my chin with his thumb, he softly uttered, "Goodnight." And then he disappeared into his room.

My chest heaved.

I shouldn't have agreed to that.

Did he love me? Did I love him? Kissing a man without the answers to those questions wasn't fair.

I closed my bedroom door and dug through my clothes until I found my pajamas. All I could think of was Levi—and Ezra.

Ezra embodied comfort—neatly tucked sheets, a lineup of coffee mugs, and the remnants of wine on his lips. In contrast, Levi represented spontaneity—a chaotic cabin, a slightly battered guitar, and a silence that spoke volumes.

And I'd kissed them both. Without intending to, I'd position myself as the girl between them.

Chapter Twenty

Levi

Although I was skeptical and reluctant at first, I took Donner's advice and didn't contact Marigold. Instead, I hoped and prayed that she would come back to me.

Two weeks passed with no sight of her.

In the meantime, my routine carried on. I went to football practice and games, hiked with Finn, and ate dry toast for breakfast instead of pancakes.

On the morning prior an important away football game, I found Finn tearing apart a paperback book in the bedroom. How he got it, I'll never know. The book was torn into so many pieces that I couldn't decipher the author, title, or genre.

As I attempted to tidy up the aftermath by plugging in the vacuum cleaner, it failed to roar to life. Sighing, I wished I could ask Marigold to fix it, but of course, we still weren't speaking. If I remembered correctly, there was a shop vac in the basement.

Paper confetti stuck to Finn's jowls as we descended to the one-room basement, and I was reminded how messy the place was. Note to self: *clean this room.* Momma might have to help determine what to keep and what to include in a spring yard sale.

If I were to judge my dad on this room alone, I'd assume he was a hoarder. Medium-sized boxes were stacked like columns. Most of the boxes were filled with books. Dad had a hard time parting with the written word. Maybe Finn's mess was a blessing in disguise. One less decision I had to make.

Weak sunlight struggled to illuminate the dark corners but didn't succeed. Instead, hazy dust swirled in the air. Unlike the rest of the house, the basement hadn't been cleaned. In a shadowed nook, a cluster of items lay scattered. The shop vac would be here.

My foot accidentally snagged a box, sending a stack of four boxes toppling down until the top one hit the floor, spilling its contents at my feet. Papers and journals surrounded me in a chaotic array; some sprawled open while others lay with their spines facing downward.

My dad's distinctive handwriting stared back at me from within these scattered pages. Could one of these be the journal I sought? The journal where he wrote someone into existence on the mountain?

Memories of an antiquated collage library filled with literary classics flooded my mind as a musty scent of aged paper tickled my nostrils. I crouched to inspect the pile. The first journal I picked up could be more accurately described as a notebook. It was filled with scribbled thoughts and novel scene ideas, plot points, character arcs, and setting descriptions. The next notebook contained poems. And the third, favorite quotes.

As I sifted through the pages and papers, a square object fluttered to the ground. Setting the notebook aside, I found an unsealed envelope with my mom's name written across the front in my dad's flowing script.

Inside was a yellowed, aged letter. I had to tilt it toward the light of the sliding glass door to interpret the faded words.

Dear Elizabeth,

I don't have the book with me, so this single piece of paper must suffice.

I must say that I love you. The loneliness in your eyes as we went to bed last night concerned me. So, like normal, I am retreating to pen and paper to tell you how I feel.

Elizabeth, I love you and only you. Feelings for Courtney no longer reside in my heart. I despair showing you my love in a manner you'll believe. If you could see yourself the way I do, you would never doubt my affection for you.

I married you, Elizabeth Charlotte Shaw, and I've loved you since the day you shared your ham sandwich with me on the playground. You know why I tried having a relationship with Courtney. You also know why it didn't work.

It's because I loved you more.

I always have.

And yet I don't regret a single moment of my life or who I've loved. Every encounter made it even more clear to me that you are my person.

You are my sunshine, my rain, and my hope. All paths have led to you. And they always will.

All my love,

Duncan

The letter fell on the folded seam as I digested the words.

Dad had dated Courtney King, which meant the initials Marigold and I found on the tree were theirs, just as I feared.

I reread the letter. The first line struck me. Dad mentioned a book. He must mean a journal like this one. He referenced it as if he wrote in it often. Could it be the one I'd searched for? The place he kept his secrets and composed someone? Maybe Courtney?

The journal may be in this pile.

The following hours were spent scouring the box for Dad's journal. But I did not find the book.

While I enjoyed grasping these pieces of my dad, they were all rather generic. They proved that the man loved to write everything on paper, which—in my mind—proved he *didn't* write the suicide note.

I was interested in clues about his killer or who he had created, but neither piece of information was found in this pile.

I read the letter a third time. Momma might know about the journal he'd referenced. Maybe she stored it on a shelf in her bedroom or tucked it into her nightstand.

I stuffed the paper inside the envelope and then shoved it into the back pocket of my jeans. Then, I loaded Finn into the truck and drove to Ghost Mountain Farm.

Marigold

My bare feet padded down the stairs and into the kitchen. The scent of coffee wafted from the pot. Other than the tantalizing smell, the kitchen was empty.

As had become my routine over the past weeks, I poured a half-filled mug of robust dark roast coffee, adding a swirl of creamer and sugar. For breakfast, I prepared a boring bowl of flakes mixed with nuts, raisins, and granola clusters. Ezra liked bland, fiber-filled cereal. Levi and I never ate cereal together on the mountain. I begrudgingly adjusted to this morning soup.

When I was done with breakfast and Ezra still hadn't appeared, I padded back upstairs and peeked into his bedroom.

The king-sized bed was neatly made with a plain black comforter draped over it and two plump pillows. White drapes decorated with black diamond patterns hung serenely from the two gabled windows that overlooked the front yard. Mounted above the sleek dark-wood dresser sat a small TV set. The door to his closet remained closed. Ezra was nowhere in sight.

The room bore few personal touches save for a series of professional photographs gracing the wall above the bed—likely scenes from Italy—and a handful of framed pictures scattered across the dresser's surface. After peeking behind me to confirm I was alone, I ventured into the room to inspect them.

The first frame displayed a picture of Ezra in a winery setting. The second held a photo of him and Lillian. But it was the third frame that piqued my curiosity.

The five by seven photograph captured a smiling family immortalized in color. They were standing somewhere on the farm, rolling fields and the setting sun behind them.

My fingers glazed over the glass, the smiles, and the family that looked whole and perfect. Ezra's father was the only person I hadn't met. His black, windswept hair touched his shoulders, and he and Ezra appeared to be the same height, both with handsome features. Courtney leaned into his shoulder, content and relaxed, while Lillian held Courtney's hand with a wide smile.

I contemplated Ezra's expression in the picture. He looked lighter. Freer. His father's imprisonment, subsequent responsibility on the farm, and delayed dreams added weight to his shoulders and lines to his face.

The sound of tires on gravel startled me. I wiped my fingerprints from the photo with the hem of my shirt and then ran downstairs.

I watched Levi's truck pull into the driveway. Instinctively, I walked outside in my bare feet and waited for him to park.

After exiting the truck, he saw me standing on Ezra's porch and stopped midway to his mom's house. A flutter swept through my belly. Levi had not contacted me since the day I'd left.

Why? Was it to give me space because he knew he'd lied? Did he wish for me to return while he was at football practice?

"Hey," I said.

He lifted his hand in a forced greeting. "Hello."

"How are you?"

He shrugged. "Busy. Here to see Momma."

Footsteps shuffled down the drive. We both turned our heads at the same time.

Ezra's stubble glittered in the morning light as he walked from the direction of the farm store.

Ah. So that's where he'd been. His office was upstairs.

He neither spoke nor looked at Levi as he passed the truck. When he reached me, he laced his fingers through mine and walked me up the porch stairs, into the house. I watched from the screen as Levi stood for a few moments. Finally, he made his way into Beth's house.

"Why did you do that?" I asked, peeling my hand out of his. "He's just here to visit Beth."

He gestured toward the kitchen. "Did you have coffee?"

"One cup."

"Would you like another?"

"I guess."

After we filled our mugs with steaming coffee, he said, "I'm sorry if I overstepped. Levi irks me." He set his hand over mine, a gesture I allowed. We'd been flirting with danger since the night we first kissed.

I didn't want the town to gossip. In my short stay in Sutton, I'd learned that being with someone was almost equivalent to marrying them.

Although Levi and I hadn't dated, and we only shared one brief kiss, the town was already whispering. Deep down, they still didn't forgive Levi for breaking up with Lillian—even though she'd married Jackson. I didn't want to continue the cycle of gossip and blame.

The problem was this: Ezra and I had grown close. Closer than Levi and me. It wasn't planned, nor was it forced. It had just . . . happened.

"Want to go to the truck graveyard?"

"Yes." I sighed, relieved for the change of topic.

———

Levi

The letter was tucked into my back pocket when I opened the worn wooden door to Momma's house. "Hey, Ma," I called, helping myself inside. "Momma?"

There was no answer.

I walked through the house to the rear deck and saw her kneeling in the garden.

The slap of the screen door alerted her to my arrival. "Levi, what a surprise," she remarked, pushing herself up with a hand on her knees.

"I can help," I said, nodding toward the bucket of weeds nearby.

She straightened, placing her hands on the small of her back. "I'd love to sit a spell."

As we settled into the porch swing, its chains protested with a screech. She sank into the cushions and let out a satisfied sigh. "I've missed having you around," she said.

Using my foot to set us swaying softly on the deck, I replied, "I miss you too, Momma." I didn't bother with pleasantries. "I found a letter."

Leaning forward, I retrieved the envelope from the rear of my jeans and handed it to her.

Tears immediately threatened to spill from her eyes. She must have recognized the handwriting. "Your dad wrote me often."

"Have you read this one?"

She pulled the paper from the delicate envelope and unfolded it. Her fingers went to her mouth as she scanned the words. A single tear ran down her cheek. "I wish you hadn't read this. I should have known you'd find such things at the cabin, but I never . . . " She wiped the tear away. "You must wonder about Courtney and your dad."

She knew me far too well. "Yes. I'm curious, but that's not the only reason I showed this to you."

"You are a mystery, Levi, so much like your dad. Your brother has always been easier to read. Have you talked to him? He called yesterday."

I leaned forward. "No. Mom, please. The letter referenced a book. Do you know which book Dad was talking about?"

She read it again. "Yes. Duncan and I wrote letters to each other in it. I must have had it when he wrote this."

"Do you know where it is?"

"No."

That's not the answer I was hoping for. "What do you mean?"

"I haven't seen the book in years. I assume it's at the cabin."

"It's not."

She let out a sigh. "Good, because I don't want you reading it. Those were personal letters."

"There were only letters in the book?"

She nodded and looked at me curiously. "What were you expecting?"

I'd hoped there would be a reference to who Dad wrote into existence. An indication of his mental state at the end of his life. Something other than love letters to my mom. That was sweet, but she was right. I wasn't interested in them.

Could Momma know who Dad had penned?

No way.

She would have told me.

"I was hoping to discover more about Dad. Mom, you must admit, he would never have written his suicide note on a computer. If this is how he communicated with you, this is how he would have done it."

She gripped my arm with a light touch. "I've made peace with your dad's death, Levi. There's been no sign of it being anything other than . . . " Her hand fell as she faltered, unable to say the word.

Suicide.

My dad's name didn't seem to fit together with the word *suicide*.

Her warm hands clenched mine as I reached for her and held her. Instead of arguing, I just sat with her, listening to the breeze in the orchard.

"Levi," she whispered, her voice soft yet firm. "Please move on. I've loved having you here, but you don't belong in Sutton. You should be in Nashville with Colton. I know your heart longs for the music. You are an artist. Don't ruin your life by staying here."

She was right. My body itched to create, but I couldn't do that until I learned the truth.

Even if I returned to my passion, Nashville might not accept me. As far as music fans were concerned, I was washed up. Old news. But Momma wasn't talking about me being successful. She desired to see me *happy*.

I squeezed her hands. "I love you, Momma."

She squeezed in response. "I love you too."

When I tried to stand, she pulled me to the chair. "I'm not finished," she said. "You mustn't think ill of Courtney because of the letter."

I sat, curious but also hesitant to hear about my dad's dating life. "How long did they date?"

She sighed. "Only a few months. I hope you don't assume I hated Courtney. I didn't. Your dad and I dated on and off. He was with her during one of our 'off' times."

This was new information. "Why did you and Dad break up?"

"You're a lot like him. Or you *were*. All passion. He'd get so caught up in a song or a book idea that he'd forget about me. It took me time to realize he wasn't disinterested when he pursued his art first. He was distracted. I learned to love that part of him."

Was she digging into my failure with Lillian? "I never forgot about Lillian."

"But did you include her?"

This wasn't supposed to be about me. *Time to go.* "Thanks for talking to me."

"You won't think differently about Courtney?"

I stood for a second time. "No. Dad ended up with *you*."

"Consider what I said. You don't belong here. I'll be fine if you move."

I gave her a quick kiss on the brow. "I'm not ready to leave yet."

"And Levi."

I stopped at the door. "If you find that book, don't read it. Bring it to me."

Was she hiding something?

Maybe it was filled with sappy love letters between my parents.

But still, I wouldn't promise. "I'll let you know if I find it."

I discovered the exact part needed for the 2018 Ford F-250 amidst the decrepit remains of a retired 1999 F-250, its body marred by rust and its engine a charred shell, while the speedometer boasted a staggering 295,392 miles.

Ezra sat on the lowered tailgate. His gaze drifted between the distant horizon, the swaying trees, and the looming barn in the distance.

"What are you looking at?"

His focus shifted to me. "You."

"I mean, what were you looking at a second ago?"

"You."

I slammed the truck door and settled beside him. The metal beneath me was warm but not too hot because of the large shady tree above. "No, you weren't."

"Actually, I was. I was thinking about you."

"What about?"

His Adam's apple bobbed as he swallowed. "My friend, Jake, who works on the farm, asked if we were dating."

I swung my legs like a nervous child. "Oh?"

"I told him no, but I've been sitting here thinking about it."

I wasn't ready to talk about such things. "I went into your room this morning," I said. "Looking for you."

He clasped his hands behind him and reclined slightly against them. "Did you? I apologize. I was attending to some business."

"I saw the picture of your family on your dresser. It was the first time I've seen your dad."

His jaw hardened as she shut his eyes. "I remember that day. I was visiting from the Bruno Vineyard Winery and Lilly was in town for a visit after she passed her NCLEX exam for nurses. Momma made pulled pork with barbeque sauce, fried green tomatoes, creamed corn, cornbread, and the best warm peach cobbler with ice cream I've ever tasted. Father was arrested the next year. We had Thanksgiving, Christmas, and Easter together before he was taken, but I remember that day more than the holidays."

Both love and grief permeated his words. "I'm sorry," I said.

His eyes opened. "I hate Levi."

My legs swung faster. "Why do you hate Levi? Don't you assume Duncan turned Samuel in?"

"I *know* Duncan turned him in." He leaned closer. "I'm sure you've heard Levi moan about his father's death, but I doubt he thinks about my father, the one who's alive but not present. Because of Duncan Shaw, my father didn't get to walk Lilly up the aisle at her wedding. He doesn't get to climb into bed with my mother every night. He can't smell the fields or feel the wheel of a tractor under his grip. He's here, but he's also not. Levi isn't the only one who lost someone."

I couldn't tie these loose ends together. Both Levi and Ezra believed things for which they had no proof. Both could be right, and both could be wrong. Living in the in-between seemed almost impossible.

"I'm sorry," I said again.

"Mari, I don't wish to talk of these things. May I kiss you again?"

For two weeks, our fingers had brushed when we were close. He'd casually hold my hand, or his fingers trailed along my back as he passed, but we hadn't kissed. Kissing was an admission that we were moving forward, and I wasn't sure if I was ready. I was still holding onto the hope that I would find my memories and learn of a love I already had.

As sunlight filtered through swaying leaves, casting playful patterns on his face while he awaited my response, I chose not to reply verbally.

Instead, I intertwined my fingers with the smooth skin at the base of his neck where delicate hairs tickled my touch, and drew him closer for a kiss.

In that moment, I resolved to embrace both hope and progress. I would be strong. I would kiss Ezra King and be his girl and belong to him because he treated me with both respect and kindness.

Despite the lingering ache in my chest echoing Levi's ominous words—a truth I struggled to accept—I pushed those doubts aside.

Ezra's lips left a trail of kisses from my cheekbone to the soft spot below my ear as he guided me back until we were lying in the truck's bed.

As he gazed down at me, I saw the faint scar on the side of his head. The injury he wouldn't tell me about. I looked at his hands. The knuckles that lovingly held me were covered with white scars from demons he'd fought over the years, along with new red marks.

He leaned in to kiss my neck. "Ezra?"

"Hmm?"

"Will you tell me the story about how you were hurt?"

His stubbled chin grazed my jawline as he hesitated before replying, "Maybe later."

And because I wanted him to kiss me again, I let it go.

Chapter Twenty-One

Marigold

September bled into October, painting the landscape in a riot of vibrant hues. Ghost Mountain stood majestically in the distance, its foliage shifting from green to a tapestry of autumn shades, interspersed with evergreen patches peeking through the crinkled leaves. The orchard peaches were picked or fell to the ground in sticky puddles. The cornfield had transformed into a maze. Families came to the farm to drink hot apple cider, eat warm donuts, play outdoor games, or pet the farm animals.

The air transitioned from muggy to balmy before settling into the perfect temperature for wearing a cozy sweater and ankle boots. As nature embraced change, so did I; attempting to immerse myself in my new life and forget Levi. The seasons were moving on faster than I was.

A bucket of candy sat on the kitchen counter, waiting for the trick-or-treaters to visit. Ezra assured me only a few kids would show, but I wanted to wear a costume anyway. I found a velvet dress at the thrift store and borrowed a bow and arrow from Ezra to complete my costume as Princess Merida. My fiery red hair was perfect for the role.

"Who are you dressing as?" I asked over breakfast. I'd ditched Ezra's bland cereal for a more vibrant, fruity O-shaped version.

He took a sip of coffee. "I'm not."

Milk dripped down my chin as I talked with my mouth full. "Ez, we talked about this. You've got to dress up."

He wiped the milk away with his thumb. "What goes with your thing?"

I almost suggested a bear. But in the movie, the bear was Merida's mother, so that would be weird. "Nothing goes with my outfit. Do you have anything here?"

"I could be a farmer." He jabbed his finger in the air. "Or a hunter. You're using the bow. I'll carry a gun."

I dropped my spoon into the cereal. "Think about what you're suggesting."

He pursed his lips and stared at the ceiling. "That I may scare the children away?"

"I don't think answering the door with a firearm on a holiday intended for childhood enjoyment is appropriate."

"Hmm. You might be right," he said with a mischievous grin. "Farmer it is. Simply because I don't have another costume. You know how I feel about farming."

In the almost two months since I'd lived here, I had discovered that Ezra didn't belong in a small town. With each new story of Italy and the places he'd been, I found it harder to see him in the context of Ghost Mountain Farm.

The problem was, I loved Sutton. The little map-dot town had seeped into my skin. I loved visiting Donner—who still palmed his rifle every time a car entered his driveway—and going to the grocery store, gazing at the mountain, watching the sunset, and participating in the slow way of life.

I ate the last few scoops of cereal and then lifted the bowl to drink the sweet fruity milk. I still missed pancakes. Although I attempted to recreate them a few times, it never felt quite right without Finn's presence under the table and Levi's guitar leaning against the wall near the sliding glass doors leading to the porch.

"Do you need me to get anything from the store?" I asked. I brought my bowl to the sink, rinsed it out, and set it in the dishwasher.

"When are you leaving?"

"Now."

He finished his coffee and met me at the sink. "Are you sure?" He set both hands on my waist and leaned in to kiss the tip of my nose.

His lips were warm and soft. I pulled away to look at him. "Yes. I need to get Donner's milk before they run out again. I have no idea who keeps buying all the whole milk."

"Donner can wait." Leaning closer, he tempted me with another kiss, causing my lower back to press lightly against the counter's edge. I lifted my face to meet his, tasting the coffee on his breath.

We'd been sharing kisses for over a month, and his closeness still made my pulse race. He'd never pushed me away. Not once.

We eased back on an exhale. After a few more seconds, we breathed in together and deepened the kiss.

And then his phone buzzed.

"Should you get that?"

He nudged my nose with his and then murmured against my lips, "It can't be as important as this." His hands moved up my arms to my shoulders.

He tipped my head back and pressed his lips against mine again, his fingers gently tightening their hold as I clutched the fabric of his shirt.

The phone stopped ringing and then vibrated with a text.

Groaning, he released me and pulled his phone out of his back pocket. His eyes widened before he ran for the door.

I clutched the edge of the counter to process his sudden shift. "Is everything okay?" What could be so urgent he'd leave me?

He slipped into his shoes without answering.

Rushing toward him, I shouted, "Ez!"

"Gotta go. Sorry. Urgent farm matter."

And then he was gone.

Unease settled over me like humidity as I cleaned the kitchen and anxiously waited for his return. After fifteen minutes passed, I slipped on my shoes and headed to the store. He'd be back home by the time I returned.

———

Ezra

Once outside, I quickened my pace without running. The lingering warmth from kissing Mari faded as I read the text I received:

> Jake: MADAY! Fred is at the barn. Get over here ASAP.

The plants flourished under my care. We didn't have any run-ins with Fred since the day he'd bashed my skull with the butt of his gun.

This visit was unannounced—the worst kind. Any meeting with Fred was a nightmare.

> Me: Be there in a sec.

Passing the last of the farmhouses, I cast a cautious glance behind me to ensure Marigold wasn't following. Then I broke into a run.

The farm was eerily quiet, devoid of even a whisper of breeze stirring the fall foliage. Dead leaves drifted from branches in lazy spirals before settling on the ground in haphazard piles. The chill in the air didn't bother me as I sprinted.

Gasping for breath, I finally reached the old wooden barn and spotted Fred's truck parked in front of the doors. An unfamiliar truck.

Barreling inside, I found Fred leaning against a rugged beam, cigarette dangling between his fingers and gun holstered at his hip. His disheveled appearance—messy hair, soiled clothes, and repulsive smell—suggested he'd spent nights roughing it outdoors.

Jake stood nearby. When he saw me glaring, he shrugged and pointed toward Fred as if to say, *don't shoot the messenger. It was his idea.*

"Look who showed up," Fred drawled.

I straightened my posture and crossed my arms. "You're an idiot for coming. Anyone might spot your truck and investigate. It's like you want to be arrested."

Fred pushed off the beam. "Don't talk like that to the hand that feeds you, boy. I can come when I please."

That's where he was wrong. *Very* wrong. This was my farm, and I chose who came and who went. "No, you can't. You're not welcome here. Ever."

Jake slid onto the dusty floor, his fingers digging into his hair as he perhaps mentally calculated the potential prison time for a felony conviction.

Fred exhaled a cloud of smoke, a malevolent smirk twisting his features. "Boy, this is why I came. You're a flight risk. You don't respect me. And if you don't respect *me* then you don't respect my bosses, and they aren't men to anger." He tossed his cigarette butt on the hay-strewn floor. "I'm not someone you wanna mess with."

The ember briefly ignited on a piece of straw before extinguishing. "I could burn this place to the ground, and you'd haveta let me," Fred said, approaching.

"Because you don't want anyone to find out what you've got going on here. I own you."

A list of indiscretions flickered through my mind.

My first mistake was to run to the barn. Running had a way of accelerating one's heartbeat, and if mine sped any faster then I might explode.

My second mistake was arriving unarmed, because I swear, if I had a gun on me, I'd shoot Fred Tanner right then and there, disposing his body in Atlanta without leaving a trace. The thought didn't alarm me as much as it should.

My third mistake was deciding to come to this meeting in the first place. Rage burned through my body like an out-of-control virus.

"Fred, get out of here. And don't come back unless I invite you." My words remained steady and calm, even as my temper roared within.

His fingers rested on his gun.

"Don't try it," I said, arms still crossed.

He unclipped the safety on the holster.

Wrong move.

I would not lose everything I had sacrificed for. This farm was all I had. This marijuana was my gold mine. The only thing—*person*—keeping me from reaching my freedom was Fred.

White-hot rage exploded in my brain as I lurched forward. I didn't register pain as I smashed my fist into Fred's face faster than he could palm the gun. His body recoiled as I held his arm to keep him from stumbling. I needed him right here. I landed another blow against the side of his ribcage. After that, I'm not sure where I hit him or the number of times. Jake's voice reached me through the haze of my violent outburst.

"You're gonna kill him," he shouted.

When I regained control, I found Fred lying in a puddle of his blood on the floor. His gun remained strapped to his waist, his eyes were closed, and his arms lay limp at his sides. He didn't move, groan, or protest. I couldn't tell if he was alive.

At the same time that I registered Fred's body, I felt a slight discomfort in my knuckles.

Jake knelt by his father and checked his neck for a pulse. "He's breathing," he said, and then he swore. "You coulda killed him. I wouldnta minded losing him, but if we wanna get paid, we need him."

He was right. I'd just beat our drug runner unconscious. My rage felt both justified and stupid. Blood dripped onto the floor from my knuckles. "I'm sorry. I didn't mean it."

"I get it, man, all right? Just let me think." Jake stood. "Help me get him into the truck. I'll drive him home. If you're anywhere near him when he comes to, he'll kill you."

"Not if he doesn't have this." I unholstered his gun and shoved it into the back of my waistband. "He's all talk without it."

"Whatever, man. Keep that thing away from me and help me get him into the truck."

We hauled Fred to the passenger seat, and then Jake ran around to hold him so I could slam the door. Fred didn't stir as his body sagged against the glass.

"You good?" I asked as Jake started the truck.

He rested his arm against the open window. "No, man. It wasn't supposed to happen like this."

"Tell him to stay off my land. He'll get the plants when they're ready. I don't want to see him again."

Jake looked at his lolling father. "I just don't know, man. This is bad."

Setting my hands on the door, I leaned in. "It'll be okay. They need us. And they need the pot. They won't get a payday without what we got in that barn. Get him home and take the rest of the day off. We'll talk tomorrow."

Jake set his forehead against the steering wheel. "You don't realize what it's like. What these guys are capable of. You haven't been on the inside."

"I know. I know. I shouldn't have lost control, but you heard how he goaded me. He had it coming." In truth, I didn't know what the men from Atlanta would do. I didn't know how deep Fred was in with them. Did they think of him as a sewer rat or a brilliant drug trafficker?

Jake slammed his palm on the truck door. "Get it together. You're crazier than me." With that, he shifted into drive and rumbled down the driveway. With luck, nobody saw him.

I stood there until my rage cooled. Growing pot was one of the dumbest things I'd ever done, but what other choice did I have?

None.

The loan payments for the farm were due monthly, and I needed a financial cushion to get out of here. I didn't have any other options.

I set the padlock on the door then made sure the chains were secure before leaving.

Blood *drip, drip, dripped* from my hand as I ambled home.

Fred was a no-good hustler, so lousy at running his own operation that he had to work as a go-between for real thugs. I just beat the crap out of the middleman. What would the thugs do? I hoped they didn't care what kind of trouble Fred got himself into. Just as long as it didn't involve them.

Mari's truck was absent when I arrived at the house, clomping up the wooden stairs.

Exhaustion weighed heavy on my limbs as I considered my hand. What would I tell her when she saw the broken skin on my knuckles?

I hated lying to her, but I couldn't share the truth. There's no way a smart girl like Mari would stay with a guy like me if she knew about the pot. I hated that her nearness to me might put her in danger. What else could I do? Send her back to Levi? No way. I couldn't bear the thought of him welcoming her home. She and I belonged together. I loved her.

The front door slammed behind me as the words repeated in my mind.

I love her.

Yes, I did. When did that happen?

I went to the bathroom to clean my hand. The wounds weren't as bad as the last time. I must've gotten the deepest cut from punching Fred's holster or belt buckle.

With the gauze wound around my hand, I paused by the doorway of Mari's bedroom. I loved how she was tidy, but not as much as me. The room reflected her organized chaos: a flannel button-up was draped over the foot of the bed. The sheets weren't tucked in as neatly as mine, and her closet door was left wide open. The dresser was a colorful mess with a brush and various pairs of earrings scattered haphazardly across its surface.

She embodied beauty and honesty, while I was shrouded in darkness and deceit.

I couldn't love her.

But I did.

She deserved someone better than me.

The creak of the downstairs door broke my reverie. "Hello?" she called out. "Ez, are you home?"

"Up here."

I heard the rustle of a plastic bag followed by her footsteps ascending the stairs. "I picked up a box of brownie mix for later when the kids are gone. I was thinking we could watch a movie." She stopped at the top of the stairs. "What are you doing?" Her gaze fell on my bandaged hand. "What happened?"

"I just missed you," I said, unsure if I should confess what plagued my thoughts.

"What happened to your hand?"

Feeling the weight of guilt, I raised it for her to see. "This? Sorry, had to rush out earlier. Mother needed help. She thought she lost her wedding ring in the garbage disposal. I had to dig it out. Ended up scratching myself trying to retrieve it."

She stood still. "I thought you said there was an urgent farm matter."

If I loved her, I shouldn't lie to her—but what other choice did I have? "Lost wedding rings are urgent farm matters." Mother and Mari didn't talk, so she'd never corroborate the story.

"Ouch."

I didn't deserve her trust. "I've got to do a few things at the office today. Will you be okay here until dinner?"

"Yes. I'll whip up some brownies and finish the book that Beth let me borrow. I had just reached an exciting part."

I lied. There was no urgent work waiting for me at the office. But I couldn't stay in her presence after lying. I felt like the sewer rat I'd scorned Fred as. Scum. Vomit. Dung. I didn't want this life. I wanted my vineyard and trust and beauty. And I wanted her to share it with me.

With a quick kiss on the cheek, I left her to hide in my office.

When I emerged at four, Levi's truck was parked in Beth's drive. The aroma of warm chocolate enveloped my home as I stepped inside.

"Hey," Mari said, walking out of the kitchen. "I couldn't resist trying out those brownies. They'll be perfect with some ice cream."

"Did you happen to sample the candy?"

She grinned. "Only one piece."

"I've had more than that," I admitted.

She furrowed her brow upon noticing Levi's truck. "He comes every Halloween to help Beth hand out candy," I explained.

She looked away and said, "Are you hungry? I tried making the chicken casserole your mom makes, but mine didn't quite measure up."

Was this what domestic life looked like? A woman who made brownies and casseroles while you went to work? She didn't have to do these things. I could've survived on sandwiches, pizza, and the blessing of Mother's home-cooked meals for years before she arrived, but I still loved it. Loved that she wanted to do these things for me. For us.

If only I could give her something in return.

"I'll eat when you tell me it's ready," I said.

She turned toward the kitchen and then back to me. "Let's give it time to cool down."

We went through the motions of routine: I took a shower while she finished dinner. Then we sat at the kitchen island in front of a flickering caramel and vanilla-scented candle. After that, we changed clothes and waited for the children to visit.

Most of the kids arrived before eight. The subdivisions in town might be busy until after dark, but only a few families came to the farm.

Mari's smile lit up the overcast night as she talked to the kids, commented on the costumes, and helped them choose the candies.

As darkness settled outside and only a faint gray hue colored the sky, we shut the door. Mari unhooked the bow from her shoulder. Even in the dimly lit living room, I noticed that her green velvet dress hugged her in all the right places.

"Are you okay?" she asked. "You've been quiet tonight."

I shrugged. "I'm fine." But I wasn't. I couldn't stop thinking about the lies I'd told her.

The room lay in darkness, save for the warm glow emanating from above the stove. Mari's delicate hands found my forearms as she asked, "Are you sure?"

Why did she have to be so perfect? I freed my right hand, caressing her velvety cheek before tracing my thumb along her jawline. "I want to give you the world," I whispered.

She leaned into my touch, her breath mingling with mine. "What makes you think I want the world?"

Our voices barely above a whisper, I clarified, "I never said you wanted it. I said I wanted to give it to you."

"I want a life brimming with memories and joy. You've provided both, and for that, I'm grateful."

She was so close I could smell the pine shampoo on her hair. When she first moved in, I couldn't figure out why she'd smelled so earthy. Then I found her shampoo in the shower caddy next to mine. A bottle of men's pine-scented shampoo. At first, I wanted to buy something feminine for her. But then I realized that I liked the aroma on her.

"But Mari," I said. "I want to give you more. You deserve a life of exploration and excitement beyond what this farm and I can offer. Trust me. I've seen what's out there, and you belong in a place of beauty with someone who—" I stopped myself from saying, *someone you can trust.*

Gently guiding my hand to her neck as she tilted her head upwards, she said, "Stop trying to fix something that's not broken."

My mouth opened as she pressed her parted lips to mine. Dropping my hands to her sides, I drew her in, holding her tight against me. Though our mouths moved in unison, it wasn't enough. I had to share something with her.

"Mari," I said, breathless, setting my forehead against hers. "I love you."

Her eyes snapped open, searching mine in the darkness. "What?"

"I love you," I whispered. "You don't have to say it back. But I had to tell you."

I felt her body melt against mine. Taking her in my arms, I carried her up the narrow staircase. Once upstairs, I set her on the landing to kiss her.

She wrapped her arms around me, holding so tightly that I lifted her again and carried her to my bedroom. We held hands as I closed the front curtains and then turned on a soft bedside light.

"Are you okay?" I asked.

She touched my healed temple. "Will you tell me how you were hurt?"

"Maybe later."

"Will later ever come?"

I kissed her cheekbone, her eyebrow, and her lips. *No, if it were up to me, later would never arrive.* "Do you think you could belong with me?" I whispered in her ear.

She shivered. "I can't think straight when you're kissing me like that."

"Do you want me to stop?"

She held the front of my shirt as she responded in a breathy whisper, "No."

Levi

Daddy's deep voice rang through the house. Momma turned on the CD player in the living room, playing the album that always hurt my heart.

Whenever I needed to hear his voice, I'd play a cherished voicemail on my phone, but Momma preferred to immerse herself in his music. "It's good for you to hear him this way," she said, taking a seat beside me on the porch. "He loved to sing."

It was the last day of October, and just like the past two years, I spent the day with Mom, distributing candy to trick-or-treaters before indulging in her extensive collection of Hallmark Christmas movies.

The aroma of chicken noodle soup simmering in the Crock-Pot wafted from the kitchen into the living room where Dad's melodies lingered, drifting outside to where we sat on the porch.

A colorful array of chocolates and lollipops adorned a bowl placed between us as we waited for the children to arrive. Momma loved seeing the kids dressed as princesses and superheroes.

At the next house over, Courtney King sat on her own porch with a friend from church, waving as we settled in. She and Momma both handed out treats so that every child could showcase their costumes to multiple neighbors. Against my will, I inspected Ezra's house every few minutes, searching for a glimpse of Marigold. I knew she was inside. I'd seen her shadow pass the windows in a green dress. She was the type of girl to dress up for the kids.

She and Ezra weren't on the porch. They must be waiting indoors behind their screen. Or maybe they were avoiding me. If so, I didn't blame them.

I hadn't seen her since the day I came to ask Momma about the letter. She didn't text me, so I did as Donner suggested and left her alone. Sometimes I thought she might truly be a ghost because her memory haunted me at the cabin. In my mind's eye, I saw her seated at the kitchen table, wandering through the hillside in search of flowers, or perched on the porch with Finn nestled at her feet.

Donner insisted that the sacrifice was made out of love, but how could love endure when the person you cherished was so far away? How could you love from a distance?

I felt a mixture of longing and apprehension at the thought of seeing her again. Did her smile radiate now more brightly since she had moved in with Ezra? Did she think of me as much as I thought of her? What would she say if she saw me?

"You haven't told me what happened," Momma said.

"How is she?" I asked. I didn't want to explain to her about how I wrote about a girl and then she came to life. Or about how, when I told her the truth, she ran into the arms of the man I hated most.

The porch planks protested as Momma rocked in her chair. "She's happy. She and Ezra have been holding hands and even kissin' some."

"Momma." I groaned.

She *tsked* me. "If you didn't want to hear then you shouldn't have asked."

I slouched in the rocker. "I didn't really wanna know. I was just diverting the conversation."

"From telling me why you two broke up?"

"We weren't together."

"You're sulking as if you were."

"It's complicated." Would now be a good time to tell her about the magic? Perhaps she knew more than I thought.

I glanced at Ezra's house again and kept quiet. It was too late. Marigold was gone. I'd tell Momma more when the pain of losing her ebbed.

"All right, Levi, I'll wait until you're ready, but I'm patient," she said, reading my mind in a way that only a mother could. "I'll be here when you want to talk."

I pretended to be cheerful as we passed out candy to my cousin's children and a few families from church. My thoughts were consumed by Marigold. I saw her head peek out of the house to welcome kids. A few times she stepped onto the porch to talk to them. But she never looked at me.

When the sun began to set, Momma and I retreated to the kitchen. She ladled steaming soup into bowls while I warmed up cornbread muffins. We savored our meal while listening to Daddy's soothing voice in the background.

"I'll clean up," I said. "Go relax. Turn on a movie. I'll be along soon."

The familiar album stopped as Momma switched off the CD player and then turned on the TV.

The kitchen window above Momma's sink overlooked the side of Ezra's house. Dusk made it easy to see that there weren't any lights on. There were no signs of life on the inside.

I finished the dishes, turned off the kitchen light, then moved to sit with Momma. We watched a Hallmark Christmas movie.

My brain was fuzzy from the cotton-candy storyline when Momma said, "Can you refill my water?"

"Sure thing." Grabbing a glass off the coaster, I shuffled to the sink. Ezra's house was no longer dark. From the kitchen I could see the side of Ezra's house. His upstairs bedroom light was on and I could see inside.

Flipping on the faucet, I searched the window for a sign of Marigold. The glass almost slipped as I saw the side of her body. Ezra held her waist and kissed her, his hands traveling *down, down, down*. I knew I should turn away, but my legs wouldn't move.

She wore a medieval green dress with her hair cascading past her shoulders.

They fell onto his bed. She pulled his face to hers. They spoke to each other before he began the slow process of taking off her dress. Inch by torturous inch.

The glass in my hand overflowed with water, but still, I couldn't force myself away.

As their intimate moment escalated, I nearly threw the glass through the window. His hands traveled to places I'd never touched. She didn't push him off. Instead, she only drew him closer.

My eyes were filmed with tears of anger. I contemplated storming over there and beating Ezra until the only bed he ever slept in was six feet underground. But killing Ezra would change nothing. Marigold had chosen this. She'd chosen him, and there was nothing I could do about it.

Only when she began undressing him did I force myself away. I should have stopped watching much sooner, but the shock of seeing the woman I loved with my enemy paralyzed me. How could she choose *him* over me? What did Ezra possess that I didn't?

I wiped the glass dry and dumped out an inch of water. "Here you are, Momma," I said as I placed it in her outstretched hand. "I'm heading home."

"Sure you don't want to finish this?"

"No," I said, keeping my voice level. "I gotta go."

She didn't argue. "I love you. Don't be a stranger."

I kissed her cheek. "I won't. Love you, too."

Crisp October air cooled the blood burning through my veins as I stepped outside. I forced myself not to look at his house as I drove away.

For the past few weeks, I'd held a thin sliver of hope that Marigold would come back to me. That somehow this backward love, this *letting her go*, would work. Now I knew it hadn't.

Loving someone who didn't return your affections was bad, sure. But seeing the one you loved entangled with another—someone who had the potential to hurt them—was torture. I didn't want to let go. I wanted to rescue her, but that would force my love on her, and I didn't want that either.

The shadow of the mountain loomed in front of me as I turned onto the main road and left Marigold behind. With him.

SHELBIE MAE

The problem?
I still didn't love her any less.

Chapter Twenty-Two

Ezra

My thumb hovered over the "decline" button on my phone. I couldn't ignore him. Not again.

The grocery store loomed outside of my truck window. Ripe maple leaves swirled in the parking lot while Marigold whisked pancake batter at home. We were out of syrup and orange juice.

I told her it would only take me a minute.

With a sigh, I answered the call and put it on speaker mode.

"Ezra, it's been too long."

I pressed my fingers to the bridge of my nose. "I know, Father."

"How are you? How's the farm?"

This wasn't small talk. He wanted to know the ugly, terrible things I kept secret. I couldn't give him this burden while he was still locked away. God-willing, he'd be out in a year or two, and then we could talk in person. I'd never tell him what I'd done to keep the farm. I couldn't bear to see the disappointment in his eyes. "We're both splendid."

"Don't lie to me. Your sister was here last weekend. She told me the crops were bad this year. How long have you got?"

Father understood the financial problems I faced better than anyone. He was in jail for a crime he didn't commit, and I was outside doing something that could land me in prison. "Don't worry about the farm."

"Son." His tone held a warning.

If growing pot worked, then the farm wouldn't be in a dire predicament when he returned. This score with Jake would grant me suitable time to make money on next year's crop. If I wanted to save enough for a down payment on land in vineyard country, then I'd have to continue growing pot on the side, surrender my dream, or pray the farm's profits shot heavenward.

"I look forward to seeing you," I said.

"Son, I don't want you to end up here."

"It wasn't your fault."

The sound of voices, bangs, and commands filtered through my father's silence. "The guilty party doesn't always pay the price," he finally said.

My gaze shot to the phone. Numbers on the screen ticked away the seconds. We didn't have much longer. "What are you saying?" Was he finally about to admit that Duncan Shaw framed him?

Shouts rang through the speaker. "Father?"

"Hold on a second, son."

"Stop!" yelled a faraway voice. "Get on the ground." Shuffles and bangs screeched through the speaker.

"Father?"

A woman screamed. There was a loud crack. It sounded like the phone fell. "Jar, put that thing down." My father's voice.

I couldn't do anything except listen.

"Both of you, get on the ground!"

My hands clenched.

"He says you'll never get out." A man's voice. Then a grunt. A gunshot that made me jolt. Yells. Pounding feet.

"Prisoners down. Call the medic."

The voices came through clearer. Someone must have lifted the phone off the floor.

Another voice. "We've got one man with a stab wound and another with a gunshot wound."

Click.

The numbers stopped counting the seconds of the call as my phone returned to the home screen. Spots blurred my vision as my heart raced.

My father had just been either stabbed or shot. The attack sounded personal, like somebody didn't want him released.

A woman with a baby pushed her cart past the front of my parked truck. Someone parked a white GMC across the lot. The vibration of carts being pushed back to the store hummed through the closed windows. A black Chevy slid into the space opposite mine.

A faraway feeling overcame me, like I was watching myself from above yet totally present in the moment.

I slammed the truck door, pulse pounding with vengeance as I stalked my prey. If Duncan Shaw couldn't pay for his sins, then his son would. My father was bleeding—maybe *dying*—on a prison floor, and the root of his fate was tied to the man stepping out of that black Chevy.

With a swift motion, I used my fist to push Levi back into his truck before he could fully step out. "I'll kill you if he dies," I said.

He braced himself on the steering wheel and kicked.

I pivoted. His heels struck my hip instead of my gut. Pain exploded through my pelvis, but I didn't let it slow me. I grabbed his legs before he could retract them and tried to drag him out onto the asphalt, but he held fast to the wheel. I punched him in the stomach, loosening his hold until I had him on the ground. The air left his lungs as his back smacked the hard pavement.

He lifted his arms, but his body was too weak without breath. I wasn't aware of what I said as I pounded my fists into his face, chest, and abdomen. The world around me blurred into a haze of red fury.

He grunted as blood spurted out of his nose.

He dodged one of my blows, causing my fist to connect with the parking lot. Blood oozed from my knuckles as bruises formed on Levi's face.

Red. Red. Red.

Strong hands heaved me off my target. Levi gasped, spit blood, and rolled into a fetal position on his side. The hands hauled me backward as I spewed curses at Levi.

Jackson, wearing his sheriff's uniform and a wide-brimmed hat, appeared in my line of sight.

"Get it together, Ezra." He nodded to whoever held me back. "Bring him to the station."

The red haze dissipated by the time the officers escorted me away. They handcuffed me to the chair outside Jackson's office. "You think he's okay? Or should we put him in a cell?"

The younger officer glanced at me. "You gonna cause any more trouble?"

Fear gripped me, replacing the anger that had consumed me moments before. What if my father was dead? What if I couldn't go to him?

The older officer patted me on the shoulder as he left.

I had to call my mother. I was working to drag the chair toward a phone when Jackson stomped in and barked, "Sit down."

I did as he commanded.

He paced in front of me, saying nothing, hat in his hands. Then he went on a tirade. "Levi claims you attacked him without being provoked. Bystanders say you repeated 'I'll kill you' as you beat him. Is this true?"

"Call the state prison. Find out if my father is alive."

Jackson set his hands on his hips as I told him what I'd heard on the phone. "I'll see what I can find," he said, then he disappeared into his office.

The next thirty minutes felt like a year. Mother needed to hear the news. Marigold would be worried. I had to get off this blasted chair and *do something*.

Jackson walked out. "Samuel King is in stable condition. They won't release any further details."

I slumped with relief.

"Ezra, you assaulted someone."

"Is Levi pressing charges?"

"An officer is driving him to Elizabeth Shaw's house. I don't know what state he's in. Let me make another call." He closed himself in his office again.

Jackson returned and uncuffed me, granting relief to my wrists. "You're free to go."

I took two steps backward to put distance between us, rubbing the broken flesh of my knuckles.

"Elizabeth Shaw is speaking on behalf of Levi. She says they won't press charges. You got lucky. I don't want to see you here again. Understand?"

There was no denying his military background at a time like this. "Yes, sir," I said.

I walked the few blocks to my truck and then sped home, parked in front of Mother's house, and ran inside.

She met me at the door. "What happened? Levi was brought here in quite a state. They say you attacked him."

I explained the phone call but intentionally left out the part about me losing control. "If we leave now, we can be there by early afternoon." Never mind that I hadn't visited my father in over a year.

She rushed to gather her belongings.

"I'll be right back," I yelled after her.

I ran to my house. As I entered the kitchen, I spotted Marigold sitting at the island listening to music, a mug of steaming coffee in front of her. When she saw me, she jumped up and turned off the music. "Where have you been? I tried calling, but . . ." She noticed the blood oozing from my hand.

I strode toward her and gripped her shoulders. "Someone attacked my father in prison. I need to bring Mother there now. Will you be okay alone for a night or two?"

She couldn't stop looking at my hands.

"Listen," I said, grabbing her attention with my voice. "Will you be okay?"

"Y–yes."

I hated that she saw me as a monster.

Maybe I was.

For the hundredth time, I wondered how I could ask a girl like her to love me. How could I expect her to stay when she didn't even know how my hands were bloodied? I couldn't explain it to her. That would give her a reason to hate me even more.

I kissed her forehead and then packed a bag.

Mother met me in front of my Bronco.

Marigold stood on the porch, watching as I drove away.

Marigold

Movement at Beth's house caught my attention as Ezra's Bronco faded into the distance. We'd hardly spoken since I came to stay with Ezra, but the frantic activity behind her windows compelled me to approach and tap on her door.

Her hair had escaped its bun, creating a wild frame around her face. "Yes?"

"Is everything okay?"

Her expression twisted in concern. "Where's Ezra?"

"He just left with Courtney. Something happened to his dad."

"Perhaps we can forgive him then."

"*Forgive* him?"

"He just beat Levi in the grocery store parking lot. He's inside if you want to see him."

The blood was Levi's? I wanted to slap Ezra across the face. How could he?

Beth and I stood in silence, enveloped by the crisp November air. Levi and I hadn't truly spoken since the day I'd left, and I felt like a limb was missing in his absence. Could I forgive him for his falsehood? The more pressing question lingered: did he even *want* to see me? The girl who had left him for the man he hated. The man who had just drawn his blood.

No, he wouldn't want to see me, and neither was I prepared to interact with him. "Is he okay?"

Beth clenched and unclenched her fists. She was like a momma bear who was willing to go to war for her son. "He'll heal eventually, but this is the worst I've seen him."

"I'm sorry," I said, unable to stay in her presence. I ran down her steps and then forced myself to walk. As my feet carried me away, it felt like my heart was split into two halves: one with Levi and one with Ezra.

Ezra and I had grown close.

Very close.

Close enough to share a bed.

In a few short weeks, we'd gone from friends to lovers, and I didn't want to lose him. Yes, I loved him—but I couldn't dismiss what he'd done to Levi.

Was it safe for me to love a man like Ezra?

The nagging doubts clawed at me, threatening to unravel my world once more. I had nowhere else to turn.

I crossed the dirt road to a fallow field and continued my brisk walk away from Levi. Facing him would be too much for me to handle. He would ask why I'd remained with Ezra, but I couldn't answer that question. I wasn't sure if I would continue to live with him after this.

Three times he'd come to me bloodied, and never once had he given me an explanation. I couldn't help but wonder . . . would he hurt me if provoked? Was I safe with Ezra? He'd been gentle and kind, but something lurked within him that I'd never seen.

A copse of trees loomed in the distance with a muffled outline behind them. I changed course to a two-track that wound toward the structure.

Since moving to the farm, I'd spent my time in the main farmhouse, the garden, and the serene orchard area, with frequent trips taken to the truck graveyard. Our days were spent enjoying campfires in the backyard or strolling through the orchards and fields. I'd lived within a few acres, and it had been beautiful. Tranquil.

Until today.

As I trudged forward, arms wrapped tightly around myself to ward off the November chill, a weathered barn emerged from behind the trees. Fresh tire tracks imprinted the soil at my boots.

Strange.

I'd never noticed a truck on this drive. The temperature seemed to drop as I entered the trees. The usual sounds of nature faded away—no more wind rustling through fields or cars humming on distant roads; only an eerie silence enveloped me with every step I took, amplifying each footfall in the unnatural hush. I squeezed my arms tighter around myself.

The tire tracks stopped abruptly at double barn doors. Glancing around, I cautiously advanced toward them. A padlock and chain denied entry.

Frowning, I reached out to inspect the lock. The barn looked old and seasoned with worn wood and faded paint, but the lock appeared new and shiny. I gave it a tug. It clanked but stayed in place.

Surveying the exterior of the structure, I noted that besides the locked doors, the only other possible entrance was a window perched high above them. I circled the perimeter and found remnants of a past celebration—four paper plates bearing the inscription "Mr. & Mrs.", two red solo cups, a smattering of wooden furniture, and a ladder that looked more decorative than functional.

This must have been where Lillian's wedding took place.

The ladder wasn't too heavy to carry to the front of the barn. Wood clattered against wood as I hefted it into place. Fortunately, it was tall enough to get me to the window.

Now, the real test: it's durability.

With cautious steps and bated breath, I ascended slowly. The ladder wobbled as I neared the top. I slowed and took the rungs one careful step at a time.

The window appeared newer than the barn. Probably an upgrade for the wedding. I pulled the latch, hoping to find it unlocked.

The hinges screeched as it opened, and I darted my gaze around. The woods remained quiet and still.

Careful not to push the ladder away from the wall, I clutched the sill and hiked my leg over the side and onto a loft. The inside of the barn felt warmer than the outside, like there was a heat source.

I crept across the wooden boards to a rickety staircase, careful not to make a noise— although I was almost certain I was alone. It would be impossible to padlock the door from the inside.

At the bottom of the stairs, I observed a series of tents against the right wall. The heat was radiating from them. I almost tripped over a toolbox on my way to a tent. The clatter of metal on concrete made me stiffen. I waited for someone to assail me, but nothing happened.

The tent stood tall and rectangle, too narrow to sleep in. Curious, I unzipped the side.

Cozy plants filled the interior. The other tents contained the same greenery. It didn't take a botanist to recognize them.

And faster than the snap of a finger, the padlock made sense. Ezra's secrecy made sense. His wounds made sense.

He was growing marijuana.

Marijuana was illegal in Tennessee.

And if he was growing pot, that meant he must be selling it too. If he was both growing *and* selling, he knew people who were willing to break the law. People who would give him a busted face. Or worse.

"Stupid. Stupid. Stupid," I whispered.

I knew he wasn't telling me the entire truth, yet I'd allowed my disagreement with Levi to propel me into a relationship with him. Falling for Ezra was easy. He was handsome and well-respected. Plus, he adored me.

But I knew better. I was smarter than this.

His secrets grew in this barn. Who had smashed his face? Why was he doing this? I'd never seen him smoke a joint, and he'd never once mentioned pot or CBD oil to me.

Tears misted my eyes. This discovery didn't surprise me. A salty drop ran down my cheek as I admitted to myself the truth: I'd been holding back my love for him.

It was easy to think I loved him when he cared for me. When we were natural friends. When we had fun together. I liked him. He let me bloom.

But he kept this from me. He'd shared his hopes and dreams, sure—but not this. His secret.

I hurried up the stairs and back down the ladder, tears blurring my vision. What should I do? I couldn't keep living with him and pretend to love him with the same ferocity he loved me.

I no longer trusted him.

The discovery made me wish to see Levi.

After returning the ladder, I ran across the field to the house and knocked on Beth's door. No one answered. I checked the driveway. Her truck was gone. She must have driven him back to the cabin.

I sank against the door and sat on her porch. *What should I do now?* I could drive to him, but the tears wouldn't stop trickling down my face. Tears of shame and embarrassment for deceiving myself. Driving might not be the best idea.

Ezra's house loomed next door.

If I left Levi because of a lie, I should leave Ezra for the same reason. He might be discovered and arrested. He was the sheriff's brother-in-law, for Pete's sake. What did he think he was doing?

He wouldn't be back until at least tomorrow.

I had time to decide what to do.

Chapter Twenty-Three

Levi

M y players moved swiftly across the field, their movements ghostly under the glaring lights as the buzzer signaled the end of the game. The end of their season. We'd lost on our home field.

If I blinked, the apparitions turned into young men.

Blink. Blink. Blink.

There was white Trevor, dark William, and the other boys, all with slumped shoulders.

Tilting my head back, I tipped two pain reliver pills into my mouth and swallowed them dry. It wasn't just my eyes recovering from yesterday's brutal hits.

My skull felt like there was a marching band inside of it. The *actual* marching band in the grandstands only added to the cacophony.

I gave the boys reassuring pats on the shoulders as they returned to the bench. I couldn't let them detect my discomfort. "Good game, guys. You still got next year."

They grumbled replies, but I continued my praise as they converged on the bench. Parents streamed out of the bleachers onto the field. The opposing team hooted and hollered as they congratulated one another on making it to the next game in the finals.

After a quick huddle with my team, I strode across the grass to shake the coach's hand. We exchanged a few polite words. He stared at my bruised face, and then we parted.

The aroma of salty popcorn and sweat filled the arena as families crowded the players. A few parents shook my hand and congratulated me on a fine season. I smiled and boasted how great their boys were.

I preferred to escape to the quiet cabin. The thought of Finn's body draped over my legs like a blanket made me ache to go home.

Until I saw her.

I'd been trying to forget her, but her memory lingered. I thought of her almost every minute since I saw her with Ezra last week.

She stood unmoving in the sea of Sutton folk, her red hair swaying around her shoulders. People passed, hiding her from my sight, but then she reappeared as they carried on.

She stared into my eyes, tilted her head, and beckoned me toward her.

My feet felt like weights as I approached. The crowd swayed around us as we stood together, unspeaking.

She peered at my face, roved over every bruise, and then lifted her fingers. She hesitated, then traced the lines. My hand found hers and tucked it against my jaw. Tears welled in her eyes. "I'm sorry."

"You didn't do this."

She averted her gaze. "I don't know how to care for you both."

I could have focused on the fact that she cared for Ezra. But instead, I gripped the part about *me*. She cared about me too. It was a wonder she saw good in either of us.

Ezra was trying to love his family the same way I was. That's why he attacked me yesterday. Momma had gotten the details about Samuel's injuries in prison.

My feelings for Ezra hadn't changed, but I could understand why he did what he did. His actions revealed his brokenness. I still believed he was a murderer. The truth would come out. I would find it if he didn't kill me first.

Marigold's left brow rose, and I read the question behind her blue-green irises.

Can I trust you?

She was considering the tale of her becoming. My acceptance did that. Not my arguments. If I begged her to stay, she'd go. If I accepted her as she was . . . I wasn't sure.

Love demanded I make a heartbreaking choice, sacrificing the one I held dear to her destructive whims. Since that fateful Halloween night when I caught sight of her with Ezra, Donner's advice about letting her go had been a constant echo in my mind. The decision wasn't easy, but necessary.

Marigold needed to learn about Ezra herself.

I'd hoped that the longer she stayed with him, the more opportunities she would have to witness his evil firsthand.

The way she studied my broken face assured me she was pondering us.

"I feel stuck between you two."

I didn't answer. Didn't need to. The bruises spoke for me.

"His Dad's okay. He's on his way home now with Courtney."

"Glad to hear that." I had nothing against Samuel.

She extended a wrapped hot dog toward me and said, "I got this for you."

The spicy tang of meat wafted from the foil as I accepted the crinkled edges. "Thanks."

"I—I miss you, Levi."

That was something. Smiling sadly, I said, "I miss you too." A startling thought occurred to me. "Ezra doesn't know you're here."

"No."

"He wouldn't approve."

"Probably not."

She deserved better than both of us. "You should go before he gets home. I don't want him to . . ." I pointed at my face. "Lose it on you."

"He wouldn't hurt me," she said with a frown of uncertainty.

"I didn't think he'd hurt my dad either." I shrugged. "Now look where we are."

"You don't know . . . never mind." Her gaze wavered over my face. "I need you to know that I don't approve of what he did."

"I know."

She nodded once, raised her hand, and waved. "Goodbye, Levi."

I watched her disappear into the crowd.

A chill swept along my cheek. I'd never felt the coolness in the valley, the foreboding.

Turning to the mountain looming ominously over the proceedings, I understood that something awaited me in the coming hours.

Ezra

The crimson digits of the dashboard clock glowed 11:01 as I steered onto Ghost Mountain Farm Road. Mom dozed in the passenger seat next to me. I gave her a light tap on the shoulder. Startled, she jerked, her eyes opening in surprise.

"We're home," I whispered.

She rubbed her eyes and then hugged me across the center console. "Thank you for bringing me. I'm not sure I could have driven myself."

"Father will pull through. The doctors gave a good prognosis."

"I wish he could heal here."

My body tightened as I recalled Father restrained to the hospital bed. "I wish so too."

She clutched my arm, likely feeling the taunt anger in me. "Don't make any rash decisions."

I forced my muscles to loosen. "Goodnight, Mother."

She leaned in to kiss my cheek. "Goodnight."

After she vanished behind her front door, I drove down the road toward my house.

A figure loomed on the top step, hazy in the night. My shoulders relaxed as I recognized Mari sitting on the top step. She cared enough to wait for me in the dark. Admiration replaced the tension I'd been carrying since the phone call with Father.

She patted the spot beside her as I approached. The night was on the cusp of cold, a beautiful evening in early November. I settled beside her.

"How's your dad?"

Letting out a deep sigh, I said, "He'll be all right. A guard shot and killed the man who stabbed him. Father won't say why it happened. I think it involves money laundering."

I rubbed her arm when she didn't move closer. She stared over the valley, her form rigid. "I'm glad he's okay," she said, her tone detached.

"What's going on with you?" I moved closer and wrapped my arm around her shoulders. Maybe she was cold.

She kept her gaze on the surrounding land. "Have you ever done anything illegal?"

My arm fell away as my answer came instinctively. "No."

288

Finally, she turned to face me. "Are you as involved in this farm as your dad was?"

"Where is this coming from?" She was leading me like a horse with a bit between its teeth, and I didn't understand why. "Say what you want to."

"You lied to me."

Fear crept into my bones at her words. She knew. She must. But how?

Rising from my seat, I made my way to the porch edge. "What are you talking about?"

She followed suit closely behind me. "I found what you hid in the old barn."

Relief and anger warred within me. She knew. I didn't have to hide from her anymore. My future was dependent on what I said next. She could turn me in. But I had to be sure we were talking about the same thing. "What?"

"The marijuana plants, Ezra. I'm guessing that's why your face was busted in and why you've been keeping secrets."

Pulling the door open, I ushered her inside where no one could hear us. "Did you tell anyone?"

She flipped on a light, casting us both in a yellow glow. "No. I needed to talk to you first. I feel like I don't even know you anymore. I saw Levi's face at the football game tonight. He looks awful. And yesterday I found the pot. How could you?"

I wanted to keep my composure. I really did. But she was treating me like a murderer when I was nothing of the sort. I was only trying to keep my family intact.

My rising anger caused me to revert back to my old accusations. "My father wouldn't be in prison if not for Duncan Shaw."

She crossed her arms. "That has nothing to do with Levi."

"It has everything to do with Levi," I shouted.

"You didn't tell me about the pot."

Headlights through the windows drew our attention toward the driveway. I hurried outside and saw twin beams approaching from the direction of the barn. Mari rushed outside and caught the end of my curse.

What was Jake doing? Anyone might see where he came from. We had been careful to water and tend to our plants discreetly. Why was he here at this hour?

I knew something was wrong when the truck swerved in our direction. Jake jumped out of the cab and ran toward us. He doubled over with his hands on his thighs. "It's all gone."

I met him at the bottom of the steps. "What?" I'd heard him, but I still couldn't believe it.

"The pot, man. It's gone."

Impossible. Mari just saw it.

"Fred must have taken it." He swore. "He was gone when I got home from the football game, and I had a weird feeling. I knew we shouldn't have involved him, but I didn't know how else we'd sell it."

"All of it?"

"Yeah. Go look for yourself. The padlock has been cut and the doors are wide open."

Pushing past Jake, I hurried toward the barn, refusing to accept what he claimed. He had to be wrong. I couldn't lose the marijuana. I wrapped my future in those stupid leaves.

A ringing sounded in my ears as I neared the barn. I'd tried to stay calm for the sake of Mari, but I couldn't contain myself any longer.

My chest heaved with the effort of pumping my legs as fast as they would go. I pulled up inside the yawning doors.

Jake was right.

It was all gone.

This was Fred's revenge.

Specks of red dotted my vision as I returned to the house. The farm was as good as bankrupt. My future was gone. "Get out of here, Jake," I yelled.

He jumped into his truck and sped off.

Mari stood in the shadows of the porch, hugging herself.

"Did you have any part in this?" My voice was hard, tinged with accusation.

She straightened against my yell. "No."

I stormed inside the house. "I was trying to save the farm."

Kicking the couch, I stumbled upon an empty wine bottle resting on the coffee table. With a surge of frustration, I hurled it against the wall. The red glass shattered across the room. The little control I had fragmented just like the bottle. Yesterday, I had a healthy father, a chance to save the farm, and a woman who loved me. Now what did I have?

Calm down, Ez, I told myself, but my blood raced, and my thoughts spiraled.

Father was healing from an attack on his life.

The farm would have to be sold.

And Mari . . .

"You went to Levi." Resentment swept blood through my veins as I remembered her saying how she had seen him. "I left to visit my father—who was stabbed, by the way—and you traipsed off to get cozy with *him*?"

She moved to put the couch between us.

My jaw clenched as she inched away. "Are you afraid of me?"

"No." She took another step back.

I moved closer. Each step I took forward she matched in a backward motion. Finally, her back hit the wall and I closed the distance between us. She had to see things the way I did. I had to prove to her that I wasn't a bad guy. "You don't understand," I spluttered.

"Tell me," she whispered, palms on her thighs.

She wouldn't meet my gaze as I growled at her. "If I didn't grow the pot, we'd lose the farm. I did it for my mother, Lilly, and Father. For Levi, too, because Beth would have lost her house. I've been risking my freedom—and what is he doing? Living up on a mountain and teaching kids how to throw a ball."

She stayed with her back pressed against the wall, unblinking, but her face betrayed her fear. Why fear? Perhaps my words came out more forcefully than I'd intended. It was hard to talk in an even manner when I could hardly think straight because of fear. Jackson might be on his way right now. The extent of Fred's revenge was unlimited. Yet, the thought of her going to see Levi still bothered me.

"Are you back together with him?" I asked. If she said yes, I might kill him.

"No. I had to see what you did to him."

She wasn't telling me the whole truth. I'd already lost the farm, as well as my dream of a vineyard. I couldn't lose her too.

Levi's face flashed across my vision, and I acted without reason. "You wanted to see this?" I slammed my fist into the wall beside her ear. Jealous rage propelled my fist into the wall again and again until a hole swallowed my hand. Drywall and paint chips stuck in her hair. Her perfect, siren hair. To her credit, she only flinched.

Reason halted my fist. This was Mari. I loved her. She wasn't responsible for what had happened to my father or the plants. "I'm sorry." I placed my hands against the wall on either side of her head and buried my face against the crook of her neck. I could make this better. She didn't have to fear me.

She jerked away, tearstains on her cheeks.

No. I needed her. "Mari, please." I brushed my fingers along her upper arm, but she shrugged me off.

Defeated, I collapsed at her feet. "I'm sorry."

She remained still a few moments before padding up the stairs. My stomach clenched, skin tingling with pent-up anger and helplessness.

She returned a moment later, dragging two garbage bags behind her.

"Mari, I didn't mean . . ."

"We'll talk later. I'm going to Beth's house." The door shut behind her like the back cover of a book. My lungs heaved. The blood in my veins flowed too fast. My muscles ached for release as my brain darkened with uncontrollable anger.

I'd lost her.

I'd lost everything.

I jumped up and lunged forward. The TV crashed to the floor. Empty wine glasses broke against walls. I toppled the furniture.

My house was almost destroyed when I heard a voice shout, *"Ezra!"*

I spun.

Mother paused in the doorway, a covered dish in her hands. Tears wet her lashes as she surveyed the room. "What's happened?"

"Nothing."

She accepted the lie. "Beth and I are driving to the Marks. We just got word that Jeb died. I whipped up a little something. Beth's bringing a cake. I'll stop by when we return."

I nodded and then fell in a heap of broken dreams.

She looked outside and then back at my pathetic form. After maneuvering around the mess, she knelt beside me and placed her hand on my cheek. "Ezra, I love you. We'll get through. You're better than this." She kissed my sweaty forehead. "I love you, son," she whispered. "I love you. Be back soon."

I didn't move or speak. Her presence had calmed the raging in my blood. I lay my head on the hardwood floor and stilled.

At least I still had her.

Chapter Twenty-Four

Levi

T he sound of grumbling stirred me from slumber. I nudged Finn, his sturdy frame unmoving. Another noise roused me further, prompting me to lift my ear from the pillow. It wasn't Finn making the sound; it was my phone.

I answered.

A familiar voice. "This is Jackson Miller. There's been an accident."

The emergency room sign shone like a beacon on the empty Chattanooga streets. Although it was an hour away from Sutton, it was the closest hospital. My truck shrieked to a stop as I slammed my foot on the brake and rushed inside. "I need to see Elizabeth Shaw," I urgently informed the woman at reception.

She glanced up with a hint of disinterest, her face etched with boredom, before slowly setting her book down and regarding me and then her computer screen. She moved slower than a grandma driving home after Sunday mass. "Please repeat the name. What is your relationship with the patient?"

"Elizabeth Shaw. She's my mother."

Anxiety gnawed at me as she sluggishly navigated her computer screen as if my mother's life wasn't in peril.

Jackson had only shared that there'd been an accident. I didn't know if I was going to a regular room, the ICU, or the morgue.

"She's in the ICU."

I couldn't wait for her to finish. I bolted toward a sign that marked ICU. My bruised ribs ached with the movement. The soles of my boots thudded against sterile linoleum tiles as I barreled past nurses, doctors, and visiting family members. The odor of antiseptic stung my nose. My arms shook and my fingers twitched with adrenaline.

Overhead, fluorescent lights zipped by in a blur as I raced down the hallway, frantically checking room after room. The first revealed an old man with a breathing tube. In the next, a woman lay asleep under layers of blankets. My rubber-soled shoes squeaked as I pivoted to the next room.

There, on the right. A nurse hovered over her body. Monitors blinked and whirred.

Mom was alive.

I let out a shuttering breath and braced my hands on my knees, weak with relief.

"Sir, you can't be in here," she said.

"This is my Momma." I couldn't control the shaking that gripped my body. I studied the woman who had loved me through every scabbed knee and broken heart. Her face was bruised and her eyes were closed. Butterfly bandages stretched across the skin of her temple. Her arm was bandaged.

Jackson rushed into the room. "Levi, come with me."

"No." I pointed at the nurse. "Please. Tell me if she's okay."

Jackson and the nurse shared a look. He nodded. She huffed before saying, "She's in a coma. You'll have to speak to her doctor for details. You must leave."

Gripping my shoulder, Jackson steered me out of the ICU. He then deposited me in a waiting room where Lillian and Ezra sat side by side. What were they doing here? The pieces fell into place.

Courtney would have been with Momma.

Ezra's face hardened when he recognized me.

Jackson propelled me down a hallway. "You know better than to go blazing through a hospital," he scolded.

"Where's her doctor? I gotta talk to him."

He still held my shoulder. "I understand this is hard. My wife's mother was injured too. We're all doing the best we can to keep our wits and let the doctors work. I'll help you find him after we talk."

"Talk about what? What is more important than this?"

"The nature of the accident."

That got my attention. I straightened, but the shaking didn't stop. "What happened?"

"From what we've pieced together, your momma and Courtney were on Pine Road heading north when a Jeep Cherokee swerved into their lane and struck them. Your momma was driving. The Jeep was speeding. Hit the driver's side. Your momma's car flipped once and landed upright in the field." He paused.

A buzzing echoed in the back of my skull. My stomach rolled like I might be sick. I should be connecting the dots, but I couldn't. "What does this have to do with me?"

"The driver and passenger of the Jeep were scraped, but their conditions were okay. They were your boys."

"My boys?"

"Football players. The Jeep reeked of alcohol when I arrived at the scene."

Shock seared through the softest parts of my brain like a whiskey shot. Wooziness followed. Drywall cooled my palm as I braced myself against the hallway. Images surfaced to my mind from the night Marigold had left me.

School parking lot. Headlights. Jeep. Beer bottles. Trevor. William.

I let them go without even a whisper to the district or to their parents.

My voice shook. "They told you."

Jackson leaned into my line of sight. "Told me what?"

I focused on him. "Why are you telling me this?"

A fluorescent light blinked on and off, casting Jackson in shadow and then light. "Because I wanted you to know that two of your boys caused a drunk driving accident involving your family."

If they hadn't mentioned my name yet, they would. They'd do anything to beat a juvie sentence.

I ran my fingers wearily across my face. "This is my fault."

Jackson crossed his arms. The brim of his sheriff's hat case his face in shadow. "Excuse me?"

I might lose my job if the board found out I withheld information about criminal activity on school grounds. Heck, I might lose my job anyway.

The harsh light ceased its flickering, casting a blinding reflection on the gleaming floor, causing tears to well up in my eyes. Or was I crying? For Trevor and William's uncertain futures? For Momma and Mrs. King?

With a trembling exhale, I told Jackson about the night I'd discovered the boys in the parking lot.

He swore. "I'll have to write this in my report."

"I figured."

"Then why would you share it?"

"It'll come up."

He swore again. "The town won't look kindly on this if—" He paused before finishing. "If lives are lost."

There it was. Either my momma's or Mrs. King's future was uncertain. I needed to talk to a doctor. I should call my brother. "Are we done?"

He released me. "For now."

———————

The monitors ticked with precision, echoing a metronome's rhythm. *One-two-three-four. One-two-three-four . . .*

Sheets and bandages covered Momma. I found comfort in her rising and falling chest.

The doctor said that the left side of Momma's body had been badly injured. He told me about broken bones, abrasions, fractures, and head trauma. There was a chance that Momma might wake up—but there was also a chance she might not. I'd texted my brother, Colton, but hadn't received a response.

The sound of footsteps drew closer. Seconds later, Jackson stood over me. "I thought you should have this." He handed me a plastic bag heavy with items. "Your mom's things from the wreck. Her car is being towed to a body shop. Expect it to be totaled."

He left me with the bag. I set it on the sterile floor between my feet. Regular car things like sunglasses, hand sanitizer, and pens were jumbled together with one of Momma's necklaces tangled at the bottom. The biggest item surprised me.

A worn leather journal that smelled of oil and gasoline.

I flipped it from front to back. Dad's handwriting covered the pages.

I swallowed. Either Momma lied about knowing where Dad's journal was, or this was a different one.

I leafed to the last entry.

Dear Elizabeth,

I realize you think I'm being dramatic when I write letters to you instead of verbally communicating. It's my way of understanding what I'm thinking, and there's been much on my mind lately.

Levi called today. He and Colton are following their dreams in Nashville. I told him we'd visit soon. I hope I wasn't lying. Things are getting complicated.

He found me at the cabin. You know who. He's angry. He doesn't understand why I continue to let people believe that I turned Samuel in.

We alone know the truth. You, me, Samuel, Courtney. And him.

Samuel didn't launder money. He did.

I didn't turn Samuel in. He did.

Samuel and I didn't realize what we were doing when we wrote in those notebooks all those years ago. Nothing happened as we imagined.

I wrote Courtney, and she fell in love with Samuel.

Samuel wrote him, and he betrayed us both.

We didn't realize the power we had, the gravity of being a writer. In a way, we were playing God without even knowing it. But when we play God in our stories, we can't make choices as well as He does.

God knew I needed you, Elizabeth. That's why it didn't work out with Courtney. I felt compelled to try since I'd made her, but things worked out as God intended.

I trust that Samuel and I still need him. The one we created. Or, more accurately, I suspect he needs us.

The reason Samuel stays in jail, and the reason I don't tell folks I'm innocent, is because of love. You know this. I know this. I wish the world could see love the way we do. Most think it's a feeling.

But we know better.

Samuel and I love him too much to let him be punished. Does he deserve it? Of course! But he wouldn't be alive if not for us. We'd hoped our sacrifices would show him that our arms are forever open.

We were wrong.

Elizabeth, you were there the day he stumbled off the mountain straight from Samuel's pen. You saw him and helped him gain a footing in life.

He won't accept it. He'd prefer to see Samuel in jail and us at each other's throats.

Our choices created him, and we'll do what we can to give him every freedom, even if he hates us for it.

Because that's what love does, right? Love gives in all things.

I love you, Elizabeth. I love you more than you could ever imagine. This trial will only bring us closer in the end.

Forever yours,

Duncan

This was what I'd been seeking. Momma had it all along. She knew everything, and despite that, she let me believe unfair things about Ezra, Samuel, and my daddy.

Why?

The journal added a new element to the Shaw and King feud. A third, unnamed party. A man who was most likely responsible for my dad's death.

This confirmed what I'd suspected: Dad was murdered.

But I was wrong, too, because Ezra *wasn't* involved after all.

The obvious question pained me: Why had Momma kept this from me?

Searching for answers, I read the letter again. She must have wanted to honor Dad's wish to protect the mysterious unnamed man.

But how could she care for him if he'd murdered her husband?

The answer rocked me to my feet.

Because she loved him. She had to. Maybe not the way she loved Daddy, but she loved him. She was there when he was created and felt responsible.

Just like how I felt for Marigold.

For the first time, I realized she wasn't in the waiting room with Ezra.

His name unhinged something inside me. Guilt tumbled through my chest like rocks breaking off Skeleton Cliff and crashing below. The pain settled in my stomach.

Ezra. My brother.

I wasted years hating him for a crime he had no hand in. He spent the same time despising both me and my daddy for the same reasons.

Dad made it clear in his note. He and Samuel chose to be punished for the fall of their creation. They wanted brotherhood, not strife, yet Ezra and I chose anger.

Momma and Courtney could have joined us over this truth instead of letting us hate each other.

Wait. The journal reeked of car fluids.

I jogged toward the nurse's station. "Where's Jackson?"

"He's on his way to speak with the other family."

I found him before he entered the waiting room. "Where did you find this?"

He looked at the book.

"Near the rear of the crash."

"Could it have been in the glove compartment or in the backseat?"

"I only took items from off the road. You can gather the rest from the body shop."

I slapped him on the back. "Thank you." Someone could have hidden the journal in Momma's trunk where it had been dislodged in the crash.

I texted Marigold.

> Me: Where are you?

> **Marigold:** At your momma's house. She's not here. I'm worried. Where are you?

> **Me:** On my way.

Seeing Marigold made my heart's rapid beats to gradually transform, like a fading drumroll, into a deep, ominous bass.

She raced onto the porch as I parked. "What happened? Beth and Courtney left last night, but they didn't come home."

Wrapping her in a tight embrace, I rested my chin on her head, released a trembling exhale, and then shared the crushing news.

"Can you take me to the hospital?" she asked. "I don't know where it is."

I showed her the journal. "This is what I've been looking for. It explains everything that happened between the Shaw and King family. Well, I hope. I only read one entry, but I suspect if it's read cover to cover, it'll tell the whole story."

"What do you mean?"

"My dad didn't kill himself. Ezra had nothing to do with his murder. This journal also suggests that characters can come to life through writing . . . which is exactly how I created you."

She backed away.

My phone buzzed with an incoming text from Ezra.

> **Ezra:** Meet me at the cliff.

My heart quickened its pace, a drumbeat of anxiety echoing in my chest. The message conveyed almost nothing, yet it explained everything. Jackson told Ezra about my involvement with Trevor and William. Ezra held me responsible and wanted revenge. I could give him the truth.

"Read on the way," I said. "We need to stop at the cabin before meeting Ezra at the cliff. We'll go to the hospital after." I handed her the journal and jogged to my truck.

I turned off the radio as we drove. The noise distracted me. If Ezra was driving from Chattanooga, we had time. If things unfolded as I suspected, I had to take precautions, but they might not make a difference.

Replaying fragments of Dad's letter in my mind, I struggled to decipher the truth from what I perceived.

Samuel wrote a man who was displeased with both Samuel and my dad.

Why was he mad?

The letter didn't say.

This individual framed Samuel in a money laundering scheme and made it look like my dad had turned him in. Then he presumably killed my dad. And now Samuel had been attacked in prison.

I imagined how my dad's death must have played out. They met at the Cliff. Dad tried to reason with him. The man pushed him over the edge. Maybe it was an accident, or perhaps it was intentional.

The part of Dad's letter that impacted me the most was how much he loved this person. He loved him enough to let the town think he'd betrayed his best friend. Samuel was willing to give up years of his life in jail.

I was moved because I understood.

Marigold sat beside me with her nose almost pressed against the pages of the journal.

I loved her enough to tell her the truth.

I loved her enough to let her walk away.

And yes, I loved her enough to let her push me off a cliff, just like my daddy let the man in the letter. I would die for her if that were the only means for her to see the depth of my love. I'd allow it.

Was that what my dad let happen? Of course, he would have fought back, tried to save himself. Who wouldn't? But when he realized his efforts were useless, did he surrender?

The bond I shared with Marigold felt paternal yet passionate, a blend of protection and freedom that transcended mere affection. A need to protect at all costs, but also to set free. We had the added benefit of attraction. I *made* her. I loved her. I'd do anything for her.

I understood my dad better than ever before.

Finn dashed toward the truck as I parked and jumped out. His tail wagged, slapping against the tires and my legs. He followed me as I sprinted inside. The sound of Marigold's footsteps trailed behind.

I found the original journal on Dad's desk, flipped past Marigold's ballad and Finn's limerick, and stopped on a fresh page.

And then I wrote.

Chapter Twenty-Five

Ezra

S carlet sparks of hatred sizzled through my mind as the nurse spoke on the other side of Mother's bedside.

"The surgeon stopped her internal bleeding," the nurse said. "She suffered three cracked ribs, a dislocated shoulder, a broken wrist, and damage to her left leg. The doctor should be able to answer your questions about her mobility."

Lilly and I were then requested to leave Mother's room to let her rest. As soon as we exited, I sent the text.

> Me: Meet me at the cliff.

I could not lose my mother too.

———

When I arrived at Skeleton Cliff, Levi's car was absent from the trailhead.

I'd chosen the cliff because it was where he harbored his deep-seated animosity toward me, blaming me for his father's death.

It would now, ironically, become the place where I killed him. Extreme? Maybe. But someone had to pay for my dad being in prison, the pot being stolen, Mari leaving me, and my mother's accident. I knew I should stop, turn around, and end this, but I couldn't.

I climbed out of my truck, slammed the door, and stalked toward the edge. Looking over the precipice made me woozy, so I backed away. The serene view did nothing to ease my loathing.

A small cry screamed from the depths of my subconscious.

Don't do this. What are you thinking? This isn't you.

No, it wasn't. But it would be. Levi and Duncan Shaw forced me to be this person. Years of being accused of murder while trying to do the right thing created a heat inside of me that couldn't be cooled. If Levi Shaw wanted a villain, he'd get one.

In all our years of contempt for each other, I'd never denied his blatant accusal of murder. I thought denying his accusations would make them seem real. Now I would tell him the truth.

I had nothing to do with his father's death.

Nothing.

I let him hate me because it felt good to mutually dislike each other. If I'd admitted my innocence, his hostility might abate, and then my contempt would look petty. Our feud worked when we had equal amounts of hatred toward each other.

The sound of a truck approaching poured water on my burning anger. He was here. Suddenly, the thought of murdering him seemed rash.

What was I thinking?

Three figures came through the woods. Levi with a dog beside him, and then

. . .

The water cooling my anger turned to gasoline when I saw her.

Mari.

With him.

Flames of envy consumed me.

She trailed behind him as they approached, a book in her hands. I was right. She'd gone back to him. She'd lied when she said the football game meant nothing.

Levi gestured in surrender. "Can we talk?"

The smell of the hospital still clung to me. I might lose another family member because of him. Just when I thought I couldn't lose anything else.

"I've got something you need to read." He tossed me a book, but it fell in the grass.

"Now isn't the time for reading."

"It's a letter that explains—"

"Shut up!"

He raised his hands again. "I know you didn't kill my daddy."

My cheek twitched. The inferno inside me sought for a foothold. My fury found its center in an image of my mother's broken body lying in the hospital bed. "You knew those boys were drinking and driving, and yet you didn't report them."

He dropped his arms as his shoulders slumped. "If I could go back—"

"And you." I pointed at Mari. "You lied. You left me for him."

"No."

"You're both liars. You don't care if your actions ruin the people around you. I have nothing because of you."

The feeling of Marigold's curves and scent beside me in bed brushed against my memory. I stepped toward her. Levi shielded her body with his. "I told you about my future!" I screamed over his shoulder. "When I imagined it, you were there. The winery. Kids. A house in the mountains. It was all with you!" Spit flew from my lips as I screamed.

I wanted that dream. I still wanted her, but she didn't want me.

The veins inside my muscles seemed to turn to liquid iron as the weight of what I'd lost coursed through my bloodstream. For once, the color I saw wasn't red.

It was black.

Mari was my second chance. Now she was Levi's. I lunged toward her without thought. I just wanted to hold her, maybe shake her or kiss her. I didn't know.

Levi set his boots and took my weight.

Mari screamed.

The dog bit at my legs.

"Stop," Levi cried. "The letter said—"

I didn't hear the rest of his sentence. It was drowned out by a piercing, hollow scream in my mind. I couldn't tell if it was Mari or the cry of my soul dying as I did what my body begged me to. I couldn't think, reason, or stop.

The dog sank its teeth into my ankle while my hands clenched Levi's shirt tightly, oblivious to the pain searing through me. My fingers bunched around the fabric as his eyes met mine. He set his feet against the rock, but dirt and pebbles kept him from gaining traction. Gritting his teeth, he struggled against me.

We stared at each other in the seconds before. He focused on trying to win solid footing. His face didn't cringe in fear. His palms pushed as his feet scrambled. Through it all, he maintained a steady gaze on me. There was a calmness there. A peace.

His expression reminded me of the Labor Day games. How, for a second, we'd been brothers again.

Sweat slicked the space between my fingers and his clothing. We moved toward the edge. Black covered my vision. The scream intensified. Levi released me, windmilled his arms, and tried to step forward instead of back.

His hands found my shoulders. He didn't clutch or grab; instead, he just placed them there. "I'm sorry, brother."

Then we were at the side. The dog released my calf as his legs went over.

I didn't stop.

I couldn't.

Levi stared right at me as he said, "I forgive you." Then he fell backward over the precipice.

Chapter Twenty-Six

Levi

F alling felt like a crescendo. The final push before the end. The grand finale.

I knew it would end like this.

The ballad of Marigold told me so.

He gave his everything to be hers
He cast his heart upon the rock

After all my hunches about the cliff—about *Ezra*—this was how it should end.

Ezra caught himself at the edge. His gaze followed me down. Hopefully she wouldn't see my end.

Marigold.

The girl who left me for my enemy and the one I never kissed properly.

The girl who wanted to fix me and who slept with my murderer.

The girl I created.

And the girl I loved.

Yes, it was true. She left me and crawled into his bed. She hardened her heart against me, but I still loved her.

In the end, I think she loved me too.

At least, I hoped.

But it didn't matter. I died for her.

And I'd do it again.

Chapter Twenty-Seven

Marigold

Disbelief gripped me as Finn and Levi disappeared over the edge. Spots covered my vision, and I collapsed to my knees. The book Levi had pressed into my hands slipped from my grasp, landing in the dirt at my feet.

Ezra retreated from the cliff.

My heart slammed against my ribcage, a desperate rhythm urging me to follow Levi and Finn.

Without conscious thought, I sprang to my feet and screamed at Ezra, *"What did you do?"*

His face was slack, his eyes vacant. He blinked and then peered at his hands. "I . . ." He swore and then fell to the ground.

I rushed toward him and pounded my fists into his chest. "You killed him! How could you? What is wrong with you?"

He caught my fist and held it until I stopped wiggling.

When he released me, I clutched my chest, sucked in air, and tried to calm myself. I wailed. A long, mournful sound that punctured the sky and sank with my soul to the bottom of the cliff with Levi.

The bottom.

I doubled over as my stomach heaved, but I'd eaten nothing. I heaved and heaved until my throat was raw. When I looked up, Ezra was kneeling at the precipice.

I didn't know if I had the strength to look. *Levi. Finn.* Why did Finn have to go too? Losing Levi was unbearable, but Finn was an added and unnecessary loss. I struggled for breath and coherent thought. Everything inside of me ached and writhed to travel back in time sixty seconds.

This couldn't be real.

Ezra slammed his palms on the rock and yelled, "I didn't mean it."

A vision filled my mind: Two figures at the edge of a cliff. An argument. One fell.

The picture was seared into my brain when I awoke on the mountain. Had it been a prophecy or a dream? I thought the falling man was Levi.

I was right.

Dizziness swept over me. This was no ordinary mountain.

The knowledge stamped the truth into my soul: I was no ordinary girl.

Everything Levi said about me was true. Duncan's journal revealed the truth that I had been unwilling to believe.

Levi's words created me. I was a full-grown woman, but I'd only lived a few months.

If that were true . . .

I picked up the book I'd dropped and the one Levi had held. I joined Ezra at the side. "Read this. He wasn't lying. Duncan didn't turn your dad in. He's innocent."

Ezra faced me. "I can't read right now." He stood.

"Take it." I threw it at him as he sulked away. It hit him in the back. He turned, grabbed the book, and took off in a run.

Seconds later, I heard his truck speeding down the road.

A cool wind touched my face like the ghost of Levi reaching from heaven to comfort me. Leaves rustled behind. The air smelled like fall turning to winter. Like death and decay. A salty tear slid onto my lip.

I inched toward the ledge with the book clutched to my chest.

The book!

I gripped the leather tighter. My sweaty hands slipped along the smooth surface.

When we stopped at the cabin, Levi had insisted on writing. He scribbled something in the book, handed it to me, and said, "You'll know when to read this."

I'd been too consumed with reading Duncan's diary, with the fate of Beth and Courtney, to care about what he wrote.

My hands shook as I turned the pages.

Dear Marigold,
I found something worth dying for.
Love, Levi

The legend about the ghost and the man who loved her resurfaced. When I asked him why he liked the story, he said, "Because he found a girl he was willing to die for."

Tears blurred my vision. How did he know?

A few verses were scribbled onto the following page:

He let her go
She went away
But his heart remained hers

-

When the time came
He chose to lay
His life in front of hers

-

He fell on the rocks
But that day
Wasn't the end

-

He lived again from the words of a pen

The last part didn't register. Did he suspect this would happen?

If the words he wrote were powerful enough to make me, then maybe they'd be powerful enough to bring him back.

My breath hitched on a sob. I crawled to the edge, looked over, and saw his form far below.

Unmoving.

"I'm coming," I choked out. "Levi, I'm coming."

My body swayed as I pushed my feet beneath me. I had to be strong. I couldn't let my sorrow keep me from going to him. If I could believe he wrote me, then I must believe words were enough to save him too.

I ran back the way we'd arrived.

The book shielded me against the forest as I navigated through the tangled undergrowth, stumbling over barren bushes, sliding down steep dirt inclines, and slipping on decaying foliage. Pine needles from intact evergreens poked and prickled my arms as hope propelled me forward at a reckless pace. The spice of tree sap and cool wood encircled me as I stumbled along the path.

Dirt gave way to rock as I neared the base. My foot caught on a slab of stone, and I flew down, pain bursting through every nerve in my left palm. Clutching onto the book with my right hand, I pushed forward.

Steep angles gave way to sheets of uneven rock and boulders. I slowed my pace and braced myself for the sight of Levi. There were two possibilities:

A broken Levi or a breathing Levi.

My throat tightened when I stepped past the jagged boulders and saw him.

Levi. My heart.

It had always been Levi that I loved. I felt it deep inside my bones and marrow and sinew. Ezra's charm and adoration drew me in, but I didn't care for him in the same way. Levi was cool drinks in Mason jars, rumbling drives, sunsets, and the scent of musty cabin. He was my best friend. The guy who brought me to meet his momma, made breakfast for me almost every morning, introduced me to Donner, told legends to me, swam with me in a frigid stream, and cared for me with all he had.

Levi was still.

Broken.

My legs went from rushing to plodding as I approached. Tears streaking my cheeks as I forced myself forward. He was sprawled half on his side, half on his stomach. A mound of cloth and flesh. Dead, but also alive. He'd always remain alive in my memory. In my heart.

And then I stood before him. My insides fractured.

I was afraid to see his face, what the rock had done to him. I wouldn't leave him in a heap.

I rolled him onto his back.

Where my body was fragmented emotionally, Levi's was shattered physically. The only broken skin lay on his head was where he'd struck the rock. The rest of him remained undamaged. When I turned him, I felt the splintered parts.

Somehow, it was easier to keep myself from falling apart and retching when I was with him. At the top, I couldn't control myself. Now, my mind and body moved practically.

Levi was dead. This was his body. Sure, all bodies reached their end eventually—but not like this.

I scrambled for a way to save him. Maybe if I read the words aloud to him.

I flipped the book open with my throbbing wrist and recited the poem.

Nothing changed.

Cold air swirled around me as I knelt on the frigid rock. Wind rustled the naked tree branches as a crow cawed from an unknown location. "Wake up, Levi," I choked out in a hushed plea, tears slipping down my cheeks.

My arm touched his as I collapsed beside him. He was still warm. I lifted his arm and tucked my head against the crook of his shoulder, the solid unbrokenness of his collarbone.

I breathed for both of us. Deep breath in and out. Inhaling life, exhaling death.

I turned my face against his shoulder, smelled his manly scent, and cried. My tears wet his cooling skin, his unmoving chest. "Why did you come if you knew?" I cried. He could have prevented this, but he didn't. Why?

Raising myself slightly on one elbow, I studied Levi's face marred by Ezra's brutality a few days ago yet untouched by the fall that claimed him minutes ago. I leaned in and pressed my lips to his.

"I love you, too," I said. Because that's what he'd said when he stepped between me and Ezra. Not with his words, but with his body.

I lay on his shoulder and cried myself into an exhausted sleep.

A movement woke me. My swollen lids fluttered open.

The setting sun cast streaks of orange and red across the sky as I shivered in the crisp evening air. Memory washed over me, and for once, I wished I could forget.

Sensing a shift beside me, fear propelled me away from Levi's side in search of potential danger lurking in the shadows. Yet there was no threat—only Levi lying peacefully with closed eyes. I rubbed the sleep and sorrow from mine. If nobody was here, then Ezra hadn't shared what happened. I wouldn't have either if I were responsible.

I'd have to hike until I had cell service to reach Jackson. Levi couldn't endure the harsh elements alone. Any wild creature could surely find him.

With arms hugged against my knees, I looked at him.

His form shocked me. Not the stillness, but the movement. His chest rose and fell.

I rushed closer and placed my palm against his ribcage, which had been broken just a few hours ago. The bones were solid and intact. His diaphragm lifted beneath my hand. With tentative movements, I brushed my knuckles across his cheek.

Warm.

Life.

"Levi," I said, inspecting the place where his head had been smashed. The spot was now rounded. *"Levi?"*

Could it be possible? Had his words truly healed him?

A soft gasp parted his lips.

"Levi," I said. "I'm here."

His chest expanded with a deep intake of breath. His eyes popped open on the exhale. Blinked. Focused. Then he tilted his gaze toward me.

"What happened?" he uttered. "Where am I?"

I eased him to a sitting position as words poured from me like water down a stream. I told him about Ezra's actions, the book, my mourning, and then his waking.

"How do you feel? Do you think you can walk back to the truck?"

He sat up and felt his chest, his head. Ran his fingers down his legs and over his arms. Then he saw Finn. "Poor guy."

"I hate seeing him like that. Too bad you didn't write him back to life."

He frowned but said nothing. I helped him to his feet and watched as he tried walking. After a few steps, he shrugged and said, "I'm fine."

"Levi, you're not yourself," I said, alarm wobbling my voice. He should be rejoicing, asking questions, piecing the day together, and running up the hill to drive to Beth. But instead, he stared at me like he couldn't quite figure out why I was standing in front of him.

"I'm sorry," he said. "I'm not sure how to say this politely."

That sounded more like him. Gentlemanly.

He continued. "I don't know who you are."

Chapter Twenty-Eight

Levi

The girl, her hair a vibrant shade of red that seemed to defy nature, nervously bit down on both her lips in contemplation. While she was occupied with formulating a response, I surveyed our surroundings. Towering beside me was a jagged cliff that rose into the heavens.

She was right; we were at the base of Skeleton Cliff.

The last thing I remembered was lying in a sleeping bag at my campsite the day before Lillian's wedding. I had a two-hour hike to my truck and then a twenty-minute drive to the valley.

But if I fell asleep at my campsite—alone—then how did I end up here with a freckled stranger who seemed to know my family's history?

"Do you know my name?" she whispered, the sunset glittering in her glassy eyes.

I hated making girls cry, but I couldn't lie. "No. I'm sorry."

"What do you remember?"

I told her my most recent memories and rubbed my arms. July wasn't this cold. Looking around, I noticed the gold leaves clinging to spindly branches. The smell of decaying forest and frosty nights enveloped us almost as if Christmas were near. But that couldn't be right.

Panic seized me. "*Wh--what?* Why are the trees bare?"

She recognized the terror shaking my limbs. "What are you talking about?"

"It feels like fall."

"Yes. It's the first week of November."

I caught myself on a jutting rock. "That's not possible."

She touched my arm. "Levi. Here's the book you used to write me and Finn to life. The poem that brought *you* back to life too."

I didn't take it. "Listen, I don't mean to be rude, but that's insane."

She snorted. "That's what I thought a few hours ago. You tried to convince me otherwise." She turned to the unmoving dog. "We can't leave him like that."

It took a while, but we finally dug a shallow grave and then piled rocks over him.

Focusing on her kept my body from shaking. I needed to get to my truck. I needed my phone—more specifically, the calendar on my phone—to sort everything out.

"Do you remember the accident?" she asked as we huffed upward.

"Accident?"

"Your momma's at the hospital in Chattanooga."

This day was getting weirder and weirder. "Tell me everything."

By the time we arrived at the truck, her version of events had unfolded to me, leaving me uncertain about its credibility. I found my phone in the cupholder and tapped the screen. It was Saturday, November 7th. A missed call from Colton and a text message awaited me.

Colton: How's mom?

Thankfully, I was seated in the driver's seat. If I had been standing, I might have collapsed under the magnitude of this revelation.

Everything the girl said had been true.

I cranked the engine. "Let's go to the hospital."

"If Ezra's there, you can get the book from him."

Gravel spun under my tires as I slammed the accelerator. "If he thinks I'm dead, he's long gone."

The skeletal trees reached their bony branches toward us in the fading light. "What did you say your name was?"

"Marigold."

A wave of static clouded my thoughts before clarity returned like an old TV adjusting its signal. Her words resonated with a distant memory.

"Your tale about being a ghost sounds like one of the mountain legends."

Her crimson locks gleamed under the fading light as she cryptically stated, "Perhaps some legends are true."

What Happened to Ezra?

F riend,

Thank you for reading *When We Were Legends*! I am so excited to get the next book in your hands as soon as possible. As many of you know, I am welcoming my second child into this world shortly after *When We Were Legends* is released.

The second book in the Ghost Mountain series, *When We Were Memories*, is already written! I just need to get it edited. Quality is important to me, so I will do this in as timely a manner as I can while also being a mom to two.

In the meantime, I would love to give you a bonus chapter from Ezra's perspective. I am setting up an exclusive newsletter for my Ghost Mountain readers called ***The Ghost Mountain Gazette*** where you can find the bonus material and get updates on the writing and release of *When We Were Memories*! Please visit https://theghostmountaingazette.substack.com/ or follow the QR code below to get your free bonus chapter from Ezra's perspective! The chapter will be in your welcome email after you subscribe!

Author's Note

Dear Friend,

I am honored that you took this journey with me.

As I wrote *When We Were Legends*, I had two hopes.

One: that you would be entertained.

Two: that maybe, through these pages you would consider the love God has for you.

If you are just here for the entertainment, that's okay, but if you'd allow me, I'd love to share a few things about the conception of *When We Were Legends*.

I started this book during the pandemic of 2020, but it lived in my head and heart much longer. Somewhere between 2016-2019, I began to feel God speaking to my heart. He said, *I thought you were worth saving*. No, I did not hear the audible voice of God. These words were more like love poured into my soul. They also surprised me because as much as people have told me they love me over the years, I've always had trouble believing them.

When I felt these words like truth stamped into my heart, my first reaction was to think; *Who? Me? Not likely. I'm not worthy of love. I don't feel like I deserve God's love. Why would He want me?*

I tried to believe the words. Sometimes it has been easy, but more often, I find myself wondering. *Why would God think about me? Why would He love me? I've pushed Him away with my actions. I've put other lovers before Him. He can't possibly love me the the way people assure me He does.*

Around the same time, I also began to explore the idea of God as an artist. I wondered: *is writing art? Yes, of course it is. What if there were an artist who created a person like God created humankind?*

Levi and Marigold were born from these humble thoughts. Of course, Levi's character is not meant to mirror God exactly, but I wanted to give him a deep love for his creation, this woman he finds in the woods. And then I wanted to explore how his love would change if she fell in love with his worst enemy. This is the story of humankind. God created us, and we constantly turn away for other things. We leave our creator, only to be wooed back, saved, and loved unconditionally. (I also understand that Ezra can not be the antithesis of God. He is a fictional character and I'm rooting for his eventual redemption and happily ever after!)

Maybe this is all new to you. That's okay, friend. Or maybe this is old news you've been taught since you were a kid. Both are okay. My hope is that this story asks you to confront God in a new way. The avenue of love. No matter what you do. No matter how far you run. No matter how unloveable you think you are. God loves you. He truly does. He would be pushed off a cliff for you and so much more. He died and came back to life so He could have a relationship with you.

Today, I just want you to know you are loved. Right now. But if you want to know more, I encourage you to pick up a Bible and read God's love letter to you. Try starting with John. (that's my favorite Gospel) Or you could ask a Christian friend who already loves you unconditionally what it's all about.

Levi, Marigold, Ezra, and some new characters will be featured in the next installment of the Ghost Mountain series. There are more stakes, more danger, and more romance. I hope you'll stick around to find out more. You can get updates at my newsletter (https://shelbiemae.substack.com/) or my Instagram @shelbiemaewrites. You can also use the QR code on the previous section and be directed to The Ghost Mountain Gazette, a newsletter specifically for Ghost Mountain book news.

You are loved,

Shelbie Mae

Acknowledgements

Firstly, thank you, God for putting this story in my heart and using me to write it. I'm thankful that You continually save me and tell me I am *worth* saving. I think it will take a lifetime to fully grasp what You've done for me. Even then, I think it will take meeting You in heaven to truly understand.

Thank you, Mason for giving me space to write. Thank you for letting me write the stories in my heart even though you're not a reader and don't always understand my love of words. This book was written and edited throughout some of the darkest days of our marriage. It's a miracle it's here and you are part of that miracle. Thank you for loving me and our kids so thoroughly.

Thank YOU, reader, for picking up this book and giving it a chance. I'm honored that out of the millions of choices you read my words. I hope they entertained and inspired you.

Thank you to my mom, dad, and sisters for humoring my love of reading and writing. You never said I couldn't do it. Instead, you've asked me questions about my work and are sometimes first in line to read it. You read and enjoy words with me. (Except for dad, who has never been a reader but is fabulous at moral support and still takes the time to ask me about my books.)

The magnitude of editing that made this book possible is thanks to several talented and wonderful ladies.

Rachel, my former small-group girl, turned developmental editor. I'm so glad we bonded over books all those years ago. I am so proud of you for finishing college and following your dream to put books in readers' hands.

To Tessa Emily Hall, I can't even begin to thank you for the hours you put into the line edits for this book. I wasn't confident about publishing it until you broke it apart and put it back together. I am so grateful.

Thank you to fellow author Taylor Epperson and friend Arliss for proofreading this for me. I'm so grateful! If you, dear reader, found any errors, they are my fault.

To my amazingly talented cover designer, Hannah Linder. I am stunned by your work! You took my gibberish and turned it into a breathtaking cover. We absolutely judge books by their covers and you've created a beautiful one. Thank you!

Thank you to my brother-in-law Clay and his wife Tiffany for helping create the chapter art and publisher logo. And also for taking my author headshot! You make my work stand out and look more professional. Thank you!

And last but not least, thank you to my son. You took fantastic naps which made editing this possible. You bring me more joy than I thought possible, and I adore your love of reading. I hope your love of words grows and grows.

About Shelbie Mae

Shelbie Mae has lived in so many states it's hard for her to pick just one that feels like home. She currently lives in Michigan with her husband and son. At the time of this writing, she is expecting her second child. When she's not writing, you can find Shelbie outside enjoying a run, mothering her kids, sailing, swimming, cooking something in the kitchen, or reading good books. You can find her on Instagram @shelbiemaewrites or her website shelbie-mae.com.

Printed in the USA
CPSIA information can be obtained
at www.ICGtesting.com
LVHW090838300824
789625LV00004B/937

9 781733 471558